The Horsemen

THE

TRANSLATED BY

Joseph Kessel

HORSEMEN

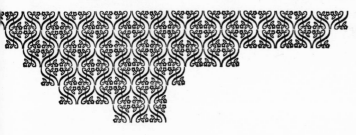

PATRICK O'BRIAN

Farrar, Straus & Giroux

NEW YORK

To the memory of my father
for his great and gentle wisdom

CONTENTS

The Horsemen

The Ancestor of All the World

THE LORRIES hardly traveled faster than the camels of the caravans, or the mounted men than the men on foot. The state of the road kept them to the same speed; for it was mounting to the approaches of the Shibar Pass, the one breach in the enormous majestic chain of the Hindu Kush, the gap more than eight thousand feet high through which flowed all the trade, all the traffic, between northern and southern Afghanistan.

On the one side, the saw-edged cliff. On the other, a bottomless void. Huge ruts and great fallen boulders blocked the road. The slope, the bends, and the violent corners grew steeper, harder, and more dangerous.

To be sure, the bitter cold and the thinness of the air were a great weariness for the men of the caravans, for the muleteers, the shepherds, and their beasts; but at least, clinging against the mountain face like lines of ants, they went along without danger. Not so the lorries. Often the road was so narrow that they took up its whole surface, and then on the edge of the precipice their wheels bit into the sagged, crumbling rim. A false move or a moment's lack of attention on the part of the driver, a failure on the part of the engine or the brakes, and the badly maintained vehicles, worn out before their time, might plunge over into the abyss. Their loads invariably exceeded the permitted weight and exceeded it by a great deal, which made them even less manageable on the steep slopes. And the excess of parcels, boxes, bundles, sacks, and bales was not the only form of overloading, or the worst.

Above their load of goods the lorries bore an overflowing human cargo on the roof—or on the tarpaulin if they had no roof. The bodies were heaped upon one another, piled up until they made a kind of shapeless, blunt, seething, unstable pyramid, topped with wisps of cloth that blew to and fro in the gusty wind, showing the tanned faces of the travelers; and the pyramid perpetually wobbled, collapsed, and built itself up again, according to the jolts and lurches of the machine.

Upon one of these lorries and at the top of one of these pyramids was perched a very ancient man. He had done nothing to get there. But he was so extremely thin that he had neither weight nor bulk, and by the mere thrust of the people who had come aboard since Kabul, the capital, layer after layer of them clinging to the ill-stretched cover, his body had risen above the others of itself. With his feet on the nape of one neck and his person wedged between two others, both powerful, he watched the motion of the chains and peaks of the Hindu Kush—an almost imperceptible movement, so slowly did the lorry make its way. Gray was the rocky crust on the mountain sides, the ridges, and the spurs, gray with a senile, dreary grayness. A kind of dismal, clotted ash shrouded the prodigious mountain and all its upthrusts, all its folds, stretching as far as the dull frozen patches of sky that bounded it.

The lorry's passengers spoke less and less. The animated talk, the jokes, the stories, and the merriment of a lively, good-humored people that had lightened the journey until the Shibar Pass grew near was no longer to be heard. From time to time a traveler uttered an exclamation, or a sigh, or a prayer. And then even these fell silent. Before such desolation upon the face of the earth, speech was no longer a defense. The only thing that could bring comfort was warmth—a shared animal warmth. Each traveler tried to edge his frame more deeply into his neighbor's. Silently.

But the very old man, perched above the others, felt neither anxiety nor sadness. Looking beyond that dead-star landscape, his inner eye saw enchanted valleys, overflowing turbulent cities, burning deserts, measureless steppes. And what he saw was Afghanistan.

He knew all its provinces: every path and every track. He had traveled all its frontiers, the Persian and the Russian, the Tibetan and the Indian. At any moment he could evoke these pictures in his mind; now, for him, living was remembering. And he made his memories spin, boxing the compass round.

Suddenly the line of the ridge and the roof of sky vanished from before his eyes. At the same moment a thin, shrill uproar surrounded him on every side and he toppled down the heap of bodies, which had lost its cohesion, loosening and shifting toward the tail of the lorry. Then the hubbub stopped dead. Terror had taken the place of surprise. The engine was no longer turning. The driver tried to start it, but in vain. The brakes were on as hard as they could go and they were shrieking wildly; but they were not powerful enough to hold the huge, overladen vehicle on so steep a slope. It was not yet moving backward. But it was already hesitating, beginning to yield to the pull. From one moment to the next its wood and metal were acquiring a weight, a strength, and a will that were no longer under human control. Very slowly the lorry slipped one inch back, and then, a little faster, another. Between it and the edge of the precipice there was scarcely more than . . . The travelers crammed into the bottom, who could see nothing but backs and heads, shouted, "The danda panj!" *

"What is the danda panj doing?"

The people clinging to the sides of the lorry replied, "The danda panj is doing all he should."

"He appears brisk and skillful."

"The Prophet be with him!"

"May Allah inspire him!"

The passengers called out their encouragements and invocations to a little boy, almost a child, who had made the journey hanging onto the outside of the tailboard, coiled against a wedge as tall and as heavy as he. At the first jerk he had jumped down. Now he had just disengaged the wedge from its hooks. The lorry was moving back faster. Its wheels had begun to turn. One more revolution would mean the plunge into the abyss. The danda panj wedged the most dangerous wheel, the one on the left. The lorry lurched once, twice, three times and then stood motionless, block-

* The fifth gear.

ing the road. In front and behind came a furious shrieking from the klaxons of the cars and lorries it was holding up. The turbanned head of the driver thrust out of the cabin window. "All out!" he shouted. "Push, and do not get in again until I tell you."

The travelers hurried down from the lorry. When it was the very old man's turn, his neighbor, a smith with uncommonly thick black hair, said to him, "Stay, sit there, grandfather. I never felt the weight of thy bones at all. Thou art lighter than a quail."

The engines started again; the lorry climbed to the next flat place. One by one the passengers hoisted themselves onto the tarpaulin. The blacksmith, because he was strong and because he wanted to, thrust his way back to his place next to the old man. Gasping and happy, he said, "I pushed and strove like a fiend. It made me forget my dread, which was very great."

"And what did you fear so much?"

"Why, death, of course," said the blacksmith.

"You should not have been afraid," said the ancient man, gently.

"It is easy enough to think that," answered the blacksmith hotly, but with kindness. "It is easy when a man is as close to death as thou art, grandfather."

"Not so close as thou, my son," said the old man. "For thou—thou art afraid of it."

"Like everybody else!" cried the smith.

"True," said the old man. "And it is in that great fear—and in that alone—that men's death has its being."

With a thumb all horn from the labor of the anvil, the smith scratched his very black, very thick eyebrows for some time. "I do not understand," he said uneasily.

"It does not matter, my son," said the old man. His face was so fleshless that it was no longer capable of expression. And its skin was so crisscrossed, cracked, furrowed, labored with wrinkles that it looked like a tightly stretched net in which his dim blue eyes had been caught and held. Yet it seemed to the smith that although the bloodless and thread-thin lips of this emaciated countenance never stirred, a friendly tremor spread from fold to tiny fold, reaching the eyes and causing them to send forth a spark. Without understanding any more clearly, the smith felt comforted.

Still another jolt once more threw the heap of bodies on the lorry's tarpaulin into disorder. The smith put a solid great arm around the old man's shoulders and said gently, "I am called Ghulam: and thy name, grandfather?"

"Gardi Gaj," said the ancient man.

"Gardi Gaj, Gardi Gaj," repeated the smith. He smiled blissfully. "A quail weighs more than thee," he said.

The ground leveled out. They were at an altitude of some thirteen thousand feet, and the Shibar Pass was in sight.

THE HALTING PLACE WAS ON THE OTHER SIDE OF THE PASS, LOWER down, on the first level spot on the northern face. It was an immense rocky table, closed to the west by the mountain and cut on the east by a gorge with a torrent roaring through it. In this predetermined place halted all the convoys which carried the trade between the two halves of Afghanistan, separated by the Hindu Kush. Scores of vehicles from either direction were always standing there. Those that came from the south were lined up by the stream, and the others against the rock.

On either side of the plain stretched a long line of primitive inns. Since tea, either black or green, was what was drunk there for the most part, they were called chaikhanas.* The mud-walled huts had no more than a single dark room within. Outside there was a covered terrace. This is where the travelers gathered. The cold was more bitter on the terrace and the wind more cruel. But what man in his senses would choose, for such a trifle, to give up such a sight as the arrival of the lorries, the dismounting of the passengers, the unexpected meetings of friends traveling in opposite directions? Where in the whole of Afghanistan but at the Shibar Pass could one see, in so small a space, men from Kabul and from the Hazarajat, from Kandahar and Jalalabad, from Ghazni and from Mazar-i-Sharif? And dressed according to the provinces and tribes to which they belonged, in wide shirts or close-fitting tunics or spreading cloaks, and wearing turbans that might be loose and flowing or wrapped firm and tight, or else astrakhan kulahs, brilliant silk caps,

* From *chai*, tea.

or tall, hairy sheepskin hats. And who were a delight to attentive ears with their astonishing and inexhaustible supply of tales, arguments, tidings, and lies? Truly this halt was a gift from fate, a treat, and only a raving lunatic would lose a moment of it.

So when the lorry in which the very ancient man was traveling took up its place on the torrent side of the platform, the passengers were too impatient to wait for it to come to a stop before they slid down from the tarpaulin and ran to the verandas of the chaikhanas. The smith himself, having hastily set the old man down, cried, "Thou no longer hast need of me, grandfather, to be sure." And he hurried off with long strides.

The ancient man slung a light knapsack over his shoulder and stood there motionless. In spite of his age and the strong gusts that buffeted his body, which had neither flesh nor muscle, he stood very straight, and slowly, prudently allowed the rare magnificence to soak into him—the splendor of this remote roadside halt at the top of an enormous mountain range in the heart of Central Asia, with its heavy lorries ravaged by the sun and the dust and shattered by the terrible roads, and the drivers and passengers squatting or lying under the porches of the primitive inns. And then barrenness all around, without the slightest transition—the everlasting sterility of rock, the everlasting thunder of water, the everlasting icy blast from the roof of the world. And Gardi Gaj reflected upon the hosts of men, the human rivers that had been obliged to take this unavoidable corridor between the two halves of the world as their bed—the torrents of conquest, the streams of religion . . .

To the old man it seemed that he had seen all this with his own eyes. He had been living for such a very long time . . . He had wandered so very far over the face of Afghanistan . . . The roots of his memories were so very deep . . . Lost in thought, he made his way toward the nearest chaikhana.

SOME OF HIS TRAVELING COMPANIONS WERE THERE ALREADY. THE first, most eager of them all, had been a tall, very thin groom wearing a brown, wool-lined caftan that covered him from neck to ankle. No man wearing a garment of this kind had to say what province he came from: the chapan was peculiar to the Uzbek and Turkoman horsemen of the northern steppes.

As soon as he reached the veranda of the chaikhana, this man behaved in a very curious manner. He made his way through the customers with an impatience that took no heed of anyone, he trod on the people who were squatting around their tea on wretched scraps of carpet on the beaten earth; he jostled against those who were sitting on battered stools or on rough wooden frames with a network of string as a mattress. Angry murmurs followed him. "What an awkward brute," they said.

Or: "The height has turned his wits."

"My mule is more light-footed than he."

But though the words might be sharp, the tone was good-natured. The only one to grow really angry was a fat, smooth mullah. He swore that the Prophet would punish the miscreant who had knocked into his nargile.

The man, without hearing a word, passed on through the crowd, craning his neck so that his black gleaming narrow eyes, watchful between high cheekbones, should have a wider field of vision. At last, against the low wall that separated the veranda from the road, he found what he was looking for—chapans. There were two of them, the one purplish-red with black stripes and the other russet with thin green streaks. As for the two middle-aged men who were wearing them, the young groom had never seen them. That signified nothing. They were his brothers by their clothes and by the life of the steppes. They alone among all the people around him, people from every village and valley in Afghanistan, were capable of understanding his feelings and of sharing them.

The purple and the russet chapans drew together to make room for the groom. He did not notice it. "Are you going to Kabul or are you coming back from there?" he asked the two men.

"We left Mazar-i-Sharif yesterday," said the stouter and more hoary of the two.

"Why then, why then, you do not know the most important news of all!" cried the groom.

The two chapan-clad travelers slowly brought their faces closer to his. Their almond eyes were alive with curiosity tinged with uneasiness. But they were far more venerable in age than this mere stable boy and their standing was far higher than his, so they could not show it. The one who had already spoken raised his voice and in an even, almost drowsy tone asked, "What dost thou, so young and devoid of experience, mean by 'the most important news of all'?"

"I mean that there is none other that can matter so much," said the shepherd. And although he was on fire to make public what he knew, he remained silent to relish for a few moments longer the power of one who possesses a great secret. On this the two travelers, speaking as one, said, "Has a new governor-general been appointed for our provinces?"

Without a word the shepherd shook his head.

"Has the duty on weaving been raised?" asked the man in the russet chapan, who owned a carpet factory in the province of Meimana.

"Or on astrakhan?" asked his companion in the purple chapan, who for his part bred long-wooled sheep on the steppes of Mazar-i-Sharif.

"If that were all!" said the groom. And unable to contain himself any longer, he cried, indeed chanted, "Hear, hear what I say: I proclaim to you that for the first time in Kabul, that great city, there will presently be seen the running of a buzkashi." The groom's eyes were fixed greedily on the two men in chapans. His hope was not disappointed. The merchants, who until then had been sitting in great dignity against the wall, their every word and movement compassed and slow, lost all control. They rose in one movement and with one shrill voice they cried, "A buzkashi at Kabul! Didst indeed say at Kabul, a buzkashi?"

"And that the most brilliant, the most memorable," intoned the groom.

"The air up here is too strong for thy young head," exclaimed the dealer in astrakhan.

"Where would these people of the valleys find the horses required? Where would they find the men?" cried the weaver of carpets.

In his turn, and louder still, the groom proclaimed, "They are to come from our regions."

For a moment amazement plunged the merchants into silence. When they tried to speak again it was too late, their voices were drowned by others.

The scraps of conversation sounding like stray words of a quarrel, the sudden, unbecoming change on the part of the two gray-haired men, had spread a happy tremor of curiosity among the travelers gathered in this part of the inn. They had clustered around the three chapans. And the tea drinkers squatting farther off abandoned their trays to discover what the others had found so interesting. And men were already starting up in the nearby chai-khanas, hurrying to learn what was happening.

Above all this hubbub one word was heard: buzkashi, buzkashi . . . It came from the far end of the veranda, it was passed from mouth to mouth, and it spread throughout the crowd. But most of the travelers did not know what it meant; they had never been beyond the valleys of the Hindu Kush or the cities of Qunduz and Baghlan; and with a great din they asked to be told what it was about. The explanation passed from row to row. "A game; yes, a game, it would appear, from far off in those parts, in the steppes."

When this message reached them, many of those who made up the crowd—a crowd whose garments fluttered wildly in the cruel wind of the high mountain—felt bitterly disappointed. Leave a good place, patiently warmed by long sitting, among agreeable neighbors—let scalding tea go cold merely to hear talk of what? Of a game that was played in the remote, unknown, arid regions of the north. A game, by the Prophet! As though there were not games in plenty, both in their lofty cities and their green valleys! And those of the finest! And calling out to one another the men of Ghazni and of Kabul, of the province of Kandahar and that of the Haza-rajat cried, "Is this buzkashi with which our ears are deafened as skilled as cudgel play?"

"Fiercer than ram-fighting?"

"As furious as battles between dogs and wolves?"

"As terrible as the fight to the death between two camels in rut?"

"As shrewd as the blows of a quail trained for the pit?"

Thus the dwellers in the mountains uttered their protests; and to drown their uproar the three men in chapans, who had been joined by certain other northern travelers, cried, "How can you understand the beauties of the buzkashi?"

"You who cannot tell an old screw from a thoroughbred."

"You who always seem to be mounted on an ass whenever you are in the saddle!"

The tone was rising, the retorts becoming insults. Over and above the game itself, the disagreement touched the honor of the tribes and of the provinces.

THE OWNER OF THE CHAIKHANA SAW HIS TRAMPLED CUPS SHATTERING and the boiling water spurting from the tottering samovars. A few moments more and these madmen would smash and wreck everything. The innkeeper clenched his jaw. He had a hard, flat face, a great solid chest, and long powerful arms. But with all his strength and determination what could he do alone? And not one of his bachas* was more than fifteen!

He thrust his way savagely through the milling crowd on his veranda and reached the edge of the road, with the idea of asking the other innkeepers and the drivers he had as friends to lend him a hand. At that moment he caught sight of the very old man with the little knapsack whom a blacksmith had helped down from the last lorry to come in from Kabul.

"Allah Himself sends him to us," cried the owner of the chaikhana. He went back into the midst of the angry crowd, but saw at once that he could never make himself heard. He was short, and because he had lived so long at such a height his voice had taken on an exhausted ring. What could he do?

The youngest of his bachas, a boy of thirteen, made his way to his side to ask, "Are the cups and samovars to be taken in?"

"Wait!" said the owner of the chaikhana. He grasped the child, hoisted him so that he stood on his square shoulders, and said, "Thou must repeat what I say with all thy strength, with all thy strength."

The bacha rounded his hands on either side of his mouth like a

* Young serving boy.

speaking trumpet and set about shouting with all his might the words that reached him from his master: "Stop! Stop! Listen! Listen!"

The boy's head raised above all the others, the young and piercing voice compelled attention. Even the most furious faces turned toward the bacha. He continued, "Why go on arguing? I see coming the one man who can decide between you . . . Gardi Gaj." The bacha paused for a moment, and then, putting forth the utmost strength of his lungs and throat, he cried, "The Ancestor of All the World!"

Then the wind of the mountain tops could be heard, so deep was the silence of the crowd. And now this silence owed nothing whatever to curiosity.

No doubt very few among the travelers had, in the course of their lives, actually met the ancient man. But not one of them did not know his name. From one end of the Afghan land to the other, and from generation to generation, grandfathers had told their grandchildren of the ancient man, repeating what they themselves had heard about him. For there was not a single village, not a hamlet, however remote, that he had not passed through. And when Gardi Gaj went by, he was never forgotten.

The bacha slipped down from his master's shoulders. The owner of the chaikhana went up to the old man, bowed very low before him, took him by the right hand, and through the passage that opened of itself in the crowd led him to the far end of the veranda. Everyone gazed wonderingly upon Gardi Gaj.

How old was he, this ancient, emaciated man, hollowed out, withered to the utmost degree beneath the vague folds of a shapeless cloak—the same color as the tall knotted branch on which he leaned? No one on earth could tell. His origin, his tribe? The only thing that could be said for sure was that he was not of Mongol blood. Apart from that he might have come from the sands of Seistan or the Persian frontier or the country touching India or from Baluchistan, that savage land. He might be a Hazara, a Pathan, a Tadzhik, a Nuristani . . . Time had so dried, worn, obliterated his features that the signs of race and the marks of ancestry could no longer be read upon them. And he spoke the languages and dialects of all the provinces. He was not a dervish or a guru or a shaman. Yet like those holy men he traveled the highways, the roads, the paths, and the tracks of the whole great Afghan land. He had made his way up its valleys, where the icy rivers churn and sing. The shores of the Amu Darya were familiar to him. He had trodden the everlasting snows of the Pamir at the far end of that deep valley which touches the Roof of the World where, without the hairy yaks, man cannot survive. And the burning deserts had scorched the soles of his naked feet. How long had he been traveling? One might as well have asked his vanished footprints. What power, what dream led him on? Wisdom? Whim? An everlasting restlessness? The unquenchable thirst for knowledge? He came; he went; many years later he reappeared. Each time he stopped he told another wonderful tale. Where did he draw his knowledge from? He had never been seen to read. Yet he seemed to remember all the happenings and all the men who had left their mark upon the mountains, the passes, and the steppes of Afghanistan for hundreds and hundreds of years. He spoke of Zarathustra as though he had been his disciple; of Iskander* as though he had followed him from conquest to conquest; of Balkh, the mother of cities, as though he had been born there; and of the massacres of Genghis Khan as though he had been soaked in the blood of slaughtered nations and buried under the ashes and ruins of strongholds.

In just the same way he told tales of the life in present times, and in these the goatherd or the nomadic camel driver, the engraver of weapons or the carpetweaver, the dambura player or the Istalif potter took on as much importance as the legendary chiefs or heroes.

When they reached one of the wooden frames set against the wall of the house the owner of the chaikhana said humbly, "I have neither cushions nor padded quilts to hold thee up or wrap thee about, Ancestor of All the World . . . In the Shibar we are poor, extremely poor."

Gardi Gaj sat on the edge of the primitive bed, put his staff between his knees, and rested his chin upon it. "Never vex thyself," he said gently. "Only my head needs a support."

In the midst of the silence suddenly burst out a loud, rough voice, filled with tenderness. "I know, I know," it said. "Thou dost

* Alexander the Great.

not weigh so much as a quail." And then, under the gaze of his neighbors, the coarse face of a blacksmith was seen to take on the color of confusion, while he shrunk his head between his brawny shoulders. Laughter broke out all around him. The master of the chaikhana said to Gardi Gaj, "They were on the point of fighting. Now see how cheerful they are. They are persuaded that thou wilt enlighten them."

These words were enough to bring apparently calm passions to life again. "Is it not true, O thou who knowest everything, is it not true that this steppe-rustic's buzkashi that we have just heard of for the first time amounts to nothing compared with the games of our forefathers?" cried some.

"O thou who knowest everything," cried others, "is it not true that for beauty, courage, power, and skill, our buzkashi is as much above the pastimes these valley blockheads boast of, as a falcon is above a hen run?"

And the men on either side awaited the old man's oracle with the same simple-minded conviction—he was going to say that they were right. But to their questions he replied with another, "And why should I decide instead of you, friends?" The crowd, at a loss, fell silent, and Gardi Gaj went on, "Each man has the right and the duty to make up his own mind. But a man must thoroughly understand whatever he means to judge. And so it is with the buzkashi. Would it please you to hear me tell of it?"

The only reply the crowd could manage was a vast sigh, an eager drawing in of breath; all were filled with gratitude. Had he not used the magic word? A tale! And told by him! By one who, as every man was well aware, did not possess an equal for age, memory, distance traveled, wisdom, and the art of the spoken word throughout the Afghan land—the Ancestor of All the World.

The blacksmith had succeeded in getting close to the ancient man. He was the first to squat at his feet. After him, row by row, the others let themselves down on their folded legs. Only the people for whom there was no room on the veranda remained standing there along the road.

Now Gardi Gaj sat above a kind of carpet made up of all the headdresses that distinguished the provinces and the tribes. And beneath the turbans, kolpaks, caps, and kulahs there appeared the lines of faces whose planes and ridges spelled out the difference of their origins—mountain, valley, desert, steppe; migration and conquest and the mixture of blood. But all these faces, with their contrasts in age and features, bore the same expression—that of childish eagerness and expectation. And the old, old teller of tales toward whom this feeling was directed, as the thirst of a pilgrim is directed toward the wellhead of a spring, was aware, deep in his weightless, fleshless body, worn almost completely away, of the one vibration of life and the one pleasure he was still capable of feeling —that of infusing into this simple and wonderful ignorance a little of what it could know, so that each man who listened to him might repeat his tale to others and that each of the others might repeat it in his turn; so that from neighbor to neighbor and from father to son it might never cease to spread in space and time like spring waters traveling through countless little channels; and so that in this way man might experience the eternity that the gods unjustly reserved for themselves alone.

Gardi Gaj let his staff fall (it was piously gathered up by the smith), straightened his back, raised his head, and spoke. His voice was exceedingly frail and thin. Yet it carried very far, like the sound of a flawed crystal bell.

And Gardi Gaj began, "It came in with Genghis Khan," he said.

And without knowing it the audience, as though it had been no more than a depth from which arose an echo, whispered "Genghis, Genghis . . ."

For throughout Afghanistan, even in the remotest, most backward hamlets, there was not a man or a child, even the stupidest and the most ignorant, who did not know that terrible name and who did not feel a superstitious horror, in spite of the centuries since the conqueror had passed by.

"Genghis . . . Genghis," whispered the travelers, and the wind of the Shibar carried the murmur toward the peaks of the Hindu Kush.

Gardi Gaj thought, "Truly, magnificent cities of which the ruins alone remain, fruitful plowland now forever sterile desert, and nations butchered even to the children at the breast do more for the memory of a leader than the noblest and the best-proportioned monuments . . . Fame has no trustier guardian than fear."

Gardi Gaj raised his eyes to look at a group of roadmen gathered at the side of the highway. They were dressed in pale blue rags, and in order to listen they were leaning on the shovels they used all day long to fill the potholes in the road with a dusty gravel that the gusts of mountain wind carried away directly. They were Hazaras, whose tribes dwelt upon the harsh plateaus and in the narrow valleys of the Hindu Kush, on the side of the setting sun.

"Genghis, Genghis Khan," whispered Gardi Gaj's hearers. For their part the roadmen said nothing.

"Do the wretched creatures know at least that the name of their nation is a Mongol word," wondered the old storyteller, "that it means five score, and that five score was the prime figure by which the Conqueror of the World raised and numbered his invincible hordes?"

The ragged descendants of the merciless horsemen whom their master had implanted in these regions to rule forever continued to direct their flat yellow faces and narrow slits of eyes toward Gardi Gaj, and on these faces he read the limitless patience of stupidity.

Then Gardi Gaj went on: "The Mongols lived in the saddle, died in the saddle. When they played, they could only play on horseback. And to all other games—racing, shooting with the bow at full gallop, hunting, hawking—they preferred what they called the buzkashi. Genghis's warriors carried it into all the countries that felt the trampling hoofs of their stallions and their mares. Even now, after seven times a hundred years, it is played in our northern plains, played as it was in those far-off days—the buzkashi."

The blacksmith sitting at the feet of Gardi Gaj could no longer contain himself, and as though he claimed the rights of friendship over his old traveling companion, he cried, "Ancestor of All the World, art thou going to let us know at last how this game is played and what it is?" And the whole crowd, emboldened by this remark, called out imploringly to Gardi Gaj, "Yes, oh yes, enlighten us!"

"In the first place," said the old storyteller, "close your eyes."

The smith was startled, and he hesitated. Gardi Gaj hid his own eyes behind one of his sandals and said to the audience, "You too, my friends."

When there was nothing before him but blind faces, the voice of the old storyteller, like a flawed crystal bell, rang higher. "Make yourselves ready for a great effort," said he. "An effort over yourselves. I desire, O men who have never left the sides, the hollows, and the shadow of the mountains, I desire to lead the eyes of your minds to the great steppe of the north." By the intensity and gravity of these faces with their closed eyelids Gardi Gaj saw that they were giving themselves up to him unreservedly. "That is well," he said. "Now you must think of a valley. A valley such as none of you has ever known . . . Wider and longer than the widest and longest you have ever passed through in the whole of your life."

Voices arose, as though in a trance.

"Greater than that of Ghazni?"

"Greater than at Jalalabad?"

"Than the Koh Daman?"

Gardi Gaj answered, "A hundred times greater." And he cried, "Come, friends: to work. Push away, thrust back all the great walls of rock . . . to the left and to the right: both before and behind. Thrust and thrust again . . . Farther . . . still farther back . . . They are growing smaller, are they not? They melt away . . . they fall . . . they exist no more."

"Truly, truly," whispered the crowd. "There is no longer anything at all!"

"Do not open your eyes," commanded Gardi Gaj. "And now look upon this valley that has no barrier, no obstacles and no end, flat, bare, free, smooth, with the sky on every hand as its only frontier."

"We see, we see!" cried the blind men, in an ecstasy.

"And there," went on Gardi Gaj, "there stretches a carpet of grass and herbs as far as the end of the world; and when the wind touches it this carpet smells of the bitter-scented wormwood. And the fastest thoroughbred can gallop until he falls from weariness, and the swiftest bird may fly until the moment its wings will no longer bear it. And still they will see nothing but grass, and grass, and grass, over which the wormwood spreads its scent." Gardi Gaj breathed with difficulty; in a tired and gentle voice like the rustling of a feather he ended, "Such is the steppe."

"The steppe," repeated the enraptured audience.

The men wearing chapans cried out louder than the rest. Not at all out of pride in their country, but because they were filled with wonder at having, through the words of Gardi Gaj, discovered in it the beauty that they no longer saw because they lived there. And when they opened their eyes again they were quite astonished to see that they were surrounded, overborn, dwarfed by great masses of rock, like huge, ill-omened jailers. And the other travelers, although they had had these mountain chains and peaks as their companions all their life, felt the same astonishment.

Gardi Gaj did not give them time to forget their vision. He said, "Yes, such is the steppe, the mother of the buzkashi. She alone of all the lands beneath the sun has a belly broad enough to bear her men and beasts and feed them."

"Tell them about our horses!" cried the groom.

"Not all of them have wings," answered Gardi Gaj. "But the wealthy lords of the north who are called khans or beys have horses bred and trained solely for the great game. Chargers as swift as arrows, as enduring as the fiercest wolf, as intelligent and obedient as the most faithful dog, and handsome as princes. They withstand both icy cold and burning heat, and they can keep up a gallop a whole day through."

"There are some that are worth a hundred thousand afghanis!" cried the groom.

"A hundred thousand afghanis . . ." repeated the unbelieving crowd (for most of the men who formed it the earnings of a whole life did not reach this sum). "A hundred thousand afghanis . . . It is not possible."

"Yet it is true," said Gardi Gaj. "And a chapandaz is needed to ride such horses."

"And not every man who chooses is a chapandaz," said the groom. "In a hundred and a hundred and a hundred buzkashis and among a thousand and a thousand and a thousand players, one horseman must be better than them all. And that is not enough. When fame has made him known throughout the Three Provinces, the oldest and most rigorous of the chapandaz come together. Before them this horseman goes through the trial. If they are satisfied, and only then, he has the right to the glorious name and to the fox- or wolf-skin hat. He no longer has any other calling but playing buzkashi. And he earns close on a hundred thousand afghanis a year."

"That too is true," said Gardi Gaj.

"Such a great deal of money . . . such a great deal of money." The murmur was as melancholy as a sigh, as painful as a groan.

"Now this is the game," said Gardi Gaj. "They choose a he-goat from the flock. His throat is slit. His head is cut off. To make his body heavier they stuff it with sand, fill it with water. They put it in a hole just deep enough for the hair to be on a level with the ground. Not far from the hole they draw a little circle with quick-lime. And this is called *halal*, which in Turkoman means *circle of justice*. To the right of the halal they set up a pole in the steppe, and to the left, another, at an equal distance. As for the length of this distance, there is no rule. It may call for an hour of galloping or perhaps three or perhaps five. The judges at each buzkashi decide as they see fit." The ancient storyteller let his eyes run over the crowd, and went on, "Good . . . The hole that has the body in it . . . Close by, the white circle. And far away, often very far away, the poles . . . The horsemen gather around the hole."

"How many?" asked the smith.

"It all depends on the circumstances," said Gardi Gaj. "Some-times ten, sometimes fifty, sometimes hundreds. When the judge gives the signal all of them fling themselves upon the headless body. One grasps it and gets away. Pursued by the others he races toward the pole on the right. For the remains of the goat must go around it, then pass behind the pole on the left, and finally come to the halal. And he whose arm throws the headless goat into the middle of the white circle is the winner. But before the victory, what battles, what pursuits, what conflicts, what escapes, what fierce confusion! Anything is fair. From hour to hour, from hand to hand, from saddle to saddle, the headless body makes its way around the two poles and travels toward the goal. At last one of the players gets possession of it, dodges his last opponents or overcomes them, gallops with the hide in his fist, reaches the whitewashed circle, waves what remains of the goat and . . ."

An ululation drowned the storyteller's voice. A high-pitched, barbarous, frantically excited, frantically exciting howl, formed in the land of endless grass, to fill it with its wild, strident clamor.

"Halal! Halal!" roared the groom from the steppes.

"Halal! Halal!" answered the men in chapans. And because the rocks and the chasms of the Shibar sent back the cry in a thousand fragmentary echoes, the mountain demons howled on and on, "Halal! Halal!"

When at last they stopped there was an amazing silence. Then Gardi Gaj observed, "Such, my friends, is the game of Genghis Khan. Now you understand it."

"Thanks to thee, Ancestor of All the World who knowest everything!" cried the crowd.

From out of this concert of praise arose one voice at the very feet of Gardi Gaj, a voice both furious and grieved. "What good is it to me, grandfather, to know the rules of so splendid a game when I shall never see it?"

"He is right . . . Truly, the smith's words are reasonable and just." So murmured the men of the valleys and the mountain towns who made up almost the entire audience. And they began to get up one after the other (for the lorry drivers were waving to show that the halt was coming to an end), sad and as it were fallen from their state of grace. But Gardi Gaj raised his staff to hold them back a moment longer, and he spoke again. "If no mortal man has the right to say 'Forever,' so none may say 'Never.' And here I bring you fresh proof of this; for the first time since time began, buzkashi is to be played on the other side of the Hindu Kush, not far from Kabul itself, the capital."

The drivers stopped calling and the travelers, as though turned to stone, remained frozen in the attitudes in which Gardi Gaj's words had surprised them—here a man on one knee, there a man on the other, here one on both, and there one with his body bent like a hunchback.

"How?" they asked.

"Why?"

"When?"

"Because," replied the ancient storyteller, "Zahir Shah, lord of the Afghan realm, has ordained that henceforth the best buzkashi players mounted on the best horses of the steppes shall come every year and run the headless goat on the Bagrami Plain, not far from the capital, for the king's birthday, in the month of Mizan." *

"The month of Mizan!"

"Next Mizan!"

"I shall be there!"

"I shall be there!"

"Even if I have to sell my last ewe!"

"My last tool!"

"My wife's chadar." †

The roaring of the engines spread, the travelers climbed in heaps onto the lorry roofs, and still their cries went on.

The blacksmith said to Gardi Gaj, "The village where my cousin is to be married is not on the road. I am walking the rest of the way. And thou, grandfather?"

"I go on," said Gardi Gaj.

"How far?" asked the smith.

"To the steppes," said Gardi Gaj. "The king's decision will change more than one life among the men of the buzkashi."

"What of it?" asked the smith again.

"A man who knows a great many dead tales loves to see one at its birth, whenever he can," said the Ancestor of All the World.

* October.
† A voluminous hooded cloak that completely hides face and body.

PART ONE

The Royal Buzkashi

1

Tursen

Dawn was just beginning to break in that part of the province of Meimana, in the north of Afghanistan, that touches the Russian frontier.

Flat on his back—and his back was so broad that it reached from one side of the charpoy to the other—old Tursen lay like a roughly hewn block of wood.

After so many awakenings of the same kind he had grown used to finding that his body, after sleep, refused the least and easiest of movements. It seemed as though all his joints, from the nape of his neck to his ankles, were gripped in irons and chains. As for his skin, it did not even feel the harsh texture of the coverings or the weight of the quilts; it was dead.

And then (how? why?) his skin began to recognize the warmth and padding of the cotton-filled sack that acted as a mattress and, beneath it, the cutting network of cord stretched over the rough frame. And then (how? why?) link by link, rivet by rivet, the chains and the irons loosened, relaxed their hold. The heavy, powerful, knotted, motionless bulk of muscle and bone began to live once more.

So old Tursen waited until his body should choose to obey him again. In all this he felt neither impatience nor bitterness. The truly strong man must accept evils he cannot avoid, and accept them with a heart unmoved. And is not age, short of death, the most unavoidable?

Gradually, as happened every morning—but every morning a little later—the moment came when old Tursen felt that he was once more in command of his limbs. Then he slowly set his two huge, horny, twisted, furrowed, distorted hands—they looked like the roots of an ancient tree—on the two sides of the frame, leaned upon them, and raised his trunk. There he paused for a short while; this was to allow for the pain that was about to seize his loins. It did so every morning (but every morning a little fiercer) when Tursen swung heavily round and let first his left and then his right leg drop to the reddish floor of beaten earth.

Two thick, primitive sticks hung close by the charpoy. Tursen grasped them, and their clumsy handles vanished within his palms. Before making use of them as levers, Tursen allowed himself still another moment's respite. This one occupied the space needed to foresee and reflect upon the suffering—a tearing and at the same time a burning—that lay within Tursen's kneecaps, whose tendons were wrenched with ever-increasing cruelty each morning by the act of standing up. This ordeal too had to be overcome without a sigh, without a grimace, without so much as a flicker of his eyelids. It was of little importance that Tursen was alone between four walls. Only one witness counted—himself.

At last, leaning on his two sticks, clad in a long shirt, he stood there in the middle of the room, in which the only furniture, apart from the charpoy, was a low table. He took two steps, threw one of his props onto the bed he had just left, moved forward again, and threw the second. His body was upright, balanced. He felt his blood moving in it, warming him, easing his joints, making them supple. He dressed: first the chapan, which covered him from neck to wrist and neck to heel, so old, worn, and mellowed that its black stripes could scarcely be distinguished from the grayish background and so molded to Tursen that it seemed to have grown over his limbs like a second skin. Then the long piece of cloth twisted into a belt to hold the floating skirts of the chapan. Then the hard leather slippers with their turned-up ends like the beak of a bird of prey.

Yet the hardest was still to come: the tying of the turban so that it should be worthy of his rank, his age, and his reputation. This compelled him to raise his arms above his head and work with them there. After the torment of the loins and the knees, the torment of the shoulders.

No doubt old Tursen—and he knew it perfectly well—had but to growl out a summons to be spared these torments. The bacha whose duty it was to serve him and who slept on the floor of the corridor outside his door would hurry in at once, very proud to dress him. The bacha was only a child; but anyone at all on the estate or in the surrounding country, anyone, however splendid in strength, worth, and freedom, would have derived glory from this domestic act. There was no degradation in serving a man like Tursen; it was an honor. Everyone was aware of this, and Tursen more clearly than any.

But old Tursen was also aware that the right to marks of respect and eager service meant real power on one condition only—that of being able to do without them. The same chapan, the same camel, the same astrakhan ram that was a token of homage when it was offered to a wealthy lord became alms, a piece of charity, when it was given to a man in need.

The more Tursen found his strength diminishing, the more he refused all kind of help. He did not choose to resemble a beggar in any way at all. And it was not only his feeling for dignity that insisted on this behavior. There was also his clear-sightedness. Should not the truly wise man be certain of the resources at his command, above all when they are dwindling all the time?

Tursen's way of finding out the true extent of his powers was to try them to their utmost limits, and try them every day. That was why his heavy, thick, cracked fingers, in spite of the torture of his shoulders, neck, and wrists, tied, untied, re-tied the cloth of the turban as often as was needed to give it the splendid dash of a diadem and the supple grace of a liana coiled about itself.

There was no looking glass in the room. Never, since he had become aware of himself as a man, had Tursen made use of such a thing. Women and children might gaze at themselves in mirrors as much as they pleased. A masculine face came away soiled from that unclean duplication. Water alone was worthy of reflecting the face of a man, and only when he leaned over it to drink. Water quenched his thirst, and water came from God.

The headdress had been built up into the waving form that Tursen's old and imperious hands required. Slowly he let his arms down to his sides. There was one last action to be called out so as to face the day worthily, but this was rather the reward and crown of all those by which he had, at the cost of so much rending effort, set his rebellious, creaking body in motion once again and dressed it in a decent manner. He took the riding whip—it was still on the charpoy where it had lain all night against his cheek—and thrust it into his belt.

At the tail of its short handle a metal joint allowed the lash its full freedom and striking power. It was a heavy rawhide plait, sharp-edged and weighted at the end with balls of lead. And since for so many years it had helped Tursen through countless raids, contests, races, and battles, and since it had ripped open so many muzzles and so many faces, it was soaked, impregnated, and lacquered with sweat and with human and animal blood.

Tursen paced toward the door. His step was heavy, to be sure; but it was confident. He leaned on one stick only, and in such a way that the prop became an emblem of command. At every movement the lash of the whip quivered all alive against the material of his chapan.

As for the old man verging upon helplessness, Tursen left him shut up in the bare bedroom. The one who stepped out through the door was the unvarying, indestructible, dreaded Head of the Stables and Master of the Horse.

THE DOOR IN FRONT OF TURSEN OPENED OF ITSELF AND RAHIM, HIS bacha, stood back to let him pass. Sleep still gummed the child's thin little face and his ragged chapan still bore the dust of the red earth floor he had slept upon. But he was up and ready for his tasks, and now he held out water in an earthern jug for Tursen's ablutions.

Of course, as he knew very well, old Tursen had but to utter the wish for all the comfort and luxury that the other important men on the estate enjoyed—the Intendant, the Head of the Gardens, the Head of the Farms—to have them in abundance. Tursen and the others served the wealthiest bey in the province, a bey whose generosity to them was proportionate to his wealth. And Tursen was the oldest, most senior among them; and the wealth of the estate in his charge the noblest—the horses.

But does the purity of water depend on the cost of the vessel that holds it? And what is the point of smothering a room with thick carpets, hangings, and dusty curtains, if one has preferred the hollow of a saddle to every other seat all one's life?

Tursen contemplated his bacha. The nape of Rahim's neck and the jug he offered had the same smooth and noble inclination. It was no longer a physical impediment that made Tursen pause now, but this particular harmony. The water trembled at the edge of the spout, about to flow; and Tursen thought, "Because it is intended for me, Rahim holds his coarse jug as though it were a costly ewer from Samarkand or the finest of Persian china. Unlike so many grown men, when this child considers the worth of an object he takes less account of its substance than of the use to which it is to be put . . ."

Tursen reflected that the whip could obtain perfect obedience, promptness, and speed from any bacha—and Rahim had experienced it, like the others before him. But there was no punishment, however severe, that could ensure this concord of body and soul.

Tursen stretched his huge old hands toward the jug. The water poured over them, still filled with the coolness of the night. Tursen sprinkled his cheeks, rough with gray bristles thick as a wild boar's, and wiped his face with the end of his sash.

His eyelids were still lowered. And so for a moment the master's person was as it were delivered up to Rahim and his wondering gaze. There was not a single man in the bacha's world who could be compared to Tursen. None had that depth of chest, that breadth of palm, that majestic forehead. There was none whose flesh and bones bore the marks of glory in such plenty—shattered nose, broken ridge of the brow, scars and gashes merging into the wrinkles, distorted wrists, and disjointed knees. Each wound bore witness to one of the raids, battles, or triumphs of the centaur, the

horseman whose legendary exploits were recounted by the shepherds, the gardeners, the grooms, and the craftsmen. To Rahim,
Tursen's age meant nothing. Heroes and idols are beyond time.

When Tursen opened his narrow almond eyes they suddenly
expressed indomitable energy and fire. He felt that the years had
lost their malignant power, that his knees were still capable of
crushing the ribs of a disobedient horse and his fingers of snatching
the goat's body from a pack of furious horsemen at full gallop—the
finest trophy in all the games and contests of the steppe.

"There. A little cold water is enough," thought Tursen.

In fact (and neither the one nor the other knew it) it was the
bacha's gaze that had had this power, for on opening his eyes Tursen had seen, shining back at him from that naïve mirror, the reflection of his strength, intact and as it were immortal.

WHEN THEY WALKED OUT OF THE HOUSE THE RIM OF THE SUN HAD
already thrust above the horizon of the steppe on the eastward
side. The light met no obstacle on the plain and it flooded the land
with an even glow. Tursen and the bacha turned toward the place
where Mecca lay, beyond the mountains, plains, and deserts. This
was the hour of the first prayer, the moment that commits the
whole length of the day in the purity of dawn. Rahim let himself
drop to his knees and touched the ground with his forehead. It
would have needed immense time and effort for Tursen's body to
take up this position. The old man remained standing, satisfying
himself with bowing his turbanned head as low as possible over the
stick upon which he rested both hands. But such was their mass
and their power that the simple bow of Tursen's shoulders, neck,
and head, bending before an invisible force, expressed a degree of
faith and humility that made the child's prostration look like play.

It was true that what mattered for Rahim was less the prayer
than the fact of praying at the same time as Tursen, at his feet, and
of feeling that breadth and mass above him, like a tree. Of repeating the ritual words that the growling murmur half spoke, half
chanted. Of sharing the sacred splendor of the morning with the

horseman, the chapandaz whose name was the most famous in all the flat lands that stretched out to the Hindu Kush.

The other bachas, who worked in the kitchens, gardens, household, or stables, or with the flocks, no doubt had certain advantages over Rahim in the matter of stolen food or freedom. But on the other hand what greed, what envy shone in their eyes when he told (or invented) the tales of Tursen!

One after another, joint by joint, the old man straightened his head, neck, shoulders. Rahim was up with a single skip and cried, "Today will be fine."

And his little thin flat-nosed face with eyes like pomegranate seeds meant "Fine, because I have the good fortune to begin it with you, O great Tursen."

"The season of the year requires it," said the old man, slowly. The great heat was over. Now was the time when the steppe lived through the luminous dryness of the autumn.

Leaning on his stick, with his turban high and splendid, his ankles cooled by the dew-sparkling grass, and his back turned to the sun's first rays, Tursen spread the nostrils of his snub nose and filled his huge chest to savor the immaculate air before it was thickened by dust raised by the southern winds, the movement of the flocks, and the galloping of the horsemen. All around him stretched the estate, with its gardens, meadows, flowerbeds, and orchards fed by the murmurous charity of the water flowing along, led through irrigation channels. Farther away the green leaves cut off the line of sight on every side. But Tursen's slit eyes, deep in the hollow of their Mongol sockets and shadowed by eyebrows like couch grass, pierced the screen of foliage, remembering and recreating the vast plain over which he had ridden so far and wide.

Meimana, Mazar-i-Sharif, Qataghan.

The inhabitants of each of these provinces (of which the first, Tursen's own, began at the edge of Persia, while the last leaned against the foothills of the Pamir) boasted of possessing the finest astrakhan sheep, of weaving the most precious carpets, and of breeding the swiftest horses. But they were all of the same blood. To conquer these steppes their ancestors had come out of upper Asia in the same hordes. They spoke the same language. Their children learned to ride at the same time as they learned to walk.

Meimana, Mazar-i-Sharif, Qataghan.

This land, faintly rippled by a few slight tawny hills and watered by occasional trickling streams that determined the existence of the fields and the settlements, was Tursen's country, his only one. Certainly, when the sky-reaching passes of the Hindu Kush had been crossed to the south, it was still Afghan country. But Tursen, a child of the steppe, knew and acknowledged nothing other than the steppe. After the Hindu Kush, according to what he had heard, a strange foreign world of high valleys and terrifying peaks began. There men wore no chapans, had long hair, spoke a different tongue. From those parts came the provincial governors, the judges, the officers, the scribes—all people who looked like sacks or logs of wood when they were in the saddle.

And it was in those parts that during the next few hours Uraz . . .

Tursen's terrible hands clenched around the handle of his stick. He had forbidden himself to think of Uraz's journey. Up until that time there had neither been difficulty nor merit in obeying. The struggle against his limbs and his clothes, washing, and prayer had taken up every one of his moments. But here he was, at the first respite . . . "I looked in the unlucky direction," said Tursen to himself. With a movement so violent that the bacha's thin and expressive face filled with astonishment, Tursen turned due north. He felt the better for it. In that direction the land stretched away forever, the same land he had always trodden.

Not far away, no more than two hours' gallop, flowed the Amu Darya, the river of the steppes. After that the Russian land began. But on the one bank as on the other and above the same flat ground floated the same dust in the summer; in the winter the same snow lay; and in spring the same tall grass grew. The men on the one side and on the other had saffron skins and narrow eyes; and on both sides Allah's most splendid gift was a noble horse.

All this Tursen had seen in the first strength of his youth, when he had gone with his father across the Amu Darya. In those days, although the amirs of Khiva and Bukhara were subject to the great northern Czar, they still ruled over their principalities. And men of the same blood and the same Law might go there freely . . .

O mosques, O bazaars of Tashkent and of Samarkand! O brilliant clothes, O silks and chiseled silver, precious arms!

Tursen's thick, fissured lips, drawn back in an unconscious half-smile, formed the words he had learned in those days. Yet it was thirty years since then, and a prodigious revolution had overturned everything on the other side of the river, mercilessly sealing off the fords and bridges. "*Khleb . . . zemlya . . . voda . . . loshad . . .*" said the old man in a very low voice.

Rahim made out the words from their shape on Tursen's lips, and translated the murmur, "Bread . . . land . . . water . . . horse . . ."

For it often happened that Tursen, to bring his memories to stronger life, would tell them to his bacha. And there were no tales that Rahim preferred to those that led him to a country so near and yet so legendary now, guarded by frightening soldiers on either side of the Amu Darya. And perpetually, by questions that might seem naïve but that were filled with subterfuge and hope, he did his best to send Tursen back along the tracks of time past.

That morning the bacha had no need of ruses. Tursen spoke of his own volition, and with a free flow. He too wanted to escape from the present. Once again, as the sun rose in the sky of the steppes, Tursen spoke, chiefly for his own benefit, high over the head of the thin, slender, puny child who stood in his shadow, closing his eyes the better to follow what the old man said—the Kirghiz caravans, the Tartar market places, the dances of the fighting men, princes' gardens and their palaces, the loveliest, most wealthy oases of the heart of Asia.

Yet when Tursen fell silent—and his stories had been longer than usual—the bacha felt disappointed. Tursen had spoken about everything except the heart of the matter. For some moments Rahim respected the old man's silence, out of politeness in the first place and also to be certain that Tursen had really finished. Then in his most offhand, innocent voice he asked, "And what of the buzkashi, great Tursen? They played in those parts also, did they not?"

The old man only jutted out his chin and drew his eyebrows together. That was all that was needed to give his face a look of pitiless ferocity—an expression that Rahim knew well. Filled with terror he thought, "What have I done wrong? He likes talking about the buzkashi more than anything in the world." In the bacha's mind arose the pictures that Tursen's stories had left behind. And Tursen did a great deal more than merely visualize these same images. The stallion who cut through the tangled mass of men and horses, flinging them down, biting, rearing, and trampling, was his own. The rider attached to his saddle by a single stirrup, racing at full gallop with his whole body bent out over the emptiness, stretching toward another mounted fiend to snatch the body of the goat as he hurtled by—that was himself. And the triumphant horseman who flung the trophy into the goal—that again was himself, great, greatest of the chapandaz.

But this thought, far from calming Tursen's rage, doubled its fury. He hated the frightened, ingenuous face that was asking him, "Why? Oh, why?" He was incapable of giving the answer to anyone. So he raised his huge fist to smash the question in the face that bore it.

Rahim neither drew back nor flinched. In the great Tursen he revered even injustice. And the old man saw this in his bacha's eyes. He brought his club of a hand down to his side and suddenly, heavily, set himself in motion. After a few steps, without stopping or turning his head, he shouted the order, "Follow me!"

2

The Mad Horse

THEY WENT THROUGH the twelve enclosures one after another, yards with low walls of dried mud, linked by narrow gaps, all alike—rectangles of bare, cracked earth, blazing hot in the sun already, although it was very far from its zenith. In each corner of these yards stood a fully harnessed horse; each had just been brought out of its stable and tethered to a picket by a short rope.

They were all of a dazzling and powerful beauty. Their long, thick, perfectly groomed manes and their coats—black, bay, chestnut, or gray—had the gleam of wild silk. Their deep shoulders, their broad rounded chests, their muscular, proudly arching necks breathed forth inexhaustible strength, endurance, and spirit.

The maze of enclosures in which these horses were picketed four by four held forty-eight in all. There could be no doubt that Osman Bey, to whom the estate belonged, was the richest man in the province of Meimana, since he could gather together, breed, and maintain so many splendid horses merely for his personal glory. Their sole function was to play buzkashi during the season— the game from which many of them came back wounded and crippled.

The real master of this princely stable, recognized by all, was Tursen. And when Osman Bey's horses won their victories, the honor went in the first place to the Head of the Stables.

What could be fairer? The wealthy man only provided the money—Tursen all the rest. He supervised the buying of the foals. He decided upon the mares' covering. He watched over the feeding and the litter. He ruled over exercise, training, and education. He determined the age at which the horses should face their first encounter. He followed them from game to game, had their faults corrected and their talents brought to flower. He treated wounds and broken bones. And if a noble animal was maimed in the contest, it was he who killed it with his own hand, respectfully.

Tursen knew the virtues and the weaknesses not only of all Osman Bey's horses but also of all the picked horsemen he engaged to ride them. And weighing, matching their qualities, he wedded the man and his mount so that the conjunction should come as near to perfection as possible.

Once again, according to his daily custom, Tursen went from yard to yard, examining the forty-eight horses under his charge one by one. He halted for a long while before each of them. The stable boys and grooms followed him in an almost superstitious silence. They fully understood the importance of this inspection.

At the end of spring the horses' weariness and the climate's burning heat brought the buzkashi season to an end. It began again in the autumn. In the meantime Tursen had to rebuild the tendons, muscles, blood, and marrow of the creatures who had been exhausted and wounded by months of pitiless struggle.

To begin with, the horses were given a complete rest. They never moved from their light, spacious, airy stables, the floors of which were sprinkled every morning with dry dung and sand so that they should be springy and gentle to the horses' hoofs. At night the animals were fed with barley and oats. By day they were given a special mixture of raw eggs and pieces of butter.

They quickly recovered their strength, but at the same time they grew fat, putting on too much weight. They therefore had to undergo the *qantar*. Bridled and saddled, from dawn to dusk in the full summer, week after week they stood motionless at the four corners of the bare yard, where the heat and light, concentrated and reflected, transformed the air into an oven. The sun's fire burned away the fat, soaked into the flesh and muscles, purifying them, teaching patience and long-suffering.

Now it was the heart of autumn. The morning had come for Tursen to make his decision.

While he had been moving from yard to yard, the group that followed had grown by ten men or so. They, like the servingmen of the stables, wore meager, worn, sun-faded old chapans, and they too had badly tanned leather slippers on their feet. But under their belts was thrust a crop with a short, hard lash like Tursen's; and instead of the greasy, shapeless rags that covered the heads of the grooms they wore round caps pulled down almost to their eyebrows —astrakhan caps with fox or wolf fur round the edge.

Rahim stared fixedly at these headdresses: they smelled of wild beasts and emphasized the fierce planes of those Uzbek and Tur-koman faces, their high cheekbones and narrow eyes. These caps could be worn only by those who had received, from pitiless judges, the title of chapandaz for their unsurpassed skill at buzkashi.

"Thou knowest their names?" Rahim asked a stable boy who chanced to be at hand.

"How should I not know them?" said the other proudly. "I am always here when they come to take a horse for training and when they bring it back. There is Yalavach . . . and there is Buri."

"Yalavach . . . Buri," repeated Rahim in a voice that quavered. Like all boys of his age he had already seen a great many buzkashis. But they were only village amusements, played by amateurs mounted on what horses they could find. The chapandaz played only in the great matches, either against one another or in contests of province against province. When those who had been spectators of these memorable encounters came home, they recounted the feats and prowess of the chapandaz over and over again. Their neighbors embroidered these tales, repeating them in the alleys of the bazaars and in the shade of the chaikhanas all along the highroads and mountain tracks. The tales traveled on and on from mouth to mouth, rapidly turning into legend. The fame of the great horsemen resounded to the remotest yurts.

So Rahim knew their names, as did all the other bachas on the estate, the little shepherds, vegetable peelers, scullions, carpenter's boys, smith's boys, gardener's boys. But these names had only been the symbols for inaccessible beings. And now all at once . . .

"There is Mengu," said the stable boy. "And that is Muzuk."

"Mengu . . . Muzuk!" repeated the bacha. Each of his sighs was a fresh source of pride to the wretched little dung sweeper who pointed out the famous horsemen. Did they not belong, as he did, to the stables of Osman Bey?

"Thou seest, bacha," he ended, "thou seest—we have both the finest horses and the finest chapandaz."

Rahim tightened the very dirty rag that belted in his ragged chapan, wiped his nose on his sleeve, and replied, "It is we who pick them."

He ran after Tursen, who was moving into the next courtyard. This was the last of the twelve enclosures given over to the qantar. Tursen stopped in the middle and made a sign. The chapandaz gathered round him.

Rahim stood in their shadow, his throat dry. He could not believe in his own good fortune. Until then he had never been allowed into these yards. Now he had walked through them all; and here was Tursen carrying out his most important function right in front of him. The bacha no longer dared blink. He felt that the slightest flicker of his eyelids would make this sight, this dream, vanish quite away . . .

In the middle of the courtyard rose Tursen's majestic turban; in a ring around him the fierce hats of the chapandaz; behind, the stable men. In the four corners, like statues in their power and beauty, four magnificent horses upon whose gleaming flanks blazed the already lofty sun. And beyond the walls, stretching out as far as the horizon, the woods, the rounded hills, and the grazing pastures of the estate.

Rahim thought of his father, a poor shepherd. Somewhere over there he was guarding Osman Bey's astrakhan flocks with his dog and his flute. "If only he could see me here, in the midst of all this glory!" thought Rahim.

How splendid they were, the chapandaz! All of them, whether very young or completely gray. Tall and slim, all muscle and bone, their faces like falcons trained for hawking; or else heavy-bodied and heavy-jawed, like the mastiffs of the nomad caravans. The horsemen's age, the shape of their features, their build—these were of no importance to the bacha. What set each of them above the ordinary run of mortals was his bruises and his scars. And also—

and this was so even with the slimmest—the massive wrists, the hands made to snatch the goat's body, prize of the buzkashi, from the opponent and to hold on to it afterwards. Above all, clearly expressed by everything in their attitude, from the way they looked about them to the way they walked, was the haughty, offhand certainty of their supreme status. Their chapans might be threadbare and dirty and their whole estate no more than a hovel or a yurt with a few goats on a barren patch of steppe, but in their fur caps they looked prouder, richer, and more free than the wealthiest khans and beys in the province.

Tursen, leaning on his stick, remained silent. And the men in fierce hats waited without stirring. Tursen's eyes settled on them one after another, making one last assessment. It looked as though he were trying to burrow beneath the skin, to reach the deep essential fibers, the most hidden springs of strength, determination, skill, and courage.

At last he uttered the names of five chapandaz, and to each he coupled that of a horse. Then he said, "Those will go to Kabul, the capital."

Rahim's whole meager body trembled. So it was true, all they said in the kitchens, the stables, the forges, and the saddler's shops . . . A buzkashi at Kabul . . . the greatest . . . the first . . . At Kabul . . . beyond the Hindu Kush, behind the tall mountains, the enormous mountains that barred the whole horizon to the south . . . At Kabul, the great city, city of the king.

The chapandaz whom Tursen had named went up to him. "What are the others going to do?" wondered the bacha. He waited in alarm, exquisite alarm, for the chorus of harsh, discordant shouts, the cries of anger, the furious protests, the calling down of divine revenge, the curses upon the iniquitous worthlessness of the decision that never failed to ring out, backed up by furious gestures, whenever a choice of this kind was made. The blood of the steppe tribes insisted upon this, even in the poorest man, even before a bey, a khan, a judge. What might one not fear and at the same time hope for from disappointed chapandaz, humiliated in their desires?

Nothing happened. The riders who had not been chosen for the wonderful buzkashi gazed at the little transparent clouds that drifted over the limitless sky, at the cracks in the walls, at the motionless horses in the four corners of the yard. They did not even turn their heads toward those who were listening to Tursen. "There you are," thought Rahim. "From him, they will take anything at all."

When Tursen had given his orders, Yalavach, the oldest of the chapandaz, a man with the silhouette of an aged bird of prey, said to him, "We have not seen Uraz, thy son . . . Is he not to go to Kabul?"

"He is to go," said Tursen.

"But with what horse?" asked Yalavach. "Thou hast given us the finest."

Tursen's huge hand came down on the shoulder of the chapandaz and in a deep growl he said, "Thy hair is gray already, Yalavach, and thou dost not yet know that another man has nothing to say between a father and his son?" The thrust was sudden. Trained though he was to contest and battle, Yalavach staggered.

"Follow me," said Tursen to Rahim.

THEY HAD GONE BEYOND THE ESTATE'S PLEASURE GARDENS AND CULtivation—flowers, orchards, vineyards, fields of melons—and were coming to the fallow land. They went on and on. Tursen walked in front, with a long firm pace. He was no longer chained fast to old age. The sun flowed in his bones like a grateful oil.

Now they were in wooded country. Tursen, his bacha behind him, followed a track that ran through harsh patches of bramble and then around a bush-topped hill. In its shade stood an almost perfectly round clump of green. Its trees were so close together and so thickly leaved that it seemed impossible to pass through the ring they made. Tursen thrust two branches aside with his stick, disclosing a path.

When Rahim came out from under the deep cover he found that he was on the edge of a wide bower of some kind, planted in a circle. In the middle was a pool, a stone bench, and, tethered to the bench, a horse. At first the bacha saw nothing but the horse. It was a bright bay stallion with long flowing mane, so big, so powerful in breast and shoulders, so vigorous and light on its legs that in strength and beauty it far surpassed Osman Bey's most precious charger.

"Where could such a horse have come from?" Rahim wondered. Had it fallen from the clouds, having carried the Prophet on his rides through Paradise? The bacha raised his eyes to the heavens and found no reply in that expanse of woven light. He brought his gaze back to earth. Tursen was going toward a big tent pitched at the edge of the trees on the other side of the pool. Before he reached it a man appeared in the doorway, bowed very low, and cried, "Welcome, master!"

"Peace upon thee, Mukhi," said Tursen.

The man straightened up. He was very young, almost a youth, and so tall that Tursen's lofty turban only reached to his chin. He had a very flat face, very high cheekbones, and a very wide mouth. A poverty-stricken chapan, too short for him, waved over calves lined with powerful muscles, and exposed wrists as thick as Tursen's. Mukhi's candid, ingenuous eyes met Rahim's, and he smiled at the bacha for no reason, merely for the pleasure of smiling.

Tursen turned back, walked round the pool, and stopped in front of the great bay stallion. Mukhi and Rahim joined him. He motioned them back and stood there alone, facing the bright bay, leaning on the stick with both hands, moving no more than if he had been a block of wood.

The horse felt this concentrated gaze, this communion. As he had been taught, he went on acting like a motionless statue beneath the sun, but in that marvelously smooth skin a muscle quivered, then gradually another and another. His chest swelled; his eyes lit up. His nostrils trembled, like those of a wild beast.

A great silence weighed upon the round clearing hidden amid the trees. In the pool, the water shone and glittered.

"I think this horse is in good condition," said Tursen at last, speaking to himself.

In two strides Mukhi was at his side. "Good condition!" cried the young man. "Oh, master, those words are too little! Give this horse wings and still he will run no faster over the steppe than he does today. Give him ten wild stallions to fight and he will eat them up. Ask him anything at all and he will understand and obey

better than the cleverest, most faithful servant . . . This horse, he
is . . . He is . . ." Mukhi clacked his tongue loudly, as though he
were tasting a marvelous dish. Then, surprised by the way he had
expressed himself, he laughed as only he could laugh, with the full
stretch of his mouth and chest; the moment one burst of laughter
died another succeeded it, and so on indefinitely. His wide lips
almost touched his huge ears, and his teeth flashed and sparkled.
There was so much health and innocence and such a total lack of
self-awareness in his joy that Tursen's face, ill-accustomed to smiling, bent into cheerfulness. "Thou art a good syce,* Mukhi," he
said, almost gently. Then in the harshest tone he asked, "Who
rode this horse last?"

"Yesterday evening Uraz, thy son . . . and this morning myself," said Mukhi.

"Well?" asked Tursen again.

"A dream," said Mukhi. He spoke in a half-whisper, and his
eyes were narrowed as though still lashed by the wind that rushes
to meet a furious gallop. Tursen's eyes went from this suddenly
mature face to Mukhi's solid great wrists and broad, thick hands.
"Thou'lt make a good chapandaz," said Tursen.

Once again Mukhi laughed as only he could laugh, and cried,
"Any man would be, upon that horse. There will never be another
like him."

"Enough prating," growled Tursen. Mukhi's gaiety dried up instantly. He felt that he took up too much room, made too much
noise. Suddenly he was ashamed of his size and his laugh. "I must
go back to polishing the saddle," he said. The tall syce vanished
into the tent, bowing his back and pulling in his head to look
smaller.

Tursen sat down on the stone bench. Above him the great bay
stallion arched his splendid crest. No, thought the old chapandaz,
never will a horse like this be seen again. Because never again will
there be a Tursen to form another. To choose the bloodlines. To
watch over the feeding of the colt for the first three years, when he
lived in total freedom. To saddle, bridle, and ride him during the
three years that followed. Then, for still another three, to shape

* Groom.

him step by step, exercise by exercise, muscle by muscle—to shape him and train him for the most terrible feats and acrobatics.

For indeed all buzkashi horses had to possess the rarest and most contradictory qualities—high spirit and patience, the speed of the wind and the perseverance of a packhorse, the dash of a lion and the cleverness of a performing dog. Without all this, how could they pass from wild gallop to dead halt, from flight to pursuit, and from dodging to attack, at the slightest hint from the knee, rein, or spur? Yet none of these astonishing animals could compare with the stallion whose warm breath was caressing Tursen's withered cheek. He was as far beyond his rivals as the old chapandaz had been beyond the finest horsemen. The horse had not yet undergone any real trials—he was only just rising ten, the age of fullest power. But in all his exercises and in all the mock contests he had shown qualities that went beyond the brute condition, the animal state of mind. It looked as though in some mysterious way Tursen had imbued him with a share of his own ferocious determination, cool courage, and understanding.

The various efforts, stages, anxieties, and rewards that had punctuated these nine years ran through Tursen's mind. And at each recollection he repeated to himself—was it with pride or sadness?—"No, never again, never again."

A sigh roused him from his musing. Rahim was standing behind him, within hand's reach. The bacha's curiosity had been too strong—this round clearing, cut off from the whole of the rest of the world . . . The old man in the middle of it, and this horse, as stock still as the bench upon which Tursen was sitting . . . And the legend that he sometimes heard whispered by the underlings on the estate. "The horse is indeed the one they call Jahil—the Mad Horse?" asked Rahim. The words were scarcely out before he instinctively raised his hands to his face, to protect it from the blow that would punish his impudence—that would surely punish it.

Tursen seemed not to have heard. The bacha swore not to utter another word, and at the same instant said, "Why do people call him that?"

"Because this horse is more intelligent than they can understand," said Tursen, without moving.

Rahim breathed again. His head was spinning. However unbelievable it might be, he had been given an answer. Very quickly he went on, "And it really is your horse? Your own horse?"

And once more Tursen replied. Perhaps, without being clearly aware of it, he had brought the bacha for no other reason than to speak his own haunting thoughts aloud. For only the trust, the ardor, and the ingenuousness of a child could justify a proud old man in unloading the burdens of his memory upon him. Tursen was not confiding in his bacha. He was building up a tradition.

With his eyes fixed on the great stallion, Tursen said, "I have always had a horse, a horse of my own. So did my father and my father's father, and his father before him. Good, sound chapandaz, all of them. They were never rich because they preferred a horse to all other possessions. Thou knowest that these animals cost a great deal and that they are not spared in a match. For my part, I have done the same as my father and those who begot him. Only I took advantage of their knowledge and I also had more luck. My first horse was given me when I was twenty, when I won against the finest chapandaz. He was a stallion from Bactria, a land famous for noble horses since time began. And he was called Jahil, just as all my horses since him have been called Jahil, because of the stupidity of mankind." Tursen took his stick again, leaned his hands on it, and over his hands his chin. "I have had five since him," he went on. "Each has been better than his sire, because I grew better and better at choosing the mares and because greater experience in forming them has come to me with age. And here is the best of them all, the last of the Jahils . . ."

Tursen stopped short. Yet as he knew very well he had only spoken so that he could utter the thought that was always with him—"Yes, here is the last mad horse. But I am no longer capable of riding him in his first buzkashi . . . and what a buzkashi!" How Tursen longed to speak those words! How he needed to say them! He could not bring himself to it. A proud old man has no right to commit his most piercing grief even to a clean-hearted child.

Tursen rose from the stone bench. He did so without difficulty. Yet it seemed to him that he was bearing a heavier weight than he bore in those moments at dawn when his body refused to obey him as though it were loaded with irons.

Mukhi came out of the tent. Above his head he waved the stallion's harness. The sun laughed on the leather and the metal, and the tall syce laughed with it. "Look, master, look," he cried. "Jahil will not lose face at Kabul, the great city, the city of the king."

"Thou'lt have my last orders this evening," said Tursen. The old chapandaz moved his hand toward the stallion's muzzle, a movement that he did not finish. "I will see thee too, this evening," he said to the horse. Then to Rahim, "Wait till I come back."

"With Jahil?" cried Rahim.

Tursen walked away without replying. Rahim raised his eyes to thank heaven for his good fortune.

3

The Two Stars

AN HOUR'S TROT was enough to carry a man from Osman Bey's estate to Daolatabad. It was only a very small town, but it stood out as a capital for the people of these parts, an immense region of steppe and pastureland so thinly inhabited that the hamlets amounted to no more than a few hovels made of dried mud or a handful of semi-nomadic yurts. At Daolatabad there was a district administrator, a garrison, a police post, an ancient bazaar in the heart of the town, and a brand new school at its gate.

Tursen was going to the bazaar. He had to pass in front of the school. The morning classes were over; yet there was a crowd of boys before the high brown wall that hid the school and its garden. They thronged together, a mingled host of big boys and little ones, and, as could be seen from the state of their chapans, sons of the richest families and the poorest.

The stout horse that Tursen had picked from the stables stopped of its own accord—the crowd of children overflowed onto the road. They were strangely silent, and all of them, on tiptoe and with open mouths, had their shining eyes turned toward the school in a fixed stare. From the height of his saddle Tursen easily recognized the man leaning against the wall, the man before whom this mob of boys—half wild, bold, confident creatures at ordinary times —stood spellbound. "Why," thought he, "here is Gardi Gaj, the storyteller, among us once again." He slackened his reins and with immense respect said, "Ancestor of All the World, blessed be thy return."

"Peace and honor to thee, O Tursen, who hast been the greatest chapandaz of this land," said the old man in a fragile voice, but one that carried a great way.

Tursen nodded. "He recognizes me," he thought. "How? After so many years of absence, of traveling . . . After more meetings than can be numbered . . ."

Upon this the children shouted, "Tell us a tale, tell us a tale at once!" And the most zealous, the eagerest of them all was a poor sickly little boy propped up on crutches.

"I will see thee again as I return, Ancestor of All the World," said Tursen. He touched his horse's side with his spur and made his way into the town.

THE BAZAAR OF DAOLATABAD WAS ONE OF THE OLDEST IN THE province; here everything still retained the color, smell, shape, and customs of the market places of Central Asia, even in the middle of this century, just as they were at the beginning of time.

It was a maze of narrow, winding lanes and blind alleys, stalls, shops, and warehouses; and everywhere the sun, flickering through the straw mats and the foliage set up to shade the alleys, produced zones of strongly contrasting light and shade in which clothes, faces, materials, metals, and provisions assumed a mysterious richness. A ragged old chapan took on the appearance of costly velvet. The narrow eyes of an ancient merchant squatting in his tiny cell-like shop seemed to contain the world's whole store of guile. The great copper samovars turned to fiery gold. On the stalls the raw joints of meat, huge grapes, newly shed blood of the watermelons blazed with a barbarous violence. The horses tethered to the door handles tossed their heads, snorting amidst swarms of flies. From time to time a kneeling camel uttered a prolonged braying roar. Thus the current of tradition ran on, the persistence of a trade that century after century had built up out of the same exchanges following the same routes, the same rites, the same bargaining, and

the same drafts of green tea or black, the same accepted poverty
and the same untroubled wealth.

The entire length of the main thoroughfares and side alleys of
the maze was an entangled, milling swarm of men and beasts.
Rank and wealth counted for little in this close-packed confusion.
It was as hard for the richest man to make his way through as the
poorest. Yet there were a few who were freed from this constraint,
and they were the chapandaz. When their hats were seen a strong,
delighted murmur rose all around. The beloved names passed from
row to row, from rank to rank. And through the body of the crowd
—even the densest, most compact—a lane opened as though by a
miracle, so that the hero of the buzkashi made his way freely along
it, walking with the awkward pace the very high heels of his boots
imposed on him. He was greeted from either side of the human
corridor with cries of welcome, praise, and blessing, and slices of
muskmelon or watermelon or bunches of grapes were held out to
him. He replied in a lordly, good-natured way with thanks, a laugh,
a joke, or a cheerful grossness.

Through the slits in the hoods of their chadars, the women—
none of whom had ever been allowed to watch the whole nation's
game in all the hundreds of years it had been played—the women
followed the chapandaz with dreamlike eyes.

In the very middle of the bazaar the wealthiest cloth merchant
kept shop on a broad, deep platform, open on the street side but
sheltered by a roof and cut off from the neighbors by walls. Important men had gathered in this cool, dark place—the district administrator, who was called "the little governor" to distinguish him
from the big governor, the one who ruled the whole province of
Meimana; the head of the buzkashi for the same region; then
Osman Bey and two other owners of famous stables whose horses
were to be present at Kabul for the royal game.

For these guests the shopmen had covered the ordinary rugs
with rare, deep-piled carpets. Now, carelessly stretched out, with
their shoulders leaning against heaps of cotton and silk from Persia,
India, and Japan, the great men sipped aromatic green China tea
out of Russian cups.

Their presence, offered to the people at the market as it were
upon a stage, attracted the curious. The merchant did nothing to

send them away: he would have preferred the whole bazaar to have witnessed the honor done to him by such a gathering at his shop. In order to reach it Tursen had to strike out with his crop and make his horse breast its way through the crowd.

He had less difficulty in dismounting. The platform where the cloth was piled stood just at the level of his stirrups. The shopmen and the bachas helped him to get a footing, set cushions for his head, and offered him tea. Before yielding to their attentions Tursen greeted the master of the house and his guests in fitting manner. And they, though higher by rank, office, or fortune, replied as to an equal, civility for civility, compliment for compliment. Then, while Tursen stretched himself out and relaxed, slowly and noisily sucking in the boiling-hot tea, everyone remained silent. It was well known that the old man disliked questions. If he had something to say, he said it when he saw fit.

A bacha placed a nargile between Tursen's hands. Tursen raised the mouthpiece to his lips and let his lungs fill with the water-cooled smoke. Only then, addressing his words to the head of the buzkashi, the little governor, and Osman Bey all in one, did he say, "I have made the choice."

He gave the names of the riders he had picked for Kabul and those of the horses; then he was silent. In a country of ready eloquence Tursen spoke little; because of this he inspired all the more respect and dread.

"Everything is perfect, as it always is with thee," said the head of the buzkashi, who ruled the teams of chapandaz throughout the entire province. He was a man of about sixty, with regular features, tall, slim, and exceedingly well bred. A sumptuous pale green silk chapan with broad white stripes covered his silver-gray breeches and his supple knee-high leather boots. Features, voice, and manners were those of a lord. But if Tursen bowed his massive head in acknowledgment of praise it was only because the nobleman knew the horses and the men who rode them almost as well as he did himself.

"The chapandaz, their mounts, and their syces will leave by lorry," continued the head of the buzkashi. "They must have a few days to grow used to the air of Kabul."

"Very true . . . It is six thousand feet higher there than it is here," said Osman Bey with the smile that he always wore on his fat, smooth, and shining face, as though to apologize for his wealth.

There was a silence once more. The nargile began to circulate. Tursen closed his eyes. Osman Bey directed a pressing look at the little governor, who touched the chief of the buzkashi on the knee and whispered into his ear, "And Uraz? Thou art the only man who can ask the question."

The head of the buzkashi, stroking the handle of his silver-mounted crop with a very beautiful and well-cared-for hand, said, "Forgive me, honorable Tursen, if I seem impatient, which does not become our white hair at all. Duty compels me . . . We do not yet know the horse though hast chosen for Uraz, thy son."

"My son was to be with you," said Tursen, his eyes still closed.

"He has been seen in the bazaar," said the little governor.

"Where?" asked Tursen.

"At the camel fight," said Osman Bey, smiling.

"He does not know that you have met?" asked Tursen, his eyelids still lowered.

"He wants to see the end of the fight," said the little governor.

Tursen slowly opened his eyes and looked at each of the three men. "Bacha," he said to the boy who was offering him the nargile again. "Go and tell Uraz that I am here."

ON ITS SOUTHERN SIDE THE BAZAAR OF DAOLATABAD WAS LIMITED by the ruins of an ancient fortress. The network of covered alleys suddenly gave way to a broad platform protected by crenelated red earth walls. A single step carried one from the mild dimness of the narrow passages into the harsh, piercing glare of the steppes, with the sun close to its height.

Usually the place was completely empty through these burning hours. All that was to be seen at the foot of the fortifications were bales unloaded by the men of the caravans lying in heaps, and their animals squatting in the thin line of shadow that ran along the worn old stones. But on that day the space was filled with hundreds of men standing chapan to chapan. And from shoulder to shoulder spread a fierce, animal emotion that turned the human mass into something like a single quivering muscle. For above the turbans and the rags that covered the heads of the crowd, two slavering mouths, borne high on two huge, twisted, swollen, reptilian necks, confronted one another.

At Daolatabad, as everywhere else in Afghanistan, the people were passionately attached to spectacles in which animals tore one another, throttled one another, devoured one another. But to all other games of this kind—fights between cocks, dogs, rams, quails —they much preferred camel-fighting, because these encounters were by far the rarest. For a camel fight animals of uncommon strength and ferocity were needed; even so, camels only yearned to kill when they were in rut.

By threefold good fortune it so happened that the season was right, that in a caravan just arrived from Badakshan were two powerful and extremely aggressive he-camels, and that their owners wished to turn this fury to profit.

Even when they were at rest, the savage malignity of the huge, black, hairy opponents filled the beholder with alarm. Now that they were locked in a struggle to the death, they looked more like things that were half wild beast and half monster. Their long, bendable, folded, disjointed legs, interwoven in the convulsion of battle, formed a knot of revolting, hair-tufted serpents. Two other great mingled reptiles rose above the dark hairy humps, quivering with the rage of the attack—the necks of the fighting beasts. At the top, the gaping jaws, their immense, flabby lips twisted in a horrible grin, flowed with streams of foaming slime in which bubbles of blood appeared, continually swelling and bursting.

Using knees, hoofs, and teeth—rearing, lying down, upright, separated, entwined, but perpetually bent on killing whether by biting, smothering, or disembowelling—the hairy black camels, their yards erect in a rut where fury of attack took the place of the rage of coition, fought a battle that seemed to stem from the darkest night of the world, while the hawks and falcons of the steppes wheeled above the ancient ruined towers, before the red and pink battlements, silhoueted against the blinding sky.

The attacks were accompanied by continuous bellows, now a roaring, now a ghastly howling: lament and fury, a war cry, an invocation to the everlasting sap, and herald of death. To every movement, every utterance of the beasts in their deathly madness, rose an answering roar from the crowd, its blood heated to a fever by the sun, its wits stupefied by the reek of sweat, blood, and urine that flowed from the monstrous brutes.

Yet there was one spectator who seemed unaffected by this frenzy, although he was in the front row of the audience. His arms rested motionless upon his brown chapan, and under his furred chapandaz cap his cruel, shrewd face never stirred. The only thing that showed his intense interest in the sight was the tension of his lips—an expression not unlike a wolf's grin. But when the cloth merchant's messenger plucked him by the hand, the narrowed, blazing glare that settled on the bacha was that of a man who had also been overtaken (though secretly) by the common madness.

"What dost thou want with me, bazaar bug?" he asked in a voice trembling with held-in rage.

The bacha shrunk his head between his shoulders and hurriedly blurted out, "You must come to my master's house at once."

"I have already given my answer—not before the end," said the chapandaz.

"But . . ."

The chapandaz had already forgotten the messenger's existence. A sharper, harsher cry than ever rose from the crowd. The camels' necks were knotted in a convulsive effort and bones had been heard to crack. Was this death for one? Which of them was going to collapse?

The wolf's grin once more drew back the chapandaz's lips. Nothing could reach him as he stood there, rapt. Yet one name could pierce through. "Tursen . . ." the bacha had said. In spite of himself the chapandaz listened. "The honorable Tursen, thy father, has come, and he is asking for thee . . ."

For a moment the man in the fur cap hoped that the fight was coming to an end and that this way everything would be in order. But the two camels had disentangled themselves and were bellowing toward the red battlements, the incandescent sky, as though to invoke them before beginning the attack again.

"Thy father . . . the great Tursen . . ." repeated the bacha.

The chapandaz left his place.

WITH HIS HEAD HELD HIGH AND STIFF, LOOKING NEITHER TO RIGHT nor left, Uraz fixed his eyes—eyes that were scarcely slit at all—on the lane the crowd opened of its own volition for him. For him still more than for the general run of chapandaz. Was he not the most famous of them all?

Uraz appeared to be blind, deaf, and inimical to this unparalleled homage and to the praise that ran along beside him. Once again he was in the grip of the conflict, that racking conflict that arose from his one true desire, his most powerful need—his lust for fame. He could not do without it. He longed for it at all costs, vital as bread, necessary as water. And fame was his; shining fame followed him, obedient and faithful. But granted by whom? By this mob . . . this scum. Sweating hides. Silly eyes. Flabby mouths . . . And he, Uraz, whom honor required to need no one at all, was obliged to depend upon this herd for his life's essence.

Glory. Yes. The sun in the sky of the steppes. The song of the wind in the tall grass. Not these voices! Not these faces!

Do not hear them. Do not see them. Walk as though in blinkers. Clench, clench your teeth.

Thus, on his tall and awkward heels, Uraz strode on, Uraz, who would not consent to live without man-given fame and who at the same time refused men the right to grant it.

On his clean-cut, cruel face, sharpened by a little dagger-pointed beard, the clenching of his jaws made the muscles quiver, bringing his cheekbones into high relief.

And the bazaar whispered:

"He is not like the rest of them."

"Never a word . . ."

"Never a smile."

"So proud. So hard."

"He has no friendship for anyone."

"Not even for the horses."

"He is frightening."

"A wolf."

Because of the astonishment and dread he made them feel, the crowd admired him all the more. And generally speaking, Uraz derived deep satisfaction from this alarm. It was a feeling his pride could feed upon—swallow whole.

Generally speaking. Not this morning. "Today I am the one who is afraid," thought Uraz. "I am the one who turns into a cringing dog. I am whistled for and I come running." Once more he saw the great black camels at grips with one another, the beasts whose battle he had not been able to follow through; and he said to himself, "By the Prophet, I need nobody and I need nothing. I fear nobody and I fear nothing. And I am going to show *him* that this is so."

THE NARGILE, STILL CIRCULATING, HAD REACHED OSMAN BEY. Of all the cloth merchant's guests he, taught by wealth and privilege, knew best how to extract the utmost from sensual delights. And his smooth face was already registering expectation of pleasure when suddenly he sat straight up on the cushions that supported him on every side.

A confused and distant clamor reached the shop, and at the same time the crowd in the alley on which it gave gradually opened, though that seemed impossible, so closely were the people packed together. Buyers, idlers, water sellers, hawkers with trays, and even the ass drivers, most obstinate creatures on earth, drew back, flattening themselves against the front of the stall. A thin corridor appeared, and at the far end of it a man wearing a furred cap.

Tursen recognized him before his companions. In a low, careless tone he observed, "Here is Uraz." And as though the crowd had caught the name from his mouth, it came back to him in a triumphant echo, multiplied a hundredfold—Uraz . . . Uraz . . . Uraz . . . Uraz . . ."

Without being aware of it, Tursen had raised his shoulders slightly from the cushions. Now he heard, "Uraz . . . Uraz . . . son of Tursen."

Leaning on his huge palms, Tursen straightened his massive

trunk completely. It was not right to welcome such a gift from fate lying down. The happiness of delighted pride, the glowing warmth of fame—Tursen had been sure that these feelings were quite dead within him. For a great while he had been living withdrawn on Osman Bey's estate, and fame no longer knew his face, since legend wipes out the features of living men. Old Tursen knew very well that although at this moment Uraz's name was coupled with his, it was only because of ancient use and custom, just as it had been for him in former times, when they had shouted, "Tursen, Tursen, son of Tongut."

What did all that matter? What he was hearing now, after that long stretch of silence, was the song of a crowd rising up toward him once again.

And because the wonderful sound was so to speak presented to him by his son, Tursen suddenly found excuses for everything that angered and vexed him in Uraz. He lacked broad, burly shoulders? Yet, on the other hand, what astonishing suppleness and speed! Was his face without scars, the chapandaz's marks of honor? But surely that was a proof of his skill! His easy bearing did not show the dignity suitable to a man of forty-five? But what an acrobat in the saddle! And in the midst of the clamor that ran their two names together Tursen saw even the insolent wolf's grin that the whip had been unable to wipe out or conquer in the child as the mark of legitimate pride.

Uraz reached the cloth merchant's platform. Scorning the steps, he leaned on the edge of the dais and vaulted straight onto the carpets that covered it. Everyone, merchant and his guests, had risen to welcome him. Everyone—except Tursen. It meant little to him that Uraz was the best chapandaz in the province and its hero. He had been that before him. And this chapandaz was only his son.

When Uraz saw Tursen's monumental trunk like a block of eternity set there on the foundation of his crossed legs under his chapan, in spite of himself he thought, "The others are richer, nobler, more powerful than this old man. But it is he who is the lord."

So in spite of his pride's resolve, Uraz bowed as duty required, touching Tursen's shoulder with his forehead and uttering the almost slavish words of respect and obedience, a son's greeting to his father, hated for close on thirty years.

And for a moment Uraz's submission in the presence of a crowd that worshipped him gave Tursen the sense of fatherhood. He stood up; raised one hand. Everyone instantly fell silent, and Tursen said, "I do not care for useless words. So listen well, for I shall be brief. I have a new stallion ready for the buzkashi; he is called the Mad Horse."

"We know the name," shouted the crowd.

"The one I speak of is the last of his blood, and the finest," answered Tursen.

"In that case," said the head of the buzkashi, "in that case he has not his like in the Three Provinces."

"So I believe," said Tursen. "And that is why at Kabul, the capital, Uraz, my son, shall have him as his mount." Tursen drew breath. What he had wished to say was said. All he had to do now was return to his place on the cushions. Instead, he once more raised his hand to show that he had not finished.

Was it that he felt the need to retain within himself, upon himself, the crowd's warmth and emotion, like a traveler who has lived a great while in the dim icy regions and cannot satisfy his hunger for the sun? Or was he incapable of remaining in Uraz's debt?

"You who stand about me," said Tursen slowly, "and who will presently spread my words abroad, I take you to witness. If at Kabul, the capital, my Jahil wins the Buzkashi of the king, from that moment he will belong to Uraz, my son, and to him alone."

Having spoken Tursen sat down, straight-backed, on his crossed legs. The movement was not completed before exclamations and comments broke out; and in them mingled truth, falsehood, and imagination. All the people were stirred by the magnificence of the gift. They shouted, they chanted:

"To give up the stallion!"

"Of such immense worth!"

"Such glory!"

"How he loves his son!"

And with astonishment Tursen reflected, "Could it be true? Since I have done that, no doubt it is because I love him."

Uraz gazed at his father; on his proud, cruel face there was an almost childish look of unbelief. He, Uraz, who had been unfaithful to the tradition, the law of his clan and his blood, never owning a mount worthy of him because he preferred to fritter away his winnings in victory banquets, costly boots and hats, and fights between rams, cocks, dogs, and quails, he who had triumphed only on other men's horses—he was to have the Mad Horse handed over to him. To him. He had ridden the stallion. They knew one another. They could not but win the great buzkashi of the king.

When Uraz bent to kiss Tursen's shoulder, he did so with a free and happy motion for the first time in his life. And as he bowed he said within himself, "My father, my real father. I am proud of him and I love him."

At the meal which brought the guests together in the back of the shop, Tursen and Uraz, sitting side by side, did not exchange many words. But when they broke a warm, soft wheatcake or plunged their fingers in one of the dishes of ten-spiced, ten-colored rice, or in a mutton ragout, a mess of chicken, or a sour milk cheese, they shared more than mere nourishment.

The feast lasted a great while. At last the bachas poured water from the ewers over the guests' hands; then the head of the buzkashi said, "I thank our host and I beg his forgiveness . . . The time has come."

The daylight was beginning to fade in the deserted alleys of the bazaar. The little governor escorted his friends as far as the main square of Daolatabad, to the front of the house that went with his office. Here stood an aged American motorcar, huge and gleaming. Its hood was folded back. Osman Bey's turbanned, chapanned chauffeur opened the doors. His master begged the head of the buzkashi and Uraz to sit on the front seat, in the place of honor. He himself and the two wealthy men of the province sat behind.

For so splendid a departure the chauffeur wrung an appalling uproar from the engine and the hooter. The car ran around the square. The travelers called out, laughed, waved their arms, the fringes of their turbans and the sleeves of their chapans fluttering in the wind. Uraz's wolfskin cap remained motionless. Tursen saw it vanish around the corner of a street. He felt a sudden emptiness in his bosom. A stranger was going away with other strangers, along that dusty road that would take them, by way of Meimana and Mazar-i-Sharif, to the passes of the Hindu Kush . . . And thence . . . There was a taste of gall in Tursen's mouth . . . It would not be he who would ride his own mad horse at the great buzkashi, the unparalleled buzkashi, the buzkashi of the king, at Kabul, that great city.

The little governor spoke. "O Tursen, wilt thou do me the honor of taking a cup of green tea or black at my house?"

"No," said Tursen churlishly. He only wanted one thing, and that was to return as quickly as possible to his stallion in the middle of the great bower, by the pool.

WHEN TURSEN PASSED THE SCHOOL HE SAW GARDI GAJ STILL leaning against the dark wall, but now he was alone. Tursen greeted the old man and meant to go on. Suddenly, without knowing why, he stopped his horse and said, "Ancestor of All the World, grant me the favor of accepting what meager hospitality I can offer."

"It will be a joy and an honor for me," said Gardi Gaj.

He set one of his feet on the rider's boot, reached out a fleshless hand, and Tursen took him up behind, feeling as he did so that his body had not the slightest weight.

"Before anything else," said Tursen, "I will show thee my horse."

"Jahil, the last Mad Horse," said the ageless storyteller. For the first time the great bay's name rang out with all the beauty, fullness, and secret meaning that it possessed for Tursen. And the old chapandaz understood that he was taking Gardi Gaj with him because after so strange a day he had need of a wiser man than himself.

They traveled fast, in silence. When they reached Osman Bey's land, Tursen took care to avoid the main house and the outbuildings, so as to come to the stallion's retreat without meeting anyone.

In front of the curtain of trees Rahim was happily gazing at the soft and gentle sky, a sky that showed the first hint of twilight. He had just lived through the finest day of his life. Seeing Tursen, the bacha ran to help him dismount. Without stirring from the saddle Tursen said, "What art thou doing?"

"Thou didst say I might stay here, master," said Rahim with a great smile.

"Why art thou not with Mukhi and the stallion?"

Rahim started back, but only with surprise. "Dost thou not know then, master?"

Tursen's look was such that Rahim stopped. "Well?" said Tursen.

"They have left . . . left for Kabul," said Rahim.

"Kabul? Without waiting for me? I gave the syce orders . . ." Tursen's voice was low and hoarse.

"What could I do?" cried the bacha. "A lorry came with the little governor's soldiers, and they had the head of the buzkashi's order to take Jahil away."

"I am the only one who gives orders here," growled Tursen. "Silence, you false bacha." From the height of his saddle, with his elbow jerking into the old storyteller behind him, Tursen lashed Rahim in the face, twice. The leaden ball at the end of the thong tore each of the bacha's cheeks. The blood spouted instantly. Tursen trotted fast away.

With his hands hanging loose Rahim let the blood run down his face. He did not weep. He felt no resentment against Tursen. To the child, the old chapandaz wore the face of destiny.

On one side the boundary of Osman Bey's estate was the Shirin Darya, a stream that flowed so slowly between banks of muddy clay that the movement of its reddish turbidity and its hundreds of pieces of floating sheep dung could scarcely be detected.

The horse carrying Tursen and Gardi Gaj carefully made its way down the steep and yielding bank of the Shirin Darya and then forded the stream without difficulty. The water did not come above the stirrups. It was harder to climb the opposite slope, which was as high, steep, and slippery as the first. At the top the horse found flat, dry, and stony ground under its hoofs. Tursen pushed it to a trot and they quickly reached a crescent-shaped plateau in front of a hill. A few wretched brown earth hovels stood against the rise. In the middle of the plateau arose a great yurt of the ancient Uzbek kind, half hut and half tent, settled and nomadic dwelling at one and the same time, round at the bottom, pointed at the top, made partly of raw wool and partly of reeds.

When the two men passed in front of the pitiable hamlet the old storyteller murmured, "Kalakchikan." And when they dismounted by the yurt Gardi Gaj said to Tursen, "Thy grandfather pitched it here, after he had exchanged a few ewes in lamb for this little piece of land."

In spite of all that he knew of Gardi Gaj and his memory, Tursen was struck with astonishment at his words. But he did not show it. He turned toward a round-shouldered peasant and a little boy, both of them wretchedly dressed, who had come from the village huddled at the foot of the hill. The little boy climbed onto the horse and took it away. The peasant received Tursen's orders. Only then, with no appearance of curiosity, did the old chapandaz ask, "How dost thou contrive to remember so much and so much, Ancestor of All the World?"

"Eyes and heart remember what they have loved with no difficulty," said Gardi Gaj. "To pitch his yurt, thy grandfather chose a place that was like him. This is a somewhat sterile plateau and it is not very high, but here a man is his own master, and his gaze travels far over the steppe."

How many evenings at this same hour had Tursen looked over the plain that glided away in a single sweep to the horizon, and how often had he felt that his heart was at peace, freed from all commonplace anxieties and transformed into something like this endless free expanse, whose meager vegetation, gilded by the setting sun, was transformed into a precious grass, light, transparent, made for riding, riding, riding . . .

But the voice and the remark of Gardi Gaj made him understand for the first time that his grandfather, whom he remembered as a repulsive broken old man, had, in the same place and with the same happiness, looked over the high steppe; and that for him, as for Tursen, it had been a great book of wisdom upon whose surface the slightest folds marked the letters of an everlasting alphabet.

"Tell me," said Tursen thoughtfully, "thy heart and thy eyes must surely have loved a great deal, for thee to hold so many places and so many men?"

Gardi Gaj gave a very slight nod. "Many lands there are under the sky, and many men that can be loved," he said. "Dost thou not agree?"

"No," said Tursen. "No. Every man's friend is no man's friend."

"Who has counted for thee, then?" asked Gardi Gaj.

"That," said Tursen, pointing to the steppe. "And fine horses. And a few good chapandaz."

The little boy had come back from the village. He dragged out a heavy, roughly shaped wooden bench and table beside the yurt.

"Presently thou wilt be refreshed, Ancestor of All the World," said Tursen.

The two men sat down side by side, with nothing before them but the empty plateau and the vast flat expanse below it. Slowly the sun sank lower. Herds of sheep passed along the ridges of the distant hills, led by mounted shepherds with rifles slung over their shoulders—black, fine-drawn outlines against the fiery sky. A few of these horsemen were playing flutes made of pierced reeds, and their pure, ancient melody traveled through the silence of the steppe to reach Tursen. He had known this lament since his childhood. For him it was an integral part of the twilight. But now all at once he had the feeling that he had never before been aware of its sadness and loneliness, and in the depth of his being he felt an unbearable emptiness, an intolerable cold. Abruptly he said, "Tell me, Ancestor of All the World, what do they call that stretch of land near Kabul where the royal buzkashi is to be run?"

"Bagrami," said Gardi Gaj.

"Is it very big?" asked Tursen.

The old storyteller replied with a question. "Why didst thou not choose to see it thyself? I am sure it was proposed that thou shouldst go with the chapandaz, to do thy province honor."

"I am too old," said Tursen in a harsh and toneless voice.

"Thou art not old enough," said Gardi Gaj. "Thou art still suffering from becoming old."

"Make it more plain," said Tursen.

"True old age," said Gardi Gaj, "is beyond all pain and anguish. It has forgotten the evils of pride, regret, and bitterness. It no longer envies the strength of its own blood."

Tursen was half standing, his hands spread over the rough table. "Why dost thou say that to me? Why?" he asked.

With his ageless eyes turned toward the horizon Gardi Gaj replied, "Thou dost hate thy son—the only son remaining to thee—as thou hast never hated any other man, because Uraz, not Tursen, may fling the headless goat into the circle of justice, at the feet of the king." The old chapandaz bowed his forehead a little lower, and leaned harder on his enormous palms. "Thou cannot forgive Uraz," went on Gardi Gaj, "for mounting the Mad Horse instead of thee; nevertheless, thou gavest him the horse thyself." Tursen's indomitable neck bent farther still. "And to take revenge upon thy son thou hast maimed the face of a happy child," ended Gardi Gaj.

Tursen sank back on the bench, weak and broken. When he had asked the everlasting storyteller to his house he had taken up truth. Now he saw it clearly—that was what he had secretly desired.

He, Tursen, so straightforward in his proceedings, so certain of what he owed to other men and what they owed to him—he who in his profound harmony had never experienced an inner conflict—he, Tursen, had spent this whole ill-omened day without knowing what he was really aiming at, had stumbled from one muddled feeling to another darker still, and in his blind fury and powerlessness had struggled like a stubborn horse in a noose. He was unable to untie the knot alone. His nature was to cut. Merely to cut, and no more. So he had called on Gardi Gaj for help.

And the help had come. This fragile voice had taught Tursen all that he had refused, out of obstinate pride and need for dignity, to understand by himself.

For a moment he was amazed at himself for accepting another man's sentence with a bowed head. Then he felt nothing but the relief of having found so old and wise and strange a man that he, the great Tursen, could show his suffering, his shame, and his unhappiness without humiliation. He raised his head, and said, "Thou art right, Ancestor of All the World. But what can I do?"

"Grow old quickly," said Gardi Gaj.

They fell silent, and the round-shouldered peasant set a dish of rice cooked in mutton fat on the table, with a cake made of pounded almonds and raisins, some curds, slices of watermelon, and piping hot tea. But Gardi Gaj and Tursen gazed at the sky.

Now this was the season of the full moon. It had just risen above the line of the horizon, and the sun had not yet reached the limit of its course; so one could see, separated by the whole vault of heaven, one of the luminaries climbing up the firmament and the other going down. Then came the moment when they were at the same height, balanced one another, suspended on either side of the naked earth. They were the same size, the same color. And now their bloody disks seemed to bound the plateau of Kalakchikan for all eternity.

Then, each following its own path, the sun took on the glow of fire and the moon the glow of gold. The one sank into his vast abyss and the other rose into the kingdom of the night.

The round-shouldered peasant spoke reproachfully to Tursen. "The rice and the tea will be cold for our guest."

"Thou art right," replied Tursen; and to Gardi Gaj, "Forgive me, Ancestor of All the World. My mind was in another place."

They began their meal. The peasant went away. "Thou hast a good servant there," said Gardi Gaj.

"Yes," said Tursen. "And Mukhi, his son, will be a good chapandaz one day. For the moment he is syce of my Mad Horse." All at once the food seemed disgusting to Tursen. He stopped eating.

"And yet thou hast seen the sky," said Gardi Gaj. "Nothing on earth remains in equilibrium. The one rises and the other goes down."

"Yes," said Tursen, clenching his fists. "Yes, but tomorrow the sun will rise again."

"We too, maybe," said Gardi Gaj.

The moon covered the plateau with the fullness of its light. Somewhere, gently, in a hovel in the wretched village of Kalakchikan a little drum and a dambura* began to play.

* A kind of primitive guitar.

4

The Day of Glory

THE CAVALRY TRUMPETS rang out.

The sky was clear, the sun was warm, and the breeze that blew from the snow-topped peaks delightful. Urged by this mountain wind there waved, streamed, cracked, danced, and sang flags, standards, pennons, and banners all around the flat ground of Bagrami, in the neighborhood of Kabul. Here, at an altitude of six thousand feet, the first royal buzkashi was about to be played.

The area for the buzkashi was very broad and long, but not infinitely vast. The horsemen could not escape to disappear for hours in the remoteness of unbounded space as they were wont to do in their native steppes. Here the watchers could be sure they would never lose sight of the galloping or the battles.

On the north side were the mud houses of a village, newly painted pink and blue, and looking like an illuminated picture against the mountain background. To the west stretched a long wall. On the east a line of brilliantly colored lorries formed another boundary. And lastly on the southern side, just behind the road, rose a hill. All this, wall, lorries, flat roofs, rose from the site, everything, covered and almost overflowing with a flood of free-fluttering cloth—tunics, breeches, fringed sashes, the ends of turbans—that waved and eddied in the shifting wind. Truly, any man looking on this multitude would have said not a single young man or an old one or a child could be left in Kabul.

The trumpets sounded.

Their piercing, heart-rousing cry, winged like the wind, kept the thousands and thousands of people, most of whom had walked the ten dusty miles that lay between the capital and Bagrami, in a state of high excitement. And others were perpetually arriving. As they traveled, so columns of dust, striped by the beams of the sun, marched before them and behind. When at last they reached the hill to the south of the road the travelers were exceedingly thirsty. They went straight to the temporary chaikhanas or to the stalls loaded with grapes, muskmelons, watermelons, and pomegranates that knowing merchants had set up the day before. The less poverty-stricken spectators called loudly for the bachas who moved about through the crowd with nargiles, enjoyment paid for puff by puff.

The trumpets sounded.

Opposite the hill, on the other side of the road that ran along its foot, three pavilions of cheerful canvas and light-colored wood stood side by side, put up specially for the entertainment; they extended onto the ground where the game was to be played. The people, filled with memories of nomadic life, called them the great tents.

High Afghan dignitaries, in Western dress and wearing kulahs on their heads, filled the stand on the right; important foreigners the one on the left. But in the central tent, with its great crimson armchair in the middle, there was as yet no one at all. It was reserved for the king.

Across this empty space the faces under the astrakhan caps continually turned toward the foreign guests. Among them were to be seen men who embodied the knowledge, wealth, and strength of the most powerful nations on earth. But it was not these ambassadors, officers, scientists, and heads of missions who drew the gaze of the Afghans. Their eyes, incredulous and fascinated, were fixed on the women they saw in that enclosure. For in the prodigious flood of humanity that flowed over the plateau not a single woman was to be seen, except in that one tiny corner. Custom had it that no woman—whether from the north of the Hindu Kush or the south, of the lowest birth or the highest, even if covered from head to foot by her chadar, her face muffled behind a triple veil—no woman should or could be present at a public spectacle, however intrinsic a part of the nation's life and being it was.

Century after century the peasant woman of the steppes had been denied sight of the game that her father, brothers, husband, sons spoke about, dreamed of, lived for. And now that at last this game had reached the capital and was to be played for the glory of the king, all his subjects down to the Kabul beggars were invited to come and rejoice in it; but not the queen, not his wife. Pensively the Afghan dignitaries listened to the loud voices and the shrill laughter of the bare-necked, bare-armed foreign women.

The trumpets sounded. The banners waved.

Two soldiers passed before the place of honor. They were dragging the headless body of a huge he-goat. Bloody streams oozed from its neck. The same hoarse and greedy cry went up from the village roofs, the tops of the lorries, and the side of the hill. The foreign women uttered little screams.

The soldiers set the hairy mass into a hole, but level with the surface of the ground, a hole dug directly opposite the empty crimson chair and not far from it. To the left of this hole was the shining goal, the lime-marked circle of justice: this too was very close to the royal tent. And still closer, all along the three stands of honor, yawned a broad, deep ditch with almost vertical concrete sides for the protection of the sovereign and his guests. This had been insisted upon by advisers from the steppes. For they knew that once the Mongol chapandaz were possessed by the devils of their game they held nothing sacred—nothing and nobody, not even the king, although it was in his honor that they were about to risk their bones.

The trumpets sounded higher, sharper still. A whirlwind of dust swirled beneath the red and white striped canopies. A line of cars stopped on the road behind the pavilions. Weapons clashed. The crowd cheered. And Zahir Shah, followed by his suite, made his way into the royal tent. Tall, slim, aristocratic, dressed in Western clothes with a kulah of the finest astrakhan on his head, he walked slowly to the rail.

Then upon that plain—lined with helmeted soldiers and

mounted lancers bearing scarlet pennons, surrounded by huge crowds of men, enveloped in color and sound, swimming in light and air, the great mountain chains of Afghanistan towering above it—the ceremonial march, prelude to the royal buzkashi, began.

At the far end of the ground, over by the pink and blue village, a scarcely visible troop of horsemen began to move, advancing with solemn deliberation toward the sovereign's tent. First came three trumpeters, one alone and a pair, and a march as gay and lively as a maiden's step rose into the sky. A few paces behind them a young colonel rode alone, reining in his Arab thoroughbred with splendid nonchalance; he was related to the king, and it was his duty to direct and govern the game in all its changing fortunes. Then, side by side, three white-haired riders—aged men, but so used to the saddle that they sat as though on padded cushions. Each had brought one of the rival teams. Each was the head of the buzkashi in his own region—Meimana, Mazar-i-Sharif, and Qataghan, the only provinces in Afghanistan where by immemorial tradition the horses had the speed, endurance, and training, and the men the skill and vigor to compete before the king. These heads of the buzkashi wore green silk chapans striped with white.

Behind them came the three teams, each twenty horsemen strong, drawn out in line abreast. Step by step, slow pace by pace, they came closer, increasing in size to take on their true height and proportion—sixty chapandaz, the best, most famous in the steppes, chosen after a hundred exhausting, ferocious trials, mounted on the finest horses in the Three Provinces.

On that day the Chapandaz were certainly not dressed in their usual chapans. Each team wore its own uniform, devised for the royal buzkashi. The men of Qataghan had white shirts with green stripes, tucked into wide iron-gray breeches that vanished into high black boots above the knee. For Mazar-i-Sharif jerkins and breeches were russet, and the tawny boots came only to the calf. The horsemen of Meimana wore the same kind of boots, but their jackets were wider and shorter, in dark brown. Over their backs, like a strange star, was spread the skin of a white astrakhan lamb. On their heads each chapandaz wore a cap rimmed with coarse fur, a pointed cap made either of long wool or untreated skin, according to the team.

So dressed and adorned—borne by splendid animals of every color from purest black to spotless white—the sixty heroes of the steppes, drawn out in a single line, rode slowly, whips in hand, behind their old chiefs and the pealing trumpets, across the whole width of the Bagrami Plain.

Each face seemed to have been carved out of wood or cut from roughest leather. Tawny sunburn, cruel lips, the long narrow eyes of birds of prey.

The line was now opposite the royal tent. The riders stopped their horses and straightened themselves in their saddles.

On the left, twenty white and green shirts.

In the middle, twenty russet jerkins.

On the right, twenty dark brown jackets bearing the irregular white astrakhan star.

Qataghan.

Mazar-i-Sharif.

Meimana.

BECAUSE HE WAS JUDGED THE FINEST CHAPANDAZ OF HIS PROVINCE, Uraz had been placed in the center of the Meimana men. But although he was supported and carried on to right and left by a hedge of bodies, each one of which he knew so well that its smell in battle was familiar to him, and although he wore the same jacket and cap and sat as stock still as his companions, Uraz had the feeling of being apart from them, above them, and even of another race. Their lumpish pleasure, their delighted vanity filled him with mere disgust. Was their glory satisfied by parading like so many trained monkeys? A glory to be shared among sixty. "If there were only two of us, it would be one too many," thought Uraz.

Standing with his right hand to his gray astrakhan kulah, Zahir Shah saluted the horsemen. Close to him, against the rail, was the banner that the winner would receive from his hands and bear back to his own province for a year.

"It is mine," said Uraz to himself. And he could almost visualize Tursen's face and shoulders darkened, wiped out by the folds of a trophy the like of which the steppe had never seen.

Zahir Shah took his place in the crimson armchair. The grin that served Uraz for a smile bared his sharp teeth. This was the end of the nonsense. The first royal buzkashi was about to begin.

THE OPENING HAD A SLOW SOLEMNITY. SILENTLY, STEP BY STEP, THE sixty horsemen surrounded the hole that held the slaughtered beast. When they stopped, it was hedged round by a tight ring. Each third of the circle bore the color of a team—the white and green of Qataghan, the brown of Meimana, the russet of Mazar-i-Sharif. For a moment this strange, enormous flower, blooming there on the ground, remained motionless.

Then all at once the lead-tipped lashes rose like a hissing nation of serpents above the fur caps, a roar of demoniac savagery, combination of all their shouts, broke over the plain, and the goat's body was hidden beneath a mass of men and horses. By a transformation so sudden that no one had been able to detect the moment of its beginning, the grave and orderly band had become mere tumult, frenzy, an enormous whirlwind. Whoops, oaths, wordless threats . . . Lashing whips ripping into muzzles and faces . . . Ebb and flow . . . Horses rearing their full height above the entangled bodies and limbs . . . Chapandaz hanging there, clinging to their horse's sides, their faces in the dust, their nails clawing, scraping the stony ground to find the headless goat, grasp it, and snatch it up. But scarcely had one succeeded than other equally fierce and powerful hands wrenched the carcass from him. It passed and passed again over the horses' withers, before their eyes, under their bellies, and fell to the ground once more. Then as though from the bottom of a foaming roller rose up a fresh surge of chess, manes, caps, and whips that swept the first away, becoming in its turn a tall wave of bodies, clothes, and blows—a wave that turned, rolling upon itself.

One single horseman alone was unaffected by the madness; on his back he bore the white astrakhan badge of Meimana. He stood just at the edge of the fray, touched by it, but so placed that he should not be drawn in by the whirlpool's suction.

"Look at them; even wilder than they are at home," thought

Uraz, his cruel eyes following the battle that brought the riders of the steppe face to face on the high plain of Bagrami. "And here, just as at home, this fury is nothing but strength spent in vain. Here, as at home, the man who gets away with the goat will be caught in a moment." Uraz made Jahil move back. The whirlpool was swirling in their direction. "And they all know it as well as I do," said Uraz to himself.

His eyes followed the collisions and the sudden leaps, the surging forward and the surging back, the hollows and crests in which these scores of horsemen were struggling, caught in the same trap and the same madness—horsemen whose smell, mixed with that of the dust, was growing sharper every moment.

And Uraz thought, "I am wrong. They no longer know anything at all."

Already the fine clothes were stained with sweat, foam, and blood. Already the faces that flashed into sight between men's shoulders and horses' manes, spattered with clay and furrowed with whip marks, swollen masks fixed in a strange grin of anguish and delight—these faces no longer expressed anything but the instinct of violence, stripped bare.

And again Uraz said to himself, "For their part, they play for the sake of playing . . . I play to win." At this moment he had to rein in sharply, for Jahil had moved forward. The stallion shook his head. Uraz slowly stroked his neck, murmuring, "O Jahil, thou too wouldst like to play . . . Not yet . . . Thou must learn to keep thyself for the last, the only victory. It is hard when the blood is noble . . . I remember . . ."

Uraz continued to watch every surge, every turn and withdrawal of the ever more furious melee. Other struggles passed in his mind's eye: he saw a very young man wearing only a simple turban because he had not yet the right to the chapandaz's cap, and the young man outdid all the horsemen in rage and furious eagerness. "And it was myself, O Jahil," said Uraz to his stallion.

For a moment he felt once more that savage violence, that barbarous happiness that fed upon itself, that without rhyme or reason gave men's blood its fire; he felt it and he regretted it.

Again Jahil moved forward. Uraz held him back with a hand so cruel that the stallion reared his full height to neigh. Uraz's pitiless expression emphasized the high cheekbones and the hollow of his cheeks. Neither bridle nor bit had taught Uraz how to play buzkashi as he should, according to his powers. No, it was Tursen's lessons. "When Allah refuses strength to the arms and shoulders, He relies upon the horseman's brain."

After all these years the words still drowned the savage din. And to the spoken words Tursen's heavy, insulting voice added thoughts, just as in former days. "Wretched abortion that thou art, look at my body. And look at thine. How canst thou hope to play the game as I can play it?"

Shattering humiliation. But so profitable. "I understood. At that moment I understood everything," said Uraz, not knowing whether he was speaking to the stallion, himself, or his father.

A wild, tumultuous surge brought the whirling mass of horses and men toward him. Once more he forced Jahil to back. And he spoke again. "It was harder than getting oneself trodden down, crushed, torn . . . like them," he said.

Uraz breathed deeply, drawing in the air of the high plateau, which for the first time bore the smell of sweat, living leather, and wounded skin: the smell of the buzkashi. He remembered the laughter and the scorn that had greeted his first stubborn refusal to plunge into the battle of the herd. He had ignored them, saved his strength and his breath, watching like a wolf, like a falcon, for the right moment, for the single horseman near the goal; and then fresh, on a lively horse and with complete self-control, he had raced in, attacked, and won, won, won. Always. Everywhere. The mockers and scoffers had been silent for a great while now. His wariness was part of his fame.

Suddenly Uraz's thighs squeezed his horse. Above the keen eyes perpetually watching the battle his eyelids flickered. The struggling mass had moved toward the stands. "They go on and on forever today," said Uraz to himself. "Wilder than ever, since the eyes of the king are on them." In the same instant he said, "His eyes are on me too, on me, who hold back, well out of danger, like a wretched cur afraid of the pack. In Meimana, Mazar-i-Sharif, Qataghan, no one would be deceived. There they know who I am. But to all these people, these princes, great men and foreign lords from the farthest countries, who is Uraz? Who is Uraz to the king? A coward, no more."

Furiously he gripped the handle of his whip. One blow and he would vanish into the darkest of the whirlwind. He brought the lash up to his mouth and bit into the leather. He would not yield to false shame. He would play his game his own way. When he threw the trophy into the circle of justice—the trophy these fools were tearing one another to pieces for—when the finest cry in the world sprang from his throat—*Halal! Halal!*—then the foreigners and the princes and the king would indeed be forced to acknowledge him.

"Patience, patience!" said Uraz to Jahil, although the horse had made no move. "One of them is about to break away; I can feel it." A few seconds later he thought it had been achieved.

One of the players rose up in the heart of the struggle, clinging to his horse as it reared, and above its mane he waved the goat, already emptied of half its blood and substance. At once twenty fiends, their faces twisted with desire and physical effort, their mouths distorted with howling, surrounded him on their rearing horses and stretched hands like huge claws toward him. But the horseman who held the hairy carcass was so tall and his horse so high that the others could not reach the prey. In vain they lashed the giant's wrists and face, in vain they tried to stun him with the handles of their whips. He was Maqsud the Terrible, most famous of all the Mazar-i-Sharif chapandaz for his legendary strength, his huge size, his prodigious wealth, and his magnificent horses.

"Maqsud will never let go. Maqsud will break through!" said Uraz to himself, and so ill could he bear the waiting that he did not notice he was wishing well to that oaf, the rich man's son, whose name he loathed more than any in the world. In his mind he gave him advice, directions, orders. "Go in, Maqsud, go in. Strike, strike now with thy left hand . . . Thou art so strong thou wilt surely throw down the two that hem thee in closest. Then lay back thy horse. And hit again. And leap and break through, break through and away! Go in, Maqsud, go in now!"

Too slow, too heavy no doubt, the huge man missed the turn by a second. And the fiends surrounding him made the most of that second. Ten arms seized him, and ten more his horse's mane and bridle. The weight of these bunches of men brought Maqsud down to the common level. He vanished beneath the attack.

"Son of a sow! Mule's head! Now everything must be done all over again," growled Uraz. And at the same time he thought, "In thy place, Tursen . . ."

Once again, as he had watched so many times, he saw his father riding the wave of fur caps, wild manes, and cracking whips, his mouth shouting defiance and insult, his fist holding the headless goat, breaking through, always breaking through. The old, burning admiration filled his heart. And mingled with the unbearable pain of being the great Tursen's son was the torture of not being his equal. Then Uraz said to himself, "But he at least always had a Jahil." And immediately afterwards, "But now today I have one too. So . . ."

Without being fully aware of it he had forced his horse back and back. Without being fully aware of it he was leaning over Jahil's neck, reins tight, knees quivering, narrow eyes mere slits with the intensity of the glare following the dark hairy thing that passed and repassed from hand to hand between the horses' flanks, before their muzzles, and under their bellies.

All at once Uraz's ululation rang out, solitary, long, and piercing like that of a hunting wolf. Jahil, launched with spur and whip, shot toward the turmoil. Not one of the chapandaz was expecting this attack from behind, this battering ram, this cannon ball. Uraz cut through the mass in a single rush, and since his aim had been exact he was instantly within reach of the headless goat. He grasped it as he raced by, wrenched it away, and, exactly as he had worked it out beforehand, made Jahil rear and turn, breaking out through the still unclosed gap behind.

Instantly came the din of furious galloping behind him. Uraz knew that in spite of Jahil's excellence he would be caught. It could not be otherwise. Even if he were to reach the first of the poles the goat's body must pass round, even if he were to reach it before any of the others, on his road back toward the second he would certainly find riders who had taken the short cut. So what was the point of spending himself, wasting his strength in a meaningless, foolish run? He had just given them all a brilliant proof of his worth. That must be enough. Now he would slow down, relinquish the goat after a show of struggle, and go back to watching for the most favorable moment. That was what insistence upon victory required. But now Uraz was possessed by another, older longing. He had done his best to overcome it and tame it completely during twenty years of training. But now he had given it a second's respite, a second's power, and he felt the fury of his youth like a sling suddenly released, hurling him in spite of himself, hurling him straight forward like a blindly flying stone. Instead of reining Jahil in and leaving the collisions, the attacks, the fatigue, and the wounds, together with the carcass of the goat, to others, Uraz, gripping the lash of his whip between his teeth and wedging the goat's warm hair and flesh between the saddle and his thigh, urged the stallion on with knee and spur and shout, sharing his furious delight in running.

What a relief, this sudden flinging away of patience, waiting, prudence, and deep-laid calculation, and allowing muscles, nerves, and blood to be nothing but speed, thrust, and passionate zeal. "Come, Jahil, come my prince, come my king . . . We are the fastest, we are the strongest!"

So shouted, chanted Uraz in a voice no longer his own but that of a devil risen up from the depths, an all-powerful devil that was carrying him away.

Jahil was the first to reach the level of the pole. Even the fastest of the chapandaz of Qataghan, smaller and lighter men than those of Mazar-i-Sharif or Meimana—a swarm of wasps in their striped jerkins—and mounted on finer built and nimbler horses, even the fastest of them were far behind. He galloped round the pole and waved the carcass like a banner, to show the heads of buzkashi of the Three Provinces, the king's representative, and the crowd that the goat had indeed passed the first stage. Then with the body crushed beneath his thigh once more he spurred toward the west, to try to reach the other pole, a good two miles off or more.

Now Uraz saw coming toward him those horsemen who had chosen to cut off his return rather than persist in a hopeless chase. There were twenty of them at least.

How could Uraz hope to make his way through the pack that was racing in on him? But for all that he tried. And as though the soft, wet, bloody thing whose hair he felt against his thigh had become more precious to him than life itself, he put all he knew into its service. All he knew and all that he was, to preserve this hide that oozed grease and guts: the astonishing speed and agility of his youth, which he had kept entire; the hardened, concentrated strength of middle age; unparalleled acrobatic cunning; his vast and well-matured experience, enriched by every trial in thirty years of the game; and lastly the intoxicating passion that had suddenly seized upon him and that was bearing him along today. As they watched him, the three old chiefs of the buzkashi nodded their heads and stroked their gray beards in admiration. They had never seen Uraz play like this, and in all their long memory they could not recall so astonishing a player. He charged, slipped aside, feinted, fled, returned, slipped between his opponents. Some he flung down; others he escaped from. Now lying on his stallion's right side, now on his left, or flat against his neck as he reared, or out of sight beneath his belly, he defied attack, thwarted trickery, rode on and on without ever loosing his grip on the hide. Jahil helped him wonderfully. It was not only in speed and strength that he outdid the finest of the horses, but even more in his intuition and his sense of the game. He did not merely carry out every one of Uraz's wishes and commands; he continually went far beyond his master's farthest hopes. In strength and in cleverness. In charge, in smoothness, and in slipping away, in cunning feint and unexpected jig. Even more. Often it seemed that Jahil was no longer satisfied with fulfilling Uraz's wishes to the utmost; or even with foreseeing and forestalling them. He invented thrusts and stratagems. He was playing for himself and by himself, with unfailing instinct.

"Thou art a great chapandaz, O Jahil," thought Uraz.

But although these feints allowed them to get away, they also forced them to slacken their speed and deviate from their line. The main body of riders was catching up to take them from behind. The roaring and snorting of the horde was already upon them. They had to break through in that living instant.

Which of them sensed the weak point in the shifting curtain of opponents that blocked the way forward and which chose the little space held by only two horsemen and they the least formidable? Uraz? Jahil? Both together? Uraz never had to touch the stallion.

The two opposing horsemen did not come to meet them head on, for their horses could not stop or withstand the charge of an animal so much too fast and powerful for them, but each ran in on one side so that they should grasp Uraz and his mount and box them in. They reached their prey together with a howl of victory. At that instant Jahil stood straight up on his hind legs; he neighed and turned his head to the enemy on the left to catch up his hand between his teeth and crush it, while Uraz, high in his stirrups, as though detached from the stallion, struck the other chapandaz full in the chest with the handle of his whip and knocked him out of the saddle.

"It is still I who shall carry the goat around the second pole," thought Uraz.

A wall of flesh and muscle rose up immediately before him. Uraz raised his eyes and there, high above his own, saw those of Maqsud the Terrible, slits narrowed to a thread, slits in a face so wide and flat that it seemed unfinished. And in the eyes of Maqsud, who knew Uraz's scorn for him, shone the savage joy of a hatred about to be satisfied. Before Jahil could make a move against the horse that blocked his path—a horse as tall and massive as himself—Maqsud brought an enormous hand down on Uraz's neck, plucked him from the saddle as though he had been a rag doll, seized the goat with his free hand, and cried, "So you made up your mind to play like everyone else? There you are then, miserable abortion!" the giant let Uraz fall to the ground, spurred, lashed his horse, and galloped toward the pole.

Empty, amazed, devoid of all feeling, Uraz watched Maqsud go. A mane touched his cheek. Jahil's moist, sparkling, impatient eyes were fixed on him. Uraz trembled. He had been thrown—thrown with such a fall—from a matchless horse. He had lost his honor in his stallion's eyes . . . Another even more heart-piercing thought came to him. Never had Tursen . . .

With the bound of a young man he was in the saddle. His spurs ripped Jahil's sides. His whip tore them. He was no longer flying after the goat, but Maqsud's blood.

The giant was not yet far away. He had had to get rid of three Qataghan horsemen who had tackled him one after another. They were small and light, but savage and obstinate. Each encounter had taken time. Now he was racing straight for the west. As for catching him, Uraz knew that he could certainly do it. His horse was as powerful as the quarry and very much faster; he himself was half Maqsud's weight and no man in the steppes could get more from a horse. Soon he had outstripped all the chapandaz and breathed easier. He had to be alone when he reached Maqsud. There must be no other bodies, man or beast, that might hinder him in the conflict, cushion his murderous thrust . . . It was done. Nobody left between him and Maqsud. And the distance was dwindling . . . dwindling . . .

Suddenly, he was on the point of holding Jahil back and giving up the chase. What was he going to do when he had caught Maqsud? How could he kill him? What use were his hands, his whip against the giant of Mazar-i-Sharif? Oh, why did he have no knife, a knife such as the chapandaz carried in the old pitiless days, when slashing reins and girths was permitted!

Meanwhile, Jahil pressed his gallop even more. The prey was within his reach. Once again he was playing for himself alone. Uraz smiled his wolf's grin. Jahil was the finest weapon. There was no point taking thought about how to use him. Instinct did this. On the right, the side Maqsud was on, he freed his leg; then he slipped out of the saddle; and then, holding on by a single stirrup, clinging to Jahil's mane, flattened against his left flank, he shrieked into the very hollow of the stallion's ear the harshest, maddest cry he could wrench from his throat. Jahil rose in a prodigious bound. Uraz howled, howled, on and on. At the same time he aimed the charge to take Maqsud's horse diagonally, so that at the moment of impact Jahil's shoulder would strike with full force on the jugular, like a cannon ball.

"It will fall flat and Maqsud with it, and his vile body, that lump of coarse muscle, will be trampled, brayed, shattered, pulped by the hoofs." So ran Uraz's thought, and his ululation in Jahil's ear shrieked higher and harsher still.

Maqsud heard him. He turned his head, and Maqsud the Terrible took fright . . . These mad, dilated nostrils and eyes . . . This wild, maddened, furious animal coming at him without a rider, under its own rage, its own furious impulse . . . To soften the shock Maqsud thrust out the arm that held the headless goat. And this arm was so heavy and vast and hard that it deflected Jahil's charge. For a second. But in that same second Uraz rose in his saddle and with a kick of his long-heeled boot broke Maqsud's wrist.

The fingers unclenched. The goat's skin slipped from them. Uraz seized it and spurred Jahil on, while Maqsud stared at a hand that hung at a strange, impossible angle and that he could not govern in any way at all.

URAZ CARRIED THE TROPHY AROUND THE SECOND POLE. ON THE other side the pack of chapandaz were waiting for him once more. This time they were all there in front of him, except for the wounded and the maimed, who clamored for the syces as their horses wandered across the plain. All there, and all consumed by a passion that touched the extreme limits of rage. The last part of the trial had been reached. From this moment on, if the man who held the skin had the strength, the skill, or the luck to touch the circle of justice by any road or path whatsoever, he became the winner of the royal buzkashi.

And now again came the turmoil with which the game had begun. Once again the goat's skin sped from hand to hand between the rearing horses in a whirlwind of fur hats, manes, whips, and faces covered with sweat and torn by the slash of leather and lead. In the end one horseman broke away. And it was not Uraz. But Uraz, like all the rest, raced after him. And like the rest he took part in every pursuit, charge, melee, and attack. The carcass was in his hand again, ripped away, snatched back, lost once more. That no longer mattered to him. He had only one desire—to strike and strike forever.

Chase and withdrawal, maneuvers and feints, hand-to-hand encounters and mass attacks, the howling, roaring band still advanced toward the whitewashed line that ringed the goal. At last they came in sight of it, gleaming in the sun. At that moment a Meimana chapandaz had the goat. He tried his luck and made a thrust to break out. A Qataghan horseman rose up at his side, snatched the goat, and galloped straight on in the same direction. A few more strides and he would be within reach of the circle of justice. But he had to turn past an unmounted horse that blundered across his path and this lost him a couple of seconds. When he was out of the turn a dozen chapandaz lay between him and the goal. He could hear the gallop of the rest behind, racing to surround him and tear his prey from his grasp. Having been so close to victory he felt he could not, could not bear it. He spurred straight forward, and there he was opposite the stands! The horde was at his heels. How escape? Jump the gaping moat that protected the great tents? Desire blazed so clearly in his staring, desperate eyes that the guests of honor all pressed back in a heap. At the last moment the man in the green-striped jerkin saw that the width of the moat made it hopeless and that even the finest leap would only mean breaking his bones against the concrete wall. He raced along the obstacle, the whole pack of chapandaz behind him. From the wind of their passage, from their faces and cries, it was clear to those in the stands that these riders from the steppes would have trampled the king himself for the pitiful hairy remnant if they could.

When the hunted chapandaz had gone beyond the line of pavilions he saw before him a wall of lorries covered with people, the loose ends of their turbans fluttering in the wind like thousands and thousands of wings. There were only two ways out for the Qataghani—to the left along the edge of the plain, where he must inevitably be brought to bay against the heavy vehicles; and to the right down a short, narrow passage that led to the Kabul road. He chose the latter. The royal cars filled the road from side to side. The Qataghani passed between them, leaped over the last line, and found himself in front of the hill at the side of the plain, an immense crowd upon its slopes, not to mention innumerable huts, tents, stalls, and enormous copper samovars.

The chapandaz spent no time in thought. A thrust of his spurs, a crack of his whip, and the horse plunged into the crowd. The other horsemen were equally resolute. The charge swept the hillside clean. Fruit, samovars, splinters of wood, turbans, and sandals flew into the air as the chapandaz went by. Men who were not knocked down by the horses were overturned by those who fled. The roaring that hung over the hill, a din made up of shouts of terror and inhuman ululations, might have been the cry of earth and rock itself.

Uraz was not one of the hunt. Had his animal fury had time to evaporate? Or was it that he had recognized the face that stood out against the crimson velvet? In front of the royal tent Uraz suddenly recovered his self-control. With a gentle hand he slackened Jahil's speed, and when the whole band of chapandaz rushed into the alley leading to the hill he did not follow.

Far away the terror-stricken crowd howled and bellowed. Uraz turned his horse. Amid that disorder, with thousands upon thousands of men running one another down in every direction, no one had the slightest chance of overtaking the Qataghani. The foot of the hill was the place where Uraz must wait for him, lying in ambush behind the stands and their protecting moat. The holder of the goat was forced to come that way, within his reach, in order to get to the shining whitewashed circle close by.

No one was in the immediate neighborhood except a single enormous chapandaz with his arm slung in a red scarf, a rider who walked his horse aimlessly to and fro, a mere spectator—Maqsud.

"Terrible to no man," thought Uraz, indifferently. He had returned to his usual state of mind. For him other men were now no more than the elements of the game. He bent over Jahil's neck, stroking him, urging him to be ready.

And everything happened as he had foreseen. The Qataghani came out onto the Kabul road, leaped across it, and raced for the goal. Uraz shot from his ambush, and before the rider had understood who his attacker was or where he had come from, or the other chapandaz had had time to catch up, Jahil's shoulder struck the Qataghani horse a terrible blow. The man in the striped shirt tried to regain his seat. Between these two motions Uraz seized the trophy and raced alone toward the goal. He reached it, reined in on the shining edge of the circle of justice, and flung up the hand that held the remnant of the goat. He began the motion of throwing it and already the frenzied cry of the halal was in his throat . . . At that moment a huge hand also seized the hairy skin, a hand that came from a russet jerkin, the colors of Mazar-i-Sharif—Maqsud's unwounded left hand. It was incapable of stopping Uraz, but it moved with him, making the same movement that flung the carcass down into the middle of the round.

There was a moment's confusion, a moment of silence. Then in a single rush the Meimana chapandaz and those of Mazar-i-Sharif thrust their horses, black with sweat and white with foam, to the front of the royal stand. And all together the forty horsemen called upon the king with savage cries across the concrete moat. Their whips whistled in their upraised fists. Those in russet jerkins and those whose jackets bore the white star-shaped skin roared with equal violence that the victory should be given to them.

"It is we who won," shouted the Meimana chapandaz. "The Mazar barely grazed the carcass and at the very last second. The thieving cur! Shameless, shameless impudence!"

"Falseness and lies," roared the men of Mazar-i-Sharif. "It was the Terrible who truly held the goat. His was the hand that threw it!"

The heads of the buzkashi of each of the provinces, venerable in age and rank, stood defying one another, brandishing their whips. The dust raised by the horses came floating in thick clouds into the king's tent; through them he could see violent, contorted, terrifying, torn faces, blood-stained and muddy masks roaring challenge, insult, and blasphemy.

The king raised his head, and all was silence. He said, "According to the law of justice, I decree that it shall be shared. Let half the honor go to Meimana and half to Mazar-i-Sharif. And let the game begin again."

THE CHAPANDAZ WERE WAITING. IT TOOK SOME TIME TO SLIT A FRESH goat's throat and cut off its head. Some horsemen, the richer ones, took advantage of the pause to change their mounts. Others quenched their thirst, biting greedily into the slices of watermelon or bunches of grapes their grooms brought out to them. Groups of chapandaz stretched out on the ground, smoking, reins in the crook of their arm. Each of the heads of buzkashi, haranguing the men of his province from the height of his saddle, urged them to play as lone wolves no longer, but to sacrifice personal glory to that of their own particular piece of steppe and act as a team.

Mounted on Jahil, Uraz remained at a distance from the other men while Mukhi rubbed the stallion down. His eyes were fixed on the mountain snows. Behind those peaks, a great way off, lay Osman Bey's estate. Had it been just or unjust, the royal decision? What did it matter? It would not prevent him from setting the king's banner before Tursen.

Two soldiers went by, dragging a headless goat.

THE CARCASS HAD PASSED AROUND THE TWO POLES. THE BATTLE WAS being fought out some five hundred yards from the goal. The rider who broke away, holding the goat, might hope for everything.

Uraz was watching over the conflict at the proper, calculated distance. He had been playing a closer game than ever. He had satisfied himself with taking the goat from a few isolated riders, without peril or glory, and on being caught he had never really contested its possession. At this moment, throughout his entire body, from stirrup to reins, he felt that kind of icy fever that made him so dangerous.

Simultaneously Uraz was aware of the pink and blue village that limited the Bagrami plateau to the north; the southward hill covered with fluttering cloth; the stands where Zahir Shah sat among his guests and soldiers and police, horse and foot; and even the light, pure sky of the mountains with the sun sloping down toward the end of its journey, shorter at this height than in the plain. At the same time his eyes never for a second left the melee, the most savage the day had seen. The chapandaz all knew that without doubt there would be no other.

And as he had done more than once before, Uraz wondered why these conflicts did not last forever. In that whirl of shoulders, chests, and rumps every player and every horse was as good as the next. Yet it always happened that suddenly one of them caught up the hairy skin, regained his seat, broke out, and set off at a gallop. Who would it be in this engagement?

Even if the rider were of his own team, Uraz was determined that he should not be the winner. That day no man but himself had the right to utter the time-honored cry, Halal! Halal!

And now the horde that had seemed hopelessly tangled and turned in upon itself suddenly split open and a chapandaz appeared in the path he was cutting for himself by flinging his horse to the right and the left, striking out on every side with all his strength. An astonishingly rapid and skillful feint freed him from the last row between him and the open ground. He burst forth, clinging flat against his horse's left flank, so that the animal masked him, hiding him from his pursuers, while his free hand dragged the soft hairy flesh along the ground. He reached the empty space that stretched away to the whitewashed circle, and flung his horse toward the goal with a long inhuman shriek, ringing with the sound of victory.

Uraz had but to slacken the reins. Jahil was fresh again. His blood was aflame with the tumult and the smell of the melee, from which his master had held him back once more. He put forth his utmost strength.

The Mazar-i-Sharif rider urged on his horse with a merciless whip. The goal was so near. In vain. The big stallion was too fast for him by far. With a few strides Jahil was up. The furious gallop carried them along side by side.

And now at last Uraz carried out the movement he had been making ready for since he began the chase: it was the great stroke, most beautiful, most difficult in the whole game of buzkashi. At the height of their gallop he swung out over the empty air, poised on one ankle in a single stirrup—a prodigy of balance—and hung there for a second with both arms flung out before him. His aim had been exact. His hands met the goat's body, gripped it, and—their strength increased by the force and impetus of the fall—wrenched the trophy free and bore it off. Now all Uraz had to do was to swing back into his saddle and run for the goal. This recovery was familiar to all the better chapandaz. Uraz was accounted best of them all.

Suddenly as he was straightening up he felt that he was losing all power over his muscles, that he was wavering and astray, weak, awkward, and powerless. At first he could not understand. He was overwhelmed by a stupid astonishment when he realized that he was on the ground being dragged along like a sack, his face flayed by the dry grass. Yet his foot was still firm in the stirrup. All he had to do was to bear on it, grasp Jahil's mane, and swing himself up. But there was no longer any communication, no message passing between knee and foot. So it was worse than a twist, worse than a strain, a ripped muscle or tendon. Uraz had had plenty of those and none had ever prevented him from springing onto his horse and winning. What was happening, then? How? Why?

Uraz had no time to wonder any more. Jahil had stopped dead and the jerk had freed Uraz's foot from the stirrup.

At the same time it seemed to him that the hoofs of scores of horses were hammering inside his skull with a storm of furious shouting. The teams of Qataghan, Meimana and Mazar-i-Sharif all flung themselves together on the goat he was still holding.

"The charge is going to trample me into dead meat," he said to himself. "Like this goat's skin." Never for a moment did he think of letting the trophy go. And he felt no fear of any sort. He was afraid of nothing, above all not of death. "This is the end," he thought. And again, "It will remind Tursen of the days he is so proud of, when there was no real buzkashi without the corpse of a good chapandaz."

The howling, raging horde burst over Uraz. They could not reach him. Jahil had set himself over Uraz and preserved him, sheltered him between his legs; it was as though Uraz were lying between four living columns. With his rump, breast, hoofs, and teeth Jahil defended him. And tighter than he had ever gripped it before, Uraz grasped the skin of the goat.

It could not last long. His fingers were hammered with whip handles. The hands of horsemen hanging under their saddles passed between Jahil's legs, catching Uraz by the belt and the hair, while others greedily tore at the goat. A chapandaz wrenched the bloodless, hairy, emptied trophy away. The rest hurled themselves upon him.

Only then did Uraz feel the shame of defeat and only then did he know that he would survive it . . . Somewhere the huge moaning of a siren arose; it grew, came closer. An ambulance flying the pennant of the Red Crescent carried the chapandaz away.

Over by the circle of justice a hoarse, intoxicated voice, maddened by its own cry, shouted, "Halal! Halal!"

Oraz beat furiously on his broken leg, so that the pain should stop him thinking.

The well-equipped hospital stood in a spacious, flower-filled park on the outskirts of Kabul. They received Uraz with the utmost attention. The king had let it be known that he considered the chapandaz his guests.

In the operating theater the house surgeon, a young Afghan who had studied under French professors at the University of Kabul, told Uraz that he was going to reduce the fracture of the tibia and put it in plaster at once. "Soon thou wilt have the entire use of thy leg again," he said.

Uraz did not answer, did not understand, did not believe anything any more. There was no room left in him for anything but shame. A nameless, measureless shame.

The ambulance, the nurses' handling of him, never would they have dared use him so on the steppe. In his own country he would have clung to a companion's shoulder, hopped to his horse, and returned to his house or his yurt in the saddle, a man. A bone-setter would have come, dressed in a chapan like everyone else. Or perhaps a healer with his spells. And everything would have passed off in total privacy, in decency. Now he was lying on an outlandish iron bedstead, a young fellow in a white gown had decided everything for him as though for a sickly child. And, crowning indignity, a European woman had stripped him, shaving the hair from his wounded leg. Compared with this dishonor the pain of the operation meant nothing.

Afterwards he had been carried to his bed through a huge, foulsmelling ward filled with miserable wretches lying there, watching him. At least the bed was in a corner, close to a partially open window that let in the scented air of the garden and the evening coolness.

There Uraz had time to reflect on his misfortune. Not for a moment did it occur to him to attribute it to any fault from

within. Such a thing was not possible for a chapandaz of his standing. Chance? For Uraz there was no such thing as chance. Everything in the area outside his own will or reason was brought about
by easily offended jinns, devils, mysterious forces that took the
promptest revenge. Had he deserved their wrath that day? Had he
washed with his left hand? Had he, during some decisive turn in
the buzkashi, forgotten to stroke the old leather bag with the herb
of good luck in it that hung at Jahil's neck, as it had hung on all his
horses before Jahil? Uraz racked his memory, but in vain; he could
not discover any ill-omened act for which he could blame himself.
It could only have been a spell; but what enemy, what envious eye
had cast it?

Uraz jerked with impatience, and this caused him to feel a
strange weight on his left leg. He lifted the blanket and the sheet,
saw the plaster and trembled. It was impossible to imagine any
more ill-omened shape in contact with man's flesh. A little coffin!
With a piercing, loving, desperately yearning regret Uraz thought
of the ointments, balms, beneficent plants, snake's skin macerated
in mare's milk, wolf's teeth, scorpion's sting ground to a thin powder and kept in a ram's horn—the infallible remedies that the
moon-faced healer brought from his knapsack, hallowing them one
by one, ritual gesture after ritual gesture, each accompanied by the
proper incantation, when he treated the Meimana chapandaz.

Were these men of Kabul out of their wits, or were they moved
by evil intentions against him? Uraz's lips were dry and burning,
the sweat of distress and anxiety soaked his forehead and hair.

Abruptly he flung back the sheet and blanket. The woman, the
European who had shaved the hair from his leg, was coming. She
was tall, robust, and still young; her features bore the marks of an
easy sensual cheerfulness. Uraz loathed her all the more for it. She
spoke to him in halting Pushtu. He did not understand a word she
said. The man in the next bed, who had been to the Kabul High
School, acted as interpreter. In spite of the late hour Uraz, by espe-
cial favor, was about to have a visit.

Mukhi came through the ward, awkward with so many eyes on
him, shoulders hunched to make him smaller. But when he was in
front of Uraz with his back turned to all the others, the tall syce
straightened with a smile that split his flat face from ear to ear.

"I have learned that the Prophet protected thee and that very soon thou wilt be as thou wast before," he said. Then in the same breath, "Jahil is in the stable, groomed and watered. Good litter. Good oats. Almost as good as at home."

"Who cried the halal?" asked Uraz harshly. "Mazar or Qataghan?"

Mukhi's great laugh echoed through the ward. "Silence, son of an ass," growled Uraz. "Why all this noise?"

"It was not a chapandaz from Mazar," said Mukhi, "nor yet a Qataghani who won the royal buzkashi, but one of ours. Art thou content?"

Uraz gritted his teeth. The worst had happened. His team had managed to win without him. "Who?" he asked.

"Salih!" said Mukhi.

"What do you mean, Salih?" said Uraz. "His horse was utterly exhausted."

Mukhi raised one of his huge hands toward the ceiling and cried, "Allah inspired him. Jahil had no rider. Salih leaped on his back."

Uraz's whole body went rigid and once again he felt the weight of the plaster on his leg. So the means of his dishonor had been his own horse. And he could not say a word, a teammate always used a fresher horse if its injured rider left it free.

Meanwhile Mukhi was laughing still, but he laughed silently, out of respect for Uraz. "Thou art blessed twice over," he said. "Meimana carries back the king's banner, and from today Jahil is thine." And as Uraz stared at him with uncomprehending eyes the tall syce bent over him and whispered, "The Mad Horse won. He belongs to thee."

Then, word by word, Uraz remembered the solemn promise that Tursen had given before the crowd in the bazaar at Daolatabad. "If it should come to pass," Tursen had said, "that my Mad Horse wins the royal buzkashi, from that moment he will belong to Uraz, my son, and to him alone."

Uraz remembered the gratitude and the affection that he had then felt for the first time in his life. Now his mouth was so full of bitterness that he wanted to spit. The finest stallion on the steppes was his. But thanks to another rider.

The nurse came back. She was carrying a little tube that seemed to be made of quicksilver. Uraz's neighbor told him that it was a thermometer and explained how it was used.

"It is not true—such things cannot be! No one on earth shall force me to it . . ." Stiff against his pillow, pale beneath his tawny sunburn, Uraz growled, stammered, and choked with shame and hatred.

"I will send an Afghan later," said the nurse.

Mukhi watched her go, shaking his big round head. Such immodesty abashed and disconcerted him. Then he said to Uraz, "Salih and all the other Meimana men beg thy pardon for not coming this evening. They are at the feast in the king's palace. Thou wilt see them here tomorrow."

"No," said Uraz savagely. "Here I shall see no one." Although they were speaking in Uzbek, which the people of Kabul could not understand, Uraz lowered his voice to a whisper and went on, "Thou shalt be under my window with Jahil and my clothes in the middle of the night."

"But soldiers guard the door of the hospital," said Mukhi.

"There is money in the pockets of my chapan," said Uraz. "More than is needed to buy them. If they will not take it, jump the wall and then get me over it. Thou art big enough. Thou art strong enough."

"I understand thy heart," said Mukhi.

Toward midnight the patients whom fever or pain kept from sleep had a strange vision. The chapandaz in the corner of the ward got up, half naked; he dragged himself and his plastered leg to the window, opened it, leaned out, and vanished.

Gently Mukhi set Uraz in the saddle. Uraz took the reins. The iron gates of the park stood ajar; they passed through. The soldiers on guard were inside their lodge.

When they had gone beyond the long fence that shut in the hospital park, Mukhi asked, "Dost think they will come after thee?"

"Certainly," replied Uraz. "They shall not catch me." He

stopped Jahil and said, "The first thing is to break the evil fortune. Go and find a stone."

Mukhi brought one of the big cobbles that made up the road. Uraz held out his plastered leg and commanded, "Break this little coffin."

Mukhi struck with all his strength. The pain that seared Uraz was so furious and unexpected that without meaning to he jerked the reins and made the stallion rear. But the accursed envelope was shattered.

"In my sack thou wilt find a paper with certain lines written on it," said Uraz to Mukhi. "They are the Prophet's. A Daolatabad mullah copied them for me from his Koran." When Mukhi had found the consecrated sheet Uraz said, "Spread it out on the wound and tie it with thy belt." As he said, so was it done.

PART TWO

The Temptation

*****

5

The Chaikhana

THE ROAD LEADING OUT OF KABUL to one side was long and, for those not of the region, difficult. But in spite of his eagerness to put as much distance as possible between himself and the hospital, Uraz thought it better to take it than to pass through the town. In a few days he had seen so many police, so many patrols, barracks, officers, and officials, that the whole place seemed to him a trap. He was convinced that all these people and a great many others besides were going to be sent the order—if it had not already reached them—to chase him, stop him, and fling him back on that dishonorable bed, under the orders of the shameless foreign woman. Mukhi shared his certainty. How could they know in their steppes that for the great men of this world the fate of a chapandaz, even a famous chapandaz, was of very little significance?

To guide them they took the line of the endless ruined wall that had once defended the approaches to Kabul and ran now along the ridges of the hills, now at the bottom of the ravines. They followed it on the outside and at a considerable distance. The lofty wall was a comfort to Uraz. For him it performed a service the direct reverse of its original intention, for it protected him from the city—the over-large city, too populous, too noisy, where no one, ever, had recognized him in the crowd.

93

THE VAGUE PATHS THROUGH THE STEEP HILLS THAT THE FUGITIVES were obliged to take were uneven, full of ruts, and scattered with fallen earth and rock. But the moon shed light enough, and Jahil was sure-footed. When the eternal snow crowning the marvelous peaks of the Hindu Kush took on the colors of the dawn, Mukhi turned and could no longer see even the farthest outworks of the ancient wall. "Kabul is far behind," he said.

"We have traveled well," said Uraz.

"What a horse!" exclaimed Mukhi. His huge rough palm stroked the stallion's coat with astonishing delicacy. Jahil whinnied with high spirits, and the groom's laugh rang out, immense and interminable. This time Uraz felt a kind of laughter echoing in his bosom. The dawn was spreading its wings of light from peak to peak, and it bore him witness: he had been able to overcome his wound, defeat, and shame, the hospital and the night. He was once again his own master, mounted on his own horse. The eagles were taking wing. One rose immediately in front of him. The best of all omens . . .

"I am going to get down," he said to Mukhi. "For the prayer. The sun is up."

"Bowing down," said Mukhi, "will make thy wound worse, surely?"

"It does not matter," said Uraz.

"Allah bears with those who are hurt," urged Mukhi. "The great Tursen knows it; pious as he is, he still prays standing. Thou canst pray in thy saddle."

Now nothing on earth would have stopped Uraz from doing what he had already decided on. It was not in infirmity that he wished to be his father's equal. With his sound leg firm in the stirrup he swung the other over Jahil's rump, steadied himself by leaning on his withers, freed his unwounded foot, and so dropped onto it, gently bending his knee and putting both hands to the ground before he stretched out the broken leg. He touched the earth with his forehead and prayed with all the power of his faith and superstition. The syce, prostrated behind him, repeated the sanctified verses in an undertone, trustful as a child.

Uraz was the first to rise, and he did so by reversing the series of movements that had brought him safely to his knees. More confident now, he moved faster. Too fast. His broken leg touched the ground, bearing something of his body's weight. Only for a fleeting moment and with an almost imperceptible pressure, but it was enough. Inside the wounded bone there was a kind of grating. So furious a pain shot through him that Uraz thought, "It is too much. I am going to fall." Instead of giving way or calling to Mukhi for help he grasped Jahil's mane, raised himself by the strength of his arms, thrust his sound foot into the stirrup, and threw his sick leg over the stallion's side. Then, between clenched teeth, he said, "Tighten the bandage, Mukhi."

Before pulling on the cloth, the syce felt his calf. "I can feel a little pointed end of bone that is coming through the skin," he said.

"What happens after prayer cannot be evil," said Uraz. He smiled his wolflike grin. Once more he had something to dominate —pain. Until then it had been numb, deadened, and as it were soft; it had left him in peace. Now it was biting into his nerves like a saw. Taking no account of it became a task, a victory to be renewed at every moment. "Up behind, quick!" cried Uraz.

Jahil set off cheerfully. "He ran the whole buzkashi better than any other horse in the field," thought Uraz. "And since midnight he has been carrying two men without a moment's rest, and what terrain he has had to cover! Yet he shows no tiredness, no ill-temper!" Uraz stroked Jahil's side. The stallion snorted and lengthened his stride. Suddenly he raised his head high, moved his ears, and sniffed the air with great force. A faint sweat broke out on his flanks. His pace became wary and prudent.

"He must have scented some animal," said Mukhi.

Uraz urged Jahil along the path that wound between the gloomy, dark, and naked rocks. Then in their turn the two men heard the rumbling din. They understood. Immediately before them, still hidden by a dip but very close at hand, ran the great road to the north.

From the center, south, and east, from Kabul and Peshawar, from Gardez, Ghazni, and Kandahar, this was the only road that led to the plains and steppes that lay beyond the Hindu Kush. It carried the entire traffic of a nation.

IT WAS AUTUMN, THE FAR END OF FIVE MONTHS OF DROUGHT; AND although the morning was still young the dust raised by countless wheels, feet, hoofs, and pads was already floating in thin screens, light, shifting clouds, wispy spirals that caught the rays of the rising sun, just as mist and vapor do in other lands. Beneath these wafting, ephemeral dusty veils ran, walked, flowed, and pullulated lorries, men, and beasts.

There were no rules for overtaking, none for passing or for dealing with knotted mobs of traffic. Everything was left to the effects of chance, personal preference, pride, meekness, nonchalance, and fate.

The din was as great as the confusion. Shouts, neighing, bleating, braying, barking, the blast of whistles, the shriek of horns, and the general roar of engines made up a single voice issuing from men on foot, riders, flocks, lorries and caravans, from Pathans, Tadzhiks, Hazaras, Uzbeks, and Nuristanis who, moving up or down it, were wearing away a little more of the ancient road that had carried Aryan hordes, Alexander's phalanxes, the disciples of Buddha . . .

In one chaotic stream, bearing the different clothes, headdresses, gear, and features of all these races, flowed trade, the search for work, the return of flocks to their winter grazing and men to the tribe, the quest for adventure . . .

From the top of a hill that stood over the great north road, Uraz and Mukhi gazed silently down on the river into which they were to plunge. Neither one thought of urging Jahil on.

"Yet that was the way we came," said Mukhi at last, with naïve astonishment.

Uraz made no reply.

"To be sure, thou wert in Osman Bey's great and splendid

motorcar, and I was in a lorry," said Mukhi again. He stroked the stallion's rump. "And so was Jahil."

Uraz looked out over the arid land to the far side of the road, a land that, from its colors, might have been burned—tawny, ocher, a warm brown. Beyond it the wonderfully pure and luminous sky rested on the motionless waves of mountains. Uraz's eyes came back to the road, its turmoil, its uproar . . .

Mukhi saw him square his shoulders, shift his grip on the reins. Jahil made his way carefully down the slope. When he was at the bottom Uraz uttered a sharp, harsh cry, pushing him into the jostling, variegated, thundering flow of the current.

For the first few moments the horsemen from the steppes were preoccupied with not being deafened, run into, overwhelmed. But the dust was no more stifling or blinding than in their own province, the throng around them by no means as dense or violent as a buzkashi.

The tall syce laughed his huge laugh and said to Uraz, "Well, I should rather travel like this, indeed. In that box on wheels that carried us to Kabul there was no way of seeing out and the jolting frightened me all the way, because of Jahil's knees and pasterns."

Uraz did not answer. He was thinking of the great distance that lay between him and Meimana, and of the police and soldiers who must be coming after him. Only pride kept him from turning his head every other moment, like a hunted man.

"Jahil too—he feels happier," said Mukhi again.

Of his own accord the stallion side-stepped, thrust, evaded, overtook, following the eddies, the calm stretches, and the perpetually renewed undulations. He was learning a game unknown to him, the game of the great Afghan road. And the road, like an enormous picture book, turned its leaves one after the other.

"Look! Look! Look!" cried the wonderstruck Mukhi again and again and again. These goats from the high valleys of Nuristan, how black they were, how well-knit, brisk, and proud! And their young shepherd—his eyes were *blue!* And that ragged, bone-thin old man Jahil had almost run into, walking alone in the midst of the shifting currents of the road, where was he going with his arms stretched out like stunted wings, his head craning up and his white eyes staring at the great round sun he could not see?

Then came a cart with solid wooden wheels, pulled by a pair of oxen, jolting along with veiled women deep-wrapped in cloth from head to foot. And now a wandering musician, bent under his immense, ponderous stringed instrument—nothing like the light damburas whose fragile notes had been familiar to Mukhi from his childhood. Now two Hindu merchants traveling beside their mules; between the packs a lidless chest full of cotton, silk, pottery, and knives, a perambulating stall bumping its way along the road. And there were mountebanks, holy men, dervishes, and nobles setting off for a day's sport with hawks, falcons, and eagles on their wrists.

And lorries.

All of them, the feeblest and most broken-winded as well as the newest and most powerful, had brilliantly painted panels in the front and along their sides, glowing pictures of bunches of flowers, little groves, familiar birds and beasts. At the sight of each picture adorning the heavy machines Mukhi uttered a happy laugh. He admired the unknown painters who had produced them. As he saw it, they were charms against weariness and misfortune on the road. "Look! Look!" he cried to Uraz.

Uraz did not reply. Mukhi's eyes returned to the delights of the road. Lorries—yes, but they traveled too fast. There was no time to see everything properly. Whereas the caravans . . . They, blessed be the Prophet, they at least went along at a walking pace, the pace of a man in no great hurry. Neither the people of the caravans nor their animals took any count of time. He could stare his fill at them all. "Look! Look!" cried Mukhi to Uraz.

Uraz did not choose to see anything. He was no child, crying out with delight at new discoveries. Little they mattered to him, the strange sights of this unknown land. He had only one concern —to travel beyond this country, leave it behind, and find his own world again at home. Uraz saw only one advantage in all this confusion that swirled around him: safety. Among so many travelers, herds, lorries, and caravans did he not resemble a single blade of grass in the midst of the steppe? Even the dust and the uproar of the highway could be looked upon as allies. They covered him, enwrapped him, concealed him, protected him. He no longer thought about his enemies in Kabul . . .

THE DAY HAD REACHED ITS MIDPOINT AND THE LIGHT ITS MOST CON-
suming brilliance. The sky was dull, the mountains colorless, the
earth devoid of shade. The heat turned the dust into burning ash.

The traffic on the road had dwindled almost to nothing. Nomads
camped at the sides of the road without unfolding their tents, waiting with their loaded, kneeling camels for a little coolness to start
their journey again. The lorries ran no more. The foot travelers and
riders gathered in crowds on the verandas of the chaikhanas.

These teahouses stood spaced out all along both sides of the
highway. Whole rows of them were to be found on the outskirts of
the larger villages, and even the smallest, most wretched hamlet
had one of its own.

Wherever they happened to be they were all equally primitive
in dimensions, clientèle, and construction, containing only what
the caravans and travelers of Central Asia had known for centuries:
a whitewashed mud cube consisting of a single dark room. The
front wall had narrow, roughly worked openings that gave onto
the main feature of the chaikhana, a platform shaded by a covering
of dried leaves and branches, held up by a few thin, twisted, coarsely
shaped trunks. On the ground, poor, threadbare carpets or ragged
bits of cloth with no color other than that of the dust. That was
all.

But the nakedness was in no way depressing. It was the same
for all and so was the welcome. Boiling water sang in the bellies of
the huge samovars. The bright pictures on the cups shone against
the whitewashed wall. The quails cheeped in their tiny cages. Ara-
besques and flowers painted in primitive, vivid colors ran along the
rough façade. And against the background of mountain chains and
peaks, valleys, and torrents, ran always this wild freedom, this un-
measured liberty.

THE SUN SEEMED TO HANG AT ITS HEIGHT, FIXED THERE UNTIL TIME
should end. The men and animals still afoot crept painfully along.

In spite of his sweat-soaked flanks and his double load, Jahil went forward with the same long, quick, clean-cut pace.

In each chaikhana they passed Mukhi saw the travelers resting in the shade of the porch; he smelled the rich scent of grilled lamb on skewers and eggs fried in mutton fat; he heard the clatter of cups, and he knew that they were filled, according to the drinker's taste, with the green tea of China or the black from India. Every part of his huge body was hot, thirsty, and hungry. And as he leaned on Uraz's shoulder he longed to exclaim, "Let us do what everyone does! Come now, let us stop!"

But he was ashamed to display his impatience and weariness in front of an older man than himself, less strong and wounded into the bargain. So he resorted to what he considered deeply cunning artifice, saying, "Look, Uraz, they have a talking bird in that chaikhana, a myna." Or again, "Look, Uraz, look! Surely that is the biggest samovar of all!" Or, "Such stories they must be telling, the people from that lorry that has stopped over there."

Fruitless labor. Motionless in the saddle, his mouth set, Uraz continued to ride the stallion straight ahead along the burning, empty road. Yet he was suffering from heat and thirst much more than Mukhi. The poison of fever was setting fire to his skin, entrails, and throat. When he slipped his foot into the stirrup to ease it a little the bone seemed to fly splintering apart. The cloth that bandaged his wound was an oozing mass, and the dust that covered it did not prevent huge flies from feeding there in swarms.

As each chaikhana approached a prayer rose from the very marrow of his being, a prayer to be allowed to go to the veranda, escape from the sun, free his broken leg of its monstrous weight, and drink, drink, drink, first cold water from the jars and then boiling-hot, soothing black tea, heavy with sugar. But the very violence of the petition his flesh pressed on him prevented Uraz from gratifying it. More than that: he felt a savage pleasure in rejecting and insulting this inner plea. He was obsessed by the need to prove to his body that however great the torture might be it was not his master; this need was more ardent than the fires of the sky and the fever combined. The need to hold his racked body in the saddle, mercilessly, hour after hour.

A rising hill, a downward slope . . . Another rise. Uraz rode

Jahil as though eternity were spread out before them . . . They reached a steeper slope. Mukhi jumped down and walked at the stallion's side. "He has felt that Jahil is tiring," said Uraz to himself. The horse's pace was the same, no doubt; but there was that slight quickening of his breath and scarcely perceptible stiffening in his rhythm. Uraz gritted his teeth. He would not give in. He would not pass from the infinite, measureless world he had attained solely by force of will to another world subjected once again to the bondage of confined space. He would compel Jahil to go on as he himself went on, to the end of an endless journey, to the end of being, to annihilation. And then Uraz's strongest instincts, his upbringing, his race, his steppe, all rose up together against him. A horseman of Meimana, a chapandaz, could not inflict such usage on a beast as noble as Jahil.

"Mukhi," said Uraz in a low tone, "find the best chaikhana for the stallion."

The traffic on the road was beginning once more when Mukhi made his choice. At the bottom of a hill lay a big village shaped like a heart, with a stream running through it. The point of the heart, to one side of the road, had an inn on it. It looked like all the rest, but clear water ran along by its veranda, irrigating a little garden in which some willows grew.

Uraz rode the stallion up to it, scorned the shoulder Mukhi offered him, and landed on his unwounded leg. "No need," he said harshly to the bacha who came hurrying with a thin cotton-stuffed mattress. Then to Mukhi, "Look after the horse."

When the syce came back Uraz was stretched flat on his back, utterly motionless on the reddish ground, his arms down at either side. Were it not for the flickering of the lids that from time to time gave life to his eyes staring rigidly at the blazing light through the leaves of a meager willow, he could have been taken for a corpse. Mukhi was overcome with shame. He had left Uraz parched while he slaked his own thirst, drinking greedily from the stream, his face against Jahil's. Now he cried, "The bacha . . . at once . . . I shall call him."

"No one but thee, no one," whispered Uraz. He could not bear any unknown voice, any unfamiliar face. Ever since he had stretched out his broken leg on the cool clay of the garden and

arranged his limbs to ease his wound, he had received so much
benefit, so much kindness from the earth and its bearing up of
him, from the stream and its song, from the tree and its shade, that
he asked nothing from others and above all nothing from himself.

"Instantly . . . I swear . . . Thou shalt have everything,"
cried Mukhi. He vanished, running toward the back of the chaikhana.

"Go along, then . . . Go," said Uraz gently.

His wish, his only wish, was to achieve the quickest possible
return to an astonishing happiness—that of no longer existing and
of being at the same time aware of it. But a man's body will not
allow itself to be overlooked for long. When Mukhi raised Uraz's
head and put a blue Istalif pot full of water to his cracked lips,
Uraz emptied it to the last drop. "More," he said savagely. And
when his thirst was satisfied, the need for food wrung his entrails.
Avidly he tore the warm, soft, thin cakes that Mukhi passed him,
wrapped the pieces around greasy lumps of grilled mutton impaled
still on the burning skewers, ripped them from the metal, and
bolted them like a famished wolf. When his hunger was at last
appeased, sleep struck him down as he sat with his back against the
trunk of the willow.

Mukhi squatted on his heels and began to eat in his turn. His
eyes never left Uraz, and after each mouthful, each swallow, he
nodded his head with delight. How Uraz had stuffed himself! How
deeply he was sleeping!

For as long as he had been on earth Mukhi's duty, as bacha,
shepherd, or groom, had been to take care of animals and men, to
make them happy. Because he was good, kind, and strong he took
great pleasure in his task. A ram grown deep in wool and fat because of his zeal, a horse whose coat shone and whose strength had
been assured by his care—these things filled the needs of his pride
and affection to the full.

He watched over Uraz's sleep with feelings of the same nature.
He never asked himself whether he loved him, just as he never
wondered whether he loved Jahil when the stallion, groomed, fed,
and watered by him, went to sleep on the fresh litter that Mukhi
had prepared. But as he nodded his broad, almost hairless face, and
as the joy of total attachment made his cheerful, honest eyes gleam

in their narrow slits, Mukhi told himself that he would bring Uraz back safe and sound, even if he had to carry him back to the Meimana steppes in his arms.

THE LIGHT AND HEAT WERE DIMINISHING. FROM THE WILLOW THAT sheltered Uraz arose the first uncertain chirping by which invisible birds announced the coming of evening. Uraz slept on. Nothing woke him until there was a great din made by travelers coming into the garden of the chaikhana. They had arrived aboard an ancient, dislocated motorcar from the north, and they were all shouting together, some calling for black tea, others for green, in voices that the dust of the roads and the icy winds that sweep the passes of the Hindu Kush had rendered hoarse.

His eyes closed, Uraz stretched first his arms and then his sound leg. Then carefully he stirred the other. Pain ran through it at once. But a familiar pain, one that could be dealt with, a part of himself as it were. He uttered a faint sigh of contentment. He felt well. Washed clean of his weariness. Freed from the devils of terror and shame that had been pursuing him.

As the choir of birds grew louder and more melodious every moment in the branches above his head, he reflected that his fall was after all no more than an accident—and a commonplace accident at that. Of course, it had prevented him from winning the royal buzkashi. But from now on there would be one every year. The important thing was to make his way back to his own province as quickly as possible and get well. Then they would see . . . He was still Uraz and he owned Jahil.

Until then his eyes had still been closed. Now he opened them, and his gaze met that of the syce, squatting there on his heels, watching over him. "I have had a good sleep, Mukhi," he said mildly.

"By the Prophet," cried the syce, "thou mayest be certain of that. And now thou shalt have the blackest, hottest, sweetest tea that ever restored a man's heart. I run."

Uraz's eyes turned toward the enormous peaks and the sky they held up. As the sun climbed down, so everything took on life and color once more. The firmament was one vast tremor of blue, and the gilded light that floated on the mountain side heralded the splendid crimsons of the evening. But Uraz was used to his unbounded plain, and he had little love for these great walls of stone. They blocked the horizon; they brought it close. He looked down and was no longer out of his element. The chaikhanas of the steppes, of the hidden valleys, of the lofty passes where the wind in the peaks and chasms sang, the chaikhanas of the inhuman desert, wherever a miserly trickle of water allowed a hint of life—there was no difference between all these wayfarers' houses. The gentle singing of the huge copper samovar, the smell of mutton fat, the scent of tea, the shouting for the bachas. Uraz felt comfortably at home.

And the travelers themselves, sitting there cross-legged, were not altogether strange to him. Kandahar merchants on their way to buy astrakhan skins in Mazar-i-Sharif and carpets in Meimana—in those two provinces he had often met their like under the roofs of the bazaars or on the verandas of the inns, and he recognized their turbans, tied according to the custom of their region, and the deep henna that dyed their spreading, massive beards.

The syce came back, his huge hands bearing a tray on which gleamed teapots and cups. He squatted on his bare heels opposite Uraz. "Jahil was wearier still," he said. "He is sleeping yet."

"He needs a long, long rest. We shall not take to the road again until tomorrow," said Uraz. He looked closely at Mukhi's eyelids, red from dust, sun, and sleeplessness, and at his chapan, almost in rags and absurdly short for his height; and he thought, "It is high time I bought him another." As he thought this Uraz did not wonder whether he loved Mukhi; but for once his smile did not bring to mind the fierce grin of a wolf.

THEY SUCKED IN THE TEA WITH LONG NOISY INWARD BREATHS, PARTLY because it was very hot and partly because they thought it better drunk like this. Quite given up to their pleasure, they did not exchange a word. The chorus of little birds in the willow had become deafening. The shade its branches gave came to Mukhi's shoulders now, and the slanting rays of the sun, shooting under the porch, revealed the full glory of the decorations on the pottery, the red-gold of the samovars, and the vivid colors in the pictures on the whitewashed front.

The Kandahar merchants had finished their meal and paid for it. The owner of the chaikhana came out to greet them. He was a very brisk little old man who, because of the color of his hair, the shape of his face, and his busy, active little eyes, looked like a gray mouse. He said, "From now on the road is safe and easy and you will soon be in Kabul. Yet it is a very great pity that you will get there too late. The great buzkashi of the king was run there yesterday, at this very time."

At these words Mukhi started and opened his mouth. With a harsh gesture, Uraz ordered him to be silent and still. Then slowly he passed his hand over his forehead. Was it possible? Yesterday! Only yesterday!

The man of the chaikhana went on with a longing sigh, "The worthy people of Kabul, I am very sure, are talking of nothing but this match. What tales they will have to tell you!"

The oldest of the merchants, whose beard, longest of them all and deepest dyed with henna, a beard that flowed over the richest garment there, observed in a tone of offended dignity, "Never fret thy spirit, they will not astonish me. Poor souls! They have had to wait for their first buzkashi until yesterday, whereas I . . . And as for my buzkashi, they will never see its like."

"Recount it to us, O man of wealth, recount!" begged the owner of the chaikhana, and without waiting for a reply he turned to the veranda and cried, "Bacha, ho bacha! *My* cushions, quickly! *My* tea, *my* cakes, *my* preserves!"

The big Kandahar merchant stroked his flaming beard for a moment, as though he were hesitating. But his legs were already bending slowly beneath him to act as a seat. His companions followed his example. They would not see Kabul at the appointed hour? How shocking! Time runs by and is gone . . . A splendid tale remains.

ALL THAT WAS NEEDED, CUPS, TEAPOTS, DELICACIES, PARTICULAR DE-lights, was brought, set out, assiduously handed round. The two bachas were as deeply filled with curiosity as their master. When they had finished serving they took their places, cross-legged, in the attentive ring.

Yet the merchant of Kandahar was in no hurry. There were duties of courtesy to be observed, and his listeners' interest must be raised higher still. So he savored the tea, the honey cakes, the mut-ton-fat preserves, and praised his host for their excellence. Then with both hands he caressed the waves of his burning beard; and now it was known that he was about to begin.

"Years and years ago," he said, "I went into the province of the north, riding my horse as everyone did in those days, and I went to choose the finest possible skins of astrakhan. That was not difficult in Meimana. There I dealt with the richest lord in the country and the most honest—Osman Bey."

Uraz, leaning against his willow, and Mukhi, squatting on his heels, exchanged a long look. Osman Bey! To hear his name so far from their steppe!

The merchant from Kandahar went on, "Now at that time Os-man Bey was marrying his youngest son, his favorite. Oh worthy men, what rejoicings!" The speaker raised his eyes to the heavens, and his beard waved like a flame in the wind. "What rejoicings! They lasted seven days and seven nights. The governors and the generals of the Three Provinces stayed with Osman Bey. So also did the chiefs of the tribes. Indeed, some of the great Kashgars themselves had come from Persia. And on the seventh day of the feast they were offered a buzkashi. The goal, the circle of justice, as it has always been called in those parts but which you people here know only since yesterday, stood opposite Osman Bey and his most illustrious guests. At his feet were heaped silk chapans, rare carpets, silver-mounted guns. Farther off shepherds guarded astrakhan sheep with splendid fleeces and high-bred camels adorned with pompoms and feathers. All these—chapans, carpets, beasts, and weapons—were intended for the winner of the game and for the horsemen who should carry out the most brilliant strokes and charges."

"Can such things be? So much wealth to be given away?" asked the owner of the chaikhana.

As his only reply the merchant raised his wide, kohl-ringed brown eyes to the sky. Such ignorance was beyond comprehension. Mukhi whispered in Uraz's ear, "What he says is true. The marriage took place in the year of my birth, and . . ."

"Silence!" said Uraz, moving only his lips—the fever was changing their color. Did this half-witted rustic understand nothing at all, then? Had he really not felt, the moment Osman Bey's name was heard, that a terrible force had been set in motion and that from sentence to sentence they had to listen for, watch over, and spy out its advance?

"Before the match," went on the speaker, "some ten horsemen, dressed in worn old chapans and round caps rimmed with fox or wolf, came to salute Osman Bey. They were his chapandaz. Among them was a man whose appearance surprised me greatly. It was clear from his lurching walk that his body had been broken again and again. His whole face was scarred with long-healed wounds. Amid the young and supple men on either hand he seemed out of place. I asked my neighbor, 'What age is he?' My neighbor replied, 'He is of such an age that that youth thou seest among our host's chapandaz can be his son.' 'Ah, truly I see,' said I, 'the old man does not ride in the buzkashi.' 'He rides with the rest,' said my neighbor. 'The only difference is that he rides his own horse.'"

The wealthy man from Kandahar, seized by the memories of his youth, allowed his hands a sudden movement that took them far from his beard. "Well now," he cried, "well now, in the name of the Prophet, from the first melee the most aged of the chapandaz proved that he was also the most formidable. He was always in the deepest of the struggle, closest to the goat's body. And his stallion surpassed all the others in strength, fire, and intelligence . . . Yes, friends, I do assure you that the old chapandaz was very splendid, very terrible to behold. And since Osman Bey, that unrivaled host, had caused a good horse to be saddled for me, I was able to follow him throughout the game."

"God and the Prophet be praised for that," said the master of the house. "And then what happened?"

"If everything were to be recounted," said the merchant from Kandahar, "I should never come to the end. Many hours had passed, many leagues been covered, and many horses whose riders lay broken on the steppe were galloping free, when the oldest of the chapandaz won possession of the goat. Unlike all the others who had had it before him, he did not try to turn back and break through to the circle of justice. He rode straight on before him. And as his horse was the fastest and strongest of them all, he led the whole band galloping across the endless plain. Had he already worked out his plan? Maybe; he knew the country better than any other man. Did he make the most of a happy chance? I cannot tell. But this is how it was . . . A lonely shepherd's hut rose suddenly from the steppe and he slackened his horse's speed. The other chapandaz caught him up. Then for the first time he struck his horse with the whip and they set off toward the hut at such a gallop that I thought they must be destroyed against it. But at the last moment the stallion was seen to leave the ground and fly, yes, *fly* I say, and land on the flat roof." The Kandahar merchant had been talking so fast and with such energy that his throat was dry. He turned to pour himself some tea. His teapot was empty. The youngest of the bachas ran toward the samovar, crying, "In the name of Allah and His Prophet, wait for me to tell the rest!"

Uraz's eyes were closed, his body as motionless as his face. But the lash of his whip writhed under the pressure of his grip like a serpent in its death throes.

"There, O man of wealth," said the bacha, returning. The merchant of Kandahar drank and went on, "Indeed it was an extraordinary leap that the old chapandaz had wrung from the stallion. The finest horsemen mounted on the finest horses of the Three Provinces of the north tried in vain to do the same. Many had been unable to stop in time and had broken themselves against the wall of the house at full speed. Others attempted to imitate the old chapandaz, but not one of their mounts was able to do what his had done. And again many of them maimed their horses. As for those who reached the level of the roof, the old chapandaz, high on his stallion, flung them back with a blow of his whip full in the face. And sometimes, to mock them, he struck them with the hairy carcass; and this turned them mad with rage.

"Yet this did not mean that he had won. Scores of unhurt chapandaz on their undamaged horses ringed the house round, like a pack of wolves round a prey that they cannot yet reach but that they are certain of killing. Then the son of the old horseman cried with all his strength, 'What can I do for thee?'

" 'Wait,' said the father, stroking the neck of his horse all covered with foam.

"Oh, my friends! That steppe under the lowering sun! The solitary hut! High on it the old man; and the scars that ran over his terrible face!"

"I see him, I see him!" cried the owner of the chaikhana. "But what did he do then?"

"He began to make game of those below, to insult them; and in this way caused them to lose their heads. At the same time he turned his horse in every direction from one end of the roof to the other, as though he were going to leap. And every time the chapandaz rushed in confusion toward the place where he seemed to be going to land. But he, perpetually watching the motions that he forced upon them, suddenly saw that the ring of his enemies was thinnest just where his son was placed, and he called to him, 'Make a path for me, boy!' And the young man flung himself on his neighbors without sparing them or himself. And the old chapandaz, with a prodigious leap, went through like the blast of a gale.

"After this, he galloped on without any hindrance—on to his victory."

The merchant of Kandahar leaned back against his cushion, crossed his arms on his belly, beneath his flowing, coppery beard, and gazing at his listeners he coughed with pleasure. From their faces he could gauge his tale's effect.

After a brief silence they all cried together, "Blessed be thou for having given us thy experience!"

Mukhi looked at Uraz and took fright. Uraz was hiding the upper part of his face with his right hand as though to shield it from the sun. But there was no sun. It was twilight now. "Art thou ill?" whispered the syce.

At this moment a voice, intensely shrill with curiosity, rose above all the others. "And the name of the old chapandaz," asked the owner of the chaikhana, "dost thou recall it yet, thou most deserving man?"

"As long as I live I shall remember it," said the merchant from Kandahar. Uraz let his hand fall back. "It was the great Tursen," said the merchant of Kandahar.

"The great Tursen," cried the man of the chaikhana devoutly.

"The great Tursen," repeated the merchants.

"The great Tursen," said the bachas after them.

Shyly the youngest of the bachas asked, "And dost thou remember the name of the son who helped his father so valiantly?"

The merchant of Kandahar gazed at the child, wagged his blazing beard, and observed, "Thou must know, O bacha, that if a memory is to remain good it must not load itself with names devoid of importance."

The travelers walked toward their motorcar. The owner of the chaikhana escorted them. The crockery and the remains of the meal were taken away. A strange silence fell over the garden; it was taking on its evening hue. Mukhi felt weariness overwhelming him. He cast a covert glance at Uraz. His face was drawn to an extraordinary degree. The look in his eyes was quite inhuman.

"I shall sleep against thee," said Mukhi, "and keep thee warm."

"Thou shalt saddle Jahil," said Uraz.

"But . . . but . . . thou saidst . . ." stammered the syce.

"I said saddle Jahil."

Uraz's voice was low and quiet. But there was complete finality in its tone. Mukhi went toward the grove by the stream that sheltered the stallion. He moved slowly, his knees yielding under him.

"Quick!" cried Uraz.

Never, never had he imagined that there could be a suffering such as that which he had just experienced in this place. Everything now, the garden, the water, the trees, the musical clamor of the birds, was poison to him. Everything sent his blood into a fever; everything heated and chafed his brain. Even the willow against which he was leaning burned his flesh. He saw its trunk and its branches no longer as the members of a tree, but rather as those of a man, an aged, knotted, indestructible man whose feats of long ago were told on the other side of the Hindu Kush, whereas he, he, Uraz, instead of winning the first royal buzkashi lay beneath his father's shade—lay there still, lay there forever.

Uraz set his two hands firmly against the ground and with a

furious thrust flung his body upward and forward. He had not gauged or even foreseen this movement. Nothing was of any importance but to tear himself away from this smothering shadow. The broken bone struck against the rough ground, and the two ends grated. For a moment the shattering pain prevented Uraz from thinking. Then he reflected, "Go? Yes. Easy. But what for? To follow the high road in total safety? Ride prudent stages? Be overtaken at every chaikhana by people coming from Kabul in lorries and hear the tale of the royal buzkashi over and over again? And at the end of it all to find Tursen there before me?" Then, without knowing that he was speaking aloud, Uraz whispered, "It shall not be so."

By what spell? What stroke of fortune? What miracle? He did not trouble his head to answer. He merely repeated, "It shall not be so."

The owner of the chaikhana had said farewell to the merchants of Kandahar, and now he came up to Uraz. Before he had time to speak, Uraz said, "Dost thou know the crossroads a man may take from here?"

"All of them," said the man of the chaikhana. "I was born in this village."

"How must one go to reach the province of Meimana?" asked Uraz again.

"Thou takest me too far," said the man. "For us, Meimana is another world. I know that one must go by Bamian, the valley of the great Buddhas; and I can tell thee about the old, old Bamian road, the road of long ago. Beyond that, thou must ask . . ."

"Very well," said Uraz. "What do I owe thee?"

"Hold!" cried the man who looked like a gray mouse, his searching eyes running busily from Uraz's haggard face to the blackened bandage that stuck to his leg. "Hold! I must warn thee—these rough tracks are far from safe and night out there is freezing ice with no chaikhanas like mine awaiting thee."

"Tell me the road, directly," said Uraz. At last his eyes had a look of life. Each time he was told of a fresh obstacle his heart beat higher.

"There, now," said the owner of the chaikhana, finishing his account. "Choose the highway."

"What turning must we take for the old road?" asked Uraz.

The restless little eyes were fixed for a moment in astonishment. "So in spite of everything thou wilt take . . . ?" asked the man of the chaikhana.

"I am in a hurry," said Uraz.

"Often it is not the shortest road that leads quickest to the goal, above all . . ." said the landlord. He stopped. Mukhi and Jahil were coming to a halt at Uraz's side. Then he went on, "Truly, to help thee thou hast a wonderfully fine stallion and a stout great follower."

Uraz raised himself on one leg. The man came to help him. "No," said Uraz. He grasped the pommel of the saddle and Jahil's mane. A moment later he was mounted. Mukhi got up behind him. Speaking quickly the owner of the chaikhana said, "Thou must take the path on the left. It will bring thee to a well. There thou wilt see a steeply mounting track. Follow it as far as the old caravanserai that stands at the top. And hurry. Thou must be there before nightfall. If not, may the Prophet watch over thee."

"Peace be with thee," said Uraz and Mukhi together.

Jahil carried them away. The owner of the chaikhana gave a long-drawn-out sigh. Once again one of the strange wayfarers who passed through his garden was taking his secret with him unrevealed.

*****

6

The Corpse

THE FIRST MOUNTAINS began at the very edge of the village.
From that point rose a zigzag path cut between the cliff and
the sheer drop, a steep and slippery path. In spite of Jahil's dash
and spirit the travelers had not reached the end of their stage
before the world was drowned in twilight.

Mukhi jumped down and led the stallion by the bridle. With
his free hand he followed the cliff face in the darkness, to be sure
of the uncertain path winding along the edge of invisible precipices.

Suddenly, in a child's voice, he said, "I am frightened, Uraz."

"So is Jahil," said Uraz. "I can feel it."

"It is not so much of falling that I am frightened," whispered
Mukhi, "But of . . ."

"I know," said Uraz. He too could sense the innumerable, un-
mentionable beings, the shapeless, winged, clawed, taloned, naked,
hairy monsters and ghosts, the blood-sucking spirits, birds, and
skull-bearing reptiles that slid, flew, crawled, and skimmed along
these mountains, on the surface of these chasms buried under the
darkness as though by a vast black lake. He could hear them hurrying by, panting, whistling, and laughing. Odious gusts of breath
froze his face and sometimes he could feel his skin prickling under
the fleeting, horrible touch of feet, wing-cases, feelers, feathers,
tongues, horns.

"Yes, I know," said Uraz again.

"And thou art not frightened, Uraz?" asked Mukhi humbly.

"No," replied Uraz, "I am not afraid." But the moment he had said it he was so astonished that he stopped Jahil. What? Was it true that in the midst of all this terrible swarming he was suddenly devoid of fear, free from dread? Uraz listened to his heart in the mountain night. Then in all honesty he repeated, "No, I am not afraid."

"Thou art brave," whispered Mukhi. "Braver than any man on earth."

Unseen by the syce, Uraz slowly nodded his head. What put him above other men, he reflected, was not courage but indifference to misfortune.

Uraz gave Jahil his head. As the stallion moved on, Uraz furtively patted Mukhi's shoulder.

"Keep thy hand upon me," begged the syce. Once again he began to feel his way along the protuberances and the rough places of the rock wall, his only guide in the impenetrable darkness. And so they made their way along the thin ribbon between the cliff and the void, the horseman leaning on the walker and the walker on the darkling granite.

When they reached a still harsher slope Uraz said, "How is the fear, Mukhi?"

"Thy hand has done it good," said the syce. Yet his voice was still faint and sickly. He added, "I should like there to be a few stars at least."

"They will be there presently, in their own time," said Uraz.

But the first they saw did not belong to the sky. As they rounded still another sinuous curve in the path, very far away, very high, a light suddenly trembled: but not far enough, not high enough, to be beyond the earth. And although it was humble indeed and weakly, it looked to them more splendid and radiant than the greatest of the planets. In that desert of stone, in the cold of their bones and souls, that star was the warmth of men and the flame of their fire.

"The caravanserai!" cried Mukhi.

He straightened himself, no longer shackled by dread and its spells. Uraz's hand left his shoulder. He did not even notice it.

WIDENING FROM TURN TO TURN, THE TRACK BECAME A ROAD AND ended by running out onto a plateau, the meeting point of other paths. At their junction stood a caravanserai.

The huge building was falling into ruins. Even in the darkness there was something astonishing about the walls, blacker than the night, and their shattered, broken line. The gaps and breaches were shown by beams of light that streamed out through them on all sides, as from a lighthouse. But inside the caravanserai this light, so pure and triumphant to the benighted travelers on the mountain side, was no more than one smoking lamp with a darkened, filthy glass. Its feeble light was not even enough to penetrate the darkness of the common hall, where men and beasts lay about promiscuously.

Uraz rode through the tall crumbling porch without difficulty. Mukhi led Jahil between the bodies and sometimes over them toward a still unoccupied corner. A few heads half rose; a lamb bleated weakly amid the tangled wool of a flock; a dreaming dog uttered a groan; a kneeling camel raised its long neck, with its slobbering muzzle at the far end. That was all. The gateway of the caravanserai might be a gaping hole, its roof a shattered dome, and each of its sides a heap of tumbled bricks; but on coming into it men and beasts felt themselves sheltered from the pains and dangers of the road; as they laid down the physical burdens so they put off that of watchfulness, and exhausted by the day's march gave themselves up wholly to sleep. Another traveler in from the depth of the shadows? So much the better. Their safety increased with numbers.

Uraz did not move from his saddle when Jahil had paced right across the huge room. Yet he felt that if he wished he was still capable of swinging his good leg over Jahil's withers, dropping onto it, and letting himself slide to the ground. But he had to want it, and he no longer wanted anything at all.

Mukhi was so used to respecting the chapandaz's pride that at first he made no sort of movement to come to his help. Finally, with a kind of shame he asked, "May I take thee down?"

"Thou mayest," said Uraz.

"It is right that it should be so," said Mukhi. "No one can see us here."

Without troubling to reply Uraz thought, "It will be the same before all the people of Kabul or Meimana."

Suddenly his whole body stiffened. Mukhi had seized his broken leg at the very point of the fracture. But from his childhood the syce had seen the broken legs of sheep, horses, and camels treated and had dealt with them himself; all this was not in vain. His huge hand knew how to enclose and hold the broken bones in such a way that the suffering was reduced to its least degree of fury. Uraz unclenched his teeth. Then he felt Mukhi's other arm lift him like a child and set him down very gently on the beaten earth. "Wait, wait a little," said the tall syce. "Thou shalt be comfortable." He picked up pieces of brick lying scattered on the ground, plucked others from the shattered outer wall, heaped them up, hollowed them out in the shape of a rude channel, and then stretched out the wounded leg in its hollow.

"Wait and thou shalt see . . . Wait . . . Yes, I promise thee," went on Mukhi. He was speaking for his own benefit alone. He needed to hear his own voice. The words were of no importance. They were a song of unrivaled happiness—farewell, goodbye to the monsters of the night! And of total devotion—to undaunted Uraz and his hand during that time of horror!

Mukhi removed Jahil's saddle and set it under Uraz's head. He stripped off his own chapan and covered the wounded man with it. He made the stallion stretch out right next to Uraz and he himself lay down against his other side. And as he did so he continually uttered a low chant, "Thou shalt have a true, perfect rest . . . Nape well down in the hollow of the leather . . . Legs and belly and chest quite warm under the chapan . . . And so well protected by Jahil from the drafts that whistle through the cracks; if thou hast need of anything I am here . . . thou knowest that, for sure?"

"I am certain of it," said Uraz gently.

The syce was lying at his side and against the darkness Uraz could see his eyes and mouth gleaming in a beatific smile.

"I am here, Uraz," murmured Mukhi.

Now only his teeth caught the faint gleam of the lamp. His eyes were closed.

"I am here; I am here . . . I am here," repeated Mukhi's breath while the deepest sleep of all was already freeing his muscles and sinews from weariness, fear, and delight—all equally exhausting.

FOR HIS PART URAZ WAS NOT ASLEEP. AND THIS HE FOUND IN NO way unpleasant. There was bodily peace after so long and dangerous a road, the physical delight of warmth after the frozen darkness, the sudden stopping of merciless pain: for the first moments Uraz as it were shut himself up in his own flesh with these treasures.

Only gradually did he emerge from within himself. And step by step he discovered a surprising harmony between his surroundings and his happiness. His head was resting in the hollow of a saddle, the noblest object shaped by men and one that had been his most trusted companion these twenty years. From time to time he stirred his head, the better to feel the shape and texture. At each of these contacts the smell of the beautiful warm leather mingled with the other scent that Uraz loved above all others—that which spread from the stallion's flank pressed close to his. Above these smells, borne by the drafts that wafted among the fissured walls, came the odors of wool, hair, and hide, and then those of the poor cotton clothes and the human bodies they covered, bodies that walked far and labored hard under the sun. And Uraz's nostrils flared wide to breathe in the emanation of his own kind and all their flocks.

The deep sleep of the caravanserai had its own language, too. Men and beasts breathed it out from the depth of their slumber; it rose from them at the same time as their smell. Groans, sighs, barks, snores, whining, whistling, coughing, bleating, neighing, bubbling, the sound of hoofs, the grinding of teeth, the stirring of bells, the rattle of bits—it all made up a perpetual undercurrent of muted sound, animal for one part and human for the rest. In this vast mingled chorus were joined the hoarse old man, the exhausted woman, the frightened child, the restless horse, the distrustful mastiff, the goat, ram, mule, ass, and camel, each following the tracks and feeding places of his dreams, according to his kind. And Uraz, putting a name to each voice, each gasp, experienced an unparalleled delight, as though he were a very little child again, hearing the familiar lullaby that at once thrust back all the threats and terrors of the night.

The night was wearing on. Through the holes in the roof Uraz saw that now there were stars. He stared at them without much attention. They had come too late. They were shining too far away. They had nothing to do with his surroundings. Uraz looked away.

His gaze settled on the squalid lamp. Its wick floated in melted mutton fat and it smoked heavily. Its cracked, chipped glass was filthy with dust and soot. But it so happened that this covering imparted to the light that filtered through it that particular essence which enchanted Uraz. It had as little color as the gentlest saffron, soft to the eye as a kiss; and its weak, uncertain gleam transfigured the filth, poverty, and squalor of the caravanserai and its sleepers.

Usually Uraz's quick, harsh eye instantly picked out the faults and defects of the faces and bodies he saw. An ignoble mouth here, a servile chin there; here a timid, a cowardly eye, here a stupid forehead, here a false and shiny smile. Flabby shoulders, drooping heads, hollow chests, feeble legs, swagging bellies . . . The limping men, the knock-kneed men, the goitrous necks, the droolers, the one-eyed . . . All this had fed Uraz's scorn for the herd of his fellow men, strengthening it more with every year; and with this scorn his pride and his loneliness had grown. But tonight the light of the smoking lamp wiped out all misfortunes, all repulsive marks from his companions; it washed them all away. They were only shepherds and travelers asleep, wrapped in clothes that were in fact wretched, dirty, threadbare, torn, and ragged, but that the magic of the half-lit darkness turned into soft and noble robes, just as it hung the walls with silk and velvet. And when an eye opened in some vague face it had the quality of a darkly glowing gem.

"Am I so different from them?" Uraz asked himself, suddenly.

It was the first time in his life that this had happened . . . His skin was on fire. He threw back Mukhi's chapan. Either this movement or a stronger draft (the lamp was flickering wildly) or perhaps

an insect's bite disturbed Jahil. The stallion raised his head a little
and shook his long thick mane. He went back to sleep directly. But
his breath and the rippling play of his muscles called his rider back
to a sense of worldly hierarchy. Uraz stiffened. The precious saddle
under his head was no longer a mere invalid's pillow.

Could these wretched foot-borne creatures, these scratchers of
the ground, these goatherds, plebs of the road, really be the equal
of Jahil's master?

Uraz's fever rose. His blood ran hotter; his head grew lighter
hour by hour. And he had a vision. He saw the grass stretching out
forever, and upon it twenty splendid horses, drunk with their own
strength and spirits and with rivalry, intoxicated with the unlim-
ited space before them, thundered across the steppe in a tremendous gallop. Their riders were the best this side of the earth. One
of them broke away, clean away, leaving the others so far behind
that they vanished in the dust. And he raced on, the first, the only
one, racing with no other aim than his ride itself. Uraz recognized
himself. His heart rang like the drums at a feast beating for success
and glory.

Then the inner singing stopped. Was it the fatigue of sleeplessness, the weight of his wounded leg, the lamp's smell of burning
tallow, or the greedy sound of a new-born suckling? Uraz was no
longer one with the victorious horseman. Every moment the rider
became more and more a stranger to him, harder to understand
than the unknown inhabitants of the caravanserai. As for them,
they were worn out, sleeping; when day dawned they would follow
their road to the next halting place; and so they would go on until
they reached their destination. Everything was plain. But that fellow, hurtling along like a madman, with that silent laugh on his
wind-swollen face, where was he going? Who was it directed
against, this charge, this onslaught? What did he hope to achieve,
what reach in his madness? The horizon? How could that be? The
horizon flees away perpetually, receding forever.

The lunatic irritated Uraz. He shut his eyes. Thereupon he saw
a wonderful bazaar. Richer than that of Daolatabad, larger than
that of Mazar-i-Sharif, more brightly colored than that of Akcha.
And the countless people who crammed its shady alleys and its sun-
filled streets, the whole crowd of them drew reverently aside at the

passage of a man who looked neither to the right nor left, walking along with the tall heels of his boots ringing and a wolfskin cap on his high-held head. It was the rider of the steppe. "Of course . . . That was what I rode for," said Uraz to himself. "Of course."

He still could not understand. So much effort, so much skill and disregard of danger, such eagerness, such vehemence and zeal, and all to obtain what? The praise of these cowardly, stupid merchants and the customers they cheated. What a farce! How precarious and fickle it was, that favor, which had to be sought at the risk of one's life in every match. A piece of ill-luck, a horse that stumbled, a muscle that yielded, and then came scorn, oblivion . . . And the crowd of the bazaars would draw aside for another.

As Uraz reflected on this he saw that the face of the horseman greeted by the crowd was no longer his own. It had taken on the features of Salih, the winner of the royal buzkashi. But instead of the agony of humiliation that should have come upon him, Uraz (and this was his greatest astonishment in the course of that night) felt no more than a lofty pity for the victor.

"Go along, young fellow, go along," he said to him within his mind. "Thy wretched brain still believes in it. Go on . . . Let thyself be taken in, deluded with happiness . . . until the next fall. Go . . . I am no longer part of this half-wit's game."

Uraz felt the fever booming, humming within him, and he had the sensation of being borne along on a river of the steppes in its springtime flood. It was strong. It was warm. He could think better. Wider. Faster.

Yes, indeed! Only too eagerly and too long had he played his part in this unworthy, dishonorable bargain. On both sides flunkeys, bondsmen, slaves! All of them. Those who ran after fame. And those who gaped and bleated when it came near. Enough!

Uraz slowly let himself subside on the beaten earth. Quite flat, the back of his neck in the hollow of the saddle, in the midst of the smells, sounds, lights, and shadows that peopled the dark caravanserai. Peaceful. Healthy. Friendly. And Uraz thought, "From now on, these are my companions."

These people did not even know what a buzkashi was, nor a chapandaz. Among them it was not necessary to hold one's head high above everyone and everything, above sorrow and happiness, accepting nothing but admiring respect and giving back nothing but pride. (Allah, what weariness to be a demi-god and nothing else!) And if he were a cripple, very well, then he would be a cripple. Neither beaten nor a failure. Merely a cripple. Accepted by the others. Men of the same road . . . the same tribe . . . equal before the same life . . . they would travel together.

Across ravines, plains, and valleys marched a very poor, very humble caravan . . . And he, Uraz, was with it. On a wretched horse, a mule, an ass. Yes, an ass . . . And even on crutches . . . Yes, indeed, crutches. They all looked at him with Mukhi's smile.

The stars had gone out. Uraz thought, "The sky has lost all its points of pride; it is happy." Consciousness abandoned him.

MUKHI YAWNED, STRETCHED, SIGHED, AND NOISILY SCRATCHED HIM-self. His body was calling out for a much longer rest, but he could not allow it. The sun and Mukhi always rose together.

Almost before his mind was awake his first care was for Uraz and Jahil. Excellent: they were both of them sleeping. Mukhi crossed the caravanserai, where human shapes, also conscious of the call of dawn, were rising up from their vagueness. When he reached the huge dilapidated porch he slowly rubbed his eyes with a languid fist. Sleep was still clinging to his body, as the darkness was still clinging to the plateau. But the higher he looked the brighter grew the surface of the naked rocks. Already on the peaks and granite pinnacles trembled a thin, delicate, translucent fringe, spread as it were by their ridges. It was shockingly cold.

Guided by the splashing sound, Mukhi walked automatically toward a little gush of water. He dipped his hands and sprinkled his face. By the time the water had dried on his skin there was not a hint of torpor or weariness left in Mukhi. He waved his arms and then began to beat his bosom with his enormous fists. Harder, harder, and harder still. The blows rang and echoed in the silent dawn. Their rhythm gave Mukhi a feeling of wild delight. He was both the smith and the anvil. Harder, harder still.

Suddenly the drumming broke off. Mukhi's head was rigid, turned toward the sky. He did not understand. Up there, defined by the mountain tops, he could see prairies, poppy-red and absinthe-green, brought into being by the approach of dawn. Day was coming fast. And since this was the first time Mukhi had ever seen the dawn moving through the enormous mountains he no longer recognized this moment, this familiar moment, at which the river of day began its course.

In the country of the steppes sky and earth woke together. Light rose in a steady flood, flowing over the whole horizon from one end to the other. The sky became a great pool of light and the plain a carpet of grass and dew.

Here morning came in leaps, piece by piece. Between two towering mountains there had been a shining stretch of country for a long while now, whereas on the peaks themselves still floated the ashes of the night. A single lonely mountain top burst into fiery life. A cliff face suddenly began to glow. But those that stood over against them were still dead, blind and extinguished.

The disorder grew steadily greater. Through every gap, cleft, fissure, or chasm that lay eastward the spume of dawn surged up, the darting arrows and fiery blaze of light appeared. Yet there was no sun.

The air was all light and the light was frozen. Mukhi breathed in deeply. The mountain dawn made its way into his whole being. The fluid was so strong, so pure, that Mukhi closed his eyes in an ecstasy. He was on the point of laughing, shouting, singing with happiness when he felt a warm and gentle touch upon his eyelids. They opened, just ajar, and through the network of his lashes Mukhi saw a crescent of pink fire.

The sun . . . at last . . . the real sun. Already Mukhi was on his face, turned toward Mecca.

And suddenly the words and motions that had been performed again and again, said and said again so often that they had lost all power and substance for Mukhi—suddenly they had a prodigious effect upon him. Emotion disturbed the beating of his heart: it turned the words hoarse in his throat. On his knees there at the edge of a new day he discovered a new form of speech in the daily run of the first prayer, a way to thank these mountains which, after such monstrous dread, were granting him so many wonders, such miracles to marvel at.

Other voices were repeating the same words. They belonged to other men kneeling beneath the porch or by the walls of the caravanserai. But Mukhi's burning forehead never left the frozen ground, and it seemed to him that he heard nothing but his own voice, multiplied by a hundred echoes.

WHEN MUKHI STOOD UP A YOUNG MAN, ALMOST AS TALL AS HIMSELF, though sickly and hunchbacked, was looking at him with a friendly expression. His big sad eyes had the shape and color of almonds. He said—and the ring of his voice was as gentle and penetrating as his gaze—"Praise to thee, since at thy age thou canst show thy whole soul in prayer."

"I?" cried Mukhi.

The fine sad eyes smiled at him and Mukhi had the feeling that their look filled him with light. He scratched the bare back of his neck and said, "It may be so, indeed . . . this time. But it is the first, I tell thee truly."

"Praise to thee still more," said the young crook-backed man, "for having raised such a prayer upon my poor piece of land."

"What?" said Mukhi. "Thou art the landlord here?"

The young crook-backed man uttered a very slight laugh, one that strangely enough gave strength and confidence. "That is a very grand name for the owner of these ruins," he said. "Yet it is true that last year I, Ghulam, inherited the caravanserai from my father Hyder, who had it from his father Fahrad, its first builder. He might indeed have been called landlord. Rich and powerful he was in his life. In those days there were no lorries. All the merchandise traveled on the backs of animals and all the convoys had to stop at nightfall in places built for them. Nowadays the only great caravans are those of the nomads, and thou knowest very well that they never camp between four walls. Furthermore thou seest the state of mine."

The freshly risen sun threw a pitiless light on the immense red clay construction. Fallen, collapsing on every side, it was less a shelter than a heap of ruins. From this retreat, this lair, men and beasts who had spent the night there were now emerging, busily preparing for the road once more.

Mukhi struck himself a shattering blow on the forehead. How could he have abandoned Uraz and Jahil to the confusion of all these departures? In the porch he was obliged to give way to an unhealthy, mangy camel, some scabbed, galled donkeys, and the ragged men who urged them on with pointed sticks. Inside, wretched convoys were taking shape, emaciated flocks gathering. The beasts stood loaded already and women were tying the smaller children to their backs. Mukhi slipped between rumps and pack saddles until he reached his companions. Then he breathed more easily. In spite of the noise Uraz was still asleep. Certainly the stallion was showing signs of impatience; but as soon as he felt the well-known hand along his neck and on his muzzle he quietened. "Patience, patience," Mukhi said to him tenderly. "Everything will be seen to. I shall be back."

MUKHI HAD BEEN MISTAKEN. ALTHOUGH URAZ KEPT HIS EYES tightly closed he was not asleep. The noise had plucked him from his tormented sleep at once. And it had done so in the worst possible conditions. The vast enchanted hall was now no more than a squalid ruin, festooned with spiders' webs. The shadows and the noble hangings had resumed the shape of wretched men and beasts, made worse by waking, and they all set themselves to shouting, barking, bawling, and braying.

Now as he leaned there against his saddle all these things vexed his sick body and disgusted his embittered heart. He no longer had anything whatever in common with that man who, delivered from his devils, had fallen into a gentle sleep. The ragged creatures all around him filled Uraz with a raging scorn that was all the more furious because he had dreamed of sharing their fate and delighting in their loving kindness. At the recollection of this crawling, ignoble wish—one that only a malignant spirit dwelling in these ruins could have breathed into him—Uraz felt his mouth fill with bile. From time to time he let his gaze pierce through his lashes and watched with morbid impatience the flowing away, the disappearance of the mob. Let them all vanish, all of them . . . All those people among whom he, Uraz, had been happy to be devoid of pride, to acknowledge pride no more.

OUTSIDE THE HEADS OF THE FAMILIES WERE PAYING THE PRICE OF their stay. It was a trifling amount, but even so it was too much for some of them. These, gravely addressing Ghulam, said, "Allah will pay thee again." And gravely Ghulam bowed his head.

Mukhi said to him, "I should like tea and then some barley or oats."

"There is no forage here that would answer for a horse as splendid as thine, since our usual guests would have no occasion for it," said Ghulam. His words were quite without ill-nature, and those to whom he referred heard them without humiliation. "The village is not far off," went on the young hunchback."There they sell what is needed. As for the tea, walk round to the other side of the building. My younger brother looks after it."

The chaikhana consisted solely of one long bench made of earth heaped up against the tottering wall of the caravanserai, on the sunniest side. It was covered by a roof of branches and dead foliage. In the middle was a tolerably deep niche dug into the wall. Here a thin youth cooked flat cakes over a wood fire and fed an ancient, battered, tarnished copper samovar with glowing embers.

Standing there, Mukhi breathed in the boiling-hot black tea in little sips, and as he did so he noticed a body lying on its back at the far end of the tamped earth bench. Who could possibly be lying in the freezing cold of the morning, wrapped only in thin and scanty cotton clothes? And so stiffly that the naked, roof-pointing feet looked as though they were made of stone? Mukhi went to look more closely at the recumbent figure. In the wizened face, diminished as though by invisible force, the eyes were wide open: they looked at nothing. Dead man's eyes.

The ring of the spoon against the cup he held brought Mukhi back from his stupefaction. He returned to the people around the samovar and cried, "There is a dead man over there!"

"Indeed, I know it very well," said Ghulam's brother from the bottom of his niche, without interrupting his work. "I found him there at dawn, quite frozen."

"For my part," said an old shepherd, "I saw him die. He came at the same time as we did, with a band of wandering potters. He was riding their only ass. He did not dismount. He fell off. And already he was no longer breathing. They laid him there."

"They have just left with the ass," said Ghulam's younger brother. And he called out very cheerfully, "Come now, come, who is for more good strong black tea? Fine scented green? Piping hot bread, well cooked and soft?"

The travelers went back to drinking, eating, telling stories, and laughing, while the corpse stared at them with a gaze that no longer belonged to mankind.

The tea had no savor for Mukhi now. Once again the mountains, with their peaks thrust into the sky like dragon's teeth, filled him with dread. He cared as little for the corpse as the other travelers, but he thought of the sleeping Uraz . . . Or perhaps not sleeping . . . Perhaps worse . . .

AT LAST URAZ WAS ALONE. NO . . . NOT YET. A MAN WAS COMING toward him, running, panting . . . Mukhi leaned over Uraz and groaned—this waxy color, these hollow cheeks, the bloodless mouth. Uraz was breathing still, to be sure; but jerkily, as though it might be a death rattle. Mukhi could bear no more. He squatted down by Uraz, holding his head in his hands. At last he looked up and Uraz's burning eyes stared at the syce's flat, kind face—a face all disordered with grief. The pinched wings of Uraz's nose flared wide with profound disgust. It seemed to him that he could smell the compassion, the pity that flowed toward him. "Where hast thou been wandering?" he asked in an expressionless voice. He left Mukhi no time to answer but ordered, "Tea!"

"Surely, surely!" cried Mukhi. "And thou wilt be better at once, for thou hast a wretched look . . . Yet thou didst sleep well and long, didst thou not?"

"Yes," said Uraz.

Mukhi rushed toward the porch. As he ran Uraz watched him

with loathing. A half-wit was presuming to take him under his protection. Uraz began to mutter, "You will see. All of you . . . You will see." He was still the man who led the race and mastered fate. What race? What fate? He could not tell, yet that in no way affected his utter certainty.

*****

7

The Scribe

THERE NOW, ALL HOT—THERE, soft as can be. They have nothing else here, but what they provide is good," said Mukhi, setting down the tray he was carrying.

Each movement was full of health, strength; and each was therefore an affront to Uraz. What offended him even more, with crueller force, was the exaggerated kindness of Mukhi's voice, like that a man puts on to comfort and hearten a sick child or a nervous horse.

Uraz avidly drank the whole teapotful: he would not touch the bread.

"Try, in the name of Allah," begged Mukhi. "This cake was cooked for thee, fresh from the fire."

Uraz grasped the bread with all his force, squeezed it into a sticky ball, and threw it to the ground. Rage reduced the flesh on his face, making the bones protrude even more. Mukhi thought, "I am killing him." With wretchedly feigned cheerfulness he said, "Thou art right . . . Forcing food down ties a man's entrails in knots. Hunger will come of itself. When it does thou shalt have the fattest grilled mutton, the best rice with saffron . . . I shall go and buy them myself. Ghulam, the landlord, is entirely at thy service. So is his brother."

"I need no one," said Uraz. "As soon as Jahil has been fed, buy what is needed for the road. That is all."

"What road?" stammered Mukhi. "The mountain again? Still higher, and colder, and so empty?"

"Art frightened?" asked Uraz.

"If thou hadst talked to Ghulam!" cried the syce. "He has told me about these terrible, horrifying tracks."

"Terrifying to a hunchback, no doubt," said Uraz.

"He has it from the travelers. And the travelers know," said Mukhi.

"Thou art as frightened as all that?" asked Uraz.

Tears came into the syce's innocent eyes. For Uraz's good he would have put up with countless terrors, a thousand times worse than those of the day before. But he could not help him to his own death. All in one gasp he said, "Yes, I am very frightened. Thou wilt never reach the far end of the mountain alive. I have just seen a corpse. I do not want to have to carry thine, dead by my own fault. How could I ever show myself before Tursen after that? How?" Mukhi regained his breath, and with the fearlessness of despair he cried, "I cannot. I cannot follow thee." He fell to his knees, kissed Uraz's hand, and said very gently, "No, truly, I will not follow thee."

His movements and tone told Uraz that however he might command, beg, or threaten he would not succeed in changing his syce's refusal. A shiver ran through him. All at once he saw that without Mukhi he could do nothing—he was nothing. He felt so great a hatred for the syce that nothing could compare with it. This hatred was the frost that crept beneath his skin, freezing every drop of his blood.

"Trembling? Art thou cold? So cold?" asked Mukhi. He noticed that the chapan he had put over Uraz during the night was covering only half his body. He tried to pull it up. Uraz snatched it from his hands, threw it furiously back. The broken leg lay open to their sight. A foul stench rose from the dirty, oozing cloth that wrapped the wound. Jahil sniffed, wrinkled his nostrils, and made as if to stand up to get away from the smell. Mukhi's hand grasped his mane and drew him down toward the ground. The stallion gave an affectionate whinny and stretched out again, his neck leaning against Mukhi's side.

"Against me, both of them," said Uraz to himself. "My syce. My horse."

Lying there at their feet he stared unwinkingly at the pair they made, Mukhi and the stallion. Powerful . . . Uncomplicated . . . Made for one another. Oh, to flay them alive!

Seeing Uraz's expression, Mukhi thrust his hand deeper into Jahil's mane and pressed closer against his side. A little yellowish foam appeared at the deep lines of Uraz's mouth. "My syce already thinks the stallion his," he said to himself. "His . . . his. In the name of the Prophet!" At that instant Uraz felt his breath cut short. He had called upon the Prophet. And the Prophet answered. The inspiration that had suddenly dazzled his mind like a stroke of lightning could only have come from Him. From Him alone. And because of it everything was wonderfully simplified.

Uraz let air and certainty flow into his chest together. Yes, by the Prophet, yes: he possessed—and in the very insult that had been offered him—the tool for the most perfect and the most glorious revenge.

When Uraz looked up at his syce the wolf's grin drew back his lips, burning with fever and gall. This smile and the strange benevolence that now shone in Uraz's eye should have horrified Mukhi. But in his innocence he thought, "His rage has passed . . . He agrees." The syce relaxed his fingers, deep in Jahil's mane.

"Thou shalt come with me," said Uraz.

Mukhi's hand clenched once more. Jahil thought it was a caress and gently arched his neck. "But I explained . . ." whispered Mukhi.

"And I understood thee perfectly," said Uraz. Little by little he hitched himself up against the saddle. When his back was quite straight he said slowly, "Attend to me and in thy turn understand. Thou wilt not come with me because thou wilt not work my destruction? That is the only reason?"

"Truly, truly, the only one, and may Allah be my witness!" cried Mukhi.

"Well," said Uraz more slowly still, "My fate is no concern of thine. As for that, I set thee free from all anxiety or care, and I too take the Almighty as my witness. Follow me well: I and I alone am answerable for my misfortune." Mukhi tried to speak. "I have not finished," said Uraz. "Whether thou comest or not, I set out; and I set out on the road I have chosen."

"Alone! Alone! It is not true," cried Mukhi. His fingers were trembling in the stallion's mane.

"What I say I shall do, that I do, in spite of everyone and everything," said Uraz. "And that thou knowest."

"It is death for thee," whispered Mukhi.

"Certainly," said Uraz. "For me and Jahil."

"Jahil!"

At the groan that bore his name, the stallion gazed at Mukhi with his proud and gleaming eyes.

"What other end could there be for him, lost and masterless in the stones of the empty land?" asked Uraz.

"Oh no," whispered Mukhi. "Allah will prevent it."

"That I too believe," said Uraz.

"How? Oh, how?"

"Because thou wilt be with us," said Uraz. Speaking faster he went on, "Thou hast youth and strength; thou canst bear fatigue; thou art patient and full of skill. With thy help we shall go through to the end."

"I am nothing, I am nothing but a poor servingman," cried Mukhi. "And suppose in spite of all I can do thou shouldst die?"

The face that gazed over Jahil's withers at the man stiff and straight against the saddle had been rendered almost childish by suffering. Uraz knew that the decisive moment had come. He lowered his eyelids to mask the brilliance of his desire. To seduce innocence, temptation must be clothed.

"Yes," went on Mukhi, and his voice was breaking, "Yes, what if misfortune should win in spite of everything. What then? What then?"

Uraz spread his hands: he let fate pass between his open palms. "Why then Jahil is thine," he said.

Mukhi started up, shook his sweating forehead, and stammered, "I . . . What . . . ? I . . . Uraz . . . I do not understand."

Uraz opened his eyes wide. Now he was certain he could control them. With a pause after every word he said again, "In that case Jahil is thine."

"What dost thou say? What dost thou say?" cried the syce. He whipped his hand from the stallion's mane as though from a burning bush. Jahil thought he was playing and caught Mukhi's wrist with his teeth, holding it with his great soft lips.

"Thou seest," said Uraz. His chest was more parched than the desert and all its thirst. "Well?" he asked.

"Wait, wait," begged Mukhi. His head was spinning. He dared not move the hand in Jahil's mouth. He had the feeling that the stallion and he belonged to the same blood, the same family. But he did not forget his own place in this kinship—the humblest. And now it was possible that he, Mukhi, the ragged groom, might become the owner, the master, of this son of legendary stallions, breed and masterpiece of the great Tursen. The sweat ran down his face, sweat as thick as Jahil's saliva on his wrist. His vacant eyes wandered in every direction and the rays of dusty light that danced through the countless fissures in the walls made his giddiness far worse. He cried, "It is impossible, Uraz. It is raving . . . It is madness . . . Thy fever."

"No, Mukhi," said Uraz. "Believe me, no." His voice was so friendly and open that he was astonished at it himself. "Is there any man on earth who deserves Jahil as thou dost?" he went on. "Whom does he love more? Who can look after him better than thou? So who then should I leave him to, when he comes out of the terrible mountains safe with thee and by means of thee?"

"Stop! Stop!" begged Mukhi. Violently he plucked his hand away from Jahil, turned his back on him, and went on in a whisper, "Stop, Uraz. Thou art speaking as though thou wert already dead."

Uraz bowed his head and once again he spread his hands so that the path of fate should be broad and smooth. Seeing this deadly pale, emaciated face, this diminished body propped in the middle of the huge, empty caravanserai beneath its lofty ruined dome, Mukhi once more thought of the corpse in the chaikhana. Jahil had stood up, and at that moment laid his head on the syce's shoulder. Both to silence Uraz and to forbid himself all hope Mukhi cried, "Whatever happens nobody would ever, ever believe that such a horse could be mine. I should be called a liar—a thief."

"Thou art right," said Uraz. "Bring the hunchback."

Mukhi hurried out to the porch, shouting, "Ghulam! Ghulam!" He was not so much trying to fulfill Uraz's wishes as escape from him.

Jahil looked after the syce until he vanished, then brought his eyes back to Uraz. Uraz stretched out his hand and stroked the stallion's muzzle. He no longer hated him. He no longer hated Mukhi, or anyone else on earth. He was making himself ready for the hardest ride, the most important race of his life.

"What can I do for thee, my guest?" asked the owner of the caravanserai with his usual gentleness.

"Thou canst do nothing," said Uraz. "But is there a scribe in these parts?"

"In the village itself," said Ghulam.

"Learned?" asked Uraz.

"He satisfies everyone in the neighborhood," said the tall young man with a smile.

"Go and fetch him," said Uraz to Mukhi. The syce made a step toward the porch. "On Jahil," said Uraz.

"Dost . . . truly . . . dost thou think it would be better?" asked Mukhi, without looking at the stallion.

"Surely," said Uraz. "Everything will be quicker; and we are in haste."

Mukhi began to bridle Jahil. He held his head down and his shoulders low; he moved awkwardly, as though afraid. Jahil was impatient to be out in the open air; he stretched all his muscles, and from his withers to his rump they ran in a splendid ripple.

"I have never ridden anything but wretched asses," said Ghulam the hunchback. "And we know little about horses here. But it would be delightful to possess this one, merely to watch him live."

"And if thou couldst see him gallop," said Uraz. "Is it not so, Mukhi?"

The syce, without replying, was about to mount Jahil bareback. "Take the saddle," ordered Uraz.

"But thou?" faltered Mukhi.

"I shall wait for thee outside, against the wall. Our host will help me."

LEANING AGAINST THE OLD WALL WHOSE CLAY WAS ALREADY BEGIN-
ning to store up the heat of the sun, Uraz saw Jahil and the outlines of the two men he carried. "How old he is!" thought Uraz,
gazing at the man sitting behind the syce. "A fine scholar, to be
sure . . . The palsy of age will prevent him from writing a single
line that can be read."

Yet when Jahil came out onto the flat space before the caravanserai, for a moment Uraz's anger yielded to unbelief. He had been
prepared to see the ancient man's face—mere bones covered with
skin as folded and wrinkled as a crumpled rag. But not those naked
brows with the kind of foam of gray flesh instead of hair, those
eyelids that might have come straight from an oven, and lastly the
scale over those terrible eyeballs that would not allow the slightest
gleam, the smallest spark, to pass through nor yet shine back.

Now Ghulam and his brother ran to greet the visitor and help
him down from the horse; they took him by the arm and guided
his steps. He held his head with a little upward lift toward the sky,
listening with that intensity which takes the place of sight in men
whose eyes are dead.

In fact the long-awaited scribe was blind. Only the all-powerful
respect that great age inspires amongst the Afghans prevented Uraz
from bursting out in fury. His rage was confined to the look he
directed at Ghulam. The landlord of the caravanserai replied to it
with his kindliest smile and settled the ancient scribe against the
wall, close to Uraz.

"Peace be with thee, horseman from afar," said the scribe.

"And with thee still greater peace, man of so many years," said
Uraz with all the politeness that was called for. But to the owner of
the caravanserai he said violently, "What now, hunchback?"

The blind man replied, "Dost thou choose to begin directly?"

"It is not a command, venerable man, but I am in haste," said
Uraz. He was above all in haste to put an end to this charade.

"Very well," said the ancient man. He took the tools of his
calling from his belt—a long black box decorated with pink flowers,
holding pen and inkpot, and then a little board with a blank page

attached to it. On either side of this sheet, and from top to bottom, little nails stood opposite one another at close and regular intervals. He put the pen case down on the ground, settled the little board on his crossed legs, and said, "I am ready."

"Well, then," said Uraz, "make it known that I, Uraz, son of Tursen, in the presence of witnesses declare and take oath as follows: Should death strike me down in the course of the journey we are about to undertake, I leave my stallion Jahil, son of Jahil, and all his harness wholly and entirely to Mukhi, my faithful syce, in acknowledgment of his devotion."

Ghulam glanced quickly at Mukhi and discovered nothing in his face—no thought, no feeling, not even any apparent life. For his part Uraz watched the blind scribe's every motion with savage eagerness. Did he really expect to get out of the difficulty—to escape unharmed?

"Tell me thy name again," said the old man. "I learned the other two from the young man on the way here."

"Uraz, son of Tursen," said Uraz.

"Good," said the scribe. He set his two long, almost transparent palms against the paper with one finger on each side touching the highest nail on the board. Then the pen-holding hand began to slide from right to left with a slow, almost imperceptible movement. And beneath the papery fingers Uraz saw characters coming into existence, characters not only legible but of extraordinary perfection. When the first line was filled between its two metallic guides, it was impossible to detect any weakness in its run, any blemish in the balance of the words and spaces, any fault in the architecture of the signs. The writing had the appearance of a work of art.

"How, how dost thou do all this, O grandfather deprived of light?" cried Uraz.

"Since the days of Abdurrahman I have had leisure in plenty to practice in the dark," said the ancient man.

"Abdurrahman, didst thou say?" cried Uraz again.

"Himself, truly." Although the blind man's voice seemed incapable of emotion it still held a trace of that pleasure which the very old feel when they remember they were the contemporaries of men and events that have become part of history.

"Abdurrahman . . ." repeated Uraz. The great amir of the last century, who outwitted the English, crushed the Hazaras, conquered Kafiristan, tamed the great vassals, reunited the Afghan lands. Warrior. Subtle statesman. Sage. The legendary amir.

"When he died, thou wast still far from thy birth," said the old man. "But I was already middle-aged. And I had been blind for years." His fingers drew the letters of the second line. "In His grace, as early as my days at school, Allah granted my hands the talent of a learned man. There were few scholars in those far-off days; so when I was still very young I was appointed tax collector in the rich valley of Koh Daman . . . And I traveled on a mule from village to village collecting, by right of my office, the taxes, tithes, and contributions that Abdurrahman, my sovereign, had imposed in his wisdom and justice."

The second line was finished, as perfect as the first. The blank-eyed scribe began the next. He was in such complete control of his art that he continued to write while telling his tale. "Now one evening," said he, "when my round was finished, I passed by a fair-sized village just as the business of the bazaar was coming to a close. By the gates was a sturdy man, walking along slowly because he was laden with three bags, small bags but very heavy. My mule overtook him easily. He was a cheerful, friendly traveling butcher, named Rustam. He was going home, having sold all his joints and mutton fat at a handsome profit. The sacks that bowed his shoulders were filled with his gains, all in good silver coin. He was going far. Our road ran together as far as the village where I lived. 'Put thy burden on my mule,' said I. 'Thou wilt be less tired on taking it up again.' He did not have to be asked twice. He was a simple man, and given to confiding in others. So that I should admire his attention to order he told me the number and the weight of the coins as he tied each bag to the pack: he had put the biggest in one, the middle-sized in another, and the smallest in the third. We traveled quietly along together. Rustam spoke of his two wives, his sons, and the ass that he was about to buy. We reached my village. There Rustam made as though to take back his property."

The blind man stopped writing, directed his eyes straight at the blazing sun, and went on, "Allah alone can know beforehand of the evil a man may turn over in his mind without being aware of it.

I had been honest and pious until that moment. But when I saw Rustam about to untie the first of the bags from the pack saddle, suddenly I thought, 'His money shall be mine.' Was it the satisfaction he had shown when he spoke of his profits? And above all of his wives? I wanted one myself, a wife from a family that should do me honor and thrust me on in life. Thou knowest the huge price a father asks the young man for a daughter of such a kind."

The ancient man had not lowered his head. His fleshless hand went on writing the letters on the paper with the same care, and his weak, monotonous voice went on with the tale. "I thrust Rustam back," he said, "and I said that the bags belonged to me. As was only natural, he shouted and cried out. Men came running. To prove to them that I was in the right, I named the sum each bag contained and the nature of the coins. In vain did Rustam claim that I had all this from him; he could not prove it. I said that it was I who had told him. In short it was one word against another. Mine was that of a tax collector against an unknown butcher. The matter came before the district judge, but he dared not decide it. Then before the judge of the province. The same result. And the same before the court of Kabul. It was then that Abdurrahman heard of the case and called us to one of the courts of justice that he used to hold in public."

The blind man stopped writing. "If I had been able to foresee that," said he, "I should never have laid claim to Rustam's wealth. The thought of appearing in my guilt before a ruler as terrible as he was wise made me tremble. But what could I do? Not to face him was to confess my crime. Once a man has gone so far he must go on to the end. And then, there was no proof—no more proof for the amir than for the other judges.

"Indeed, the interrogation that took place before him showed nothing fresh. Minute by minute I felt more sure of myself. In his high justice the great amir could not crush me. I waited for his sentence with a tranquil mind. But instead of pronouncing it Abdurrahman suddenly gave an order. 'Let a great jar filled with boiling water be brought.' And first he asked Rustam and then me, 'Dost thou agree that if thou art forsworn thine eyes shall be seared with this water?' 'Yes, lord,' said the butcher, without the least hesitation. And what could I, who had carried my falsehood and my greed even to the throne of my prince, what could I do but cry even louder than Rustam, 'Yes, lord!'?

"Abdurrahman said, 'Very well.' And he had the coins for which I had sworn so many false oaths thrown into the steaming jar. Every man there fell silent—the judges, the scribe, the soldiers, the executioners, and spectators. None understood the amir's mind. But at last he turned toward me and there was a dreadful calmness on his face. And he said to me, 'O tax collector, faithless to honor as to honesty, use thine eyes for the last time. Look on the surface of the water and at those spots rising from the coins that lie beneath it. Dost thou not recognize the fat of mutton? And whose hands are commonly deep in mutton fat? The hands of a tax collector or the hands of a traveling butcher?' He signed to the executioners, and they, tearing my eyelids, poured the boiling water on my eyes."

Each of those who had listened to the story of the punishment inflicted on a young tax collector sixty years before reacted in his own fashion. Mukhi groaned and covered his face with his hands, as though to protect it against a burning jet. Ghulam and his brother, who had heard the tale many times, shook their heads and sighed with compassion. And Uraz said, "To think of the judgment of the boiling water, it had to be a sovereign like Abdurrahman."

"The greatest of them all," said the blind scribe with mild certainty. "And he had me brought here, to the village where I was born. I learned to write without seeing so that I might be useful to those who ask me, as thou hast done today." The aged man laid his pen upon the board. He had so gauged his tale and his task that he had brought both to their conclusion together. Beneath the last line of the declaration he had just written his signature. "Canst thou write?" he asked Uraz.

"Only my name," said he.

"No more is required," said the scribe. And he addressed Ghulam. "Write in the usual way. Certify for thyself and for thy brother, since he is without instruction." The blind man carefully put away his writing implements, took out the little nails that held the paper to the board, and handed the document to Uraz. Uraz folded it and put it under his shirt, in the place where the belt held it tight to his hollow belly. He paid the old man and said,

"Most learned of all scribes, mayest thou live a great many years longer still."

"If Allah should grant them to me," said the blind man, "it shall be to expiate my fault for a greater space."

Ghulam, the gentle-eyed hunchback, added, "And to set us all on our guard against temptation and its mortal claws." And as he spoke he looked at Mukhi. The syce was still hiding his face in his hands.

THEY DRANK TEA. MUKHI PUT THE BLIND SCRIBE ON JAHIL'S BACK and carried him back to the village. There he bought what Uraz had ordered him to buy—certain provisions and utensils for the journey, four blankets, two big long-sleeved postins* lined with dark wool, and a dagger. He forgot nothing, but he hardly knew what he was about. He had no real thoughts or distinct feelings.

When he was back at the caravanserai he set about preparing for their departure with the same indifference. When it was all done he helped Uraz into the saddle without uttering a word.

"There. That is very well," said Uraz. "It is still daylight. Where is the hunchback? Does he not want to be paid?"

As he went toward the chaikhana Mukhi met Ghulam wiping his earthy hands upon his trousers. "We are going," said Mukhi. His voice had no ring in it, his look no life.

"I am sad, truly," said Ghulam, "to have missed thy last moments here. I was burying that poor potter."

"The potter . . . The potter," repeated Mukhi stupidly. He began to tremble. His face was contorted with extreme distress. He laid his arm on Ghulam's hump and held it against his shoulder. "O brother," he groaned, "I beg thee, make a wish that may protect me on this journey."

"I pray that it may still be granted to thee to greet the sun as thou didst greet it today," said Ghulam softly.

Attracted by their voices, Uraz came toward them on Jahil, his whip between his teeth.

* An embroidered leather coat lined with wool.

8

The Dambura

WHEN URAZ, MUKHI, AND JAHIL left the caravanserai and traveled westward toward the formidable passes of the Hindu Kush, the sun was already touching the line of the mountain tops. But on the other side of the tremendous range it was far above the horizon of the steppe. Indeed, in the province of Meimana it had not yet reached the point immediately over the peaceful plateau that bore the village of Kalakchikan.

There, in front of his yurt, Tursen was drinking green tea with Gardi Gaj, the ageless storyteller. They sat cross-legged on a meager carpet laid on the ground itself—a carpet that did more for their dignity than their comfort. A tarnished, battered copper samovar and a tray bearing rough crockery stood between the two men, the one sitting like the trunk of a powerful tree, the other thin almost to transparency. Gardi Gaj's mouth was no more than a bloodless fold; Tursen's had the color, thickness, and cracks of a burst fig; yet they both wore the same expression of tranquility.

This last part of the day was their own property. Morning loves the young horseman full of hope and expectation. The solid, copious food of noon and the heavy sleep that follows is right for middle age. But the edge of the evening is the place reserved for men's old age.

The sun had poured out its fire in the career that had taken it from one end of the steppe to the other; now it filled every wrinkle with an unscorching heat, helped the blood flow without making it run too fast, warmed the cold marrow in the hollow of the bones, and caused balm to ease every painful sinew. The light was no longer dazzling. It had grown gentle to eyes cruelly tried by watching it flame and blaze for so many summers. Shadows were beginning to well up from the depths both of the heart and the earth; their shifting, dancing play peopled, defined, and colored the unbounded expanse, the little streams, the tufts of bushes, and even the very shores of the sky itself. The fact that these faint wisps were the forerunners of night, or of death, was of little significance. Between this time and that each moment was pure detachment and wisdom, and each held within itself an eternity.

The voice of Gardi Gaj arose, fine-drawn as possible and yet as clear as the bells of a caravan. "It is deep within my body that the sun goes down," he said.

Tursen slowly nodded his flat face, all plowed with scars and ancient wounds. He too knew what it was, as he sat contemplating, unburdened of all physical substance and all awareness, to become a hollowness and no more—something that opened itself to the twilight. A container for its honey. A ewer for its coolness. A quiver for its rays. But Tursen could not preserve that perfect marriage with the day's end as long as Gardi Gaj. In the very heart of the blessed fullness in which the mind's motion was suspended a kind of worm began to stir, return to life; and the worm was thought. At this the radiant world closed itself off and handed the man back to loneliness and distress.

"We came here the evening of the day the Meimana chapandaz took the Kabul road for the king's buzkashi," said Tursen to himself. "I had only meant to spend one night in my yurt. But the seventh is at hand and the Ancestor of All the World does not appear to notice it at all."

At this same instant Tursen observed that in his turn Gardi Gaj had cut himself off from him, just as the wonderful twilight had done. A moment earlier the three of them had made up one vast and single happiness. Now there was an inaccessible sky, and far, far from it two beings, each separated from the other. Tursen felt a bitter sadness. He had begun to think. There was no cure for the evil. However frail and indeed almost impalpable the form on the other side of the ancient samovar might be, it nevertheless had its own inner charge, its fate, its secret places.

"He travels unceasingly," went on Tursen in his thoughts, "he is never two nights under the same roof, and now he has suddenly taken root. It is not need of rest—I wake before dawn and I always find his place on my charpoy empty. Food? He only pretends to touch it, out of politeness. He spends his time in the village, a place unmatched for poverty and lowliness. There he listens to the old men and the children and even the women, whom he may speak to without impediment because of his age." Tursen was almost on the point of crying out, "Tell me, tell me, Ancestor of All the World, what is it keeps thee here?" Once again he could not bring himself to do it. Would not Gardi Gaj answer with a question, as he so often did? Would he not say, "And then, Tursen?"

The old chapandaz's hands were flat on his wide-spread thighs; now they closed in fists the size of clubs. Another equally heavy fist closed about his heart. There was no more joy, no more friendship on the hills and the evening grass. Tursen thought, thought of the litter and forage he had not supervised for more than a week, of the brood mares, the sick or wounded animals, the colts being weaned, the young horses being trained—all left to the irresponsible grooms. Yes indeed, he would cut a fine figure if he were to ask Gardi Gaj with astonishment what kept him here—Gardi Gaj, who had neither office nor duty and was as light and free as a tale, while he, Tursen, laid his Master of the Stable's whip in the shade of his yurt as though he were a cripple, a sick man, a pensioner. "Why? Why?" said Tursen to himself again. His head bowed and he began to twitch it from side to side, as though he were being tormented by an intolerable gadfly.

In the transparent silence a dambura began to play over by the village, and the sound came rapidly toward the yurt. Tursen's fists unclenched: he had the right to speak—without dishonor he could escape from himself. "Listen, Ancestor of All the World," he cried, "Niyaz is coming."

Gardi Gaj let a moment pass. His ears were less keen than Tursen's. Then he said, "Now in my turn I can hear him. Indeed, it is his hour. The sun has reached the level of our eyes."

A gray-headed, winking, nodding, lousy, ragged dwarf appeared round the yurt. He came by skips and leaps: everything in him danced—shoulders, joints, wrinkled cheeks, his lips with their distracted smile, the distended veins of his neck, his Adam's apple. In time with them danced the dambura of the steppes, the stringed singer, slim and graceful between his hands. And from it came so pure and true a sound that Gardi Gaj murmured, "Truly, the innocent dwell close to the gods."

By way of greeting the dwarf threw his instrument into the air; it turned twice, fell back into his open hands still humming, and went straight on with its song.

"Often enough," reflected Tursen, "Niyaz forgets who we are, the neighbors who feed him and I who saw him born. But he is never wrong about the Ancestor of All the World."

Playing still, the dwarf sat on his crossed legs quite close to Gardi Gaj. "It is for him alone that he is here," thought Tursen again.

Once more the dambura spun in Niyaz's hands, and suddenly it changed its rhythm. A thin, long-drawn lament ran along its strings, starting over and over again without end. And Gardi Gaj, the ageless traveler, recognized it: forty or fifty years before or even more he had heard it on the other side of the Himalayas, on the Tibetan roads.

Where and how had this dwarf, from so remote a hamlet, learned the chant? Apart from his hill and the lands of Osman Bey he only knew the small town of Daolatabad, and that very little. And what of all the other songs whose tunes and words he repeated without the slightest error? Songs of shepherds, fighting men, lovers. Those of today and those of long ago. Those of his own province and of Tashkent too, Bukhara and Khiva and Samarkand. Afghan, Russian, or Chinese, from the whole of Central Asia, that vast world of grass and sand, camel caravans and tireless horsemen.

Of course, Gardi Gaj reflected, people of every kind were to be encountered on the steppe, and travelers from every land mingled under the roofs of the bazaars. But what accuracy and delicacy of ear to retain music and verse heard once only, on flute, shepherd's pipe, dambura, tabor, or in wandering voice—to hold and catch them as a fowler catches birds in his net.

Indeed it was right and full of wisdom that tradition from the earliest dawn of time required madmen and half-wits to be treated with veneration. The gods had taken away their reason merely to leave room for their own spirit in the empty head. To some they gave the prophetic word, to others second sight, to others the power of cursing, to others again holiness. This one's inheritance was undying song. "Both of us, simpleton and sage, are in the world for the same purpose," reflected Gardi Gaj. "The one gathers tales and the other songs, but here the half-wit takes precedence over the wise man. Even the most wonderful tale has to go forward slowly, word by word. Song has wings. I bow to thee, my outcast brother, my master." And Gardi Gaj, who had forgotten the nature of desire, wishes, felt a sudden and strangely powerful urge to give the innocent the present of a beautiful song.

Where could it be found? Niyaz had already stored up so many and Gardi Gaj's memory was far less reliable for tunes than for the tales men tell. He was near to despair when, as though by its own volition, through the deep layers, material strewn by the long-dead years, a frail, pure, childish music began to well up. No one on earth but Gardi Gaj could know this lullaby. It was mingled with the first origins of his life; and those were still the days when the high-perched villages and the happy valley of Kafiristan had not been so utterly destroyed that even their names were wiped out. In those days the amir Abdurrahman had not yet brought fire and sword to crush the fighting men, the descendants of the warriors of Iskander, that invincible Greek; had not yet destroyed the great images of the gods, carved out of massive wood.

The innocent was playing still. A long finger placed suddenly on the strings put his instrument to silence. Niyaz turned to Gardi Gaj. He had a flat, dull face with lifeless folds and a lifeless mouth; but in his eyes, like those of an animal, showed primitive feelings in their simplest and most concentrated form. "Thou! Thou! My only friend, thou dost not want my dambura more? Thou dost not want me?" questioned the dwarf's eyes.

Under his heavy eyelids Tursen was eagerly watching the two men without seeming to do so: then something happened that surprised him beyond measure. The Ancestor of All the World raised

his right hand and with it covered the innocent's face. Then he
began to chant words in an unknown tongue, singing them to a
strange melody. In spite of its frailty Gardi Gaj's voice was wonderfully clear when he told a tale, but when he sang it showed his
age—discordant, cracked, senile. Nevertheless he went on, on, singing the lullaby that had sent children to sleep a hundred years before in an eagle-haunted village of which nothing now remained
but scattered, fire-blackened stones.

Every fiber of his old body was gently following the rhythm.
And now for Niyaz the hand over his face, though drier than winter leaves, came to life like a welling spring. The wave of sound
flowed over his forehead, his neck, his fingers, and into the strings.
Gardi Gaj fell silent. He needed to sing no more. The dambura
was doing so in his place, and in a voice that sang without effort,
with all the calmness, purity, and gentle kindness of the evening
and its light.

A strange shiver ran over Gardi Gaj's infinitely wrinkled skin.
When he had set himself to find the lullaby again, he had only
meant to hand it on as well as he could, with what means he had.
Now that it was coming back to him, true, fresh, new, and artless,
it seemed to him that he had tossed a handful of pebbles into the
air by mere chance and that now he was suddenly hearing them
clatter into the abyss of time. From the bowels of that mysterious
pit their fall called up the sounds and sighs that its black depths
had inhaled since time began. And now Gardi Gaj, who in the
extreme frailty of his bones was virtually disembodied, and whose
wonderful length of years had dried up his whole capacity for emotion, Gardi Gaj began to tremble with anxiety and tenderness.

Although his memory went very deep it had never been able to
reach those first days when color, sound, touch, smell, and taste
begin to adumbrate the world to the new-born. But every note of
the dambura was drawing them up from the chasm in which they
lay buried. And in spite of his age and experience, which had led
him beyond the human condition and which caused him, like a
tree whose roots are worn away, to bow willingly toward death,
Gardi Gaj could not prevent his ancient heart, his tranquil heart,
from leaping until it almost failed, because he was rediscovering,

cloudy and iridescent as milk and rainbows, those moments when he was still wrapped about with the darkness of his beginning and just starting to have foreknowledge and comprehension of his own life in the world.

The smell of burning wood . . . The crackling of logs . . . dancing sparks . . . The waft and caress of fire-warmed air . . . The comforting, enclosing presence of walls, the domed ceiling . . . well-known shadows moving . . . The peaceful ease of a body, wrapped all about, entirely held . . . blessed inward being, filled with a warm, rich, life-giving fluid whose taste remained on his lips together with that of its source, that smooth, inexhaustible, soft roundness. And in the very heart of this wonderful fullness a voice as good as firelight, as warm as milk, repeating, repeating to the very boundary of sleep, a winged chant that sang the abundance, safety, and kindness of love.

The sun sank lower and lower. Now its light spread from the very edge of the steppe toward the top of the hill. The light was of an almost unbearable delicacy and tenderness, and the dambura traced its transcendent perfection so well that its song might have been made to reach out beyond the cradle and soothe the heart of the whole world, terrified by the coming of the night.

The end of the day . . . The end of the song.

What is the point, thought Gardi Gaj, what is the point of a life longer than all others, since it must soon, very soon, melt away like the shortest of them all? And what was the point of so much wisdom when its only valid function—he perceived this suddenly—was to make a man accept this dissolution?

Far away over the steppe the uppermost edge of the sun's disk was a single crimson thread.

The sound of the dambura no longer penetrated Gardi Gaj's hearing, but he saw that Niyaz's fingers were still brushing the strings and that Tursen was beating time with his massive head. Gardi Gaj almost cried out to the innocent, "In the name of thy friendship for me, do not stop!" Through this supplication he became aware at last of the full extent of his unhappiness. He did not fear death, for he had lived far too close to it far too long, but he longed, oh how he longed, just once again at the moment of death for his mother to wrap him in her loving voice and dispel the loneliness that was now so old it had become all he had as a family—wrap him and send him to sleep, ancient man, wanderer, sage, in a kindly twilight like a child.

Now the fingers of the innocent rested motionless on the dambura, commonplace, repulsive worms.

All at once the steppe took on the color of ashes.

TURSEN STIFFENED HIS BACK. THE FIRST NIGHT AIR WAS STEALING abroad so softly that his skin did not yet feel it. But his joints could make it out. The half-wit's head nodded, sagged forward, and came to rest, with open mouth and drooping jaw, against his hollow chest.

Gardi Gaj had closed his eyes, filled with boundless pity for himself and his fellow men. Then he thought, "No one on earth has the power to help me. But it may be that I for my part am still able to bring aid . . ." He said to Tursen, "I saw Aygiz."

"Aygiz," growled Tursen. "Aygiz . . ." He thought it strange and improper that he should be reminded of a wife who had become barren after Uraz's birth and whom he had at once repudiated. According to the law, according to custom and honor. For forty years he had forgotten her existence. "She lacks nothing, I believe," said Tursen. That was true. He had furnished Aygiz with a house in the village and had seen to her maintenance.

"She would like to speak to thee," said Gardi Gaj.

"By what right?" asked Tursen harshly.

"She is dying," said Gardi Gaj.

Tursen swayed his huge shoulders from side to side. If a man on his deathbed had called for him he would have been on the way by now. But could he rightfully comply with a woman's whim, even if it were the last? He said, "She is dying. Well, and is she not old enough?"

"One is never old enough to die alone," said Gardi Gaj.

"Dost thou think so?" muttered Tursen. And although he still could not understand the remark he got up painfully, to obey the curious wish he detected within the Ancestor of All the World.

THE VILLAGE OF KALAKCHIKAN AMOUNTED TO A SCORE OF HOVELS IN all, a miserable row of mud huts clinging to a wall of rock. Aygiz's dwelling was the last on the way to the stream. Like all the others, it had a porch made of dead branches in front and its mud walls enclosed one low-ceilinged room without window or chimney.

Tursen walked in fiercely. He was no longer under the influence of Gardi Gaj. This ridiculous visit filled him with shame and anger. As he stood on the threshold his body, wider than the opening, wholly blocked out the last light of day. He took a step into the bare cabin, and at the far end, next to a samovar, made out two old women. Which was Aygiz? The fat one, no doubt, squatting with her back to the wall on a heap of cushions; the one whose breathing was so loud. And indeed it was she who spoke. In a sibilant, whispering gurgle she said, "Tursen, oh, Tursen!"

Suddenly the prostrate, helpless body sprang into motion. And the voice rose stronger than the rattle. Impatient, anxious, happy, she begged, she gave orders. "Quickly, quickly, useless woman . . . Something to sit upon . . . to drink . . . a light."

Tursen made another step forward. "I want nothing," he said. "I have no time."

"Hush, hush," replied Aygiz. And to her maid, "Come now, quickly . . . quickly."

The servant drew a cotton-stuffed mattress from a dark corner and spread it on the beaten earth at Tursen's feet; she lit an oil lamp; she poured boiling black tea into a cup. Then with little steps she left the room without looking back. As she was closing the door again Tursen observed the people of the hamlet gathered in front of the hovel. The master of Kalakchikan, the great Tursen, was in the house of his repudiated wife. What an event!

Tursen had the feeling that his cheeks has suddenly taken on the color and heat of bricks from the kiln. He breathed deeply. At once his nostrils wrinkled with disgust. Undoubtedly he had known more stifling and pestilential smells. The stables and cowhouses of his childhood . . . The chance caravanserais, the chaikhanas, the huts where the families lived with their flocks. But the stench of the dirtiest men and the worst-kept beasts and even that of excrement—a stench to which he was accustomed—seemed to him in their thickness and their piercing strength less poisonous and vile than the sour, sweetish, thinly, weakly rotten exhalations that filled the hovel through and through. Impure, mawkish, sickening smell: the smell of a sick woman.

Tursen was still standing, his arms at his sides, his fists clenched against the skirts of his chapan; beneath the perfect folds of his turban his eyes gazed fixedly at Aygiz's enormous breasts and belly. He remembered certain mares he had given up trying to cure. Their putrid bowels had yielded, burst, and overflowed, turning their bodies into monstrous wineskins. "This one will die in the same way," thought Tursen. "Only before she does so, this one has to have me pity her."

Just at that moment Aygiz spoke again. She said, "Peace be with thee, O Tursen. Wilt thou not . . . grant thy servant . . . the honor . . . of entertaining thee?" The voice was hoarse, gasping, interrupted by spasms and hiccups; but it expressed modesty, propriety . . . All his life Tursen had made it a rule to be inferior to no one in civility. He was forced to acknowledge Aygiz's politeness, so in spite of his repugnance he behaved in fitting manner. He returned thanks, and, sitting on his crossed legs in the hollow of the cotton mattress, noisily sipped the tea that had been made for him.

His head and Aygiz's were now at the same level. The light of the lamp set down on the ground close to the old woman rose toward her face, and against the background of shadows it picked out a round swollen mass of purplish-blue flesh in which every wrinkle was like a dreadful furrow. "Truly, if I had met her, how should I have known who she was?" thought Tursen. And he asked, "How didst thou manage to recognize me at once?"

"How could I fail?" said Aygiz. Between the sick, horribly swollen, and almost closed lids the eyes woke with a feeble gleam. "Thy shoulders," went on the old woman. "Still the same . . . and also, for all these years . . . every time thou didst go to thy yurt and back . . . I saw thee pass . . . as upright in the saddle as in our time." Aygiz had freed her back from the supporting wall. A strange power enabled her to bend the mass of her body toward

Tursen. And with a hurried gasp, she finished, "Like a true chapandaz."

Tursen had drawn his head back. He thought, "There she is, moving about and smelling even worse."

It was not so much the vile stench that increased his torment and his anger. It was the discovery that unknown to him and at a time when he no longer even remembered her presence on earth, this repudiated wife had never throughout her solitary life ceased to follow him in her thought. What was her intention? Did she dare to claim some kind of right over him? Was she trying to bewitch him? And had she not succeeded, since here he was, in her house, sitting at her misshapen feet?

"A true chapandaz," said Aygiz again. "A true . . ." Suddenly her voice failed. She struck her hands together, opened her purple mouth wide, and uttered a loud, harsh groan. A sort of heave convulsed the fatty masses of her belly and thrust her head back against the wall.

Tursen looked at her with harsh disgust. She was certainly going to die. And having induced him to be present at her end . . . To pity her . . . to comfort her . . . Women! Women!

Aygiz's eyelids flickered, and she said, "Stay . . ." Then, "It will get better."

Tursen waited, one hand on the whip thrust into his belt. The huge belly subsided, grew quiet; the spasms gave her throat some rest. "There . . . there . . ." murmured Aygiz. With an immense effort she raised her eyelids. In front of her colorless pupils trembled an old woman's white tears. Tursen's fingers gripped and twisted the lash of his whip. Now Aygiz was going to weep to force him to pity her. The white tears did not move; they hung there like tears in the eyes of the blind.

"Tell me of Uraz, my son," asked the old woman.

"Why should I?" said Tursen with strong reproof.

His voice frightened Aygiz. Her great drooping cheeks trembled. "Do not be vexed, Tursen, I beg thee," she groaned. "He is thy son, thine alone: I know it very well."

At first Tursen did not understand at all. Then confusedly, as though it were part of a life that had nothing to do with his own, he remembered the blows with which he had punished a beautiful young woman because she tried to win over and soften a very little boy with her kisses, her spoiling, her songs, and her weak-kneed stories—a little boy who came home flayed, broken, and filled with pride from his first riding. A harsh grin moved Tursen's heavy lips. The poor woman was out of her wits. She thought she was still his wife and that she was competing for their child. For Uraz . . . who now belonged to no one except his fiends of pride and of the pursuit of fame.

Humbly Aygiz went on, "I only hoped thou might tell me the news of Kabul . . . Dost thou know who won there?"

"I know nothing," replied Tursen in such a way that terror once more made Aygiz's cheeks and dewlap tremble.

"Forgive me," she murmured, "forgive me. Truly, a woman has nothing to do with a buzkashi."

"Silence!" cried Tursen. There was no doubt she had spoken indecently. Never since the beginning of time had a woman been present at the great game of the steppes. But that was what she was certainly talking about.

For the last week Tursen had been hearing the question Aygiz asked so timidly buzzing, ringing through Osman Bey's stables, gardens, and the places where his people ate, and every day it grew more impatient. Tursen wanted to stop his ears to smother the din. For in the end it obliged him to acknowledge the feeling that had made him go to his yurt and that was keeping him there, so that he need not participate in the fever of waiting, count the hours until the royal buzkashi, and then the minutes of endless unavoidable delay while the name of the winner should travel to the house of Osman Bey. To deaden himself, to send himself to sleep, he had turned to the tales of an ancient man and the music of an imbecile.

"Dost thou forgive me?" whispered Aygiz.

"Forgive what?" asked Tursen. He was only too happy that she should stop the run of his thoughts. He now felt only one desire— to be a great way from this smell, this body, this face. Tursen stood up and said, "It is time . . ."

"Thou art hungry?" asked Aygiz.

"Very," said Tursen. He would have made any answer at all to get out of the hut as quickly as possible.

Aygiz raised her face toward him and the folds and swellings that made up its features began to stir, as though there were a seething beneath the surface.

"She has held out until now," thought Tursen. "Now she is going to let herself go." He looked down at her, determined to leave at the first sob, the slightest complaint, the gentlest moan. But however keenly he watched, he could not detect a single mark of despair or even sorrow on her face. On the contrary, it seemed that some mysterious working in the depths of that dead flesh was gradually setting the huge, swollen countenance free from its ugliness.

For the first moment Tursen could not believe what he saw. To make sure he leaned down toward Aygiz. Then he shivered, as though he had been witness to a stroke of magic. Aygiz's eyes, freed from their thick and morbid lids, were looking at him wide open, filled with peace and gentleness. They grew larger still and shone, but their brilliance was not caused by tears. Tursen brought his forehead still closer to hers. And as he did so the fragile, trembling folds at the edge of her mouth, so horrible a moment earlier, expressed such gratitude, such affection and happiness, that in this old and dreadful dying woman Tursen recognized the smile, the shape, and the curve of the almost childish smile he had discovered on his wedding day, reflected in the looking glass in which a young couple are allowed to see one another for the first time.

"Go, Tursen, go and eat," whispered Aygiz. "Thou still hast that great splendid hunger that must not wait?"

And Tursen lied again, "As in former days," he said. That look, that smile, that voice. He could no longer bear them. But disgust had nothing to do with it. He thought, "She is anxious for me . . . She! For me!" Without understanding why he did so he said, "Never again have I eaten a pilau such as thou couldst make." Abruptly he touched Aygiz's hair and growled, "Peace be with thee!" He left before she had time to return the ritual answer.

TURSEN WENT BACK THROUGH THE WARM, GENTLE NIGHT, WALKING slowly. He thought of nothing as he listened to the sound of his rawhide sandals on the dusty gravel of the path. When he saw his yurt, lit by a hurricane lamp, he knew that for him it had lost its power as a refuge.

Niyaz had disappeared. Gardi Gaj was sitting on a bench at the table where they ate, his head in his hands.

"This is my last evening here," said Tursen.

"I knew it," said Gardi Gaj. "The messengers from Kabul cannot be long now." He spoke through his long fingers, so fleshless that the light of the lamp pierced their translucent skin to the bone.

"Thou art weary, it seems, Ancestor of All the World," said Tursen.

"It is not my body," said Gardi Gaj. "We will leave together."

The round-shouldered peasant who saw to Tursen's needs brought hot wheatcakes, curds, hard-boiled eggs, a mutton-fat preserve, and some grapes. He poured out tea. Gardi Gaj touched nothing.

Tursen shook his head; sitting down, he abruptly pulled the dishes toward him. None of them tasted good. He pushed them away one by one and said, "When she thought I was very hungry, a complete change came over her."

"Aygiz?" asked Gardi Gaj.

"Just so," replied Tursen. And he told how the dying woman's dreadful old face had for a moment recovered the look and smile of a very young and beautiful woman. Gardi Gaj said to him, "See, thou didst not go in vain."

"It was witchcraft," cried Tursen. "And I am not a wizard."

Gardi Gaj stretched out along the bench, resting his head on his little sack. "Witchcraft?" thought he. "Maybe. But compounded of man's essence and as old on earth as himself."

Gardi Gaj had forgotten Tursen. He was hearing the flow and rhythm of the oldest legends and most beautiful love poems. Sometimes the verses rose to his lips. He spoke them in an undertone.

When this happened Tursen nodded in approval. He knew them, and they did not astonish him. From the Caspian Sea to the passes leading into India, from century to century, these noble verses had been sung and recited under the domes of the bazaars and in the keen-witted competitions of the learned, at the family hearth and round nomad fires. They were the inheritance common to man of letters, wandering singer, and the most unpolished shepherd. Far away in the remotest mountain hamlets the women knew enormously long epics by heart.

"Firdousi," murmured Tursen. Or, "Khayyam." Or again, "Hafiz."

At last Gardi Gaj stopped and opened his eyes. The sky of the steppes was blazing with stars. In the light of the hurricane lamp Tursen's face looked like a piece of carved wood. Quietly Gardi Gaj observed, "That witchcraft of love has its being in every man and for every man, O chapandaz." Gardi Gaj leaned on the table to keep Tursen well under his gaze. "Aygiz did not expect thee, did not hope for thee. But thou didst go into her house. Then she knew that she still counted for her oldest, dearest friend." Tursen made as though to reply. "No," said Gardi Gaj, "Listen. For a great while, a very great while, she was nothing for thee. For her, Tursen was always the husband, the splendid horseman, the only man."

"Women," growled Tursen.

"Women," repeated Gardi Gaj, but with a completely different intonation. The Kafiristan lullaby hummed in his head: he let it sing on for a moment, then continued, "Aygiz thought, 'Tursen is concerned for me; Tursen protects me,' and she felt happy. And thou, speaking of thy hunger, didst still more. Thou didst restore her to the days when her hands worked upon thy food, thy clothes . . . This evening every moment of thy presence was a priceless treasure to her. Yet she urged thee to go to thy meal. She was protecting thee once again."

"Women," grunted Tursen.

"Not them alone," said Gardi Gaj. He drank tea, and said, "Believe me, O chapandaz: if he is not to stifle all alone inside his own skin, every man must feel himself necessary to another being."

"I care for nobody and I get along very well for all that," said Tursen.

"Truly?" said Gardi Gaj. "And what would happen to thee, Master of the Stables, if suddenly thou lost thy office, looking after the horses? Would thy heart still be so hot and proud?"

"I must reflect on that," said Tursen. He saw the animals awaiting him in the stables of Osman Bey, the unsteady colts in their first play, the magnificent stallions formed by the sternest of trials, the sick mare whose great eyes had begged him to cure her and shone with gratitude when he succeeded. And he felt such eagerness to be with them again that his old blood (even older than Aygiz's, he said, in spite of himself) began to run as hot as though it were new. It was not sense of duty or desire for gain or fear of a master that spurred him so. What he wanted, with these manes, shining coats, whinnies, and soft horses' eyes, was to be reunited with his cares, his anxieties, successes, his pride, his power—his whole life. For truly without these creatures what would be the point of his living?

"They are only animals," reflected Tursen aloud.

"Comfort thyself in this way, by all means," said Gardi Gaj. "Thou art very strong, Tursen, I know . . . Only there are days when the strongest, just as much as the weakest, needs to find himself helped and to love that help. A man needs to be now the protector, now the protected."

A fist as heavy as a piece of rock appeared on the table beside the lamp. "Not I," said Tursen.

"Art thou quite sure?" asked Gardi Gaj. His voice was no more than an exhausted sigh. His loose clothes fell in on all sides, as though there were no body within their folds. Only a few ridges of his face could still be seen, frail as spun glass. In his alarm Tursen said to himself, "Allah All-Powerful, he is about to vanish away . . . Allah All-Powerful, let it not be." And through his dread he understood the immense help that he had begged and received from Gardi Gaj since the evening they had watched the setting sun and the rising moon balance one another in the sky. By the side of the lamp his fist unclenched, turning into a kind of soft root.

THEY WERE LYING SIDE BY SIDE IN THE YURT. FROM TIME TO TIME the charpoy creaked.

"But thou, Ancestor of All the World," said Tursen suddenly, "if thou hast need of help, who can give it thee?"

"A dambura," said Gardi Gaj.

Tursen let a few moments go by and then he asked again, "Thou who canst foretell everything, dost thou think Uraz has won the buzkashi of the king?"

Once again Gardi Gaj answered with a question. "Is that thy real wish, O Tursen?"

9

The Whip

Tursen, with Gardi Gaj riding pillion behind him, was already on Osman Bey's land when a horseman came galloping to meet them. Tursen recognized one of his grooms.

"Peace be upon thee, Master of the Stables," said the groom. "I was going to thy yurt."

Gardi Gaj saw the huge shoulders in front of him stiffen.

"That means the news has come," said Tursen.

The syce nervously plucked his horse's mane and said quickly, "Not all."

"Speak out," growled Tursen. "What of Uraz?"

"Allah has not favored him," said the syce, looking down. "But . . ."

"Silence," said Tursen. "Where is the messenger?"

"Sleeping at our place, in the stables," said the syce.

"Hurry and wake him," commanded Tursen. "I will hear nothing but from him."

The rider vanished behind a screen of trees and Tursen breathed out an oath. Then in one rush he said, "Shame on thee, useless son, cheap-jack chapandaz! Thou hast failed in the first buzkashi run for the king, whereas thy father and thy father's father and his father were never beaten in any great encounter." He stopped, feeling Gardi Gaj's hand on the back of his neck.

157

"Art thou suffering, Tursen?" asked the storyteller.

"And shall go on suffering until my death for the honor of my blood," said Tursen.

"And for thyself?" asked Gardi Gaj again.

"I shall think about that later," answered Tursen. The tone of his voice was savage. He jerked forward as though to loosen the reins but in fact to escape from contact with Gardi Gaj. Those weightless hands, that disembodied voice—suddenly he could bear them no longer. For a whole week they had made him unsure, weak, anxious, unlike himself. That was over. He was back in his own country. He was on his own feet again. Once more he held the laws of right and wrong, of what was fitting and what was not.

Tursen turned his horse toward his house, saying, "While I go about my business, do me the honor of taking thine ease beneath my roof."

"I thank thee for that," said Gardi Gaj.

Rahim was waiting on the threshold. On his right cheek there was a long wound, covered with scabs and flies. Tursen hated him. "Help my guest down," he called to the bacha. "And take more care of him than of me myself."

When he was on the ground Gardi Gaj said to Tursen, "Peace be upon thee, chapandaz."

"And upon thee too, Ancestor of All the World," said Tursen. "I shall see thee very soon."

"May fate so wish it," murmured Gardi Gaj.

TURSEN FOUND THE MESSENGER SENT FROM DAOLATABAD IN THE first of the courtyards reserved for the horses. He was a very small, thin man, dressed in a ragged chapan. But because of the importance of his mission he was slowly and pompously doling out his words to the stable boys and grooms who crowded eagerly around him. Tursen spoiled his performance. He grasped the sleeve of his chapan, spun him round, and said, "Thou givest the news to me alone. Quick."

"It is not my fault that I left so late," said the little man humbly. "The telegram took two days to reach Meimana and still another to get to Daolatabad."

"Very well. What did it say about Uraz?" asked Tursen.

"Uraz, son of Tursen," recited the messenger, "broke a leg. He is safe in the fine hospital of Kabul, which has not its equal in the country."

A murmur, both of sympathy and hope, rose from the listeners. Tursen's face expressed nothing. That was how it should be. Yet he thought, "The charpoys and the healers of our country are no longer good enough for my son." With a gesture he commanded silence and spoke to the messenger again, "The horse that Uraz rode, what dost thou know of him?"

The little man straightened and almost sang, "The mad stallion . . . the glorious stallion! It was upon him that Salih—may the Prophet bless him—won the royal buzkashi."

A great cry arose. "Honor to Salih! Honor to Osman Bey, who has such a chapandaz!"

"Honor!" repeated Tursen, his head high, his face unmoved.

The veins of his neck swelled with the furious rage of his shame: he had formed the most splendid charger that time and the steppe had ever seen, formed him with all his science and all his heart, only that he should carry the emptiest chapandaz in his team to victory! And in a few days he would behold Salih's triumphal entry. All the great men of the province and all the chiefs of tribes in their finest clothes would come to celebrate his return. And he, Tursen, would have to pronounce the eulogy. Meanwhile the son to whom he owed this affront would be lolling at his ease in Kabul. From the pocket of his enormous breeches Tursen plucked a handful of notes and threw them to the messenger. "Thou hast carried out thy duty well," he said. Then, as though the man no longer existed, Tursen said to the head syce, "Are the horses at their stations?"

And the head syce replied, "As usual."

And as usual Tursen walked with his slow, strong pace into the maze of courtyards where the sun was crackling the dried-up clay.

AFTERWARDS THE MEN WHO FOLLOWED TURSEN SWORE BY THE
Koran that there was nothing about him to foretell the way he was
going to break out. And indeed what man could have pierced
through Tursen's customary bearing to detect his unbearable fury
and the violent urging of his muscles so filled with red anger that
they no longer felt the shackles of age?

The inspection continued in all its usual orderliness, all its severity. From yard to yard, picket to picket. With a somber gaze
Tursen studied the tethered horses. He made few observations.
While he had been away nothing had been neglected to keep the
horses in their finest condition. Suddenly in the third courtyard he
walked straight up to the animal farthest from him. It was a young,
medium-sized, entirely black stallion, most uncommonly vigorous
and well built. As soon as Tursen was at his sweat-covered side the
horse began to toss his head, whinny, and rear.

"Too fat. Too restive," said Tursen. "How many days has he
been unridden?"

"Seven," said the head syce.

"Why?" asked Tursen.

The old groom stared at his master with anxious astonishment.
"Thou knowest this horse was meant for Uraz, thy son, before
thou didst grant him Jahil. And Uraz forbade me to let any man
ride him but himself."

"That was before he left," said Tursen.

"Since then . . . I have . . . I have had no fresh orders," said
the head syce, avoiding Tursen's look.

And Tursen thought, "He is blaming me for not having been
here." For a moment everything before his eyes was wiped out, as
though hidden by a veil of furious blood. Then he saw the stallion
again. The wide-flaring nostrils and rebellious eyes expressed challenge and contempt. Tursen said to the head syce, "Let my racing
saddle be put on this horse."

"For whom?" asked the old groom.

"Hast thou ever seen my saddle used for another man?" asked
Tursen.

"But . . . What? . . . This horse . . . The wildest of them
all in any case . . . and after seven days of . . ." The head syce
stopped short.

A great powerful silent laugh widened Tursen's scarred and battered face. The black stallion shook his stake furiously and pawed up a column of dust.

"See," said Tursen, "he has understood."

It needed two men to hold the stallion while a third harnessed him. Not that the animal was really against it or unwilling. But he was so impatient that he never stopped dancing for a moment. When the bridle and reins were in place and the girths tight, Tursen very slowly walked right round the stallion and stopped at his head. There he seized the horse's lower jaw with one of his great hands while the other rested on his forehead. Grasped in this vise, the stallion was obliged to let Tursen's unmoving stare pierce his moist, brilliant, mad eyes to their depths. Gradually the stallion stopped trembling. Only his long-lashed eyelids still quivered. Tursen passed his thumb over their folds as though to smooth them out.

"Good," said Tursen. He released the horse's head. A syce was holding the stirrup, ready to hoist him into the saddle. "Get back," growled Tursen.

The words were still in the air when he grasped their full significance. Usually, like all men of his age and standing he did the grooms the honor of accepting their help in mounting his horse in public. This was generally understood to be a right and even a requirement of high rank. In this way the possibility of a weakness or an ill-timed movement was done away with; mockery and pity on the part of the watchers was ruled out; the aged rider was spared the pain of humiliation. By refusing, Tursen put himself outside convention, outside the protection of the law. Custom would no longer revere his crown of years. His age, his office, his legend, were no longer of any use to him. He had himself determined this state of affairs.

For a moment Tursen had the feeling of being naked before all these eyes and of exposing his body's tired flesh and distorted joints to their curiosity. "And if I slip," he thought, "or stumble . . . or if I drop flat like a sack . . . No man of my age would face it."

This thought filled him with so proud, so wonderful a delight that it raised and bore him up. There was no longer any heaviness about his body. Every joint from ankle to neck was a quickly moving, obedient instrument. Tursen was in the saddle, holding the reins, all in one movement, a swing that stunned him with pleasure, so strongly did its sureness and economy carry him back to another period of his life.

What did it matter that beneath him the horse was trying to race away without waiting a moment longer? To deal with this wild excitement Tursen had his massive weight, the viselike grip of his knees, the unshakable strength of his wrists, and the whole weight of his knowledge. The horse felt it, and felt it so fast that Tursen was disappointed. He would have liked a hand-to-hand battle with the rearing, bucking horse, a battle in which he would have used all this sudden new strength that was so miraculously rejuvenating his marrow and blood. He was tempted to provoke the too quickly tamed stallion to rebellion by jagging the bit or the spurs—he was tempted to bring on the fight he had been denied. But in time he remembered his rank and his seventy years. In front of these men who were his servants and who could never be taken in by even the cleverest trickery it was not permissible to indulge in the antics of a beardless chapandaz. Accompanied by the respectful murmur that greeted the horse's obedience, Tursen rode out of the courtyard at a walk and so through the others at the same slow pace. The stallion suffered from this restraint in every muscle. The old rider who imposed it upon him suffered quite as much.

AT LAST THEY WERE AWAY FROM THE ESTATE AND STRETCHING EASTward before them lay nothing but the steppe in its immeasurable, awe-inspiring extent. Now Tursen leaned over the stallion's trembling withers and right against his ear uttered a roar, an ululation so long-drawn and piercing that it seemed to reach out beyond the horizon, endowing a human cry with the power to shake both earth and sky.

The stallion leaped forward in a furious, passionate bound. Tursen was ready for it. It was what he had wanted.

What a ride! Tursen had never known one so splendid. He had thundered over this steppe in countless gallops. But they had all been of right; they had been usual; they had been his due. This one, in which he was racing over the steppe in spite of his years and his age-bound body, was something that came from heaven, something given him by Allah. His last, no doubt; by their very nature, wonders could have no future. And because it was the last, it was the most beautiful of his life and the most precious.

The bitter incense of wormwood rose from the trampled ground, a scent so intoxicating that all the others Tursen had breathed over his years on the steppe seemed to be contained in it. And Tursen had the feeling that the breeze the horizon was wafting in his face summed up all the morning winds that had ever bathed his forehead.

His lips were drawn back and he bit harder and harder into the leather of the whip he held between his teeth, while its handle swung against his shoulder to the rhythm of the gallop. Whip: guardian spirit. Older than himself. His father's only gift: copper-bound, thicker and rougher than the whips of today, bearing a heavier piece of lead at its end. In the raw leather, hardened by the years as wood is hardened by the fire, Tursen could taste the sweat, foam, and blood that had so often wetted it. "Thou shalt follow me to the grave," thought Tursen. "And meanwhile, for this day of glory, sing and sing again, beauty, beauty, my cruel beauty."

Tursen plucked the crop from his mouth and flourished it toward the light-filled sky. There was no need to bring it down. The whistle was enough. The stallion increased the rhythm of his gallop.

"See, see!" cried Tursen, "the limits are always farther than they seem." He stroked the horse's flank with the lash. And again and yet again. At each of these touches, half caress and half threat, his speed increased in fury and in madness.

"Like a torrent . . . like the lightning . . . like an eagle . . . like youth," thought Tursen, one cheek pressed against the stallion's neck and his face wet with the foam that was whitening the animal's muzzle and lips. He laughed silently. Then he clenched his jaw. Like a torrent . . . But the torrent carried away trees and stretches of the bank . . . Lightning destroyed villages . . . An eagle stooped on its prey . . . Youth ran toward the future. Whereas he, the old fool . . .

Far away to the right appeared a kind of smoke. Tursen

launched his horse toward it. At the speed they were going they quickly covered the distance between them and the curtain of dust. Beneath the drifting cloud was a herd of sheep, driven by three very ragged men and two hairy dogs.

Which made up his mind? The young stallion trained for the buzkashi, or the old horseman yearning, hungering for the game of which he was one of the legends? In fact the horse's neigh and the man's ululation rang out together as they flung themselves upon the terror-stricken flock.

And in spite of the dash and speed of the charge, in spite of the wild dartings of the woolly mob, the stallion did not hurt a single creature. At the critical moment Tursen was able to lean right out of the saddle, dive on the biggest ram, and seize it by the scruff. As he was straightening up, a belt of fire ran round his loins, so blazing with pain that he thought he would never carry the movement through. But there he was in the saddle once more, galloping, the whip between his teeth and his prey gripped in his hand.

The torrent . . . the lightning . . . the eagle . . . youth. The limits are always farther than they seem.

With the ram flung against the horse's withers and held there, Tursen came tearing back toward the flock and amused himself by gathering the sheep together, dispersing them, and leaping over the bodies clamped together in terror like so many hairy islands.

The shepherds had flung themselves flat on the ground, their faces buried in the grass. But the two dogs, red-eyed, mad with rage and courage, raced after Tursen. And he, as though they were human opponents, challenged them and insulted them, rushing past right by their snapping jaws, waving the ram in their faces, sometimes with his right hand and sometimes with his left, twitching it away at the last second. The stallion feinted, wheeled, lashed out. And Tursen laughed silently, splendidly. Suddenly he felt one of his ankles seized and pierced. A dog had managed to grasp it. With the lead that weighted his lash Tursen hit the dog right between the eyes. It rolled on the ground as though struck by lightning.

Tursen reared his horse over the shepherds flattened in the grass, flung the ram down with such force that its legs broke, plucked a handful of afghanis from his chapan, and scattered them once, twice, three times over the wretched men's heads, crying, "For the sheep! For the dog! For the fright!" He galloped furiously away toward the east.

The dreary bleating of the tormented flock dwindled away and died. As soon as Tursen was within the circle of silence he let the stallion slacken his pace to a trot, to a walk . . . He wiped his cheeks and sweating forehead with a hand still reeking of the ram. He rubbed the back of his neck. His fingers brushed against floating cloth. "My turban," he said to himself. That monument of exactitude and dignity was nothing but a wild, streaming rag. For a moment Tursen saw himself as the shepherds must have seen him —a white-haired man who charged an innocent flock of sheep and played buzkashi against two starving dogs. "An old madman," thought Tursen. And then, "Truly, I ought to be in torment for such indecent conduct." Instead of which he was riding over the steppe in peace. Old: quite certainly. Mad: perhaps . . . But what a victory over himself.

Tursen stroked the stallion's lathered neck. His hand meant to give delight and it knew how to do so. The stallion whinnied gently. For Tursen this reply was clearer than human speech. "Praise to thee, thanks to thee for what thou hast done with me today," said the horse. "I am thy slave, and I love thee . . ." Tursen stretched out his arm and with the tip of his horn-hard nails scratched the stallion's skin just between his eyes. A shiver of pleasure ran the length of the beautiful coat, all shining with sweat. "Certainly he cannot come up to my Jahil," said Tursen to himself, "but he is not far behind." He had a strange kind of feeling for this horse. The first Jahil had been like a brother to Tursen. The others like his sons. For this stallion he was riding now, moving slowly across the immensity of grassy space under the sun at its height, for this horse, so young and new, so inexperienced in the great game and yet the tool and the witness of this triumphant morning, for this horse Tursen smiled like a grandfather.

At that moment he saw the hut.

He recognized it at once. For those who traveled the unvaried steppe, horsemen, shepherds, nomad tribes, it was a familiar and precious landmark. But in Tursen's eyes it was far more than that. In former days he had made a prodigious leap to reach its flat roof, and then had fleered at, defied, and defeated the best chapandaz of the Three Provinces. The feat had been celebrated in songs and tales from that day to this.

Usually when Tursen passed within sight of the shepherd's hut he turned aside. The horseman he had become no longer had anything in common with the rider of earlier times. But that magical morning Tursen stared straight at the roof on the block of clay. The chapandaz who was at this moment letting his horse pace idly along could look at the other chapandaz without shame or regret. They were equals. They were simultaneously the man who was slowly approaching the hut and the man who reared his horse on its roof, insulting, maddening a pack of frenzied, powerless opponents. Once again Tursen felt the joy and pride of that day. Raised toward him he saw the faces twisted with rage and jealousy. He heard the abuse, the oaths, the curses hurled up at him. And above all this hate-filled din sounded a clear young voice that bore within it measureless devotion, pride, and friendship. "Father," it cried, "Father, what must I do now? . . . Father, Father, art thou pleased with me? . . . Father . . ."

And as he had felt it then, so now Tursen felt an astonishing joy take him by the bowels, and he whispered, "Uraz . . . my son . . . my boy . . . my little son."

The stallion stopped. His ears quivered. There was nothing to be seen that could account for his uneasiness. The steppe lay dead and baking under the glare of noon. Not a breath to stir its sensitive surface. Not a single hawk in the sky to send its shadow over the carpet of herbs and grass. Tursen had done nothing to startle his mount. Knees, heels, whip were all motionless. The reins still hung loose. But the stallion's instinct went deeper than the coarse language of movements. This quicker breath, these tensed muscles . . . There was no longer a trace of peace or friendship in this body that had until now been almost merged into his own.

And indeed it seemed to Tursen that the bitter sap of all the wormwood on the steppe was filling his mouth. That same mouth which a moment earlier had uttered words of tenderness to a boy standing in his stirrups at the foot of that same shepherd's hut. "My child . . . my little son . . ."

Tursen said these words over again. But his voice hissed be-

tween his clenched jaws and an evil grin stretched his heavy lips.
Now the gentle words, chanted like a lullaby, had as their object a
hard, arrogant, secretive chapandaz in the prime of life.

"My boy . . . my child . . . my little son," muttered Tursen
very deep. His teeth ground together. He thought, "I am no better
than Aygiz . . . I snivel over shadows . . . Like a doddering old
woman."

Tursen spat out his bile—a thick jet. It touched the stallion's
leg and he took two quick paces out of fear. Tursen's hand came
down with brutal suddenness. It wrenched the bit with such force
that the stallion felt the flesh tear at the corners of his mouth and
tasted his own blood. He reared.

Then, as he sat there, raised high on the rearing horse, Tursen
saw himself on the roof of the hut. And the unconquerable chapandaz hurled insults and challenge across the blazing steppe. But
there was no longer anyone to receive them. No one but Tursen,
Tursen alone.

"Hey, carcass! Hey, stiff knees, thick loins, weak ankles! Hey!
Try to catch me!" Tursen's double shouted to him. And there was
Uraz, fixing him with his unwavering, pitiless eyes.

Tursen drove his heels into his horse's sides, lashed with all his
strength, and raced him toward the little house. Over and over
again as they galloped, with every muscle in his body ready for the
leap that should carry the stallion and himself up to the roof, the
goal, Tursen inwardly spoke to his horse, repeating his words like a
prayer, an order and a threat, "Thou shalt go up, thou shalt go
up . . . Thou canst do it . . . Thou must . . ."

And the stallion, raised and borne up beyond his natural powers by terror, surpassed himself and leaped an impossible leap. His
belly was on a level with the roof. All that was needed was to hold
him there. Tursen had victory within his reach. A furious pain
clawed into his back. Moved more by surprise than by the agony, for
an instant he let himself go in his saddle. The horse was at the
topmost point of balance. He slackened. Only the slightest fraction
and yet too much. His hoofs struck the air at the height of the
ridge. He only had strength enough to avoid the wall and fall back
to the ground.

Now, as Tursen stood beside the hut, it seemed to him to rise to a prodigious height. Beneath him the stallion was trembling, trembling . . . Tursen's violence had carried the horse along, raised him, worked a miracle upon him so that he had been capable of that astonishing effort. But it had left him broken and empty. It was pointless and absurd to begin again. Tursen knew it; he felt it through his whole being. Nevertheless he took the stallion back the necessary distance and tried once more . . . And once more . . . And once more.

Each time the leap was heavier and more blundering. Tursen went on furiously, like a gambler in the grip of his passion, who defies all common sense and goes to his last afghani. At last the horse could not leave the ground at all but merely ran into the wall of the hut. The game had been played and lost. Tursen stared at the roof with expressionless eyes. "I ought to be up there," he said to himself. "The horse did all that was needed the first time."

The reins hung slack on the stallion's neck. Everything was calm beneath the noonday sun. Tursen said to himself again, "The fault lies with me alone . . . In my place, Uraz . . ." His mind remained hanging in the void. All at once a revolting sneer disfigured his face and he cried, "That may be. But even mounted on the Jahil I gave thee, thou couldst not manage to win the royal buzkashi, worthless boy." And at these words Tursen felt what may be the most intoxicating (because the most impure) joy a man can experience: envy's revenge.

Whether it was the surprise of hearing his own harsh voice in the peace of earth and sky or the extreme intensity of his happiness, he was unable to delight in the poison for more than an instant. In spite of the midday heat he felt cold, cold to the center of his bowels. And he recognized fear.

Fear of whom? Of what? Tursen shook his head, and the drooping ends of his turban brushed against his cheeks. Above all, above all, no self-questioning . . . No thought . . . He had managed that at Kalakchikan. And once again when he had learned of Uraz's fall. Sometimes by dull torpor of mind. Sometimes by furious rage. What should he do now? He felt the dark places deep down in his consciousness, the shadows in which he hid himself, growing smaller and smaller every moment. There was only one way out—flight, flight so fast that its speed would prevent all thought. With a terrible blow of his whip Tursen launched his horse on the homeward path.

The stallion did his best. But after the insane attack on the roof of the shepherd's hut his fundamental resources were all exhausted. His first strides showed it: whatever his rider did, the horse could no longer quicken his pace or even sustain it for any length of time. No one on earth understood this better or felt it more deeply than Tursen. No one could more clearly foresee what would happen to the stallion if he were pushed any harder. Nor was there any man it could hurt more.

Tursen remembered the enchanted game they had played so well together, their shared happiness, and their friendship. The strongest instinct of a whole lifetime, the sense of duty, the rules of honor, in short, all the old chapandaz's strongest, most imperative impulses commanded and at the same time begged him to dismount, to fondle, and thank his horse, to rub him down with grass plucked from the steppe, and then, having given him all the time he needed to recover his wind, take him slowly back to the stables. And Tursen would have given one of the eyes from his head to do so. But the fear was there. Fear that had changed sides and passed from the horse—too much and too unjustly punished to feel it any more—into the man. Tursen lashed the already bleeding flanks with an even crueler blow.

The foundered horse lunged forward, but the movement was so short and pitiful that when Tursen raised his whip again shame clamped his shoulder joint. But he said to himself, "There is no help for it. I meant even worse by my own son."

The lash dropped limply, without sound or stroke. Tursen loosened the reins. Running away was no use. And the state of his horse had nothing to do with that. To escape from the confession that his vile, ignoble joy had extracted from him in front of the hut, Tursen would have needed the Prophet's winged stallion.

Timidly the horse slackened his pace to a trot and then to a walk. Tursen left him alone. What was the point of hurrying now; where was there to hurry to? Now that he saw himself stripped naked, saw himself with total clarity and certainty . . . "Go on, poor, brave, generous horse, go at thy own pace," thought Tursen. He needed time to grow used to this new face of his—a face he had so long, so furiously, and with such determination refused to acknowledge.

He who bore the fame of a long line of chapandaz crowned by their victories, he who ruled the glorious stable of Osman Bey, he who had bred and trained legendary horses, he, in a word, who was Tursen, father of Uraz, had betrayed everything in one betrayal: he had betrayed what he owed his ancestors, his lord's trust, the Jahils in their generations, and even more he had betrayed his own blood. Since the moment the great news of the first royal buzkashi had spread abroad, he, Tursen, had lived in dread, yes truly in dread, lest Uraz should win it.

Oh, he would have been entirely on Uraz's side in the Three Provinces, even if it had been for the most famous match with the most splendid prizes. On this field of glory he allowed him everything; he himself had reaped and harvested the golden sheaves long before. But not Kabul! Not the banner received at the hands of the king, when for the first time since the beginning of history the name of a chapandaz other than Tursen was acclaimed and chanted on the other side of the Hindu Kush! And if he had to bow to fate, that is to say to old age, and if at Kabul there had to be a winner who was not Tursen, then at least that winner must not, could not be the thin and silent boy who had depended upon him for so long, who had lived in his shade and then cut himself off, unloving, taciturn, arrogant, grinning like a wolf. Yes, a man could put up with seeing himself stripped, uncrowned toward the end of his life, since that was Allah's will. But that his own son should become the tool of his downfall and should pride himself immeasurably upon it—no, that for sure the All-Powerful, the Just, did not allow!

"That is why," said Tursen to himself, "hidden from everyone and from myself also, in the hidden places of my heart I have continually borne the hope and made the wish that Uraz should be beaten, and that thereby his pride should be brought down and mine left standing high." Again he thought, "And there it is . . . Uraz fell."

In the end the stallion came to a halt. The sun stood so directly above them that their shadow made no more than a line, a thread. A completely unconscious impulse made Tursen grasp the reins.

Uraz had not fallen alone—by his own volition. Oh no! Not an acrobat, not a horseman like Uraz. Some force outside him had thrown him down, broken his leg. The evil eye. A spell. And who under the arch of heaven was better provided, better armed with evil spells against his own blood than a father?

This certainty had not quite pierced home before Tursen's heels were crushing his horse's sides, his whip lashing with redoubled strength.

It was no longer a flight. For Tursen it was not a question of escaping from thoughts that could not be acknowledged. His distress had Uraz as its only object. The best hospital . . . The best care . . . No anxiety. That was what he had been told. Untrue. Too simple. Too easy. A father's evil eye had quite another power. An appalling, unimaginable spell was on Uraz. For he, Tursen, had so wished it.

Once more a young voice crying "Father, Father, what can I do for thee?" rang in Tursen's ears. And with all the strength of his arm and shoulder he brought the whiplash down. The stallion's smoking skin split and burst under the cutting edge. The pace of his gallop lengthened. "Only the cruelest suffering can make this horse run," thought Tursen.

From that moment on his arm was but a busy flail. And there was nothing steady or mechanical about the motion. Tursen knew only too well that unless he was to see his horse flag and stop forever he must not let it grow used to suffering, numb to the pain. The pain must continually be sharper and more alive. And without cease he varied the torture. He sought out the whole and breakable places on that filthy coat, a mass of sweat and blood and foam. Or he lashed the wounds, the raw flesh. The stallion's breath had grown so loud and hoarse that it drowned the drumming of the gallop. No language could speak clearer to Tursen. He was in the act of murdering a valuable horse that did not belong to him, a horse that was under his care, one that had given him all that courage could give. But what did this crime amount to compared with the crime he had committed against Uraz? Get there . . . Get there . . . Know as soon as possible. That was all that mattered. And with his knees, his loins, and his arched body Tursen held up the dying horse and bore it along. He succeeded in what he set out to do. The black stallion did not collapse until he stood in front of the stables.

FOR THE FIRST MOMENT THE SYCES SCATTERED IN ALARM. THEY SAW nothing in this fiery-eyed, glaring old man without turban to hide his ragged hair, nothing in this filthy, lacerated, blood-stained horse, to remind them of the rider and the stallion who had left the courtyard, clean-cut and proud. At last one of them cried, "Allah Almighty, it is the great Tursen."

And another, "Would there be wild beasts on the steppe at this time of the year?"

"Or brigands?"

They came toward Tursen and then jumped back at once. The horse fell in a single mass. The grooms rushed to help the old chapandaz. There was no need to pull him free or pick him up. For a great while Tursen had known that this was how his ride would end, and he was ready. The syces found him standing beside the dying horse. In trembling voices they asked him, "What has happened? What happened then, Tursen?"

Tursen—had he even heard them at all?—growled, "Uraz? What news?"

This question seemed to frighten the grooms more than anything that had happened. They exchanged glances full of superstitious dread.

"Where . . . How hast thou learned . . . ?" muttered the oldest of them all.

Tursen grasped him by the neck of his old chapan. The worn cloth split wide. "The news!" said Tursen.

"Another messenger from the little governor," stammered the man. "Uraz is no longer in the hospital . . . He broke a window and vanished . . . Since then nothing has been heard . . ."

Tursen staggered. It looked as though he were going to fall onto the stallion. He recovered. Respectful murmurs arose. "How he suffers! How he loves his son . . ."

Tursen's eyes were on the horse. Bubbles of reddish foam ran from its nostrils. It died.

"Did I punish him in place of myself?" wondered Tursen. "Did I want to punish myself in him?" He thought of Jahil . . . who had not made Uraz win but another man . . . who had broken Uraz's leg. The nonpareil, the unequalled horse, the best trained in the Three Provinces . . . The instrument of the evil spell . . . Jahil . . . Tursen did not even possess Jahil any more. Nothing, then? Truly nothing?

Abruptly he set off in the direction of his house. Gardi Gaj was resting there. Gardi Gaj, the only being on earth who understood everything, who knew everything beforehand, and did not judge. Oh, how he needed Gardi Gaj!

"THE ANCESTOR OF ALL THE WORLD WENT AWAY A LITTLE AFTER thy leaving," murmured Rahim.

"Where?" asked Tursen.

"He told nobody anything," said Rahim, still in a very low voice. "He said that I was to give you great greetings from him and very great thanks."

Tursen lay on his charpoy, closed his eyes. He was so entirely alone that he felt even his own heart refusing itself to him . . . "Uraz! Uraz! Where art thou?" he cried, deep within himself. And suddenly he felt that all that counted for him was his son, nothing more. "But in that case, in that case," Tursen asked himself, "I must love him?" And immediately afterwards, "And what if he had come back the winner?"

Tursen saw the proud, scornful, triumphant face and for a moment loathed it . . . Then in that face he saw the eyes, merciless for others, seeking his with the hope, the hidden need for approval, recognition . . . The same eyes as those on the steppe in front of the hut in former days.

"Uraz . . . Uraz . . ." whispered Tursen. He had set his hand over his lips to smother the sigh of despair and tenderness in which his strongest pride was dying . . .

It was impossible for Tursen to go on thinking beyond this point. From every part of his body shocking pains came rushing in on him. His whole flesh was racked with their torment. When the shock of suffering was over, Tursen remembered his ride. "I am paying for my morning's youthfulness," he reflected. "At my age these things are not forgiven." And it seemed to him that he heard the voice of Gardi Gaj. "Grow old quickly," it said.

"WHAT MAY I DO FOR THEE, O TURSEN?" ASKED RAHIM.

Opening his eyes, Tursen saw the scars on the bacha's cheek. His first injustice . . . His first unworthiness. The whip. It was there, at his bedside. The object preferred to all others, holy . . . the lash close to his face. What a revolting smell of leather, blood, sweat . . . The murdered stallion.

"Take the whip," said Tursen to Rahim. "Hide it; bury it . . . I do not want it again . . . ever."

PART THREE

The Wager

10

The Jat

THE PLATEAU on which the caravanserai stood did not run far. Uraz and Mukhi soon reached the gorge a torrent had sawn out of the mountain. The huge, ruinous building vanished behind a wall of rock.

Uraz turned his head toward the syce, who was walking behind Jahil, and said, "We shall not travel far today. Look at the sky."

The setting sun was going down between two peaks, as though some immeasurable depth were sucking it in; and because of the narrow space in which it flamed, its globe seemed heavier and more fiery. And its light, reflected by the two enclosing columns, had a strange color, a deep red verging on black. In a stifled voice Mukhi said, "The night is already in the sun."

"Go in front," said Uraz to him. "I shall feel safer with you there."

The tall syce obeyed. As he came level with Uraz his unhappy, humble eyes questioned him. "Why dost thou speak to me so?" they asked. "How art thou threatened if I am behind thee?"

Mukhi passed Jahil and walked on with his head down, his shoulders drawn in, his back bowed. "Wet, feeble wood," thought Uraz. "Yet when the moment comes I shall know how to set thee on fire, for all that."

They soon found a place to camp. The twilight had not yet

taken on the quality of night before the path up which they were climbing suddenly flattened out and led into an oval corrie, where the stream, gentle now, made a natural pool. All around, growing from the rock and conveniently near at hand, were harsh bushes and knotted little trees. It was impossible to imagine a better site.

"Get me out of the saddle," commanded Uraz.

"I come. I come. Directly," said Mukhi.

And yet, although he was generally so quick to help and so happy to do it, he came doubtfully toward Jahil. And his strong kindly arms were clumsy, weak, and awkward. It took him a great while to raise Uraz and set him down. And all this time he felt pain tormenting and contracting the body he handled with such a blundering hold. As he touched the ground Uraz let out a harsh, strident kind of sigh. It was the groan of a man who did not know how to groan, who was incapable of groaning.

"Did I hurt thee so, then?" cried Mukhi. Uraz's left leg was bent at an impossible angle. "Thy leg, thy leg . . ." whispered Mukhi. He kneeled and stretched out his hands toward the injured limb. Uraz thrust him back, seized the broken bone with a powerful grasp, and straightened it without uttering a sound. Then he let himself lean back a little. His face was opposite Mukhi's. Was it the last of the twilight or exhaustion that gave him that gray, corpselike color?

"Did I hurt thee so?" said the syce again.

"Not enough to kill me," said Uraz. His voice was a breath of fever and bitterness.

Mukhi's knees trembled so that he staggered. "Uraz . . . Oh . . . Uraz," he cried. Then again, in a lower voice, with a rhythm like that of prayer, "Uraz . . . Oh . . . Uraz."

And again, gentler than the sound of the water in the pool with the stream flowing through it, "Uraz . . . Oh . . . Uraz."

But the man for whom these sad, sad words were meant had vanished. Far down in the gloom—dark night already at the level of the ground—Mukhi was sure he could make out a vague shape lying there, less like a body than a fold in the ground or the shadows. Uraz buried? Swallowed up . . .

"It cannot be," whispered Mukhi. He wanted to touch the doubtful substance at his feet; but then he remembered Uraz's hideous suspicion. The son of Tursen, his master. Suspicion of him, Mukhi, the faithful syce.

"It cannot be!" said Mukhi again. His head was aching cruelly. Slowly he stood up. He stared right round the corrie and did not recognize it at all. In a few moments the night had come with its dark, quick, silent feet. It had covered the slopes and now only the circling skyline stood above it. Mukhi shook his head in a desperate gesture of refusal. He could no longer understand anything, believe anything, in the surrounding world. Why was he there, and how? In this pit, this trap?

"No, no, it cannot be," he cried into the mountain night. A whinny answered his hoarse, choking voice. Jahil. He was calling him . . . He needed him. Jahil, his friend, his child . . . Mukhi had the feeling that everything around him was taking on life again, meaning, sense, truth. Once more he knew what he had to do and in what order he had to do it. Take off Jahil's saddle and the bags. Water him, feed him. Light a fire. Prepare a meal. The stallion snorted with pleasure as Mukhi took him by the bridle.

"Come, brother, come!" whispered the syce. "Thou shalt lodge like a prince. Come!" Before he could take a single step a voice that had recovered all its aggression spoke out of the darkness. "The horse will stay where he is," said Uraz. "Next to me."

Mukhi's throat went dry. The force of habit alone enabled him to reply, "And watering him, Uraz? How is it to be done?"

"Hobble him here, right here, with rope enough for him to reach the pool," said Uraz.

"Beside thee and in thy fever, will he not hinder thy sleep?" asked Mukhi.

"Believe me, my sleep would be hindered still more," said Uraz with a short laugh, "if I left Jahil at thy mercy, and myself at the same time . . ."

Mukhi was quite unable to understand the inner significance of these words. His mind was closed to their meaning. But a feeling of hopeless distress, of unbounded loneliness, overwhelmed him. "I shall do thy bidding," he said.

Jahil was unloaded; his girths were undone and he was tethered by a long rope to the boulder against which Uraz leaned. The padded blankets came out of the bags. And the cooking pots. And the food. Cut branches piled up on the fire. Mukhi carried out these tasks with his usual conscientious attention. But the happy good temper that always went with him in his work was not there. And even when the flames were leaping in the heart of the cold and silent darkness and the water pot sang in the embers, in Mukhi's heart was no reflection of that fiery dance or any echo of the song—things that ordinarily gave him so much happiness.

Uraz ate voraciously. He greedily thrust his fingers into the simmering pot, grasped the pieces of mutton, wrapped them in thick rice, and swallowed the boluses almost without chewing and often without taking breath. As he did so his gaze—a gaze lit by red sparks from the blazing wood—never left Mukhi for an instant. Because of this it seemed to the syce that his hunger was neither healthy nor right. "If the belly is truly calling out," thought Mukhi, "one stares at one's food and nothing else. I am what he seeks to devour as he bolts down his pilaw." And as he did not know how to hold in whatever entered his mind he said aloud, "Never have I seen thee eat so eagerly, Uraz."

"Never," said Uraz, "have I had so great a need of my strength."

"True, true," cried Mukhi, delighted with a natural exchange at last. "Thou must defend thyself against thy malady."

"And against the advantage some might take of it," retorted Uraz. He licked his fingers, drank three cups of black tea one after another, and belched with deliberation. Then according to custom —the follower eats the master's leavings—he pushed the bowl he had more than half emptied over to Mukhi. Mukhi ate the rest, finishing the last crumbs. With no pleasure, no appetite. Simply because a man as poor as he had no right to refuse fate's gift of food, above all mutton pilaw.

Uraz's eyes were closed. The gleam of the fire made his hollow cheeks hollower still, and his nose seem even thinner—the bone looked as though it might pierce the skin. And when a gust of air blew from his direction the stench of rotting flesh from his wound was enough to pollute the wonderful purity of the air completely.

"He smells of carrion already," thought Mukhi. A few hours earlier the idea that Uraz might die had darkened his mind with terror and panic fear. The end of Uraz was the end of the world. Now he no longer felt any emotion when he thought about it. Everything was in the hands of Allah . . .

Yet, do what he might, Mukhi could not prevent his thoughts from returning by one byway or another to that folded sheet which Uraz had slipped under his shirt.

Without opening his eyes Uraz murmured heavily, "I am going to sleep a little."

"Peace be with thee," said Mukhi from mere habit. He stretched out, with his back to Uraz and the stallion, gazing at the fire and following its living motion. The curves, peaks, falls, and stabbing points of flame that moved one after another in a single flowing arabesque carried his thoughts a great way off. He forgot everything. He was one with the peace sheltered by the night. He was in harmony with the stars—in the ring of sky outlined by the edges of the corrie some of them shone so brightly that they seemed to crackle—with the reflections of the sparks that filled the pool with golden flowers, and with the song of the stream, the scent of the water, the grass, and the bushes.

For Mukhi Jahil's neigh was the most frightening sound in the world: it broke a silence whose nature was that of the trembling of the stars. The syce ran to him. Jahil, at his full height on his hind legs, was pulling so violently on his tether that Uraz's backrest, the great boulder, shook.

"Very close at hand there is a wild beast," said Uraz.

Mukhi put his left hand over the stallion's eyes and stroked his muzzle with the other. He whispered, "It is coming toward us . . . Jahil is trembling more and more."

Then on the edge of the corrie, the far edge from that by which Uraz and Mukhi had approached, they heard a strange voice. It was both harsh and caressing, hoarse and full, sometimes high and sometimes deep, and it spoke with a chanting rhythm. "Peace be with you," it said, "brothers who have the night for your yurt. And peace upon the companion with the long mane. There is nothing wild about my beast but his smell."

In the darkness the voice came gradually closer. In the play of light and shadows that flickered on the shifting edge of the field of vision around the fire appeared an outline, one that might have been devoid of substance. It came forward very slowly, with light, untroubled majesty.

"Who can it be that speaks like a poet of another age and steps like a king?" said Uraz to himself.

A woman came out of the shadows and stopped on their edge. In spite of everything that separated them Uraz and Mukhi pressed together, one against the other. Terror drove them to it, terror of the other world. How could any man indeed believe that by night, in this place, a woman—yes, a woman—should be walking her untroubled way?

"But in that case," thought Uraz as his eyes grew used to the apparition, "why is she wearing a postin and furred shoes under her long dress? And that knapsack? Ghosts do not feel the cold; ghosts are not hungry. A witch, undoubtedly." He remembered the words that had come out of the darkness and he said to Mukhi, "Was it not a man who was speaking just now?"

The answer did not come from Mukhi. The motionless unknown observed, "Among my people, the women who are born to sing have more than one voice in their throats."

"What people?" asked Uraz.

The woman ignored his question, and without moving uttered a few words in a foreign tongue. From the night rose a human-looking shape, very short and squat, swaying from side to side, leaning on a heavy staff. When it came and stood by the woman Uraz and Mukhi saw that it was an ape, covered with a thick coat of brown fur.

Instantly Uraz's fear, uneasiness, and even his curiosity vanished. He knew what he was dealing with. "A Jat," he said, as though he were spitting.

His scorn was so much older than himself and seemed to him so right and natural that in expressing it he had no notion of wounding the race that had been its object since the birth of time. And these people of language and origin equally unknown, possessing no houses, no pastureland, no weapons, no flocks—what else did they deserve? Mingling with all nations and foreigners to each. Always traveling, and yet with no kind of destination. Tinkers, fortunetellers, leaders of bears, trained dogs, and apes.

"Yes, a Jat," said Mukhi. Although it seemed incapable of doing so, his round, flat face also expressed repulsion and distrust. Who could fail to loathe so dishonest a race? Mukhi had never actually seen any of their misdeeds, although he had often seen Jats cross Osman Bey's estate. But so often and from such early days had he heard everyone cry out against these everlasting wanderers that he could have sworn he had himself caught them redhanded. After they had gone, ran the general cry, there were always chickens or sheep that could not be found. Sometimes, greatest crime of all, even horses. Mukhi held Jahil tighter.

Yet the Jat did not seem to have noticed the insult flung at her people and her. Was this dissimulation? Habit? Pride? Indifference? She watched the fire, without moving, without blinking. The flames shone on her with a violent light. She was tall, and the weight of her sack pulled her straight, high shoulders back a little. She was old, and the short hair that strayed from under a worn fur cap shone with a steely gleam. She was beautiful, with that pure, wild majesty that time gives to features upheld by a noble bone formation. And as he looked at her Uraz was no longer surprised that she should go as she and her fate saw fit, through the darkness and along the icy paths. The old woman pulled on the chain that held the ape and took a step forward.

"She has understood," thought Uraz. "She is moving off."

The Jat only moved as far as the fire. There she unslung her knapsack, squatted, and spread her hands out over the embers. The ape copied her.

In the old woman's motions there was neither challenge nor coarse assurance. No fear or servility, either. She was only exercising a natural, ageless right. The traveler's right to a welcome. Not only did Uraz acknowledge it, but he was glad that the old woman had had no doubt that he would respect it. And when she gravely said, "Peace be upon my host's fire," he replied in the same manner, "Welcome to the traveler who is so kind as to honor it." Then he cried, "Quick, Mukhi, boil the water for tea, heat the rice and wheatcakes."

"How can I leave Jahil?" said the syce. "He keeps trembling all the time."

With her long dry hands still stretched out over the flames the

Jat said to Uraz, "Let thy syce leave the stallion for a moment and I will calm him."

"How wilt thou do that?" asked Uraz. "He does not know thee."

"Thou wilt see," said the Jat.

Uraz said to Mukhi, "Do as she says."

The syce uncovered Jahil's eyes and stood back. But only a very little way, ready to step in. There was no need.

With two fingers at the sides of her mouth the old woman began to whistle. Her first phrase was short and brisk, but without any shrillness. A simple warning: "Listen to me." Jahil's ears stood high and he turned his head toward the shape squatting by the fire. She whistled on. The calls drew out, grew sweeter. Jahil snorted. The trembling that had run over him stopped. There was no wildness or terror left in his large, swimming eyes.

"Come . . . Come . . . " said the soft, tender, enchanting sound. As though led by an invisible rope Jahil made one pace toward her, then another, and still another. The Jat's lips were closed now, and through them came a smooth, steady sound, in its simplicity very like the stream that made its gentle way through the unmoving pool. When he reached the old woman Jahil bent his neck to touch her cheek with his muzzle. His mane flowed over the steel-gray hair. With a jealous impulse the ape placed its chin upon the Jat's free shoulder. She half-opened the knapsack at her feet, brought out a handful of sugar, and gave each creature her open hand to lick.

"There," said the old woman. "They are friends. In their own manner they have broken bread and salt together."

"Thou art a witch!" cried Mukhi. "Like all Jats. Indeed I had been warned . . . A witch."

The old woman pushed aside the ape, pushed aside the horse, and stood up slowly. A look of proud anger spoiled the regularity of her calm and steady features. "Witch! Witch! That is the name silly frightened children always call the people whose knowledge and power they do not understand."

"Where do thine come from?" asked Uraz.

The old woman thrust her hand into Jahil's mane—he was pressing against her—and standing there tall and straight said with tranquil pride, "I am Radda, the daughter of Cheldash. From Siberia to the Ukraine no one could buy, sell, and train horses as well as Cheldash the Tzigane."

"What tribe is that?" asked Uraz.

"It is the Russian name for the Jats," said Radda. "In other lands they call us Roms or Gypsies. But from one end of the earth to the other, ever since the world was a world, we are one people and we speak the same language, which comes from India."

Mukhi prepared the tea and the rice.

"So thou art Russian?" said Uraz to the old woman.

"My father and my husband were," she said. "Since they perished in the great rebellion I am no longer anything but a wandering Jat."

"Alone?" asked Uraz.

"No," said Radda. "Sometimes with one animal, sometimes another."

"And for how many years?" asked Uraz again.

"Count them, if it pleases thee. I have nothing to do with time," said Radda.

She sat down on her crossed legs in front of the three fire-blackened stones that stood a little way from the blaze, for boiling the water and cooking the food. She drank and ate in silence, with respect for what she was doing.

From time to time she took pieces of an indefinable dough from the sack and gave them to the ape. Around the fire no one spoke until the Jat and her companion had finished their meal. Then in the most natural voice in the world she said to the ape, "Hast thou eaten well, Sashka?"

The ape nodded its head and rubbed its belly. Then with a hand to its heart, it bowed very low before Uraz and Mukhi.

"Truly, truly, he is returning thanks!" cried the syce. His round, flat face expressed all the intense wonder of childhood. He no longer thought of anything but this toy. He had never seen or dreamed of anything like it. The ape bowed lower still. At this the silent icy night rang with the great laugh that Mukhi had imagined to be silenced in him forever. And the ape's muzzle widened with pleasure. It liked laughter. Through laughter it felt the success of its work. And this laugh, in splendor and generosity, surpassed all those it had ever heard. It felt the urge, the need, to make it sound again. Its sad and lively eye ran from the staff lying on the ground to the old Jat's face. She gave a slight nod. The ape seized the knotted branch, clapped it to its right shoulder, straightened, and with a very rigid pace took six steps forward, turned about, took six steps back, and halted in front of Mukhi.

"A soldier! I have guessed it! A soldier, that is what he is now!" cried Mukhi, clapping his hands. "More!"

The ape was a horseman, then a drunkard. The syce's joy was coming near to ecstasy.

"Enough," said Uraz, suddenly. He did not like these games for fools and still less did he like Mukhi's happiness. Then, speaking to the old woman, "Is it always thy animal that works, Radda? Dost thou know nothing thyself of the arts thy people understand so well?"

"Fortunetelling, for instance?" asked the old woman.

"For instance," said Uraz. He knew that he was in complete control of his face and voice; he was certain that no one could suspect the superstitious faith that dominated him now, at this decisive moment in his life. Yet when Radda, squatting by the fire, raised her unfathomable eyes toward him he saw that his secret had been pierced.

"I do not read the future in the lines of a hand or in tea leaves," said Radda. "I look through men into their depths, to see what they hide from others and from their own hearts. It is for them to understand."

"Do as seems best to thee," said Uraz.

The Jat almost entirely closed her eyes. "Pride," she said, "does not take the place of liking for oneself. Nor hardness the courage to live."

"Is that all?" asked Uraz. His words were arrogant, but in spite of the cold his hands were damp and he was relieved when the old woman turned her head away, saying, "If thou art the man I think thou art, that should be enough."

A humble, childish whisper came from behind the old woman. "And me," asked Mukhi, "what canst thou tell me, grandmother of an unequalled ape?"

Without granting him so much as a movement or a glance, the

Jat replied, "A simple mind is not always a pledge of innocence."

Uraz shrugged. "What is the use of talking to him?" he said. "Just as well speak to my stallion."

"Thy stallion?" asked the old woman gently. "Dost thou not know that he bears the thread of thy fate in his mane?"

Uraz did not attempt to reply. He was heavy, heavy. As heavy as stone. But then a strange power came to him and he turned to the old woman, who was leaning over the fire. For she had begun to sing. And her song rose toward the sky, its darkness and its stars, like a jet of flame. In it could be heard the vibration of a gong, clashing cymbals, the harsh cry of trumpets, hoarse languishing strings forced to their lowest pitch. Truly, it called for a voice of bronze and velvet, this song that seemed to be filled with the demons and spirits of night, fire, and solitude, and to be ridden by them. Uraz had never known an enchantment like it. That furious and magnificent soaring flight, that great proud liberty . . . that calling out to the infinite which cut off his breath, gave it back, took it once more, and then restored it again. His broken, rotting leg no longer hurt him. He was so far removed, so high and far: his chest split wide open that, fully winged and at their ease, all lightnings, all hurricanes, all stars might enter in.

The voice stopped so short it might have been cut off with a scythe. Uraz experienced an unbearable void, an intolerable need. He wanted to recover, to repeat at least a few words of that song of courage and glory. And then he realized that the language the old woman had used was unknown to him. "Thy words were Russian?" he asked her.

"No . . . Tzigane. Or Jat, as thou sayest," said Radda. She gazed at all that was left of the embers in the hearth—a few glowing twigs, constellations of little rubies in the ash.

"The words, are they worth knowing?" asked Uraz.

To look straight at him the old woman turned slowly on her crossed legs. As she moved, a tall flame lit her face diagonally and surrounded it with a halo of fire. So framed, the fine severity of her features and the strength of the underlying bone took on the appearance of a time-blackened bronze.

"She is more than weather-beaten," thought Uraz. "The clay of all the roads has made her a second skin."

"So thou wouldst understand the words?" said the old woman to Uraz. Uraz bent his head. "Thou art right. It is a song for horsemen," said the Jat. She closed her eyes and added, "Give me time to translate in my mind." For some moments nothing was heard but the rattle of a chain. The ape was scratching itself. The old woman said to Uraz, "I warn thee, it will not be as beautiful as it is in Tzigane. For words to take flight they need the language that was their nest. In any other they lose their wings."

"Go on, go on!" cried Uraz.

As though to increase the ardor of his waiting, the old woman began with her lips still closed. This made the sound even harsher and more magic.

"The clay of the world is in her voice, also," said Uraz to himself. He was no longer impatient; he let himself be taken, carried, borne up by the deep rhythmic murmur that issued from the motionless face and rose and rose, becoming a hum, a rumbling, a deep cry. At last the song broke forth. It ran:

> *Heï! Heï! The fire in my blood*
> *And the steppe stretching wide*
> *When he will my horse can outrun the wind*
> *And my hand is his master.*
>
> *Heï! Heï! Run, comrade, fly!*
> *Gallop on, straight on.*
> *The steppe wears the gloom of night*
> *Dawn waits for us below the horizon.*
>
> *Heï! Heï! We go to wake the light*
> *Leap as far as the sky, my charger,*
> *But take care lest thou graze*
> *The Moon Princess with thy mane.*

The old Jat, with her sharp chin in her hands, stared into the camp fire. The two men were motionless.

"Mother, O Mother! Where dost thou draw such strength?" suddenly exclaimed Mukhi, without realizing that he had called the most despicable of women by the most holy of names.

"Silence!" said Uraz savagely. To recover the enchantment, to bring it back, he murmured, "The Moon Princess with thy mane."

. . . The Moon Princess . . ." It was no use. The spell had gone. He turned toward the old woman and said, "If the Prophet were a chapandaz, that song would have been made for him. Thanks to thee for having sung it to me."

"It was not for thee. It was for the stallion," said Radda. "My father would have admired him." With these last words a surprisingly gentle tone ran through her voice, like a flaw. She leaned farther over toward the fire.

"Thou dost not know any other songs?" asked Uraz.

Now the flaw reached the old Jat's lips and eyelids. As for songs, she knew them by hundreds. All those she had heard as a little girl, when she followed her father from fair to fair, market to market, on the Don and the Dnieper, the Ural and the mighty Volga. At the feasts he gave when he had outdone the most cunning of the horse copers. At the caravan encampments, round a fire like this at which she was warming herself now. And later her husband, famous for his guitar, had taught her other songs, as old as their nation itself. No voice could serve them, help them, better than hers. And the women and girls of the tribe were only allowed to accompany her with the choruses and clapping, while around them dancing men and women whirled in their frenzied ring. Sing love! Sing orgies! Sing the wandering forever! Beautiful, intermingled, the words and the melodies stirred and hummed in Radda's memory and deep in her throat. But joy, rejoicing, riot, and passion, those two men were deaf to such cries and their lament. And the shades of dead time were never to be woken; they destroyed the strength that made it possible to survive them. Memories . . . The fire was their place. The ashes . . . Her whole past was contained in that sack lying at her feet. The old Jat took it, threw it over one shoulder. "I know nothing more," she said. Without putting her hands to the ground, she rose in a single flowing movement.

"The rise of a young woman," thought Uraz. He felt an immense weariness.

"Thanks be to thee for this meal," said Radda to him.

"And more still to thee," said Uraz, "for having made so rich a gift."

Mukhi watched them without understanding. His hand, lying on the ape's velvety head, began to tremble. The creature gently took it off and joined its mistress. Mukhi cried out, "Mother! O Mother! Why plunge into the night instead of sleeping in the camp of friendship?"

The old Jat drew in the skirts of her postin—opened for the warmth of the fire—settled her knapsack on her back and said, "I like going to meet the dawn . . . As it is in the song." She took the ape's chain and added, "Peace be with you."

"Peace with thee," said the two men.

Their eyes went after her as she walked with straight back and firm head across the warm lit space, followed by her half-human companion. When she reached the shifting, murky border beyond which the night resumed its icy kingdom, Uraz thought, "Braver, prouder, freer than anyone on earth . . . Yet a woman . . . an old woman." Against his will he whispered, "Walk on . . . Walk for a great while yet, Radda . . . Thy steps do a kindness to the earth."

The Jat walked into the darkness. Jahil whinnied very low. "Mother, O Mother!" called Mukhi. The Jat turned . . . She herself was no longer visible. Only the fire reflected in her eyes and the pale embroideries of her postin allowed them to guess her presence. Mukhi called out, "Mother, I beg thee, I beg thee, tell us it is not true thy people are horsethieves . . ."

Out of the huge darkness the bronze voice answered, "A fine horse, like a beautiful woman, belongs by right to the man who best knows how to love it."

Uraz let himself slip down against the boulder to which the stallion's tether was fastened, and then down to the ground. He was suffering terribly. In a tone of great friendliness he said, "Didst thou hear, Mukhi?"

He stretched out flat on his back. At once the great and little bells of the fever filled his ears. He could never tell which it was, the Jat or his illness, that sang far away,

> Take care lest thou graze
> The Moon Princess with thy mane.

Mukhi had piled up the fire again and was sleeping close to it, curled into a ball. Patiently Uraz watched his deep and noisy breathing. He straightened, undid the loop that tied Jahil's tether to the boulder, and gently pulled on it, inch by inch . . . When the stallion was within reach he lashed his muzzle with his whip and let go the rope. Jahil reared with a furious neigh and vanished into the darkness, toward the singing of the torrent.

"What is it?" cried Mukhi, up even before Uraz's call had reached his understanding.

"The horse has run away," said Uraz.

"Where?"

"Over there," said Uraz.

"I will bring him back . . . Rest easy," said Mukhi. He was already running when a harsh shout stopped him.

"By the blood of the Prophet, come here," said Uraz. When the syce had obeyed he went on, "Swear by the Koran that thou wilt not go off on Jahil to leave me to die and to keep the stallion."

Mukhi flung back, as though he had been struck in the eyes. His only answer was a pitiful stifled cry.

"Swear," ordered Uraz. "On the Koran."

"Yes, yes, on the Koran," stammered Mukhi, merely so that he might no longer hear that horrible voice.

Jahil had not gone far. He let himself be caught the first time Mukhi called him.

"He must have undone his tether, pulling so hard when the Jat came," said Uraz as the syce retied the knot round the boulder.

"No doubt . . . To be sure," muttered Mukhi. His words had no sort of meaning for him. He could not prevent himself from thinking, from thinking with as much sorrow as horror, of the tenderness with which Jahil had rubbed his neck against him over there in the darkness. And perpetually the Jat's voice said and said again, "A fine horse belongs by right to the man who loves it best . . . best . . . best."

Mukhi went far away from Uraz, far from the fire, into the shadows; and there he threw himself down on the frozen ground to stifle his cry, "Mother! O Mother, why am I so alone?"

And now Uraz went to sleep.

DAWN WAS COMING. THE FIRE WAS NO MORE THAN DULL EMBERS. In a bed of ashes and faint smoke, three precious carbuncles still glowed fiery red. A cold that bit right through to the marrow of their bones wakened the two men . . . This did not change Uraz's rigidity at all. As for Mukhi, his first care was to revive the fire and make tea. He drank a cup so eagerly that he burnt his mouth. The glowing warmth of his draft and of the fresh flames ran through his tall body. Then he carried tea to the prostrate figure—frozen stiff, one might have said. Uraz did not stir. The glow of the fire lit a dull, unmoving face, sunk to the bone, on which thin strips of waxy skin were rimmed with jagged beard.

"Dead," said Mukhi to himself. And his free hand moved of itself toward the inert body, just where the document drawn up by the blind scribe lay hidden.

"Thou art in too much haste," said Uraz. "First the tea." Mukhi had to raise him and hold his head before he could drink. "Another, blacker, sweeter!" ordered Uraz. After that without help he leaned against the rock. "Why didst thou prevent me from freezing?" he asked.

"A man cannot let a believer die," said Mukhi, gritting his teeth.

"I see," said Uraz.

Mukhi brought icy water in a bowl. Uraz dipped his hands, sprinkled his face. The cold made him tremble. Instantly the pain shot up and spread.

"Straighten my leg," said Uraz to Mukhi.

With a skill that did not seem to belong to them the groom's big fingers undid the sticky, fetid cloth that wrapped the wound. The wound itself showed naked in the uncertain light of the flames. It was surrounded with scabs, swellings, and reddened cracks: it was the color and consistency of rotten eggplant. Through the broken, corrupting skin the protruding edges of the broken bone could be seen. Mukhi jerked his flat face. "It will hurt thee," he said. "I should not like to see that in an ox."

"Go on," growled Uraz.

The syce seized the leg above and below the break, then with a movement so fast, powerful, and exact that it could hardly be seen, he fitted and joined the two ends of bone together. Uraz's cheeks sank hollower still and on his high cheekbones a reddish tinge appeared.

"Do not move," said Mukhi. His movements continued to be extraordinarily quick and efficient. Their perfection arose from his indifference to Uraz's hurt. He tore the sack that had held yesterday's rice. He used one half as a dressing, which he put over the infected flesh. From the other he made long strips, and these he knotted with all his strength over the rough bandage.

The dawn took on an odious smell.

"The strips have broken the pockets of evil matter," said Mukhi. The new dressing had suddenly become as slimy and foul as the old; he fixed it with two branches that he whittled into splints. Then he went off, struck camp, saddled and bridled Jahil. When everything was ready he came back to Uraz and said, "I can put thee in the saddle."

Uraz, still leaning against the boulder, said to him, "Hast thou grown as impious as the Jat's ape? Look!"

Mukhi turned to where Uraz was pointing, and even before he knew what he was doing, fell to his knees. All the fires, the gardens, the orchards of the dawn had already colored and adorned the ridges and the higher slopes, and above them was rising the sun that required men to begin their first adoration.

Mukhi remembered how the morning before a wonderful prayer had raised someone within him to ecstasy at this moment. Today the banners and wings and lacework of the rays were as far from his heart as they were from his eyes and as frigid as the ground on which he was kneeling. He heard himself reciting the words of the prayer faster and faster; he did not understand their meaning.

When he had mumbled them out to the last, Mukhi looked at Uraz and saw that he was transfigured. He was bent forward, with his body away from the rock and his hands flat on his chest; his cheeks had come to life again under the flow of blood and his eyes were sparkling.

"As for him, he is still praying," thought the syce. "And what a prayer!"

Truly, never in his life had Uraz given himself up so wholly, so intensely, to an invocation. Not for any buzkashi, not even the king's. The stake that he was wagering now went so very much farther and meant so much more than all those engagements! And when the day was at its full brilliance Uraz was still speaking to Him who knew all, who could accomplish all.

11

The Night Voice

IT WAS DURING THE DAY that the wild mountains made the travelers understand the full extent of their cruelty to those who do not belong to them.

Treacherous screes. Tracks and paths reduced to the width of a man's body. Breakneck steps cut in the rock. Chasms opening suddenly at the turning of a gorge. Never a single safe, straight, level line. Never a place where the eye could see all round. Either the rock face or the night of the abyss. The least error—a slipping foot, a failing knee, a body out of true—and death was there, vertiginous, solitary, calling with its wide-open, bottomless maw.

Fear seized Mukhi's bowels in the first minutes of the day, and it never left him. Everything was on his shoulders. He had to scout forward, search out, discover a path through this chaos of boulders, peaks, defiles, and precipices; he had to plan their way up hellish climbs and descents; he had to encounter sudden barriers at the end of blind corridors, go back, find another way out, creep and stagger on the edge of towering cliffs.

At the same time, throughout all these operations, these terrifying acrobatic feats, for which a steppe shepherd's muscles, nerves, eyes, and instincts were in no way formed, he had to guide, restrain, uphold, and encourage a horse that was also accustomed to the grassy plains.

To begin with, when it seemed impossible to overcome some obstacle or thread some maze, Mukhi looked at Uraz's face for advice or help. There was never any reply. Uraz was concentrating all his powers on holding out in the saddle against weariness, fever, pain, jolting, pitiless climbs and descents. Nothing else existed. His face remained closed, his eyes inaccessible.

Mukhi gave up turning to this mask. But the feeling of being alone in an immense danger redoubled his terror. And terror begot hatred. "Thou didst compell me to this madness," he said in thought to Uraz. "And there thou art, quite careless of the dangers we have to run, I and this wonderful horse at thy command. May thou be accursed."

The hours went by. The sun wheeled over the sky. Nothing changed in the confusion of rocks, sharp peaks, ridges, and winding gorges like clamps with twisted, tormented jaws.

Then there was that terribly long, terribly dark tunnel in which they heard the whispering of the devils that haunt the depths of the mountains. And that ramp so steep and hard to climb that Mukhi had to lighten Jahil by taking off all his packs, letting pots, clothes, blankets, and food trundle away as they chose. And that ledge path they reached at twilight, from which at last they saw a valley; but a path so narrow that as he went down its zigzags Mukhi often had to keep his eyes closed so that he should not give way to the call of the abyss whose sawlike edge was beneath his feet.

ALL THE TIME THEIR LIVES WERE AT STAKE NEITHER URAZ, MUKHI, or Jahil had felt the need of water. Once they were on firm ground they were eaten up by thirst. Of the three it was the animal that was best equipped in senses and instincts for the search. Uraz and Mukhi knew it.

Jahil raised his long head very high, and slowly, slowly he turned it through a half circle. His nostrils and lips, crusted about with a dry yellow foam, smelled and tasted the light evening breezes. Uraz and Mukhi waited for his decision with a kind of humility. At last the stallion neighed, set off, lengthened his stride, and broke into a gentle trot. Mukhi had to run to keep up with him. Every jolt echoed through Uraz's shattered body. Every stride forced a hoarse gasp out of Mukhi's throat, so parched and wizened by thirst that spittle would no longer go down. Neither man noticed it. It seemed to them that under the murmur of the wind in the bushes they could hear another sound, almost the same but with a different note, a wonderful song. It was no longer the breathing of the leaves and the branches. It was the rippling, wet, unutterably lovely voice of water.

It became a loud song, a thundering, an uproar, all the most delightful in the world. At last, in a deep cleft, appeared the water-fall. Its beginning was very high up, halfway between the foot of the cliff and its top. The setting sun still touched it, and the low rays turned the spring, fed from deep in the mountain, into a leap-ing fountain of gold and scarlet. Then, in a single stream, the light-filled jet shot into the zone of twilight, spread down the run of the rock in an immense black undulating motion, gathered in a deep, deep cauldron that it had hollowed out for itself over the centuries, sprang out again to fall into a shallower basin, and so continued its drop from pool to pool until it reached the valley in a brisk but steady and well-conducted stream. The last of these natural reser-voirs stood almost at ground level.

All Mukhi had to do—the stallion was already there—was to bend his head for the icy water to flood his mouth. He was aware of nothing but his happiness: the happiness of a plant suddenly overwhelmed with rain after an endless drought. So much so that he hardly felt the blow of the whip on the back of his neck. Another tore his ear. He stood up without yet understanding.

Uraz—and Jahil drank on—Uraz was before him, standing high on one stirrup. His ashy face, his deep, blazing eyes, his bloodless lips shut with dry spittle, frightened the syce more than the lash that whistled over his head. Groping through a red mist he unfas-tened the goatskin bottle from his belt, plunged it into the pool, set it all swollen, shining, dripping, on the saddle. Uraz drank very slowly, almost drop by drop. It looked as though in this way he meant to give Mukhi a lesson. In fact he found it hard to tilt the skin to his mouth.

Suddenly the breeze freshened. It was only a passing gust, but a dismal, mysterious whisper rose from the bushes, the grass, and the dark pool—the murmur caused by the wind that brings the night. Already the eagles were climbing with all the power of their wings toward the mountain top; the sun no longer touched it, and in its side the spring of the fall was no more than a black hole. Mukhi followed the eagles with his gaze and as he did so he reflected that Uraz and he were about to face long, long hours before the next day's sun in that high, high valley, its darkness and its cold, without any food, without a single blanket. Their possessions had all vanished into the chasm when they had had to lighten Jahil's load. Now there was nothing between them and the breath of the night.

"If the cold freezes me this time, what shalt thou do?" asked Uraz suddenly.

"Nothing," said Mukhi.

"Because of thy mortal hatred or to have the horse?"

"Both," said Mukhi.

Through all his weariness Uraz felt a moment's joy. He had brought Mukhi to the point where he wanted him. He said, "Good. Come on."

He had to go on because he was suffering too much. The splints that held his broken leg had come undone long ago. At the point of the break the edges of the bone were tearing and inflaming the flesh. From this spring of torments shot up thick, burning jets, spreading branches of pain with unbearable thorns. Their fire and their poison attacked his muscles, his bowels, his joints. His ankle and knee were so painful that they could not, would not come into any contact with Jahil's side. And what is a horseman deprived of his knees? Everything wavered and spun: the dark mass of the bushes, Jahil's ears, an outline that was Mukhi, though Uraz no longer knew it. And when a harsher jolt jerked up his head, the sky swung right over and sent the first stars falling on him. Like fiery pebbles. And the metal rings of fever clanged at his eardrums so as to deafen him.

On the other hand he was aware, and with a sharpness that he had never known before, of the smells of the world that was shut out from his other senses. The scent of grass, water, and bark came to him from a great way off, each in its most subtle vividness. Between the gusts he could even make out the stony smell wafted from the mountains. So he rode, touched only by the odors of the valley. Suddenly he lifted his forehead above Jahil's ears and reached his face out into the scents borne on the darkness. From far down in the night one smell was gliding toward him that had nothing to do with the plants, the stream, or the rocks. He wondered aloud, "Where is that smoke coming from?"

Mukhi stopped Jahil at once. What? Smoke . . . Fire . . . People . . . "What dost thou say? What dost thou say?" he cried.

Uraz did not hear him. The violent halt had almost thrown him.

"Raving," thought Mukhi. And walked on. Uraz stayed in the saddle without even knowing that he was doing so. He had fainted. When he came back to half-consciousness the smell of smoke was stronger. It filled and comforted his body. He opened his eyes. He was no longer dizzy. He was suffering less. "Where is the yurt?" he asked.

"What yurt dost thou mean?" asked Mukhi.

"The yurt where the smoke is coming from, fool," said Uraz.

"The smoke. Ah yes, the smoke," muttered Mukhi. "The smoke of thy poor brain . . . The smoke . . ."

He stopped muttering; he even stopped thinking. In his turn he too had just breathed in a smell that wiped out all the others, a smell that had none of the scent of water or of trees: the thick, almost tangible reek of a smoke that was heavy with the greasy smell of melted mutton fat, as though impregnated by a nourishing incense. Mukhi led Jahil at a run.

"Quick," said Uraz, "quickly to the yurt!"

In the cold that pierced to the hollow of his bones and veins, in the solitude and exhaustion imposed by his illness, the odors of burning wood and of cooking carried with them, so to speak, the loveliest of images. A great fire . . . a glowing copper samovar . . . walls . . . a pointed roof . . . On the ground and the charpoys, richly colored carpets, cushions, quilts . . . And chapans: and whips . . . And well-known, peaceful faces, filled with kindliness. The yurt of the steppe in which Uraz had begun his life was like that; heavy at the bottom, sharp at the top, made of reeds and felt. And as he no longer had any sense of time or place, it was to this yurt that the spirals of his fever led him. And the swaying of the saddle was like the rocking of the cradle.

"Here we are!" cried Mukhi. "Here we are!"

Uraz opened his eyes, closed them, opened them once more. In vain. Where was the magic round? The refuge of former days? Why this wretched and smoky hearth, ill fed with brushwood? These scraps of brown cloth, ill slung, squalid, full of holes? These poverty-stricken faces? These ragged clothes?

A tall, thin man and an enormous woman came and bowed very low before the travelers. "Welcome to you, and may you find our poor encampment auspicious," they said together.

The slavishness of their posture and voice were so revolting that they brought Uraz back to a notion of reality at last. The yurts of the steppe do not spring up in the high valleys of the Hindu Kush; it was not to a family of noble horsemen that he had brought his weariness and pain, but to people even more despicable than the Jats. The little nomads. They lived on theft and begging. They hired themselves out for seasonal work at trivial wages. The contempt that went with them everywhere did not arise from their poverty. A proud destitution compels respect. But among them the poor man's anguish had abolished honor and decency. There was no unworthiness for which they were not prepared so as to gain a very little money.

The fat, great woman and the spider-legged man stood before Jahil with bowed heads. As the stallion's splendor became clearer in the light of the fire, so they bent their necks and spines further still.

"Allow us, O noble, powerful, wealthy man, allow Smagul, the head of our family, and me, Uljan his wife, to serve thee this evening," cried the woman with grasping zeal.

Very low, so that he could scarcely be heard, her husband whispered, "Uljan has spoken well."

Uljan to the left and Smagul to the right took Jahil by the bridle to lead him with honor over the few paces to the ragged tent. At the doorway the little nomads, men, women, and children, rushed forward to pay the travelers the attentions due to their rank. Some bowed to the ground, others knelt, others sought hands and stirrups to kiss.

"Back . . . Go in . . . Sit," cried Uljan.

The members of the wretched tribe hastily retreated to the middle of the tent, where they squatted down. Now Uraz saw them as they were. Emerging from his strange state, his eye, like that of a seer, for a moment had the power to pierce shadow and flesh and, beneath the mask of features and the veil of skin, detected the motives that they hid. It was not the greasy rags of these men and women that were in question, not the age and condition of their bodies, nor even the expression in their eyes. It seemed to Uraz that at the heart of these beings he could see fear in motion, venality, submission, wariness, falsehood, and shamelessness. Already in their gentle, plaintive smiles the children had all these qualities.

"They are born like that—cowardly and corrupt," thought Uraz. "The freedom that is happy to live under the roof of a tent is lacking here; and here the poverty is baseness."

Squatting on rags set down on the bare earth, lashed by the night wind that whistled through the holes in the canvas, four gray-headed men and five younger women gazed at Uraz with eyes full of a strange, eager desire to obey.

Again Uraz thought, "These slaves give themselves, without even knowing what they expect from me. Theirs is the very lowest servility: servility for its own sake." He remembered his vision, the yurt, the horsemen of the steppes. Once more his fatigue was so great that he was on the point of yielding to it again.

Then Uljan said, "Lean on my shoulder to dismount, O lord, and come into our tent." Because her tone had a caressing note it jerked Uraz into consciousness. It was as though he had felt something obscene touch him. He looked at the woman's swollen, shameless, cheaply overpainted face, and pride gave him the strength to speak in a loud, strong voice. "I shall spend the night outside: my syce will look after everything. I shall pay well," he said.

He walked Jahil round the tent and stopped behind it, close to a makeshift pen in which a few asses were shivering. A feeble, smoky light lit up the rocks and thorns that surrounded him. He could vaguely make out Mukhi's form behind a torch made of plaited straw dipped in mutton fat.

"The ground is too frozen for me to take thee down at this moment," said the syce. "But we shall have what we need directly. Uljan—she is the chief here—is seeing to it."

Two women appeared, their widespread arms overloaded with chapans, postins, blankets, carpets. All mere rags. Uljan followed them. She cried, "I have stripped my people of everything they had on their backs, and they were happy to be of service to thee, lord."

Although the materials and garments were in tatters, their quantity made a deep bed. Mukhi set Uraz down into the hollow of it. The women came back with armfuls of branches and glowing embers from the camp fire. A soaring blaze crackled so close to Uraz that the tongues of flame almost licked his face. Within hand's reach he had a scalding pot of tea and a dish of very greasy rice.

"Peace be with thee under the stars," said Uljan. At that moment in spite of the paint her face was open and generous. But at once she added, "At thy command, lord, and only at thy command, I have told the syce what it costs."

Uraz drew a handful of notes from his belt. Uljan received them in her fat hand, fingered them with an excited, sensual laugh to make out their thickness, and led away the two other women.

Uraz could not manage to quench his thirst with the black tea that burnt his mouth. Mukhi ate the rice to the last grain. In silence.

Jahil, tethered close to Uraz, whinnied. The little nomads had nothing to give him. Mukhi stepped over to stroke his mane. He reflected that during the *qantar* the great buzkashi horses ate nothing for days on end. But that was in the season of burning heat . . . With his fingers wandering in the stallion's mane he dreamed of the steppe and the bitter scent of wormwood rising up from it under the sun.

The heap of rags weighed on Uraz's broken bone. The pain was increasing every moment. He was about to order the syce to free his leg when a head leaned down toward him. It had long hair in plaits, and it was intolerable to Uraz that a woman—and a woman of such a kind—should stand over his powerless, sagging body. He thrust the face violently away and cried, "Who art thou? What dost thou want?"

"I am called Zereh," said the woman. "I helped to bring the fire, the blankets, and the food." Her voice was very low but very clear, as though it were used to secret speech.

"I need nothing," said Uraz. Mukhi had come near. He added, "I have my syce."

"He cannot help thy leg, which is very sick," replied Zereh. "I know herbs that are good for the blood and there is skill in my hands to make ointments, potions, and powders from them. I learned it from my mother and she from hers."

"Is Uljan quite insatiable, then, that she sends thee here?" said Uraz with disgust.

"I swear to thee Uljan does not even know I left the tent," said Zereh. "I waited until they were all asleep before I came." The voice was muted, but it bore the accents of a most unusual tenacity.

"I see," said Uraz. "Thou wouldst have me pay thee in secret."

"Offer me anything at all, and I shall not take it," whispered Zereh, and there was the same determination in her whisper. "I came . . ." She suddenly dropped on her knees. As she did so she leaned her plaits against the syce's hand just behind her. ". . . Only for thy wound, lord," she ended. Before Uraz was able to reply she had raised and pushed aside the ragged coverings and bared the wounded leg. Uraz suffered more than he had ever suffered before. Until this moment he had not allowed himself to be concerned with his pain. Now all at once this woman was forcing him to it.

Zereh threw back her head to speak to Mukhi, and her hair touched his hand again. This time the contact was longer and more firm. "Bring the kettle, tall syce," whispered Zereh.

In the wavering firelight her eyes gleamed strangely, and as Mukhi looked down into their shining, fathomless water he felt a kind of dizziness. Before he could recover his freedom of movement and do what she told him, he had to wait until Zereh looked away.

There was no more tea in the pot. Zereh turned it upside down, gathered the sticky leaves, and made them into little swabs. "Now, tall syce," she said, "light the torch again and come here." When the smoky, grease-smelling flame was lighting the infected wound, Zereh leaned far over, the better to understand its putrid stench. "It is time," she murmured. "Oh, it is time indeed!"

Then with the tea leaves she began to press and wipe the skin. Her fingers were extraordinarily light and skillful. Uraz could not master the contraction of his muscles. Zereh stopped, murmuring, "Do I hurt thee too much, lord?"

Uraz raised himself a little on his elbows and looked fixedly at Zereh. She was quite unable to put a name to the expression that made his fever-blackened eyes gleam with such hard brilliance. She was well acquainted with fear, envy, submission, cunning, and even anger. But pride had no currency in the world to which she belonged.

"Who allows thee to question me?" said Uraz. His breath was heavy with such disgust and his gray lips held such scorn that Zereh learned the existence of a feeling that had also been unsuspected by her until that time. And one harder to bear than insults or blows. Those were things she was used to. She was born for humility alone. Through Uraz she was now discovering humiliation. At the moment she did so she felt a hatred for him, a hatred such as no one had ever raised in her before. Her fingers returned to their work with the same diligence and the same gentleness.

The suffering grew less and less. Gradually the pus voided itself from the wound. When Zereh had pressed out the last drops she felt in the top of her dress, produced four flat cloth bags, and held them up toward the flame of the torch that Mukhi was holding. Each was marked with a different colored thread. Zereh put three back into the hollow of her bosom and opened the one embroidered with a little blue circle. It held a dark paste. A strong smell of rotten bark reached Uraz's nostrils. He scorned to move his head or even change the direction of his gaze, fixed on the stars. This woman with her remedies was a mere tool, and one so base that her existence did not signify.

"I do not need the light any more, tall syce," whispered Zereh.

The torch that had been burning close to Uraz went out. He felt an agreeable languor invading him. He thought it was caused by the return of darkness. But the peace grew in depth, intensity, and power. And Uraz was conscious of a strange confusion, as though a part of him that was essential for his balance were slipping away, leaving him. The pain had stopped. It was unbelievable. Instinctively he felt for his broken leg. It was there, daubed with a sticky substance. "Zereh's herbs," said Uraz to himself. "So she did not lie."

His eyes moved toward the woman who possessed this knowledge. Until then he had paid no attention to her features. The campfire threw a severe, searching light on her face, one whose bloom the years, the sun, dust, and weariness had not yet taken away, and it showed the high, sharp cheekbones, the big, long-lashed brown eyes, the very dark skin.

"Shameless bastardy," thought Uraz. "Uzbek, Pathan, Hindu, all mingled in her. And what is surprising about that? In these families the husbands or fathers sell their wives and daughters to the first traveler that comes by for a few afghanis."

This was how he thought; and he was pleased with so much dishonor. He had no wish to be under any obligation to this woman. The extremity of the defilement liberated him from any kind of gratitude toward her. No noble emotion could be attributed to Zereh. In contact with her, it became impure. "I shall pay her with an open hand," said Uraz to himself. "Truly, that is all she wants."

This thought was the last he granted to people or to things. Nothing outside himself could concern him now. There was too much happiness within. That marvelous resting place, a body that no longer hurt, closed over him.

Zereh raised her hands and held them over the wound for a moment, ready to go on with her task if it should be necessary. Not a nerve, not a muscle stirred. The young woman dropped her arms with a deep sigh. Her body relaxed entirely. Mukhi was in the same place, just behind her. He felt Zereh's head and shoulders lean against his side and his knees. All at once a strange and delightful weakness came over the syce. A whisper, as though from a great way off, reached him: it said, "Now he needs nothing more . . . He is asleep . . ."

In a single movement, as quick and supple as the stretching of an animal, Zereh was on her feet, turned toward Mukhi. He saw how small she was. Her forehead reached no more than halfway up his chest. It only increased her magic fragility.

"Come," said Zereh. "I am cold . . ."

He followed her to the other side of the fire, throwing on an armful of branches.

URAZ PERCEIVED THE CRACKLING OF THE FIRE, THE BLOWING OF THE night wind, the shivering of the trees, the purling of the stream; he took them in without knowing it. For him these muted songs were no more than the echo of the deep-lying sounds that traveled throughout his body—those of his blood, his breath, and his fever. They were his rest, his happiness.

When the noise that was not in harmony with these hidden voices arose, Uraz did not consciously hear it. Only a strange sadness came over him. He was still not suffering, but he felt that the harmony of the darkness and the earth was withdrawing from him. He was still not suffering, but he was there with himself once more, lying under the rags. The noise increased, hindering and overpowering those which came from the sky, the mountains, the leaves, the water, and the fire. Because of that, Uraz heard it at last. A hoarse, regular gasping, as though wrung from the depths by a delicious torture, combined with a drawn-out, flawed, continuous moaning—human but very like the cry of beasts in their ecstasy. Uraz recognized its nature at once. "Mukhi and Zereh," he observed to himself.

Their coupling left him unmoved. A brisk young fellow: venal loins . . . What could be more natural? Himself he had taken advantage of those wenches who were open to all. He thought about them for a moment. He had not known many—the opportunities had been few—and he could not remember them clearly. Always the same kind of meeting: the chance of a day's halt, a squalid camp, the darkness, the harsh, short-lived satisfaction. The contempt before, during, after. Through his memory an unobtrusive form passed . . . his wife. Cholera had killed her, pregnant, in the very year of their marriage. "Then I was afraid of an evil omen," remembered Uraz. "I was wrong. That was when I won my first great buzkashi at Mazar."

On the other side of the fire a sigh rose, loud and prolonged. It was as though some all-consuming thirst had at last been slaked. Behind their burning bush the two were silent. Uraz forgot that Zereh existed; he forgot Mukhi. What they did, what they were, did not matter. Now once again only the sounds of the valley filled the expanse of darkness. Once again they cradled Uraz; no longer burdened with thought, once more his innermost being discovered the untroubled freedom of the wind, stones, and trees.

But at the moment he was about to sink down into their heart the sound of a voice stopped him. Yet this voice did not disturb, did not spoil the concert of the night. Clear, gentle, and liquid, it was no more than a murmur in harmony with the murmuring of the earth. Indeed, its very purity brought Uraz up to the surface of consciousness. What woman was it who could own that voice innocent as a child's waking from a delightful dream, happy as those of birds that greet the dawn? To whom could it be speaking? Uraz listened, listened. At first he could not make out the words. Then the wind changed and brought them to him.

"Tall syce, my tall syce," the voice was saying, "I came for thee alone . . . As soon as I saw thee by our tent I made the vow." There was a very short silence and the voice went on, lower, but still as clear, "Tall syce, tall syce, tall syce."

The wind veered again. But Uraz had heard enough. He was forced to believe the unbelievable. The child's voice, the voice of the welling spring, belonged to Zereh.

"A bastard wench," he said to himself, "and of the lowest gutter! A whore, and the most venal of whores!" As though some trap kept him from advancing, he could not carry on his train of thought. Venal, certainly, and from her birth . . . except for this night. There was no money on earth that could buy that tone, those words.

"What is it, then?" Uraz wondered.

Sheltered behind the curtain of flames, Zereh's voice was flowing once more, so fresh and young. The breeze still robbed him of what she said. He did not care. Rhythmic words ran in his head, following Zereh's voice like music.

Now that I know
The light thou givest
All other roads
Will be roads in the darkness
Oh, I shall love thee
While I have breath
Love thee, all drunken with love . . .

Uraz had never felt the beauty of this poem of Saadi's, which he had learned at school. But when he rode past a yurt and saw a girl inside, or when he was invited to a marriage feast and thought of the bride, the lines came into his head. And when they did so, these verses that had lived for centuries in their lovely flow did not move him to longing dreams or to tenderness; rather, they stirred his senses to fury, to savage desire to possess, rape, hurt, and spoil these innocent creatures, these virgins with little breasts and timid eyes. And now again, although he was lying there broken and sick, they set him on fire. All the strength that was left to him gathered in the middle of his body and ruled him like an impaling stake. He madly wanted the woman hidden from him by the veil of smoke and fire. She was no longer Zereh. She was the dreaming song of purity, the unreachable flower of the poem. And Uraz was possessed with the furious urge to crush, bruise, rape, and tear her. He would call her, he would . . .

Suddenly he wanted nothing at all. The panting, the animal gasps and moans had taken the place of the voice of the child, the bird, the spring.

"A bitch . . . a bitch," said Uraz to himself. He never knew, so deathly was his weariness, whether at that moment it was sleep that struck him down or whether he fainted.

A FINGER OF LIGHT TOUCHED EACH OF HIS EYELIDS. THE SUN'S DISK was rising above a three-horned mountain top. Uraz's first glance was for Jahil. His first movement was to touch his will. Quite near at hand the stallion was cropping the dew-softened grass. The sheet of paper lay there under his shirt.

"Never again, never again until the end of the road will I sleep like that," thought Uraz. He ran his hand along down his broken leg. It was still in a state of grace.

He saw Mukhi, lying there stretched out by the dead ashes of the fire as if he had been struck by lightning. He was alone. Uraz picked up a stone and aimed straight. The cutting edge of the flint struck the syce's brow, cutting it. Mukhi's head scarcely stirred. Another stone hit him full on the forehead. He shook himself, saw that it was broad daylight, stared all round him, saw no one, covered his face with his huge open hands as though to protect a threatened treasure, and then slowly stood up.

Once he was standing he uncovered his face, and Uraz held his breath with astonishment. Mukhi's countenance looked entirely new. Its artless self-confidence, its gentle ardor, the exaltation that lit up its eyes, and the unconscious half-smile of its fuller, redder lips gave it a kind of nimbus. Uraz thought, "He is almost beautiful." And then again, "He has missed the first prayer, and yet he looks as though he had just uttered the most passionate and best-answered."

Mukhi began to move toward the tent of the little nomads.

"Where art thou going?" asked Uraz.

"To fetch tea," said Mukhi.

"No," said Uraz. "We leave at once. The delay has been long enough as it is."

"But . . . but . . . Thou hast need of rest to recover thy strength."

"All I need is something to hold my bones together," said Uraz.

Mukhi went to cut two strong branches and returned to tie the broken leg between them. As he did so he said, "It no longer hurts thee, I see."

That was true. But because of the hands that had treated it Uraz was exceedingly unwilling to acknowledge the truth to Mukhi or even to himself.

Mukhi cried, "Thou art healed, healed by Zereh." He closed his eyes, and with a soft, enraptured laugh he repeated "Zereh . . . Zereh . . ." again and again.

Uraz's strange look did not worry him. Uraz could not know anything. His sleep had never varied. Zereh had vouched for it . . . Zereh . . .

Mukhi was still repeating this name when Jahil, saddled and bridled, gave a snort, impatient to be moving again to warm his muscles, all stiffened by the mountain cold. And Mukhi had the feeling that the course of life was coming to a stop. He had just come to understand that he was leaving the encampment of the little nomads. His panic-stricken eyes searched for an object, a piece of work that would delay their going. In vain. They no longer possessed so much as a bag, a knapsack. He remembered that everything had been surrendered to the precipice.

"What art thou waiting for?" shouted Uraz.

"Listen, listen," stammered Mukhi. "We cannot . . . go off . . . straightaway . . . like this."

"Why not?" asked Uraz.

"Because . . . Because," repeated Mukhi. Inwardly he begged and prayed, "Allah, O Allah! By my heart and my body, give me reason to stay a little."

He found it in the very cause of his distraction. "Dost thou not think," he went on, "that the care thou hast received deserves reward?"

"I shall pay, never fear," said Uraz. "For everything." His eyes never left Mukhi, and he added, "I shall do so when we pass in front of the tent. So give me my horse."

"Here he is, here he is," cried the syce.

All that counted was to see Zereh again, speak to her, perhaps touch her. Time did not go beyond that.

Uljan bowed very low to the travelers. The men of the family were around her. The women stood in the background. Zereh was not among them.

The Bridge

THE GRASSY PATH ran close by the river. It was so smooth and the sound of the water was so clear and steady that a blind man could easily have made his way along it. And indeed it was as a blind man that Mukhi walked, his eyes wide open. The golden morning, the fresh green valley—he saw none of it. He had not yet left the bosom of the night. At this moment Zereh's smell, the taste of her skin, the warmth of her breath, and the sound of her voice were the plants and their scent for Mukhi, the sun and its rays, the stream and its song.

All at once he stopped believing in it.

Was it possible that he, a pauper among the poor, one who had never gone near a woman and whose poverty-stricken fate forbade him even to think about it—he, Mukhi, with his thick and awkward bones, his outgrown chapan, was it possible that he should have had that wonderful girl, and that from her mouth he should have heard the most beautiful words in the world? No. He must have dreamed those images and those words. Allah had merely granted him an hour of happy madness. How otherwise could Zereh possibly not have come to say farewell?

Mukhi brought both fists up to his forehead and turned suddenly. He wanted to be sure of at least one reality, the tent of the little nomads. It was no longer there, shut out by the undulating ground. The only trace of it was a humble gray smudge in the trembling air.

Mukhi's tall body barred the path. Jahil stopped against his chest. Uraz's look fell straight down on a despairing face, obsessed and hopeless. "It was thy first woman?" he asked.

The emotion that stirred Mukhi was not embarrassment or even surprise, but joy. Uraz knew: so the dream was true. "The first, yes indeed, the first," he cried.

"And now that whore is all thy thought," said Uraz.

"Zereh asked nothing for what she did for thee; and as for me, thou knowest very well I do not possess a half afghani," said the syce. As he spoke his flat, unprepossessing face took on a remarkable nobility and handsomeness.

Uraz struck the handle of his whip violently into Mukhi's ribs and growled, "Get along. Enough talk of that bitch."

"Thou dost not understand anything at all, O Uraz," said Mukhi gently. His heart was strengthened by a great certainty. The kindness of the sun, the morning's beauty, the splendor of the mountains made their way into him through his eyes, his nostrils, his lips, and his entire skin. The grass and the leaves with the last diamonds of dew on their tips were a countless field of stars. Mukhi bent, gathered his muscles, tightened his shoulders, and set off in long and rapid strides.

Seeing how fast the syce was going, Jahil lengthened his pace. Uraz did not interfere. They overtook Mukhi. The syce was walking with his head in the air, humming. As Uraz passed him he smiled.

"So where is yesterday's longing to see me dead?" wondered Uraz.

Mukhi's song followed him. But Jahil went fast. Presently Uraz could hear nothing but the wind and the water. The river took a sudden very sharp bend, and this brought him to a halt. Uljan had said that they must cross at this point. There was no other bridge anywhere else in the valley.

He hesitated. Two beams, or rather, two roughly stripped, badly set trunks with their wet bark on them, led across to the far lower bank opposite, bowing heavily as they did so.

"Do I still need a wet nurse?" said Uraz to himself, and he rode

Jahil toward the narrow, slippery gangway. The stallion only set out on it with extreme reluctance. Slowly, lightly, he ran his off forefoot over the rough wood, scratched and felt with his hoof, and at last set it down. The near foot followed in the same manner. And one after the other his hind feet. The stallion made one pace forward and stopped. All his muscles were trembling. Uraz thought of going back to the bank he had just left. Impossible. The thinness of the bridge prevented him from turning; its slope from going backward. He had to run the risk. For although the river here ran with the speed of a torrent, it also had a torrent's narrowness.

Uraz did not have to urge Jahil. It was growing harder and harder for the stallion to stay where he was. He moved forward of his own accord. One uncertain step . . . Another. They were half over the bridge. At that moment Uraz was flung sideways with such force that only his acrobat's instinct saved him from a fall. As soon as he was back in the middle he saw the disaster. Jahil's off hind foot had slipped on the wet bark and forced its way down between the two trunks. They had closed on him at the level of his pastern, like the jaws of a trap.

For an instant the stallion remained motionless, his flanks heaving unsteadily, his head down and heavy, as though he refused to believe what had happened. Then with a fierce neigh he arched himself and with all his strength pulled on the imprisoned foot. In vain. He tried, he tried once more. In vain.

Then, shaken by this convulsive, terrified, impotent strength, for the first time in his life Uraz felt panic overcome him. And he heard a voice. A voice that said over and over and over again, "Jahil wounded, crippled, maimed, lost . . . Wounded, crippled, maimed, lost . . ."

A stronger jerk than all the rest jolted Uraz out of his frenzy. The horsemanship he had inherited from the finest riders of the steppe told him that this time Jahil was on the point of breaking loose. One more fraction of a second, one last fury in the effort, and the trapped foot would be free. But Jahil had given all that he could give. His hindquarters relaxed again.

"Shame, shame on me!" said Uraz. "If I had helped him instead of weighing him down like a dead log he would have succeeded."

Jahil had returned to the struggle. Uraz perceived every one of his movements as a clear message. He was waiting for the deepest, the most violent, the one in which strength should reach its utmost extremity, to lift and help his horse. Just in that very crucial moment he was struck, grasped, paralyzed on the left side by an anguish all the more atrocious since he had forgotten its existence. He let his broken leg hang and huddled there on his saddle. Zereh's salve had exhausted its power.

Jahil moved no more. "He is telling me that he will no longer try with me here on his back," thought Uraz.

And his hatred for himself gave him the necessary strength. He lay against Jahil's withers, slipped his sound leg out of the stirrup, swung it over to the near side, and grasped the stallion's mane; hanging by it, with his bad leg bent, he let himself down until he touched the bridge. There he was racked by such a torment that nausea and dizziness overwhelmed him; the one foot that upheld him slipped and he fell. As his back was to the river he flung his body forward in a last convulsive spasm and came down on his face, lying on the beams under Jahil's belly.

He thought he was going to lose consciousness. The pain prevented him.

MUKHI CAME UP A LITTLE WHILE AFTERWARDS. URAZ AND HE DID not have to speak. A look was enough; Jahil first.

Mukhi knelt behind the stallion, pushed his huge hands between the two beams, closed his eyes, held his breath so as to let out none of the strength concentrated in his arms whose muscles started out like levers, and then with a short, strong thrust forced the trunks apart. They scarcely yielded at all. His eyes red with blood, Mukhi gave a second heave. The gap opened for a split second, just to the width of the imprisoned hoof. No more was needed. The stallion was free.

Mukhi crept along Jahil's side, grasped the reins, and walking backwards guided and pulled the horse to the bank. He came back to pick up Uraz, used the inert body in his arms as a means of balancing himself, and put him down close to Jahil.

They examined Jahil, Uraz stretched out and Mukhi on his knees, still without speaking. A piece of skin near the fetlock joint had been torn off by rubbing against the wood. The raw flesh was bleeding a little. There was no other hurt.

Mukhi washed the wound with plenty of water and bandaged it with grass to keep it cool. As though it were part of the same treatment he tightened the splints on Uraz's leg.

Uraz stared steadily at the bridge. Two beams . . . Two wretched beams. He had not been able to get across them. And Mukhi could and would tell everybody. Uraz's nails clawed the grass and the earth. No, that could not be. By the Prophet, no! "Put me back in the saddle," he ordered.

The syce did not obey at once. His arms hanging by his sides, he gazed at the opposite bank and searched in himself for the sun of happiness that had never left him for a moment over there. Not a single spark of it was left. The line of turbulent water cut life in two, just as it divided the valley. Zereh on one side and himself on the other. What chance had they of ever seeing one another again?

"Well?" said Uraz.

Mukhi hoisted him onto Jahil and set off along the track. It was a very thin ribbon of stony ground that had been laid bare in the greensward by centuries of men's feet and the hoofs of their animals. It ran quite straight toward the mountain range that closed the horizon to the west, a vast rough table of rock without peaks or clefts.

"A child could not mistake the road," Uljan had said. "After the bridge there is one track and one track alone that runs across the valley. After it comes one path and one only, going easily up the mountain. And it comes down directly onto the old Bamian road. Two days' march at the most to reach that town. It is so, believe me—we go round and round these parts like asses drawing water from a well."

Uraz remembered her words. He trusted the huge woman's knowledge. Not for nothing was she the little nomads' leader. The day after tomorrow Bamian would be in sight . . . The halfway point.

Jahil was following Mukhi with a cautious pace. Uraz reined in, as though his horse were going too fast. "Halfway . . ." he said

to himself. "Halfway already . . . And where have I got to?"
Mukhi's head was low, his back bowed, and his knees weak; he was
not so much walking as dragging himself along. Uraz thought, "I
had succeeded. He had come to hate me. He coveted the stallion
. . . Crime was swelling in his heart. Then that whore appeared.
She is all he has in his blood now . . . lost dog . . . spineless
fool. All to be done again . . . How?"

Meanwhile the character of the valley was changing. The vegetation was a far darker green than it had been on the other side of
the river. The grass grew short and harsh, the bushes stunted. And
although the sun was climbing higher and shining hotter the two
travelers wrapped their chapans tighter to shield themselves from
the blast of an icy wind. For the mountain was coming toward
them. They made their way into it by a gorge. It was noon, the
time when shadows die. There was not even so much as a fringe of
darkness at the bottom of the gleaming cliffs. Yet Uraz saw a
brown shade thrown by a rocky spur. It could not possibly be so.
Uraz shaded his narrow, hawk-bright eyes and discovered that the
impossible shadow was a woman sitting under the ridge of stone. A
moment later he recognized her. "The whore!" muttered Uraz.
Then louder, "Zereh!"

The syce was still walking with his head down, and he felt as
though Uraz had struck him between the shoulders right through
to the heart. He turned toward him, showing a face whose motionless features and half-opened mouth had the appearance of a mask.

"Over there," said Uraz.

In his turn the syce saw her and made as though to run forward. Uraz gripped him by the collar of his chapan and whispered,
"As Allah is my witness, if thou shouldst defile men's honor, I shall
lash out thine eyes with the lead of my whip. Dost thou no longer
know that it is for her to make the greeting?"

And Zereh came up to them: she did not grant Mukhi so much
as a glance but flung herself on her knees before Uraz and with her
forehead against his stirrup uttered her supplication. "Take me,
lord, oh take me on thy journey! Never shalt thou have so humble
and silent and faithful a servant, so attentive to thy wishes! I beg
thee, do not leave me with the people of my tent. Since my husband's death they have kept me as a slave. I work for them. I eat

their leavings. The men lay me under their bellies as they choose. And for that the women scratch me and beat me without mercy. Let me follow thee, Magnanimous. I want no pay. A handful of rice and a blanket are enough for poor Zereh."

Uraz's first thought was to reject this unseemly bastard who presumed to cling to him. He was not deceived. She was there on her bended knees for Mukhi, and for Mukhi alone. Just as he was about to strike her head with his heel she lifted her face toward him. And now the sun, shining straight down on her, stripped her features of all their falseness. Beneath the slavish begging and the paint running with fictitious tears, Uraz suddenly detected a most uncommon strength, eagerness, and resolution. He cast a glance at Mukhi. The syce was trembling like a child, like a sick man. Adoration, hope, and intense anxiety one after another passed through his eyes.

The wolf's grin that had not appeared for so long stretched Uraz's pale lips a little. Zereh was frightened: she pressed her forehead against the stirrup again. "Pity, lord," she moaned.

The echo of the wild gorge sent back the plaintive cry. Uraz touched Mukhi with his whip and commanded, "Get on!"

Jahil stepped forward. Zereh was still on her knees; the metal of the stirrup scraped and grazed her cheek.

"Thou mayest follow," Uraz said to her.

Zereh rose; as was proper, she walked behind the horse.

THE CLEFT RAN FROM TOP TO BOTTOM ACROSS THE MOUNTAIN IN A straight line. The path that followed the bottom of this chasm had no excessive slopes. The travelers crossed the range easily and fast.

At the very high top end of the gorge, an arch-shaped rockfall ran from wall to wall. When Mukhi, Uraz, and Zereh were through this tremendous gateway they found a road. On the far side of it stood a chaikhana, hung there as though above an unending landscape. The horizon was all that bounded the infinite ocean roll of empty plateaus, the color of baked clay, and of shallow green valleys.

Uraz rode Jahil to the chaikhana. Mukhi tied him to one of the twisted branches that held up the veranda, lifted Uraz, and laid him on one of the wretched charpoys, set at the back of the veranda so that they should be sheltered from the north wind by the wall and from the sun by the roof. What would he not have done for the man who had given him back Zereh?

The inn was in a state of extreme desolation. The scraps of worn-out carpet even the poorest refuges offer were not there; nothing whatever covered the rotten straw of the benches or the lumps and hollows of the floor. Beneath the roof of dried leaves there were only three old men sitting round a nargile. They had square faces and snub noses, and their eyes formed such narrow slits that among all the other wrinkles they looked like slightly deeper folds with two black tears in them.

"Hazaras," thought Uraz. "This is where their country begins, no doubt."

Mukhi bent over Uraz and said, "This is a strange place. I see no bacha at all. No one inside."

The Hazara who sat nearest the samovar said lazily, "The child of misfortune fled at dawn this morning with a caravan. He wanted to see the world."

"Then I want the man of the place," said Uraz.

The Hazara turned slowly toward him on his crossed legs. "It is myself," he said with a sigh.

"What art thou waiting for to serve us?" asked Uraz.

"Serve you what?" The man scratched his ankle and went on, "The son of a sow left me without cooking anything. I only have stale wheatcakes."

"And for the horse?" said Uraz.

"My ass finds quite good grass in the meadow thou seest along the road," said the man.

"And tea?" asked Uraz. Before the man had time to reply he added, "Thy ass finds it equally to his taste, I imagine?"

The Hazara looked put out for a moment; then the black drops sparkled deep in their slits and his mouth opened in a silent laugh that showed his bare gums.

"Did you hear? Did you hear?" he cried to his companions. Already the other two were sharing his gaiety with all their wrinkles. Then the proprietor said to Uraz, "I like thee, horseman: in spite of thy hurt thou dost prefer mockery to anger."

"And I like thee too," said Uraz. "In spite of thy trade, thou dost prefer idleness to avarice."

"It is not my fault," said the Hazara. "For a man who has been a slave for a great while, work is never pleasant again." Sighing, he stood up. "I will make thee some very strong tea," he said. "But not in clean cups. The bacha, that son of a bitch, left without washing anything." He moved off with little steps, deeply bowed.

"He must be seventy at least," reflected Uraz. "I was still a little boy when the amir Habibullah set free the tribes who had been punished with slavery for their perpetual risings." He shook his head. Slaves . . . The descendants of the horsemen left by the great Genghis to hold the country.

Mukhi said, "It seems there is no longer any need for me . . . May I lead the horse to the meadow?" His voice was low and ill at ease.

"Thy words are of the horse and thy thoughts of the whore," said Uraz to himself. He gave his consent with a wave.

Mukhi saw Zereh as soon as he was out of the shadow of the veranda. She was sitting against the low wall that enclosed the meadow along the road. Her tattered cotton clothes were the same color and much the same texture as the dried mud against which she was leaning, and they gave her the look of a little heap of rags forgotten there in front of the chaikhana. The sight of her, so close, so accessible, after the long, long road that he had had to travel far removed from her, separated from her, not even daring to turn for fear of Uraz there between them on his horse, moved him so much that he could not stir. Nor did Zereh move or speak. The passion that had carried her along and had thrown her across Uraz's and Mukhi's path took possession of her now with a strength she had never known. She felt her loins and belly all aglow. How handsome and powerful he was, the tall syce, at the splendid stallion's side! It seemed to Zereh that she had never seen him before. The heave of her bosom stirred her ragged dress. But all the strength and knowledge of dissimulation that she had learned in the course of a very hard life helped her not to betray herself any farther.

"Take care . . . take care. Patience . . . patience," thought Zereh. "I have already gone far enough in daring. Now step by step, inch by inch, I must make myself accepted. One move too far and all is upset. The master watches me with his wolf's eyes."

Thus innocence in the one and profound calculation in the other concealed a love both felt with equal violence and total purity.

Mukhi came up to Zereh. The young woman's forehead, tanned as leather, only reached the level of the syce's knee. Wrapped in these rags, her face seemed to him more beautiful than it had been when lit by the fire. But to the wonderful joys he had experienced then and was recovering now—tenderness, desire, admiration, gratitude—was added a new feeling, one that frightened him and hurt. It was begotten, fed, and magnified by all the others; it had taken its sweetness and intensity from each; and it had turned them into instruments of bottomless, unbearable suffering. And this pain had the strange power of binding Mukhi more strongly to Zereh than the sharpest happiness had done. The sight of the woman of his love against his knees in supplication like a beggar acquainted Mukhi with the almighty power of pity over a man who loves.

The state, the condition of the very poor had never surprised Mukhi. There were the poor, and there were the rich. That was nature's law. But because Zereh, squatting on the ground without tea, without bread, had to wait until Uraz and he had exhausted the chaikhana's resources, the syce was revolted by the world's cruelty.

"What art thou doing there?" he cried.

"Dost thou see another place for me?" asked Zereh very gently.

Mukhi swayed to and fro, to and fro, as though he had been knocked off his balance by an unexpected blow. What answer could he give? The weight, the order, and the holiness of the most ancient of customs spoke from Zereh's mouth. Come, what was he thinking of? A woman. And of the lowest rank. And without a husband. And without money. And without a chadar . . . She should be allowed in a public place? He himself, Mukhi, would have been amazed, shocked, to see such a thing. So it was fair, it was right that Zereh should be outside, like a thirsty, hungry dog, while they, the men . . . ? No, not Zereh. But why only Zereh? Behind the woman he loved Mukhi saw the unending line of her outcast sisters, and he felt himself guilty of a crime of which he knew nothing except that it had half the human race as its victim.

He put his hand—it was trembling a little—on Zereh's hair and whispered into her ear, "I shall come back, by Allah! I shall come back . . ."

The tea tray had not yet appeared at Uraz's side. However, he seemed to be in an equable mood. Mukhi came and squatted close to the charpoy.

"Was the grass for Jahil as good as the man said?" asked Uraz.

"Even better," said the syce, who had not even looked at it.

"So all is well, then," said Uraz.

"No, all is not well," cried Mukhi. He thrust his head forward, and face against face, he spoke in a breathless, urgent murmur, "I saw Zereh outside . . . She set out before us at dawn . . . Nothing to eat, nothing to drink. We must help her."

"What dost thou suggest?" asked Uraz mildly, his eyes half closed.

"I am ready . . ." began the syce.

"To carry her food and drink," interrupted Uraz in the same tone. "I know it . . . and I would rather kill thee. The baseness of a syce dishonors his master."

"Let her come here," whispered Mukhi.

Uraz's eyes were no more than gleaming slits. His voice grew even more friendly. "Here?" said he. "Here? Indeed? Even if I were in a position to force such an outrage on the owner and his guests, who would choose to serve a wench of that kind? The most pitiful of bachas would refuse. And there is no bacha."

Mukhi's body sagged over his crossed legs; his head shrank between his shoulders. He had promised Zereh to come back. But with empty hands? How could he?

Between his almost shut eyelids Uraz watched Mukhi with a kind of sensuous delight. This great lump, so flabby, void, and inert only yesterday, how quickly it had grown sensitive and manageable!

"Get up, fool," he ordered, "and go and find her."

"But . . . but . . . Thou hast just said . . ." stammered Mukhi.

"I said that a servant has no right to be served," retorted Uraz. "But she may, she must, serve. Tell her that."

Mukhi leaped over the little wall to go faster. From the threshold the man of the chaikhana said to Uraz, "Is it true that that woman is here to look after thee?"

"It is true," said Uraz.

"By the Prophet, if all travelers did the same, this place would be the antechamber of his Paradise!" exclaimed the proprietor. He reflected for a moment and went on, "A good woman servant is worth all the accursed bachas on earth. I remember in the days when our nation was set free, some masters married toothless slave-women to their sons to keep them in the house." The old man went back and sat with his friends. They smoked in silence. From the back of the building came the sound of pots being moved, the clash of crockery.

Zereh appeared, carrying a very heavy tray with no apparent difficulty.

"How clean everything is!" said one of the Hazaras.

"The tea smells good," said another.

"She has warmed and softened the old bread!" cried the third.

Without being aware of it, Mukhi nodded with a beatific smile. Zereh served Uraz. He did not touch the food. It made him feel sick. In spite of his hunger, Mukhi only took a piece of wheatcake.

"He is leaving it all for the whore," thought Uraz. "If I do not set things in order she will no longer look on him as a man." Uraz caused her to fill his empty cup and said to Mukhi, "Jahil is growing rusty, never going faster than a walk. Stretch his legs!"

"What . . . thou sayest . . . truly . . . Here, in front of everyone?" cried the syce. He said "everyone": he thought only of Zereh.

"Go on," ordered Uraz.

Mukhi ran to Jahil, who was grazing fully harnessed, and with a hand on his withers vaulted into the saddle without touching the stirrups. Those who watched him from the terrace had the feeling that in a single moment, before their eyes, they saw him turn into another man. No more awkwardness, no constraint left in that big body. All at once Mukhi managed his height, bulk, and strength—usually such an embarrassment to him—with all the ease in the world. At ordinary times it seemed to him that his arms were too long, his hands too big, his wrists too massive, and his legs too thick, but now they instantly fell into their true balance and took on their full dignity. His shoulders were no longer hunched and drawn in. In their splendid breadth his head stood up high and free. And lastly, instead of the usual childish simplicity there was a new strong, commanding look on his face; and long before its time the set expression of watchful experience placed the mask of maturity on it.

Mukhi jagged the bit with a quick, harsh jerk. Jahil returned to his full height. Although he had not touched the stirrups the syce's massive body did not fall back an inch, being held to the horse's sides by the vise of his knees and thighs. So the two heads reared high side by side, and the wind of the high plateaus waved the streaming mane and the wings of the turban with the same breath. On the veranda the three old Hazaras squatting round the nargile let their mouths droop open. By way of riding animals they only knew mules or sad little donkeys. It seemed to them that in this man and horse they saw one single, astonishing creature.

Now Mukhi held Jahil on his hind legs until the stallion began to lose his balance. His forefeet struck the air with irregular, unordered force. The hocks that held him upright trembled more and more. Still the syce would not let him come down. It looked as though he were trying to hold the two-headed monster up toward the sky forever. Strength, skill, experience, instinct—he brought them all into play to correct and counterbalance Jahil's disconnected motions. Flung back and leaning pitilessly on the bit when the stallion lurched toward the ground, pressing forward with all his bulk against the withers when Jahil threatened to fall over backwards, Mukhi straightened, gripped, and upheld his mount.

All at once he slackened the reins, loosened his knees, and hurled the stallion forward. In a single stride Jahil was galloping. The meadow was far too short, far too narrow for such a career. A few moments, a few strides more, and the stallion would run full tilt into the chaikhana. The old men covered their faces with their hands. Zereh, pressing back, her wide eyes motionless, her mouth open in a silent, inner cry, said to herself, "He will kill himself . . . Kill himself."

None of these fears affected Uraz. He knew what was in the syce's mind. And indeed at the last moment, right against the wall, Mukhi swung over, laying his whole body along Jahil's side, and with his knee, chest, and arm turned him, making him fly along the front of the chaikhana with no more than an inch to spare. The hammering of the gallop shook the earth of the veranda. Mukhi had already swung round again, flinging the stallion across the grass, and he was racing back.

Uraz no longer leaned against the wall. Bending forward on his charpoy he could see the syce's broad rounded chest, barred with splendid muscles, breathing under his ragged shirt. And he had the feeling that he was within that breast, so strongly had he foreseen, understood, and shared each one of Mukhi's reactions. For Uraz at this moment Mukhi was simply another man exactly like himself— a horseman.

Then, very close to his charpoy, he heard a voice whisper, "On his horse, he looks like a prince."

Uraz turned his eyes toward Zereh and became himself again. That voice filled with wonder, that dazzled face . . . He had succeeded beyond expectation. The reticent, secretive girl had quite lost her self-control. She would never forget Mukhi upon Jahil. *His* horse, she had said. *His* horse . . .

Uraz signed to the syce to dismount. Mukhi got down. His chapan was too short once more.

"We go," said Uraz to the man of the chaikhana.

"At nightfall thou wilt find a good caravanserai," said he. "There thou wilt lie at ease."

Uraz asked for the reckoning.

"There is no reckoning," said the old Hazara. "I am far more in thy debt for what thou hast given us." Uraz was about to insist. The old Hazara gently added, "Leave a poor man his only wealth."

When the travelers—Mukhi in front, Uraz on Jahil in the middle, Zereh behind—had set out on the road for Bamian, the owner of the chaikhana came back to squat by the nargile and smoke. His friends waited for their turn, and the former slaves silently watched the gray mist rising from the waterpipe toward the withered leaves of the veranda roof.

*****

13

The Crown of the Road

THE OLD BAMIAN ROAD bore the marks of its age, which went back to the beginning of time. It was narrow and winding; in the dry season it was covered with a layer of dust as deep as a quilt; in the wet it was a river of mud; its sides were battered and full of holes; its middle was scored with enormous ruts—it was in fact no more than an indifferent track. Wheeled vehicles could not use it at all. All the traffic, trade, and exchange between north and south traveled by the great road that Uraz and Mukhi had followed for some hours after their flight from Kabul.

The old Bamian road, deserted and peaceful, was used only by the people of the province—peasants, craftsmen, shepherds, pedlars, chance travelers, and above all by the caravans of migrating flocks going up to their pastures in the spring and down from the mountains in the autumn. It was October now. Some went by every day.

During the course of the afternoon Uraz, from the height of his saddle, was the first to see a kind of reddish-brown smoke that was coming toward them from the skyline. This slender plume grew fast. Others rose from the ground. Gradually they united and between them they made up a clay-colored cloud so high, so thick, that it hid the sun as it stood there, halfway down the sky from its height to the western horizon. From time to time a powerful gust blew gaps in it, and they could see a confused moving mass, herds and herders, beasts and men; from this mass shone the sudden gleam of steel weapons or brass harness, caught by the slanting rays.

Mukhi stopped to wait for Jahil. And Zereh came up with them, without going beyond the horse's rump. She said, "The great nomads."

In saying the word "great" her voice had remained even. But by the mere strength of conviction she had given it its fullest ring, its true and total force. For Zereh there was no common measure between the little nomads of her kind and those who were marching in a tawny halo which the sun edged with gold.

"What tribe?" Uraz asked the young woman.

"The Pathans of the high frontier, where the sun comes up," said Zereh.

"Pathans . . ." said Uraz.

He had never met their caravans, which passed well to the south of the steppes in their migrations. Yet their name and fame were more than familiar to him, as they were to all Afghans. The Pathans of the eastern passes, of the high-perched mountain castles . . . Unconquerable shepherds and warriors. They forged swords, spears, and rifles in their secret workshops. They had conquered the plains as far as the Amu Darya, had reduced the Hazaras to slavery, compelled the heathens of Kafiristan to the true faith. Even the soldiers of the English king, invincible elsewhere, had been thrust out of the Pathans' valleys and mountains, after a hundred years of fighting. Pathans, the rulers' race . . . King-making clans . . . And people who set off with their migrating flocks every spring as they had done for thousands and thousands of years; without troubling about laws or frontiers they crossed the entire country, weapons in hand, from India to Persia.

"Pathans," said Mukhi. There was fear in his stifled voice. At Meimana all those who were in command, all those who had the power of supervision and punishment—the district governors, tax collectors, heads of the army and the police and their assistants— were always Pathans. Men of a different blood, sons of the conquerors, sent by Kabul from the other side of the Hindu Kush to make the people of the grassy steppes obey.

"Pathans," repeated Mukhi.

The moving curtain of dust now spread from one side of the great valley to the other and spiraled up to blot out the sky. It might have been still hot ash of the burning world.

"Get on," said Uraz to Mukhi.

The syce took a few hesitating steps, then turned, and with his eyes on Zereh as she walked along behind Jahil, he said, "It might be better for us to take a path through the meadows."

"Why?" asked Uraz.

"The Pathans fill the whole road; they are as numerous as a cloud of locusts; and they are armed."

"The road belongs to all who travel on it," said Uraz. "Get on!"

Mukhi hunched his shoulders and obeyed. And the vast confusion of dust was upon them: it flowed over their heads. They could see nothing. They could only hear an enormous confused trampling, the clink of metal, a faint sound of human voices, and above it all the uproar of beasts whinnying, bleating, bellowing, barking.

Zereh ran to Uraz, gripped his right leg between her two hands and cried, "I beg thee, master, let us at least take the side of the road."

"Why?" asked Uraz.

"The Pathans always follow the ridge road," said Zereh. "They think they will bring bad luck on themselves if they do otherwise."

"That is what I think, too," said Uraz.

The dust was beginning to powder their faces. The ashy mask increased Zereh's look of terror. "Woe on me," she groaned, "lowest, humblest of women, little nomad that I am. They will trample me underfoot."

"Do what thou wilt: I give thee leave," said Uraz.

The young woman kissed his ankle and in three leaps reached the hollow that ran along the road. Mukhi made a movement as though to follow her slight, waiflike form, but he dared not carry it through.

"Go along, then," said Uraz in a disgusted voice.

Mukhi joined Zereh, took her hand, and felt it trembling in his enormous palm. "Look!" she cried. "Thy master is moving on. He is mad."

"Proud," said Mukhi softly.

"Proud of what?" cried the young woman again. "Is he so rich, then?"

"What does that matter?" said Mukhi. "There is no finer chapandaz in the Three Provinces, and he is the son of the *great* Tursen."

Zereh knew nothing whatever of the buzkashi or its famous men. When she saw the syce's face express the same feelings as those she felt for the great nomads it angered her. No one, no one on earth, could be compared with the Pathan lords! "Chapandaz or not, it does not signify to me if he is cut to pieces," said she. "But he has no right to have thy horse killed or maimed."

Mukhi's skin grew too small for him and too hot. "Jahil is not mine," he said.

"That horse was born for thee," cried the young woman with an almost ferocious violence and stubbornness. She pressed herself against Mukhi and added in a whisper, "In the chaikhana meadow thou wast like a prince."

Uraz, who rode on, keeping strictly to the ridge, raised himself in his off stirrup, shaded his eyes with one hand, and halted the stallion. At the same moment Zereh flung herself from Mukhi with the motion of a terrified animal and cried, "Here they are! Here they are!"

The caravan was emerging from the depths of the cloud. This was merely its tip and yet it not only filled the whole of the road but spread out over its edges. Uraz in his saddle and Mukhi and Zereh at the side of the road peered through the folds, the hanging drifts and veils whose depth and texture the sun and wind kept in perpetual change, and behind the vanguard they saw the main body of the flocks. It had no end. It had no shape. It filled the valley from one mountain wall to the other. Uraz, Mukhi, even Zereh had never seen an animal deluge like it. It was as though an immense river in spate were rolling its wooly flood toward them. For the dust imparted something that resembled a short fleece to the horses, mules, asses, and horned cattle too.

There were currents that stirred, halted, slowed, and pushed on the motion of this tide. And at these moments could be heard barks, shouts, the cracking of whips. The shepherds and dogs remained unseen, lost in the sea whose pace they controlled. As for the half-submerged riders, seen from afar they were no more than half a man on half a horse. The only creatures who proudly stood out from this flowing mass were the statuesque camels. They marched two abreast in close-packed lines. Whether they were pack camels or racing camels, whether they were loaded with tents, shining pots, and carpets, or palanquins with whole families inside them, their pace was the same—indolent and haughty. Their heavy-jowled, barbarous muzzles swayed and bellowed on their long, serpentine necks. The biggest and strongest led trains that undulated above the groundswell of the flocks. These leaders wore astonishing ornaments. From top to bottom they were decked out with fringes, ribbons, pompons, nets, and feathers in plumes and falls. There were little bells on these violently colored ornaments, and at every pace they rang. These sleepy, sumptuous, hairy dragons rolled and pitched, voyaging on the dusty waves of the riverlike caravan.

The flood advanced toward Uraz with the slowness, the power, and inevitability of an element. He gave it only a single glance: all his attention was focused on the extreme point of the caravans and the two beasts that led it. They were from Bactria, that ancient land, and from time out of mind they had been unequaled for size, hardiness, strength, and fighting spirit. They were far larger than those that came after them, though indeed these followers were huge. Their deep, thick, rough-haired coats were dyed with henna, dyed all over, head, neck, back, humps, belly, and legs. On this red hair were arranged pieces of cloth, talismans, charms, and plumes, and they all moved, sparkling and shining with gold. Their saddles were made of tooled red leather.

The monster on the right hand bore a man; the monster on the left, a woman. The man was still young. There was not so much as a single gray hair in his beard—a short, thick, rough blue-black beard that ran up to his turban. It was like an ebony frame for his weather-beaten, sun-tanned skin, his proud-hooked nose, and his eyes, which had the deep, hard, lusterless color of lava. A badly healed scar ran in a broad furrow just under his lower lip. There were two daggers in his belt, and a very long gun with a damascened butt lay on his thighs.

The woman was not yet twenty. Everything bore this out—the

smoothness of her cheeks, the brilliance of her eyes, the softness of her forehead, and the bloom of her lips. But her features had a strange fixity that gave them greater age, pride, and strength. They had simultaneously the brilliance of a flower and the imperious immobility of a mask. The flowing silk in which she was dressed was of harsh blue, strong crimson, and fiery yellow. There were so many broad, thick silver necklaces round her throat and so many heavy bracelets on her arms and ankles that she seemed to be wearing armor. In the crook of her elbow lay a gun as splendid as the chief's.

High on their enormous Bactrian camels the man and woman had long ago seen the horsemen standing right in the middle of the road, on the very top of the ridge. Yet nothing in the attitude of either showed this. They let their hump-backed mounts go on at the same pace. Their faces remained motionless. They did not turn their eyes to one another.

Uraz played the same game. He gave the appearance of not seeing the two huge animals coming toward him, already so close that the smell of their henna-soaked coats pricked his nostrils and tiny wind-borne drops of their slaver wetted his forehead. He did not suppose for a moment that his pretense would be believed. In a game—and this was the basic, mortal game of dignity and honor —likelihood was of no importance, provided the rules and customs were strictly observed. That was why he waited, rigid and motionless, like a statue set up in the middle of the road, gazing fixedly at the narrow space that separated the two Bactrian camels, master of his muscles, his mind, and his nerves to such a degree that he could forbid them all movement, thought, or reaction. The only thing by which he felt the beat of life and time was the regular throbbing— pain's pendulum—in his broken leg: stab, lull, stab, lull.

Suddenly the space between the two huge beasts closed. Before his eyes Uraz had a kind of hairy wall—the chests of the two animals side by side. Above him spoke a harsh, toneless voice. "Peace be with thee!" it said.

Only then did Uraz raise his head: his slit eyes met those of the man with the scar—very large, deep eyes, the color of lava. He replied, "Peace be with thee, chief of a powerful tribe. And through thee upon the whole of thy people."

Uraz had made no reference to the woman of the highway, sitting there as lofty as her husband with a gun in the crook of her arm, on an equally prodigious mount, decorated with even greater splendor. And he turned his face from her as much as he could in order to make it quite clear that he did not acknowledge her existence. If the great nomads chose to treat their women as equals Uraz could do nothing about it. But a chapandaz, the son and grandson of chapandaz, could not humiliate his people's law and lay it at the feet of these camels—creatures painted like a pair of whores.

The Pathan prince was silent. The vast uproar of the caravan, its innumerable discordant cries, battered Uraz's ears. His fever was rising. His wound hurt atrociously. He had difficulty in keeping Jahil still.

Something very hard drove suddenly into his ribs on the right-hand side and made him turn his body in that direction. This brought him face to face with the woman with the gun, who sat astride her scarlet leather saddle, dominating him by the whole height of her mount. Carelessly she put her gun back in its usual place, the crook of her arm.

"She struck me with the butt," said Uraz to himself. It called for a shocking effort not to betray his rage. Perched so high and protected by her camel's reptilian neck she was out of his reach, even with his whip. Honor required that as he could do nothing he should set himself above the insult by indifference.

So he did. And the woman with the gun—her voice was harder than her husband's and loaded with arrogance—asked him, "What art thou doing here, drinking our dust?"

Uraz spun Jahil about so roughly that he showed the mistress of the caravan his rump. It was to the Pathan chief that Uraz spoke. "I am waiting for my road to be free," he said.

As though he did it in spite of himself, the great nomad glanced at the enormous horde of animals and men advancing, spreading, flooding the valley; then his eyes came back to Uraz and he said, "On seeing us, then, why didst thou not take the only road open to thee, the lower path at the foot of the mountain?"

"My path always follows the ridge road," said Uraz.

A mauvish tinge colored the edges of the scar on the face of the tribal chief. "Dost thou claim . . . ?" he said. Without finishing or turning his head he swung his arm to point out the mass behind him, the mass of his flocks and armed men. "I do not even need the warriors," he said. "I march on, and in a moment thou and thy horse are no more than scraps of flesh and bone."

"Truly thou canst do so," said Uraz. "And that indeed is why thou shouldst let a single unarmed man go by."

"On the ridge road?" asked the great nomad.

"Am I not on it already?" replied Uraz.

The chief's wife stiffened her back. Like two shields her breasts rounded the silk of her garment. Her bracelets and silver necklaces jingled. "Thou hast listened to him too long," she cried to her husband. "If he is mad, let Allah take back his remains."

The eyes of the great Pathan, fixed on Uraz, still had the color of lava. "Thou hast one instant and one only to leave the road," said the master of the tribe.

But then an irresistible wave of movement confused everything all round him. The camel men of the vanguard, marching two by two close to their chief and his wife, had seen why they stopped and understood. And they had followed their example. Those who came behind, without knowing the reasons of the men in front, had also halted their beasts. But because of the distance and the lie of the land the great mass of the caravan, spread right across the valley, could not know that the front rank had come to a halt. The camel men, the riders, and the men on foot carried steadily on. The shepherds and dogs still urged the flocks forward. One wave piled up behind the other. At last the tide reached the two Bactrian giants.

They resisted. Their masters had not signaled to them to move on and they were too proud of their strength, their size, and their office to yield to the pushing of inferior beasts. Gripping the road with their huge elastic suckerlike feet, leaning back with all their weight and strength against the pressure that built up against them, they succeeded in holding it back. The state of balance lasted for some moments, those very moments in which the chief of the great nomads finished speaking with Uraz. Then under the perpetually increasing thrust the two huge camels began to give ground. The flow was stronger than they.

It shifted their grip on the dusty earth, and inch by inch they began to slide toward the horse and its rider, standing there in front of them. Pushed from behind, shouldered, rubbed, pricked by metal and leather ornaments and plumes, harassed by innumerable little bells, their understanding became incapable of receiving their riders' orders. A furious roaring, a flood of slaver flowed from their drawn-back lips.

This primitive rage called for an object. None could suit it better than the dwarfish animal and man, ridiculous obstacle fit to be trodden down, trampled into mess, paste that should vanish into the dust of the road. They took a step toward the horseman.

Jahil's reaction was faster than Uraz's thought. The stallion hated the two monsters. Their strange smell of henna, their bells and feathered crests, their drooling slaver that wetted him, their stubbornness in not letting him go by—everything had warned his instincts against them from the first moment they met. When they decided to attack, Jahil moved first. In its strength and harshness his neigh drowned the voice of his enemies. At the same time he drew back for a pace to give himself more room, reared, and charged. This creature suddenly upright before them, his challenging roar of fury, and his speed so astonished the Bactrian monsters that it threw them off their balance. They had no time to get under way before the leaping stallion was on them. In spite of their size and weight they took fright and started away from one another. To Uraz, lying over Jahil's neck with his head buried in his mane, it seemed as though he saw a gap opening in a wall covered with thick, dark moss. The stallion hurled himself into it. Uraz's legs scraped against swollen, hairy sides, and a pain so unbearable rose from his broken bones that it gave him a longing for death. When he saw that a line of camels, each pressed tight to its neighbor, barred his way, he thought, "What of it? If they kill me, at least it will be on the ridge road."

Faced with a huge, close-packed herd that he could not possibly thrust through or pierce, Jahil reared once again. The nearest animals recoiled. The rank behind them did the same. And the one after that. There was a moment's balance between the opposing thrusts.

The stallion let himself fall back to the ground. His breath was short and harsh, his eye wild. There was no longer room to wheel, to fight. One step in front of him was the mass of camels whose anger was rising fast. On either side were the huge Bactrians, so close that he could hear fury rumbling in their bellies. Together, Uraz and Jahil felt that the moment of being smothered and crushed was upon them.

The bandage had been torn off Uraz's broken leg, the lower part of his breeches ripped. The broken bone and the putrid flesh lay bare. The prince of the great nomads gazed at them thoughtfully. "A man in thy state is no rival," he said to Uraz. "Pass! I spare thee because of thy wound."

"And I for thy stallion," said the woman with the gun. "Pass . . ."

The chief turned, shouted an order, and set his huge mount in motion. The camel that carried his wife moved on at the same pace. Their bells rang out. The dust of their going rose as high as Uraz's neck. And Jahil went straight forward, along the narrow pathway that opened before him between the lines of camels as the chief's order was repeated back and back to the farthest parts of the caravan. He followed the ridge road.

"Lift me up," said Zereh to Mukhi.

The tumult up there, along the road, had hidden Jahil and Uraz from them. When the caravan moved on once more they knew nothing whatever of their fate.

Mukhi raised her above his head with ridiculous ease—lifted this body so rich, so loaded with delights. In the dust and the rays of the declining sun, Zereh saw a kind of furrow run through the mass of the caravan, and in its midst, opened by a horseman who traveled in the opposite direction to the flocks.

"It is he for sure," said Zereh. "He has gone by the ridge road."

"He would never have borne anything else," said Mukhi.

With a movement as unexpected, supple, and quick as that of an angry cat, the young woman plucked Mukhi's fingers from her waist and slid to the ground along his length. Under her rounded, stubborn forehead, anger darkened her eyes. "Thou art very proud of him, art thou not?" she cried. "Even if the horse is lost."

"But Jahil is safe, since Uraz is riding him," said Mukhi.

"It is not over yet," cried the young woman. "He has not gone through half the caravan."

"Then we must go with him," said the syce.

Zereh did not hesitate for long. The couple that had filled her with holy terror were far away, hidden in the dust. Now men and women were passing by, people whose clothes, duties, and behavior made them less dreadful. And with them came the main body of the flocks. Zereh was as accustomed to animals as Mukhi. They plunged into the wooly flood.

It was a long voyage. It was all very well for them to know by instinct and experience the quickest, liveliest way of sliding between the rumps, shoulders, and heads of animals on the march and to dodge kicking feet, biting teeth, and stabbing horns—for all that they were sometimes stopped by an impenetrable wave, sometimes carried along by the force of a current. The dogs chased them. The mounted shepherds threatened them with their whips. They made their way in sudden darts, following a broken line, submerged in dust and uproar. Yet gradually the flocks thinned out. This was the rearguard of the caravan. Mukhi and Zereh could go faster, running between the stragglers. They reached Uraz just as Jahil came out into the open.

There, as though by instinctive agreement, the stallion, the syce, and the little nomad stopped and drew the evening air deep into their lungs. Emerging from that animal stream, all three of them needed a pause to recover their sense of being on solid ground. And behind them they heard the dying roar of the flood-like caravan.

"By Allah the Merciful," whispered Mukhi. "Look, Zereh . . . Oh look at his leg!"

The young woman gazed at the round, gaping mouth of the wound, its inflamed, torn lips, and the pus and blood that oozed from it. "The rubbing against the beasts," she said.

"Canst thou do something for him directly?" asked Mukhi.

"I can," said Zereh.

The syce made as if to tell Uraz, but Uraz, making an effort to move the bloodless lips—his face was hollowed to the bone—said, "I heard." And pushed Jahil on.

At the end of the day they reached a caravanserai lying somewhat off the road, with the bend of a stream running around three sides of it. On the fourth it leaned against the side of a steeply rising hill. It was a massive, thickset building, far less spreading than that in which the scribe blinded by Abdurrahman had written Uraz's will; on the other hand, it was well-kept and solid. Two torch-carrying bachas received the travelers in the courtyard, and after the usual greetings the elder asked Uraz, "Wilt thou sleep with all the rest, or in a separate place with thy servants?"

"I wish to be alone," said Uraz, speaking with difficulty. "I and my horse."

The bacha took Jahil by the bridle and led the newcomers through the common sleeping room. It was strikingly clean and had none of the disorder that was usual in such places. The muleteers were all together, the goatherds were all together, and the camel drivers also. Their animals surrounded them in clearly defined rings. The men traveling alone or on foot or mounted, the craftsmen with their tools, they too had a place of their own. The groups were lit by paraffin lamps with clean glass shades. Then came a broad corridor. On each of its sides opened a domed cell, big enough for several people and tall enough for a horse. Near the entrance stood a trough full of water and a rack full of hay. Against the far wall trusses of straw to lie on.

When Uraz was stretched out on one of them the harsh light of a lamp hung in the corner showed the full horror of his wound. The stench that arose from it made the bacha recoil. Zereh whispered to Mukhi, "Ask him for boiling water and clean rags."

The syce obeyed. A little nomad woman could not give orders even to the youngest servant in a caravanserai. The dust that covered Uraz's face had turned it into a mask of clay. Zereh washed his wound and opened her bag. Instead of thrusting her hand into it, she darted it back. The whip that Uraz never dropped had lashed her arm.

"No more ointments, no more herbs, no more powders," said the clay mask with the dead eyelids, scarcely opening its lips. Uraz's hissing voice, hardly distinguishable, ordered, "Bacha . . . black tea . . . very strong . . . very sweet . . . at once." The little servant left at a run. "Mukhi . . . Tomorrow, at dawn . . . Tighten my leg. Now . . . She and thee . . . outside."

The syce and Zereh found the bacha in the corridor, flattened against the wall, listening. "Tell me, tell me," he asked Mukhi in a whisper, "He is not going to die? It would be the first time here . . ."

"No, I promise thee," said the syce. "He is only very weary after a very hard day. The tea will revive him."

"We always have two samovars, boiling and ready," said the bacha. They had reached the general room. Now there was only one light burning. For the most part men and beasts were already asleep in their due order and place on the clean floor.

"The master of this place," said Zereh, "has a head on his shoulders."

"Oh, as for him," said the bacha, "he is not much older than I am. His mother, the widow, runs everything."

Mukhi and the girl stood there, poised above the sleep of the men and their animals. Unconsciously the syce swung his big body from side to side; it was tormenting him again . . . Only that night, in the doorway of the great vaulted room with its hushed murmur, it was not so much Mukhi's awkwardness and size that irked him, but rather an impatience whose nature he dared not acknowledge. He moved uncertainly toward the corner where the solitary travelers lay and said to Zereh, "Shall we go and sleep?"

She said nothing. Mukhi found that he had to go on. And his voice seemed false and lying when he said, "Thou art surely dead with weariness . . . Come."

The young woman dug her nails into the syce's wrist and led him outside without a word. They came into the outer courtyard. The lantern hanging above the porch shed a feeble light. Zereh pressed her bosom against Mukhi. "Tall syce," she said, "my tall syce, I have been waiting all day long."

She started back. A sharp, determined woman's voice in the silent gloom said, "Enough!" The voice seemed to come out of the wall of the caravanserai. In it, above the lantern, Mukhi and Zereh discovered a long, narrow window, once a loophole. The smoky gleam of the wick dipped in melted mutton fat showed them, deep down in the slit, a shapeless being wholly covered with floating black cloth, a garment that ended in a cowl. Only the eyes could be seen, and they shone in the ghostly light.

"A spirit, Zereh!" whispered Mukhi.

"Never fear," she whispered back, "It is only the mistress of the caravanserai, the widow . . . On the watch."

The voice under the cowl spoke again. "There is no room in my house," it said, "for shamelessness. Go elsewhere!"

Mukhi drew Zereh hurriedly toward the courtyard gate. She turned back on the threshold and made a three-fingered sign in the direction of the shapeless black figure, a sign of exorcism and insult, and between her teeth she muttered, "Cholera strike thee, foul old prude, wearing a chadar even in the night! Cholera strike thee, old witch, dying with jealousy of women young enough to be loved."

Outside, a bitter icy wind made Zereh shiver in her rags. Mukhi opened his chapan, wrapped the girl in one of its skirts, and clasped her to his side again. His shirt was as tattered as the little nomad's dress. Their skins touched through the holes. They walked straight ahead of them, stumbling as they went. The only light they had was that of the stars. The stream that ran half around the caravanserai only stopped them for a moment. Mukhi picked Zereh up and crossed it in a single stride. He held her crushed against his chest and plunged on into a thicket of close-set bushes. Thorns clawed them. They were quite unaware of it. Presently there were no more brambles and under his feet Mukhi felt the spring of grass. The clearing was just the length and width of a human body. Zereh clasped her hands around Mukhi's neck, her legs around his waist, and with astonishing strength she pulled him down to this mossy, frost-soaked bed.

Afterwards, in the gentle peace that filled them, they were both confusedly aware that their relationship was no longer quite the same. There was their desire for one another and the extreme pleasure they derived from it; but now trust, sensual friendship, and safety were added. Their happiness was without blemish.

The cold wrenched them out of it. They would not yield to it at first. The warmth of their tight-pressed sides and interwoven legs was so strong that it spread all over the rest of their bodies. Zereh gently ran her fingers over Mukhi's chest, stopping where she found the holes in his shirt. Then, her desires appeased, for the first time in her life she experienced a feeling of which she was not herself the object. As she touched this bare skin, she was laying her hand on the injustice of the world.

"Why," Zereh asked herself with so vast and tender a pang that it made her feel almost dizzy, "Why have men so managed it that the best among them has rags for his whole earthly fortune, and that others . . ." Suddenly, in a very calm voice, Zereh said, "Thou must have that horse."

Mukhi, paying less attention to Zereh's words than to gentle movements of her hand, replied easily, "Jahil will not be mine before Uraz dies."

"Why?" asked Zereh.

"The will," said Mukhi.

"What will?" cried the young woman. "Tell me quickly. I must know everything."

So Mukhi told how and where Uraz had had his testament drawn up. While he spoke Zereh, so as to hear better, drew away from him. When the tale was done the syce and the girl felt their bodies, no longer touching, flayed by the cold.

They both stood up at the same moment. And Zereh said, "Dead or alive, it scarcely matters. We shall find a way of taking the horse."

"Without the will I should be punished," said the syce.

"Why shouldst thou be taken?" asked Zereh.

"Everyone knows that stallion worthy of the Prophet," exclaimed Mukhi.

"Everyone? But where?" asked Zereh.

"Everywhere," said Mukhi. "At Meimana and at Mazar-i-Sharif . . ."

The girl gave a short, affectionate laugh and said, "For thee, the whole world is in those steppes at the back of beyond." She stopped laughing. Her teeth chattered with the cold. Mukhi took her under his chapan again. "It is long, long and broad, the Afghan land," went on Zereh. "And every valley is a country to itself . . . Come, tall syce, we can go from one to the other until the end of our days without anyone ever recognizing thee or the stallion."

"No . . . I beg thee, I should be too afraid without the will," said the syce.

Zereh stroked his hand as though he were a frightened child. "We shall take the paper too," she said.

"And how shall we live?" asked Mukhi in a low voice.

"Thou wilt win races," said Zereh.

"There is no buzkashi except in our country," said Mukhi.

The girl laughed again and slid her hands between the cloth and the shoulder that warmed her. "There, thy steppes again," she said gently. "There are other games on horseback besides buzkashi. And with that mount a horseman like thee will always be the best . . ." She fell silent for a moment and added, "Thou wert like a prince, back there at the chaikhana." Because of this mental image she felt herself go weak and soft with desire; but she overcame it. Afterwards, afterwards . . . When they were alone, free . . . When they had the horse. "Let us go back," she said.

Mukhi took her up in his arms again, and while he was making his way out of the thicket, striding over the water and walking up to the caravanserai, she whispered, "With a horse like that we need good clothes, so as not to be suspected. Thou art strong. I am clever. We will work at some little trade—any little trade. We will save a few afghanis. The clothes will soon come. Then . . ." Zereh pushed so hard against his muscular chest that she seemed to be wanting to hollow out a nest for her forehead. "Then attend, attend to me, tall syce," said the girl, and her words had the hot eagerness imparted by telling a dream dreamed long and passionately. "Attend to me. If thou goest from this place toward the setting of the sun, after days and days thou comest to the Hazarajat. It is a great free land of mountains and open plateaus. There are no roads for wheeled things there. In the very middle, high, high up, lie pasturelands that have no equal in the world for beauty. I have never seen them, but I know, I know." The shape of the caravanserai loomed up vaguely in the darkness. "Stop: wait until I have finished," said Zereh to Mukhi. He held her tighter and bent his head down toward her burning mouth. "In those parts," she went on, "there is no one for half the year. Everything is covered with snow. But in the spring the grass rises up, fresh, thick, and green—a delight to the heart. Suddenly there are flowers. And they cover the mountain side until the depth of the summer. There the caravans come in, one after another, week after week. Pathan caravans like the one we saw today, which was going back to its own country because it is autumn now. Yes: every year the great nomads lead their flocks, their numberless flocks, into the Hazarajat for pasture. And when they are all there together— listen, tall syce, listen—then there is an enormous fair. The tribes all so proud and fine in their holiday clothes . . . Fifty, a hundred thousand, I cannot tell how many, with their tents, their carpets, their precious weapons. And the lute players, the tabor players, and the dancers delight the whole assembly. And we shall be with the great nomads too. Not poor at all, not fearful. In our fine new clothes, mounted on the finest horse in the world, with me riding pillion behind the biggest, strongest, best of horsemen—everyone will envy us . . . "

Zereh's voice, smothered and at the same time intensely eager, sounded right against Mukhi's bare chest—bared by the holes in his shirt—and it seemed to him that it came from inside his own body. He was in such a hurry to give Zereh this wonderful city of tents that he put her suddenly down, bent, and said in her ear, "Let us fetch Jahil."

Zereh took his face between her two hands and drank in his breath until they staggered.

IN THE COURTYARD OF THE CARAVANSERAI THE LANTERN WAS GIVING less light and more smoke. There was very little melted fat left. Mukhi and Zereh cast a furtive glance at the old loophole, and then they breathed more freely. The space was empty.

"And when we lead Jahil out, what if the noise brings the widow?" whispered Mukhi.

"Thou shalt say thou art going to wash the horse in the stream, at thy master's command," whispered Zereh.

Very quickly, without a sound, they passed through the common sleeping place: they stopped on the threshold of the cell where Uraz was lying. He had not stirred. His face was still a death mask.

"See to the horse," said Zereh, scarcely parting her lips. "As for the will, mine is the lighter hand."

Mukhi untied Jahil and made him stand. The stallion gave the faintest snort and licked his syce's cheek. Zereh leaned over Uraz and ran her fingers over his body, fingers so slim and delicate that they seemed incorporeal. She touched a paper folded in two; the tips of her nails grasped at it. Upon this, in an undertone, the mask said, "To have it, thou must kill me first."

Zereh darted her thieving hand to her mouth, to stifle the cry that was on her lips. Mukhi held himself up by Jahil's mane. His knees were yielding under him.

"Tether Jahil again and stay by his side," said Uraz to him. "First thing in the morning, thou shalt see to my leg. Let the whore get out. At once."

Zereh fled. Before he let himself drift into sleep at last, Uraz felt as clear-minded and pitiless as he was in the opening moments of a great buzkashi.

*****

14

Thunderbolt and Flail

THE SUN reached the middle of the sky. They had been traveling since dawn, traveling easily. The road had risen all the time, but in an even slope, through clumps of poplars, little fields of wheat and beans, and sometimes vineyards. There was water in abundance. The ground was hatched with a gleaming network of streams, books, rills, and rivulets. Even in the rocky places the grass grew happily and thick. The houses were gathered into hamlets now, and they met more and more people. These men going along the road were grave and kindly. They greeted the travelers with words and movements of the hand. Some stopped to call down Allah's protection on the proud horseman and his faithful servant.

Their praise overwhelmed Mukhi with guilt. Even before that, as they left the caravanserai, after he had washed the earthy crust from Uraz's face, cleaned and dressed his wound, binding the broken bone between two splints without the pain producing the slightest groan, Mukhi had cried out in his heart, "Forgive me, forgive me, son of Tursen! A devil in me wished to rob thee and leave thee there without defense." And now over and over again he repeated, "I thought him uncurable, lost for sure, because I coveted his stallion. I was a murderer . . . Oh never, never again, by Allah shall I even in thought lay a hand upon the man who gave me Zereh!"

Often, looking over his shoulder, Mukhi gazed at the nomad. She was walking with her head deeply bowed, and because of this her forehead, under the rag that covered her hair, seemed even more rounded, stubborner still.

And so they went until the evening. Then they came to the gorge that the Bamian River had cut out since the dawn of time, and there they stopped; they could not tell the nature of their feelings.

The whole world was suddenly on fire. It was not so much the rays of the setting sun glancing down the length of the prodigious cleft that caused this blaze but rather the color of the rock itself. From top to bottom and on every side was redness: red walls rising sheer, with the river foaming and singing between them; red colonnades, pediments, porticoes, reliefs, and clefts. Every ridge, every fold, blazed and gleamed with brilliant red, scarlet, and crimson. Where the rock wall was smooth, flames leaped from it, as though reflected from enormous mirrors hung above the water and set deep in an all-consuming fire. And the tremendous ruins of the ancient fortified city that overhung the gorge, high on a rocky pedestal and built from its own glowing substance, had the appearance of a pyre that had blazed through all past time and would continue to do so for all time to come.

"Allah! O Allah!" said Uraz.

"The Omnipotent!" cried Mukhi.

"The Merciful!" murmured Zereh.

In spite of everything that set them apart, they felt the same emotion, and a very strange one. This was not a dread to crush the bowels or freeze the blood, this apprehension that made them hold their breaths yet spared their hearts. It was like a kind of dizziness, a whirling of the spirit so dazzling that they feared it and yet at the same time longed for it to go on forever.

"Allah! O Allah!" said Uraz again.

And Mukhi, "The Omnipotent."

And Zereh, "The Merciful."

They spoke all together once more, for—chapandaz, syce, or nomad girl—they were all made of the one clay, and they needed Him who had worked that clay to defend themselves against the outer world.

Uraz could not bear the spectacle for more than a moment. He set his stallion onto the track worn by innumerable feet and hoofs between the foam-colored water and the flame-colored rock.

Rising continually, they traveled along by the racing stream, the waterfalls, whirlpools, and rapids. The sparkling river deafened them with its triumphant song. The heavenly blaze traveled with them as they went. At last the slope grew less steep and the river more smooth. The flaming rock walls stood wider apart. All at once the Bamian Valley appeared.

On its threshold the travelers stopped once again. This time their surprise was pure delight. A vast oasis—almost unbelievable at a height of close on ten thousand feet—was spread out before them. It was all crisscrossed with the quicksilver of water channels, all shining green with woods of deciduous trees, copses, gardens, and orchards, all sprinkled with hamlets. Far away on the left and softened by the evening light, wild mountains rode up to the sky. On the right, against the track, the crimson cliff rose on and on.

Flocks went by, following their shepherds, and caravans moving above at the untroubled pace of their camels to meet the night and to camp. Smoke began to show houses hidden among the trees. Above one deeper patch of green rose a thicker cloud. From these two signs the travelers saw that the village of Bamian lay close at hand. At once they felt quite destroyed by the long road's weariness. They were seized with a longing for a place for the night. Yet a little farther on they stopped again.

In the towering wall under which they were making their way —a sheer, smooth rock the color of clearest blood—they found an enormous opening. This cleft was no chance natural formation, but the work of men. Its shape was that of a cube with a kind of cupola above it. At the far end, with dimness behind, a colossal being stood. His size was greater than the height of three watch-towers, set one on top of the other. His body filled the entire sheltered space; his head the whole of the cupola. The oval of the head was smooth and gentle, and it was faceless. The face had vanished, as though cut off. Nevertheless it seemed that the forehead was living and thinking in the light and shadow of the niche.

From the tales that storytellers, travelers, and those who went with caravans had told from century to century, Uraz, Mukhi, and

even Zereh knew that there were prodigious monuments at Bamian, raised for a former god by the name of Buddha. But after so
much weariness and so many trials this gigantic being terrified
them. A horseman was a mere trifling insect beside that mass in the
blazing rock.

"Allah, Allah alone is the truth!" cried Uraz.

"Truly, truly it is so!" said Mukhi and Zereh together.

A few moments later, behind a screen of poplars, they found
the village. The houses, mud-walled whitewashed cubes, stood
along the road. They sheltered craftsmen's stalls and humble
shops. The best was used as an inn. It had more space to offer and
more ease than the common chaikhanas.

Uraz had a place for himself alone and Jahil a corner in the
stable. "Let my stallion be watched over as though he were a
prince," said Uraz to the man of the house.

He went to sleep instantly, wholly. This safety in sleep was too
precious for even a minute of it to be wasted. It would be long
before he experienced it again.

The syce found Zereh squatting against the wall of the inn,
where the veranda ended. Against the whitish background of the
mud wall she was no more than a very small brown patch. Mukhi
sat down next to her without touching her. Dark forms passed
slowly by. In the next door house a phonograph with a horn,
playing its loudest, roared out a heart-rending, monotonous song,
broken by the scratches on the old record.

"I have seen the stable," whispered Zereh. "There is a tall
bacha lying by the horse. We will not try tonight."

"Nor the next, nor any, any other night," said Mukhi.

"Art thou so afraid?" murmured Zereh, "because yesterday we
did not succeed?"

In the darkness she could see that Mukhi was shaking his head
desperately. "The stolen horse would bring me misfortune," he
said.

For an instant Zereh slid her hand under the sleeve of Mukhi's
chapan, stroked his arm, laughed gently, and said, "I know all the
masterwords against the evil chance."

"No, no, the Prophet be my witness!" cried Mukhi. And shut
his mouth, frightened by the clamor of his voice.

"Calm thy heart, I beg thee, tall syce," said Zereh. "Why worry so? Of us two I know very well who decides and gives the orders. Not I, truly. I am only a woman."

Mukhi believed these words and drew comfort from them. Never had his love been so strong and humble.

Zereh went to sleep in the serving-women's quarters and the syce on the straw of the stable. A powerful young fellow lay between him and Jahil. Mukhi was happy to see him there.

The moonlight ran along the cliff of the Buddhas. In the depths of the niches, those great holes of blackness, the vague forms of the colossal statues showed faintly. In the next-door house the same scratched record still turned on the loud-horned phonograph.

MUKHI ROSE WITH THE DAWN. THE AIR OF THE HIGH PLATEAUS WAS all freshness, strength, and purity. The syce washed in one of the countless irrigation canals through which the river fertilized the oasis. The icy water was as sharp and clean as the air. At that very moment the crest of the red cliff burst into a brilliant glow. Mukhi said his prayer with a direct and easy faith. Allah's grace and the beauty of the world were beyond encompassing.

He felt a yearning for tea and wheatcakes and hurried to the kitchens. At this early hour he expected to find no more than a single bacha stretching himself and yawning by a new-lit fire. He was astonished to discover all the inn's people, men and women, hard at work. Some were stuffing the great copper samovars with live coals. Others were kneading dough and rolling it out. Others were setting crockery on trays. And others were cooking mountains of rice and hills of cakes, cutting open muskmelons and watermelons, filling bowls with curds, baskets with grapes and almonds, breaking eggs and beating them, cleaning poultry, cutting out rounds of meat and mutton fat and threading them on skewers.

"Today is the great market," shouted a bacha in Mukhi's ear. "It takes place twice a week."

"Truly, truly," said Mukhi.

The confusion of voices, laughter, orders, and oaths, the tin-
kling of cups, the clashing of pots and frying pans, the sizzling of
hot fat, the singing of boiling water, the smell of burning grease
and of spices, all stunned Mukhi and amazed him. He caught sight
of Zereh in the midst of the other women, preoccupied, like them,
with the fever of preparation. While her skillful, nimble hands
were working her avid eyes ran from the meat to the curds, from
the pilaws to the mounds of delicacies. She had never seen such
rich food, or in such abundance. Mukhi did not presume even to
wave. As soon as he had hold of a teapot he went out onto the
veranda.

He was not the first there, either. Pedlars were unpacking their
wares and spreading them out on the cloth that had wrapped them
—old watches, padlocks with enormous keys, delicate, childlike
pottery from Istalif whose ocher, brown or blue glazes showed
lions, goats, cocks, men mounted on horses or dromedaries. There
was also a blind musician tuning his stringed instrument. His
guide, a boy of about ten, was still asleep with his head against a
tabor.

On the ancient road that served the village of Bamian as its
high street, shepherds were driving sheep, goats, asses, and mules
toward the places at either side where they would pen them.
Craftsmen were bringing loads of carpets and cloth on their camels. A family of Jats went by. At the end of a chain a Himalayan
bear followed the chief of the clan. On their shoulders the women
had little monkeys brought from India. And Mukhi marveled at
the sight of all these people flooding in from the hamlets, the
farms, the solitary houses, and the everlasting road to sell their animals, their wares, and their skill at giving pleasure.

The morning wore on. The crowd of sellers and buyers grew
continually. The oasis was losing all its inhabitants to the market.
The stalls, the traveling shops, the heaps of melons and pomegranates, the flocks arranged according to the color of their wool—all
overflowed the village on both the right hand and the left; and on
both sides reached as far as the foot of the great bays cut into the
red rock. Looking from the veranda Mukhi could see an enormous
being in each of them, gradually emerging from the shade. He felt
a shiver run from his neck down to his loins and looked question-

ingly at his neighbors. Not one of them took the least notice of the terrible statues. The dead gods were part of their life.

A bacha ran along the veranda, shouting, "The syce of the finest stallion in the stable! The wounded rider's syce! His master calls him . . ."

In the courtyard Mukhi met Zereh. The little nomad's eyes had the hard, set brilliance peculiar to thieving magpies. "Hast thou seen, hast thou seen," she whispered, "hast thou seen the market? I only had a moment for it. But Allah, what cloth, what combs, what girdles, what necklaces!" She repeated, "O Allah Omnipotent!"

Her longing for the cloths and jewels showed on her face like a torment. The syce, who had never troubled about money in his life, felt guilt for his poverty. Why, why could he not give the girl all these wonders from all these stalls! Without looking at Zereh he said, "I cannot stay any longer."

In Uraz's room there was a stifling reek of decomposition. Uraz himself had fever in his eyes and high on his cheeks. "We are leaving," he said.

"What? Straightaway?" cried Mukhi.

"This minute," said Uraz.

"And the things we are to buy? All we possessed was lost, as thou knowest," cried Mukhi again.

"We shall buy them on the road," said Uraz. "Go and make Jahil ready."

"But it is market day here," said the syce plaintively.

"What market?" asked Uraz.

"A huge market, truly, and splendid," cried Mukhi. "Jats, musicians, storytellers . . ."

Uraz shrugged impatiently. In a curt voice he asked, "Are there any fighting animals?"

"Indeed, indeed there are!" exclaimed Mukhi. "I saw two fighting rams go by—terrible rams. One is called Thunderbolt and the other Flail."

"Thunderbolt and Flail," repeated Uraz. Then he said, "Come and fetch me in time for the first battle."

To the north of the road lined on that particular morning with market stalls soared up the cliff of the Buddhas. To the other side a gentle slope led down to the river. Close to it, where the ground was flat, a primitive kind of semicircular arena had been laid out, its limits defined by upright stakes with thorny branches linking them. Within the half-moon there grew short, soft turf. The straight hedge that closed the far end had a little gate in it. Behind that a few deserted hovels, and hedges of willows, tall reeds, and poplars hid the running water, whose silky murmur could nevertheless be heard. On the roadside, however, there was nothing to interrupt the view, and the slope of the ground made a series of natural steps. Along the barrier itself were spread carpets and heaped cushions for those who were distinguished by their office or wealth.

When Uraz reached the place, riding on Jahil led by Mukhi, a close-packed and eager crowd barred his way. He did not have to ask to be let through. The crowd opened of itself, with the most spontaneous, generous impulse. Hospitality was due to the stranger. To the wounded man, protection. And the master of so beautiful a horse and so upstanding a syce could sit only in one row— the front.

There Mukhi took care to choose a place where Uraz would have his back to the sun; he lifted him out of the saddle, settled him against a pile of cushions, and went to tether Jahil as close as possible.

As was fitting, Uraz expressed his gratitude to the two men who had obligingly drawn aside to make room for him. There was no possibility of mistaking that they were important figures. In the cloth of his garments, the leather of his slippers, the bloom of his spreading cheeks, and the gleam of his graying fan-shaped beard, the man on the left bore all the blessings of great wealth. It had not turned him tyrannous or vain. In his good nature and his unpretentious ways, thought Uraz, he was very like Osman Bey of Meimana, that worthy master of noble horses.

Uraz's other neighbor had spotted, dirty clothes, a bitterly ill-tempered face pitted all over with smallpox, expressionless eyes, and a pointed chin on which stood tufts of dull, meager gray hair, growing in every direction. Yet it was to him that the chapandaz's first acknowledgments were due. His headdress, the green turban allowed only to those who had made the pilgrimage to Mecca, raised him above the wealthiest and most powerful.

"O holy man," said Uraz to him, "be assured that to my far-distant province I shall carry the praises of the Hajji of Bamian who was so kind as to yield his place to a passing horseman."

"On condition that thy corrupted leg allows thee to live that far," said the man in the green turban in a piercing voice. "Look." He pointed a finger toward the sky. Uraz looked up. A huge raven was wheeling very low, just above him. No worse omen could there be. At that moment the syce's head bent over toward Uraz, filling his field of vision.

"Jahil is settled and I am here," said the syce. Uraz's heart grew lighter. Mukhi had intercepted the evil chance. "Hast thou need of anything?" asked the syce.

"Thou hast done what was needed," said Uraz. He turned toward his neighbor on the left and asked, "Wouldst thou tell Uraz, son of Tursen, thy name, so that he may pay it all due honor?"

"I am called Amjad Khan," replied the big man, with kindly majesty.

"I shall remember it all my life," continued Uraz. "And if I speak to thee so late, O Amiad Khan, it is not—Allah be my witness—ingratitude or gross ill-breeding. As thou hast seen, the holy man prevented me . . . in his kindness."

At this everything about Amjad Khan began to laugh silently: his eyes, so shining and soft that they might have been anointed with butter, the florid substance of his mouth and cheeks, the silk that covered his belly, and even the lapis lazuli rosary whose beads ran through his smooth, fat hands.

"Do not pay too much attention, son of Tursen, to the words of Zaman Hajji," he said gently. "Whatever comes into his head, that his mouth repeats directly."

"Mouth of Truth," barked the Hajji.

"Truth, Truth of Ali," cried another voice, a very strange one. It was deep, harsh, and broken, and it came from a ragged man who had come and set himself behind the green turban, next to Mukhi. He was the same height as the syce, but he seemed far taller because of his spectral thinness. His ribs could be seen beneath his rags. A great hooked nose sprang from the bones of his face. "Ali, Ali," cried the strange voice.

Uraz thought that he was calling on the Prophet's son-in-law, the martyred Caliph, as revered in the northern provinces as Mahomet himself. He remembered the mosque with blue domes sparkling in his honor in the midst of Mazar-i-Sharif, the capital of the steppes. And he thought he saw the wonderful swarms of pigeons that settled in thousands on his tomb.

Suddenly he thrust himself violently back into the cushions supporting him. A fluttering of black wings blinded his eyes . . .

The raven settled, croaking, on the head of the man who spoke with the same voice as the bird. His feathers mingled with the blue-black hair that fell to the man's arms. Against this background the bird's claws and beak stood out with extraordinary violence: they were blood red.

"Do not be astonished," said Amjad Khan softly. "His master, Kohzad, paints them with lacquer, to make Ali more beautiful."

"Ali . . . So it is the bird?" asked Uraz.

"What can I say?" said Amjad Khan with a sigh. "Kohzad is persuaded that the spirit of the Caliph breathes in his black bird." Then, lowering his voice, "But look at his thinness, look at his eyes . . ."

"I see: mad with hashish," said Uraz.

"There is not a single line in the Book of Books that forbids the faithful to nourish himself with herbs if he chooses," barked Zaman Hajji.

A cracked laugh and a long croaking answered him. Uraz shuddered. He could not tell which was laughing and which was croaking, the raven or his master.

Now there was a great deal of movement around him. Everyone was getting up and bowing. Amjad Khan did the same. The only men to remain seated were Uraz, because of his wound, and the Hajji, because of his green turban.

A man dressed in European clothes and wearing an astrakhan cap made his way through the crowd—a young man. He had a harsh face and a hard mouth. A uniformed officer of the police followed him.

"At last the chief of the district deigns to appear," said Zaman

Hajji. "This little civil servant makes a pilgrim to Mecca wait! And he does not hurry. He takes his time . . ."

"Why such haste, O holy man?" asked Uraz.

"I am here to gamble," exclaimed Zaman Hajji. Until that moment his features had been dead and dull; now they took on intense life. His lackluster eyes had sparks dancing in them; and because the demons of chance dwelt in Zaman Hajji, Uraz felt more akin to this odious man than to the good Amjad Khan, who went on peacefully counting the beads of his rosary.

The chief of the district sat down next to Amjad Khan. The police officer gave a blast on his whistle. The doors of the ruinous huts on either side of the door into the arena opened. In each of the openings the head of a ram appeared.

THE CHIEF OF THE DISTRICT LEANED TOWARD AMJAD KHAN AND said, "They are well matched and very handsome."

Uraz was of the same opinion. The two rams were of the same size, tall but not over tall; they had the same thick astrakhan fleece, ashy gray with brown streaks in one and bluish patches in the other. Their foreheads were framed by tapering horns that turned in long whorls like coiled snakes. Zaman Hajji tossed his head and said to Kohzad, who was stroking his raven, "They are pampered and lazy."

Uraz did not think him mistaken. As they made their way into the arena by the little gate neither ram attempted to dominate, to thrust the other aside and pass through first. They followed one another, two well-behaved rams. The first to come in was the one whose handler pulled him by the horn. From the crowd, swollen by all those who had deserted the market, good-natured voices called out, "O Gamal, thou art in a greater hurry than thy beast."

"And as for thine, O Ahmad, take care it does not go to sleep in thy lap."

"These rams take the arena for a sheepfold."

"Rams . . . rams . . . Who is certain of that? There are wethers more dangerous."

Gamal and Ahmad, very young men in freshly washed breeches

and jerkins, reddened under their carefully knotted turbans. And each, at the top of his voice, began to cry up the virtues of the animal he had brought.

"The sharpest, the strongest . . ."

"Lord of his flock . . ."

"Unconquerable fighter . . ."

"Back my ram and thou art a wealthy man."

"Mine brings in as many afghanis as he has locks of good wool."

These observations were mere patter. Everyone, including the shepherds, knew it. But the sound of their own voices excited them. They began to believe what they said. Face, body, hands, the folds of their clothes—everything expressed the most ardent conviction. It infected the spectators. They longed to be deceived.

"Begin the fight! Begin the fight!" they shouted.

Bets were already being made. Uraz found himself fingering the bundle of notes deep in the folds of his belt. How many afghanis had he there? He had no idea. He loathed casting accounts. Full pockets or empty pockets were his only landmarks. At all events the crackling wad was of handsome thickness. When Uraz had set off for Kabul, both Osman Bey and Tursen had been generous. Before the great buzkashi he had had neither the wish nor the time to spend anything in the capital. And after . . .

"Which of the two rams wilt thou take?" asked Uraz, speaking to his neighbor on the left.

"Neither," replied Amjad Khan, with an apologetic smile. "They are both mine. I have given them for the people's amusement. If I were to bet they might suppose that I was profiting by my knowledge of the animals or my power over the shepherds."

Then Zaman Hajji's bitter voice was heard, "Dost thou not think, oh stranger, our guest, that a pious man's afghanis are as good as those of the richest Khan?"

Uraz looked at the face under the green turban. In addition to the cupidity he had seen there already, the features and wrinkles now expressed the arrogance of challenge. "He is as eager to humiliate me as to take my money," reflected Uraz. A sudden warmth came into his cheeks. And he felt gambling take on that strange, absolute rule over him that it assumed when it went beyond the idea of winning and became a struggle against another man, a trial of fate.

In the hollow formed by his upper half, propped up by the cushions and his outstretched legs, Uraz scattered a shapeless bundle of notes. Zaman Hajji piously raised his hands to his green turban, and from its folds drew a long wallet made of strong wild silk. He clasped it lovingly between his knees and drew out a heap of hundred-afghani notes, so flat and cleanly folded that they might have been smoothed with a heavy iron. He counted out five, one by one, lined them up on the carpet of honor that he shared with Uraz, and asked him, "Does the stake suit thee?"

Beside the Hajji's money Uraz put down notes so crumpled that they might have been waste paper. When he had unfolded it and counted it, Zaman Hajji found there was a little excess of small change and he handed it back to Uraz. Without turning, Uraz passed it over his head to Mukhi, saying, "Amuse thyself."

The shepherds had finished marching round. Gamal led his ram to the right of the arena and Ahmad to the left.

"Who has the choice of the beasts?" asked Uraz.

"The guest," replied Zaman Hajji, bowing his green turban.

"I thank thee," said Uraz. He would willingly have done without this civility: he knew nothing whatever about the rams. He pointed to the animal held by Gamal, merely because he saw it on the right, the noble side.

The district chief raised his arm. Ahmad and Gamal put their hands on their animals' hindquarters and thrust them toward the middle of the arena. The rams walked out to meet one another, pacing very slowly, along an absolutely straight line. It was as though in the hollow of his lowered head each had a magnet that drew his opponent toward him. Those in the same row as Uraz with a side view of the animals' heads could see the eyes deep in the wool, and in those eyes appeared a settled, stupid rage, first spark and then fire.

"No wickedness in those creatures . . . No interest in the game," thought Uraz. He leaned back on his cushion. There was no chance that his stake would either ruin or enrich him: only one amusement remained—that of foreseeing and accurately predicting the phases of the battle.

"Now the challenge," he said to himself. At that very moment the rams came to a stop, raised their heads, and stared at one another, their eyes blazing with anger of the most primitive kind.

"Now the attack," he said again. The thought was not wholly in words before the rams charged.

An inner spring, astonishing in its power, suddenly raised up these slow, heavy creatures, thickened, hampered, made bulky by their enormous fleeces. The line of charge was as straight and direct as that of a bullet. The lowered heads did not vary from it by the breadth of a hair. The meeting, in full flight, was a brow-to-brow collision.

The air rang with it. In its harshness and strength the impact brought to mind the clash of cymbals. The crowd echoed it in a great hoarse growling rumble that climbed the slope row by row, crossed the road, reached the line of red cliffs, and made its way into the huge niches. Like enormous conchs, they hummed at the Buddhas' feet.

By all rights the attack should have crushed the rams' skulls entirely; it only stunned them for a moment. They shook their heads, backed a little, and charged again in a still more furious assault.

"Ugh! Ugh!"

"Ho! Ho!"

The audience groaned and gasped in time with the shattering impact as it was renewed. Uraz took little notice. This stupid rage had nothing in common with courage, intelligence, or imagination. Mere smashers, nothing more. They would use their heads as hammers until the moment one of them collapsed, destroyed. It mattered little which.

Another attack and another and another. There was the continually repeated crack of bone meeting bone. "The stupider they are, the more they hold out," thought Uraz. He would have been happy to see the animal he had backed lose so that another fight could start directly. His eyes wandered to the lines of tall poplars that stood along the Bamian River lower down the slope, from one end of the valley to the other. The next stage would carry them up the stream.

Suddenly his attention came back to the arena. Amid the regular hammering of the two foreheads there had been a missing stroke. Uraz saw why at once. One of the rams had avoided the crash. "Is he perhaps the less stupid of the two?" wondered Uraz. The movement had revived his interest: the animal was the one he had chosen. The other ram, thrown off its balance by this charge into emptiness, stumbled and fell to its knees. "Mine is going to take advantage of its fall, charge it in the side, fling it down . . ." And the people around him and behind him called out what he was thinking. Ahmad, the standing ram's shepherd, encouraged it with voice and gesture. The animal never stirred. Its eyes were turned toward the front row of spectators and they traveled along it from one to another. When they reached Uraz he no longer saw any spark of the savage, murderous fury with which they had blazed. These eyes expressed nothing but dazed stupidity. Its enemy had time to get up: it charged with a fury doubled by its fall. Now, stupefied, amazed, wild-eyed, Ahmad's ram took flight. A deafening uproar of gibes, sarcasms, insults, threats, and curses went with it. In all this din, Uraz, his jaws clenched, heard nothing but the voice of his neighbor in the green turban. It was the loudest, the most insulting, and the most filled with mockery, and Uraz had the feeling that, using the animal's unworthiness as an excuse, this scoffing and these blackguard words were addressed to him.

"A fine breeding stock thou hast! And one which does thee honor indeed," he cried to his neighbor on the left.

Amjad Khan's florid lips remained pursed round the mouthpiece of his nargile. Slowly he let the smoke escape from his mouth, and while it drifted away in the pure air he gently observed, "As for my animals, O horseman of the steppes, I am not concerned with training them to fight to the death. I merely provide them so that the worthy people may be amused. And when the Prophet wills, I succeed. Listen!"

The harsh raillery and insults had suddenly stopped. And an enormous laugh was running from row to row. There were men who hugged their bellies, others who wiped their eyes. Still others beat on the backs of neighbors they did not know at all.

For in the arena the frightened ram was running away. Blindly. In wild, lurching bounds, convulsive leaps, clumsy darts, and heavy galloping rushes. Its wool skimmed the ground. Its fat rump waggled, flapping like a badly fitting sack. Immediately behind it charged the other ram. More than once it was on the verge of reaching its victim. But each time panic shot the fugitive out of reach. Again and again they went right around the arena. At last the fleeing ram saw the open door—the door that had been open for a long while and that it had brushed past several times without noticing. The ram darted through and vanished.

AMJAD KHAN TOOK THE MOUTHPIECE OF HIS NARGILE AGAIN. BEFORE carrying it to his eager mouth he smiled at Uraz and said, "It was fury pursuing terror. But the wings of dread are faster. The sight was worth a few afghanis, was it not?"

Before Uraz had time to reply, a clutching hand settled on his thigh. "I think," said Zaman Hajji, "that I may take up the stake."

With a flick Uraz scattered the notes the holy man had folded with such care, sending them toward the Hajji. "Call that a stake!" he cried. "An old woman's alms would enrich thee more, for certain. As for me, I propose a bet that is worth calling a bet." He threw the money he had left onto the grass.

"What . . . What is that?" asked Zaman Hajji in a voice that no longer had its usual confidence.

"My next stake," said Uraz.

As he put away the notes he had won, Zaman Hajji's fingers trembled a little. "There are many, many afghanis there," he said.

"Am I to teach a gambler like thee, O holy man, that the greater the sum, the greater the delight in the match?" His tone and the look in his eye were provoking and insulting. He would have liked to go on in the same way for a long while. But Zaman Hajji no longer heard him. He was wholly possessed by avarice. He spread out, smoothed, stroked the shapeless notes, and counted them in an undertone. The murmur of figures sounded like a litany, a prayer.

"Thirteen thousand, two hundred, and threescore and four," said Zaman Hajji at last, with a deep sigh. He gazed at Uraz. In his eyes was the veil of cupidity and yet at the same time the blaze of desire. "Thou knowest thy stake?" he said.

"I know it and I intend it," said Uraz.

"Thou also knowest," said Zaman Hajji, "that it is my turn to choose the ram?"

"Rules are rules," said Uraz, "and it is the rules that make the game."

Zaman Hajji covered his face with his hands and began to swing his body very slowly to and fro on his crossed legs. Then he cried, "Kohzad, O Kohzad!"

"I am here," replied the croaking voice of the raven's master.

"I await a sign," said Zaman Hajji.

The skull-like face leaned against the raven's head and the bloodless lips moved noiselessly. The raven left Kohzad's left shoulder, walked round his neck, and stopped on his right shoulder.

"Well?" asked Zaman Hajji.

"Judge for thyself, O worshipful," croaked Kohzad.

The holy man waited until his swinging brought him farthest back before he turned his head and shot a look between his fingers. "The right is Allah's favorable reply," he said, in a whining chant. When his body had returned to its natural position he dropped his hands and said to Uraz, "Upon thy own head, presumptuous horseman."

These quiet exchanges had not attracted the attention of the people around Uraz and Zaman Hajji. They were busy settling their lost bets and arranging new ones. Only Mukhi, who had followed every one of Uraz's words and movements, realized the frightening risk his master was taking. "If he loses again, we shall not have an afghani left," thought the syce. "And we still have to buy everything against still higher and emptier mountains!" Mukhi watched the man in the green turban draw the big notes from his wallet one by one and pile them up in front of him in a faultless heap. From his innermost being he cried out, "Oh, Uraz, I beg thee, stop, stop his hands! Cut thy stake by half or at least by a quarter . . ." But he said nothing. He was only a very young servingman. He had no right to make Uraz lose face.

A buzz of voices announced the appearance of the next rams. These had by no means to be led, but rather restrained, otherwise their eagerness to be the first in the ring would have brought them into conflict at the very threshold. Instead of poorly paid shepherds these rams had their own breeders to direct and oversee them, men in the prime of life, tough and dignified. These rams were not newcomers to the arena either; they knew its geography beforehand, its ways and rules. At once of their own accord they hurried to their proper places. One had a deep, white fleece with ink-black patches. The other's was the color of scorched earth and the reddish kemp that ran through it looked like burning twigs.

They were greeted by a general chorus of praise. "Glory to thee, O Flail, and thy merciless stroke," said the crowd to the first. And to the other, "Honor to thee, O Thunderbolt, who dost always crush and beat down, never falling to the ground."

From these tributes Uraz could measure the worth of the two animals and the extent of their shining fame. They had survived years of fighting in the ring. They had stunned and flung down dozens of opponents—had stupefied them, knocked them unconscious, or killed them. Now they were matched for the first time. It was a great day.

The rams delighted in the praise and grew furiously excited. They raised their heads toward the applauding voices; their forefeet scraped the ground.

"Thou dost prefer these creatures to mine, I am sure," said Amjad Khan to Uraz.

And Uraz replied, "Forget, I beg thee, and forgive my burst of ill-bred temper; but admit that thou too wouldst rather see these rams."

"How canst thou tell that?" asked Amjad Khan.

"Thy nargile is forgotten because of them," said Uraz.

Amjad Khan laughed in his fine broad beard. "Thou art right, horseman of the steppes," he said. "Men are so made that even the least bloodthirsty loves a spectacle at which death is a guest. And of these two animals, one will not leave the ring alive. They have too much pride, too much honor to defend."

"Truly," said Uraz. "Thunderbolt or Flail, either is worthy of my stake."

✳✳✳✳✳

15

The One-Horned Beast

THE SHOUTING had stopped. The spectators were arranging their bets. The rams no longer stirred. Under their lowered foreheads, each was studying the other.

Their masters stood beside them. They did not encourage them either by words or caresses—nothing at all. At the most they rubbed their feet from time to time. As they did so the appearance of the fighting rams changed unbelievably. Each body lost its savage tension. The muscles relaxed, gave way in trust and friendship. Of itself each ram raised one foot after another, and before placing it in the asking hand, softly scratched the palm with its rough and horny tip. Then, as gently as a lamb, it laid its head with its coiled horns on the man's shoulder like a tender pledge, and kept it there all the time the skillful fingers massaged its flesh and sinews.

"Well," said Uraz abruptly, turning to Zaman Hajji. "Well, holy man, hast thou fixed on thy choice?"

Neither the rigid profile beneath the tall green turban nor the tight mouth among the bristly hairs stirred in the least. With his sparse little gray beard buried in one hand, his eyes reduced to gleaming slits under the soft overhang of his lids, Zaman Hajji was watching first one ram and then the other with piercing attention, acuity so intense it reached the point of torment.

Thunderbolt or Flail?

They were equal in size, weight, training, and their number of victories: there was nothing in their appearance or stance to give a clear preference. Beyond qualities that could be seen, beyond strength, skill, and speed, he had to seek out, discover by his intuition the secret springs that would decide the match—courage, endurance, strategic cunning, the urge to win.

Zaman Hajji clearly remembered the battles each of these rams had fought up and down the whole valley. His passionate gambler's mind had the most vivid recollection of their fighting powers. But they had never had to display them against one another. So how could one tell? Oh, if only they had met, even a single time! Ridiculous wish . . . With creatures of this rank, this blood, there could be no question of two encounters.

Thunderbolt or Flail?

Flail or Thunderbolt?

So much money depended on the choice. Again and again Zaman Hajji's eyes, sharpened and rendered fanatical by greed, slid toward the stakes lying there within hand's reach, as though to beg them for favorable inspiration. No advice emanated from the notes.

"I am waiting, holy man," cried Uraz. "All the bets have been laid."

Zaman Hajji closed his eyes, and without changing his position called, "Kohzad!"

The skull-like head, shaded by the black feathers, leaned to touch the green turban. Zaman Hajji whispered a few words in its ear. Kohzad passed them on in a muffled undertone to his guardian raven. The bird took to the air heavily and flapped over the arena. Three times it flew around it. The movements of its great wings grew slower and slower, softer and softer. At last it hung motionless in the air immediately over Thunderbolt. Its shadow covered the ram entirely. A bloody sweat seemed to drip from its crimson claws and beak.

"I take Flail," said Zaman Hajji.

The death's-head came away from the green turban. Inch by inch, Kohzad straightened the bones of his long, fleshless body. The raven returned to his right shoulder. Heard by Uraz alone, Mukhi dropped to his knees behind him, and speaking against the nape of his neck begged, "Take back thy money . . . Thou hast the right . . . There has been witchcraft . . ."

The syce's whisper was cut short; Uraz struck him a savage blow in the neck with the handle of his whip.

"The half-wit!" thought Uraz. "Do I not know how to recognize one who casts an evil spell? And thwart his power?" Under his shirt he tightened his grip on the leather amulet he always wore round his neck. He had grasped hold of it the very moment the raven took to the air and he was not going to let go until the end of the match.

It began. The district chief had raised his arm. And the owners of the rams made the same motion, a very slight pause that was at once an order, a message of confidence, and an affectionate caress, sending them toward their fate. Having done so the two men squatted on their heels, their faces blank, their eyes unconcerned.

Thunderbolt came from the right, Flail from the left: they moved toward one another with the greatest caution. Their hoofs felt and gauged the ground. Their low-hung heads swung in a slow, regular rhythm, and their hard, shrewd eyes never for a moment ceased their scrutiny of the enemy's head, chest, flanks, and feet.

There was not a sound from the rows of men. With every step of this approach the spectators could feel the growth of relentless will. Their hearts were filled with the most delightful anxiety.

At last, when they were within about fifteen feet of one another, the rams stopped. The space of time for which they kept their feet still spring-pressed against the ground was so fleeting that no man could conceivably measure it. The impulse of their thighs and loins shot them forward with such fury that the spectators scarcely saw them cross the intervening space—it was as though they heard the crash of heads the moment the rams began their charge. And yet Thunderbolt and Flail had bounced back like two immense woolen balls, to a greater distance than before. And they were gathering themselves for a fresh attack.

The quickest was the ram flecked with the red-brown marks that showed like flames in the sun. He was only one instant and one bound ahead of Flail, but this was enough to give his bulk the advantage in speed and power. When the heads with their splendid triply-rounded horns crashed together, Flail was thrown backward. The crowd uttered its first cry. But the white ram with black patches neither fell nor flinched. He had kept his balance entirely and full possession of his knowledge of the game. Thunderbolt drove in without pausing for breath. Flail leaped to one side. The enemy slid along his flank. Only the wind of the charge stirred his fleece. In his turn he thrust home to surprise and unbalance the enemy he had tricked. In vain. Even before he had come to a stop, Thunderbolt had spun about, fixed his hoofs into the ground, and darted his head back between his shoulders. Flail's forehead met another forehead like his own—it might have been made of stone.

Still sitting on their heels with no emotion showing in their faces, the rams' masters called to them with a long, strangely pitched cry. Thunderbolt and Flail came back to their stations at the men's sides. Each man set about examining his animal's joints. Now while the inspection was still going on Thunderbolt charged. And no man there could tell whether he had obeyed his own instinct or a motion of the fingers buried in the wool. With a foul oath Flail's owner started up and launched his ram with both hands. There was not time enough. Thunderbolt was halfway across the arena. The turf was echoing like a muffled drum under the thud of his hoofs while Flail was still in his first stride. And instinctively Flail knew that in a head-on collision he had no chance whatever. At two paces from Thunderbolt he bounded to the left. But his enemy was not one to be caught twice in the same trap. In full charge and at his utmost speed he swerved and struck, catching Flail on the shoulder. The guttural roar from the crowd's belly seemed to spring up from the impact. The breeze was blowing from the river and it carried the cry to the red cliff, where the niches of the colossal Buddhas sent back the echo.

Mukhi's cheek was against Uraz's and his lips sang, "By the Prophet, it is thine the stronger. Thou wilt win."

With his elbow in his face Uraz thrust the syce back (luck forbade that anyone should speak for it, if it were to remain favorably inclined) and gripped harder on the amulet in his sweat-soaked hand.

The blow that had struck Flail knocked him to the ground and flung him over on his back.

The shouting became an enormous uproar. Uraz had to exert

every effort not to join in. Thunderbolt collected himself, squared himself, and flung himself upon the enemy lying there powerless with his belly in the air . . . It was the deathstroke.

In the same second Flail, with stupefyingly nimble speed, spun twice on himself. The charge shot over the empty turf exactly where the crushed grass was flattened with the imprint of the massive body that had been hurled down on it.

The roaring of the people, violent as ever, changed its object. Flail was up. Flail was racing toward the returning enemy. Neither ram had any advantage in impetus. Their strength was balanced. They no longer tried to dodge. A common rage blazed in their narrowed, bloodshot eyes. And the din of their clashing foreheads was a sound beyond all reason. Yet there they were, unshattered, without having withdrawn a single step, nose to nose. Their masters called them back.

It was clear at once that Flail was moving toward him too slowly. His walk was tottering, his breath came in gasps. Some cried that he had a broken collarbone, others that he had a sprained knee, others that the terrible blow had emptied his lungs of air, and still others that he no longer had any heart for the fight. They were all agreed in predicting that Thunderbolt, faster now and stronger, would win the match.

The first thing Flail did when he reached the man who had bred him, brought him up, and trained him, was to raise a foot, all sheathed in white wool above the hoof, and weakly shake it. He set it on the hand that opened beneath it, then gently pulled it away again.

There was silence among the spectators. When the talk had begun again the voices were hesitant, uncertain. They said, "Is he looking for encouragement?"

"Is he saying farewell to his master?"

"And to life?"

"Is he asking for the fight to be stopped?"

Instead of fixing his eyes on the ram that carried his bet, Zaman Hajji turned his back on him. His livid face was turned to the death's-head behind him. His narrow, feverish lips whispered, "Kohzad! Kohzad! When the bird covered the other ram with its shadow, it did mean that I was not to choose him? It was to tell me of his unlucky star?"

And artlessly Kohzad replied, "How can I read the omens, holy man? I am not the one who has been to Mecca." Humbly, greedily, he added, "But for all that I shall have money for the herb of dreams, shall I not?" All his eyes saw beneath the green turban was a fat and wrinkled nape. Zaman Hajji was no longer thinking of him.

Flail and Thunderbolt set out once more for battle. And then something happened that left the oldest and most experienced lovers of the sport amazed and at a loss. In the middle of the grassy arena Flail, whose step had been weak and heavy, fell on his side and kicked a white-sheathed foot in the air. Taken aback by this sight, the opponent slowed down, and with measured, careful steps, approached the prostrate ram. The white foot stretched out to one of the reddish feet and began to stroke it with a wretched caressing motion.

The audience exploded into a deafening outcry.

"He is asking for mercy!"

"Coward!"

"Traitor!"

"Impostor!" shouted those who had betted on Flail.

And the others, "No quarter!"

"Play it out to the end!"

"Strike!"

"Disembowel!"

"Slay, O matchless Thunderbolt!"

And the first, eager for revenge, joined in with those who thirsted for blood. Uraz too was wholly possessed by that same avid greed, and leaned forward abruptly. At this a pain from his broken leg struck him so unexpectedly and with such strength that he clapped his hand to the place—the hand that held the amulet . . .

At this same instant Thunderbolt drew back a step and lowered his death-carrying head. Simultaneously Flail arched his spine and loins and struck with all his might from below upward, driving in a terrible blow against the muzzle that hung over him. There was the sound of shattering bone and sinew. Flail struck again, and in the same way. His enemy's head swung to and fro as though to escape from unbearable pain. Its lower part was no more than a mess of flesh, blood, and foam. There was no nose left, no jaw. Out of this horrible pulp the great fighting ram uttered a lament as clear, frail, and artless as the bleat of a little lamb. Flail straightened, stepped unhurriedly back for his run, and charged. His forehead struck the moaning, bewildered animal full on the carotid. Thunderbolt staggered but did not fall. It took Flail three attacks to bring him down. When this was accomplished, the victorious ram came back to his master and gave up his white-wooled foot to his care.

In the front row of frenzied spectators Zaman Hajji grasped the notes heaped up at his side and waved them like a trophy. Uraz put his hand automatically to his amulet and then let it fall. Behind them Mukhi was weeping. And over and over again Kohzad said to his raven, "O Ali! The spell-singing herb . . . O Ali! The singing herb . . ."

WHEN THE UPROAR AND TURMOIL HAD CALMED A LITTLE, AMJAD Khan was seen to lean over to the district chief and speak in his ear for a moment: and the chief nodded. "Come near, O Ayub!" he cried.

Flail's master, followed by his ram, came and stood in front of the two great men. There he bowed with deference and dignity.

"The wealthy and noble Amjad Khan and I are of the opinion, O Ayub," said the district chief, "that the usual reward and thy opponent's stake are by no means enough to honor the deserts of a man who has succeeded, as thou hast done, in teaching so much knowledge to an animal. And Amjad Khan grants thee the choice among his flocks—they have not their match in this province—of the two young rams that please thee most."

Ayub set his right hand on his heart and bowed his head very low before Amjad Khan. "As for me," went on the district chief, "I declare and command that from this day forth Flail shall by one and all be called the prince ram of the Bamian Valley."

At these words the fringed ends of Ayub's turban almost touched the ground. For a long space he held himself bent in two.

At length he straightened to his full height and his right hand left his breast to settle on one of Flail's magnificent horns. His eyes were full of happiness. "May Allah be inclined to thee, lord, and to thy sons' sons," he said. "My people will never forget thy high favor."

The audience shouted, "Glory to the prince ram of Bamian! Glory!"

The district chief raised his arm. The shouting stopped. "Then let it be so," he said, "Unless—and it is but justice . . ." He paused, waited for total silence, and continued, "Unless a rival should come forward to dispute the title. Am I not right, Ayub?"

Flail's master tightened his grip on the curving horn under his hand and cried, "Wisdom and justice are in thy words, O lord. My ram asks nothing better than another fight, and for my part I will stake all he has just brought me." Ayub fell silent. A half-smile, made up of confidence and pride, lit up his face. The district administrator turned toward the audience with a questioning gaze. Their mouths remained closed. Not a hand stirred.

"No man in this place takes up the challenge!" said the chief. "I therefore declare . . ." He was unable to finish. A voice rang out from the very rear row. Rough and very bold. It cried, "One moment, if thy lordship allows . . . One moment. I come."

The man made his way through the crowd without difficulty. He was so brisk, so hard-muscled, that the outlines of his body seemed to be sharp-edged. When he reached the barrier that ran round the arena he vaulted over it directly and came to stand by Ayub, whom he topped by a head. Now the spectators could see his face—long, weather-beaten, very deeply lined, with aquiline nose in the middle hooking down over jet-black, thick short hair. The man tightened the full cartridge belt that held a great rough brown cloaklike coat to his gaunt flanks, straightened the long gun with its decorated butt on his shoulder, and said to the chief of the district, "Forgive me, lord, for speaking so late. I was in the row farthest from thee and I thought for certain other men would put themselves forward first."

The administrator looked at the unknown man with a curiosity he was unable to hide. "And just what dost thou desire, stranger?" he asked.

The man with the gun displayed a simple openness that might have seemed genuine had there not been an irreverent spark deep in his eye. "Nothing but what thou hast proposed, lord—to match an animal of my own against the new prince of Bamian."

From all sides rose cries of astonishment, and the chief of the district said, "Truly, truly, traveler, didst thou see Ayub's ram defeat his terrible opponent?"

"Truly, I saw him indeed," said the stranger.

"And dost thou believe thine fit to try conclusions with such a conqueror?" asked the chief of the district again.

The stranger lowered his eyes to his big feet, which a pair of rawhide sandals with pointed, backward-curving toes made look devilish. Modestly he said, "Thou shalt judge of that thyself, lord."

The district chief was not deceived by this feigned bashfulness, and without trying to conceal the sarcasm in his voice he replied, "And where is he, this unknown champion?"

The man looked steadily at the administrator. Boldness and irony still danced in his brilliant eyes. Unmoved, he answered, "I ordered the bacha who is with me to lead my ram to the entrance of this arena."

"Show him to us, then," commanded the district chief.

The man set three fingers to his mouth and whistled a blast so shrill and fierce that every man there, from the front row to the farthest, gave a start. The simple people out of plain surprise. The rich out of fear. The adventurous from a strange kind of delight.

A boy, dressed in the same coarse cloth as the man with the gun, thrust open the wicket into the arena and let go the short rope to which the ram was tied. In a few strides the ram was by his master. At this all the feelings that had been acting on the spectators' minds were reduced to a single emotion: refusal to believe what they saw. The creature scarcely reached the unknown's knee. Its meager, dusty coat was of no clearly defined color. In some places the wool was lacking altogether and cracked pink patches that were the skin showed through, though it was difficult to distinguish. And lastly it had only one horn, that on the left. The other was broken off short close to the skull, so much so that the line of the break could only just be made out in the wool. As the ram rubbed against his leg like a dog, unbelieving eyes ran from the base little creature to the massive Flail, splendidly covered with his black and white coat. The stupefaction grew heavy with anger. Had this stranger come to Bamian to make game of its people? To insult its hospitality? Ferocious laughter and ugly murmurs were heard. Ayub drew Flail some paces off, as though to avoid a contact that might defile him. The voice of the district chief arose, filled with threat and indignation, "What demon, thou unknown man, has urged thee to mock, to insult these good people and, in my person, the king thy sovereign? Dost thou hope that I shall leave this unpunished?"

The man with the gun set his right hand on his heart to show that that was the source of his words. "Mock?" cried he. "Who mocks, then? Could it be I, since I back my challenge with this stake I show thee?" From inside his coat he brought out a rawhide purse, untied its strings, and gave it to the district chief. The chief thrust his hand in and brought it out filled with gold.

"Thou has left more than twice as much behind," said the unknown man.

The chief of the district opened the purse wide, gazed into it, weighed it in his hand, and said in a low voice, "Truly . . ." He raised his eyes to the stranger's face—there was quite a different expression in them—and with a respect that showed through in spite of himself, asked, "What is thy name?"

"Hayatal," said the other.

"Thy province?"

"The high passes of the east, where men know how to forge fine weapons themselves, and to use them well," said the man with the gun.

The chief of the district passed the bag to Amjad Khan, who looked at what it held and nodded his broad beard with its hennaed gleams. With the full power of his voice the district chief cried, "O Ayub, O Hayatal, you shall match your rams." Then he asked Flail's master, "Dost thou maintain thy whole stake?"

Ayub shrugged and growled, "Why should I hesitate? At least I want the shame set on my ram to bring me in as much as possible."

"Go and take thy place again, then; and thou, Hayatal, stand in the other," ordered the chief of the district. "And wait until the end of the betting before you begin."

Now—and it was indeed the first time at any ram fight—there were no bets. Everyone insisted on staking his money on the same side, on Flail. Only a sick mind, said the spectators, only a sick mind could grant the slightest chance of success to this dwarfish, scabbed, tattered, one-horned beast whose master was obliging it to face the prince of fighters.

Zaman Hajji said to Uraz, and his voice was both honey and gall, "Thou too—I quite understand—thou too art afraid to back the stranger . . . For I, in all decency and fairness, I cannot but stay with my winner."

Uraz stared straight in front of him, hearing nothing, seeing nothing. He had the feeling that he was a man struck with the plague, an accursed man. Not because he had lost. But because he had nothing to lose any more.

Mukhi cried, "What more dost thou want, O holy man? Thou and thy raven have taken everything from my master. Everything! Everything!"

Mukhi's lament made a great deal of noise. Amjad Khan turned toward him. The syce's round and almost childlike face expressed the most pitiful distress, utterly undisguised.

"Horseman of the steppes," said Amjad Khan to Uraz, "believe me, I shall be happy to advance thee whatever sum thou wilt do me the honor to name. I shall have no merit in doing so. There is certainty in a loan to one who owns a horse like thine."

In his daze, Uraz did not understand the words. He only felt their generous warmth, and he leaned toward Amjad Khan. Then a huge hand seized him by the elbow and he heard an anguished whisper. "Uraz, by the Prophet, O Uraz, by Allah the Omnipotent, do not bet, oh, do not bet Jahil!"

Had Mukhi guessed what his master did not yet know himself? Uraz pushed Mukhi's arm away and said straight into his face, "Why not?"

Mukhi strode over Amjad Khan's head and knelt before Uraz. "Thou must not, canst not, thou shalt not do that," he said.

Since Uraz was stretched out on the ground, Mukhi was forced into the attitude of prayer; but his voice did not beg. His words contained a rigid insistence. On Mukhi's hardened, matured face the chapandaz could easily read the feeling that lay behind the words: "Jahil does not belong to thee only," said the syce's eyes. "He belongs to Tursen, in the first place, who has made him what he is . . . To me too, for having cared for him and loved him more than my own eyes . . . And then to Meimana and our steppes. And thou wouldst dare fling him, like any common meat, into the market of chance, and see him led away no matter where by no matter whom."

The wolf's grin made Uraz's face sharper and fiercer than it had ever done. Never before had he so relished the delight and torment of pride and cruelty concentrated on men, fate, and his own person —never before had he felt them so strong, so living, and complete. In a single action he was combining risk and blasphemy, each to the supreme degree. He was outfacing, defying the heaven of the future and the consecration of the past. And at last he had found the strongest tool of all for breaking Mukhi's loyalty quite beyond healing.

Uraz called to the chief of the district, "Give me a few moments, lord. I offer Jahil, my stallion, as my wager on the fight."

These words made the deepest possible impression. All those present at Uraz's appearance had admired his horse.

"But where wilt thou find men to bet against?" asked the chief. "As thou knowest, they are all on the same side."

"That is not my side," said Uraz. "To defend my stake I choose the ram belonging to Hayatal, the stranger."

The murmur that ran through the audience was like a sigh of distress, a sigh of compassion. They whispered, "Oh, lamentable!"

"So noble a horse . . ."

"Lost . . ."

"Thrown away . . ."

"Because of his wound, his master no longer has his wits."

Still on his knees, Mukhi buried his face in his hands.

"Since that is thy wish, O horseman," said the chief, "and so that the worth of the stake may be judged, let the stallion be brought forward."

With the handle of his whip Uraz touched Mukhi's shoulder and said, "Thou hearest, syce?"

Walking as heavily and clumsily as if his ankles were hobbled by chains, Mukhi reached the poplar to which he had tethered

Jahil. He tried not to hear the happy neigh that greeted him or to feel the warmth of the tongue that licked his hands. Or to see the gentle brilliance of the great soft eyes that sought his own.

He was untying Jahil's headrope when the voice he loved best in the world whispered behind him, "Syce, tall syce . . ." Mukhi whipped around and in front of him saw a shapeless being, wrapped in a kind of dark shroud, its face hidden by a black mask.

"Zereh . . . Thee . . . How . . . ?" stammered Mukhi.

Breathless and impatient she pointed to the top of the hill and replied, "Over there . . . With the other women. They are allowed to watch, far from the men and wearing a chadar. I took one." She plucked wildly at her veil. "This sack, this cloth is stifling me," she said. "The daughters of the nomads, great or little, never wear them."

"I should know thee by thy eyes among a thousand. They are my stars," said Mukhi.

The girl angrily shook the cowl that covered her and cried, "Will my eyes prevent our horse being lost forever?"

"Thou knowest . . . Already?" murmured Mukhi.

"The children are continually bringing the news," said Zereh. "Those words I could not believe. But now I have seen thee . . . So it is true?"

"It is true," said Mukhi so low that the girl made out his reply only by the shape of his lips. She seized the syce's arm, drew him toward her, and stood on tiptoe. Her eyes, sparkling through the slits in the black cloth, took possession of Mukhi's. "And thou wilt let this horse be stolen?" she asked. "Thou wilt let him be stolen without making any attempt—stolen, our only wealth, our only chance?"

"I shall kill Uraz," said Mukhi, very slowly.

"When another man is Jahil's master!" exclaimed Zereh. "Thou hast not a moment to lose. Mount . . . Take me up behind. We will fly like the wind."

The passionate boldness of her voice, the dazzling brilliance of her eyes through the mask prevented Mukhi from foreseeing, from thinking . . . He wrenched Jahil's rope from the tree and set his foot in the stirrup. Zereh clutched the skirt of his chapan. "Stop," she said. "We have not even time for that. They must have thought thee too slow."

An armed policeman was coming in their direction. Zereh disappeared behind the poplars. Mukhi led Jahil away toward the arena.

In the middle of the ring Jahil showed against the background of reeds, flowering bushes, and trees that lined the course of the river. From time to time he pawed the ground and snorted with impatience; and as he did so his strength and beauty, restored to their full luster by the grooms at the inn, brought a respectful murmur from the rows of spectators. And standing at his side Mukhi felt an appalling shame and bitterness. He was putting this horse, his pride, his treasure, his heart, up to auction! Uraz smiled on and on.

The district chief spoke first to the audience. "Good people, you have seen the stallion clearly?"

"There is no more splendid horse," was the universal response.

Then the chief spoke to Uraz. "What dost thou set him at, horseman?" he asked.

"Let the noble Amjad Khan decide," answered Uraz. "There is no man here who equals him in judgment and upright wisdom."

Amjad Khan had taken up his lapis lazuli rosary again; he let a few beads run through his fingers and then said unhesitatingly, "Such a charger has no price. A man getting him for a hundred thousand afghanis—which I am willing to pay this very day— would make an excellent bargain."

"I accept," said Uraz.

"A hundred thousand . . . A hundred thousand . . . A hundred thousand . . ." The figure ran from mouth to mouth and all present were filled with wonder, particularly the poorest. And even more the one man in a green turban.

"Oh why, why have I not the whole sum?" said Zaman Hajji feverishly into his sparse and patchy beard. "This madman from the steppes is a gift from the Almighty." He called over Uraz's head, "Thou art the only man who canst buy this horse, O Amjad the Rich. The only man with a use for it. So thou must take whatever stakes the horseman will accept."

"Agreed," said Amjad Khan.

"I stand to all bets," said Uraz.

The district chief bade the scribe who accompanied him write down the wagers and names. With greedy haste, Zaman Hajji emptied out the whole contents of his old wallet. He was the first to announce his stake: "Fifty-two thousand, three hundred afghanis."

From natural respect, the scribe next looked questioningly at Amjad Khan, who said, "In my name thou shalt write what is wanting of the sum I named, after all those who choose to bet have done so."

No one held back. Every man was sure of winning. Every man emptied his pockets, whether they held little or much. Even the head of the district. And the scribe last of all. Amjad Khan took the list, laid it on his knees under the lapis rosary, and said to Uraz, "The hundred thousand afghanis are covered, bold cavalier."

"I return thee thanks," replied Uraz. His politeness was entirely external and quite automatic. A hundred thousand or five hundred thousand or two afghanis—little did it matter to him! The sole essential glorious fact was that he was about to stake his return to Meimana, his victory over Mukhi, over himself and the world in general—he was able to stake his honor and his whole being on one throw, one single stroke of chance and instinct. And alone against all of them. The power of a king. The wild freak of a god. Were he to lose he would in truth be the winner. Such power was worth the whole of life and the whole of death.

Hayatal came over to Uraz. His ram—it had no leash—followed him like a dog. "Thou hast trust in my animal, horseman," he said curtly. "It is either great courage or pure madness. I love and revere them both. I thank thee."

Uraz looked keenly at the stranger with the damascened gun. The spark of mockery was no longer dancing in his eye. Hayatal went back to his place.

"Let the stallion be led away and kept under strict guard," or-

dered the chief. "Until the end of the match he belongs to us all."
Then, "Ayub and Hayatal, begin the battle."

The crowd supported his words with all the weight of its impatience. Long had been the writing of the wagers, oppressive the heat of the sun, worn and frayed the spirits of the people, for they had passed through so many strange and violent emotions. And to all this was added the burning desire for wealth. The gain was certain. They might just as well feel its weight in their pockets as soon as possible.

The first attack left their haste unsatisfied. There was no crash. At the moment of collision the little ram's sidestep was so quick and skillful and so much helped by his size that although Flail was on the watch he let himself be caught. His black and white fleece brushed by his opponent's dull, sparse coat, but left it quite untouched. Flail recovered at once and charged. His lowered forehead, a hammer in full swing, did not prevent him from aiming straight. The knowledgeable spectators shouted in their joy. "It was only a trial pass."

"He was testing the vile beast."

"He was taking his measure."

"Now he has him."

The two heads, one splendid, one ridiculous, came together. Or at least they certainly looked as though they did. Yet the usual shattering crash did not ring out. Indeed there was no noise at all. And Hayatal's ram, unhurt, light-footed, nimble, was the first to spin round. Whispering spread along the rows.

"He dodged again, the fiend."

"How?"

"He led with the side that has no horn."

"Truly, truly! To be sure. I see!"

"Flail's head slid and carried him too far."

"But now he knows, and now he is going to strike."

And indeed everything about Flail gave proof of a furious yet at the same time prudent will. He no longer charged. Against so slight a weight he had no need of speed. He moved in short strides, his head swinging to leave the enemy no way out, and in his little narrowed, bloodshot eyes good sense counterbalanced rage. "Attack . . . Attack," said his eyes. "This time I have thee."

And the spectators, who for their part had the gift of speech, shouted aloud what Flail was thinking.

But there was no attack. Although Hayatal's ram was charging at full speed he stopped dead within two paces of his opponent and began to dance round Flail like a dog. On his right, his left, in front, behind. And each time he butted with a hard, sharp blow. These strokes carried no danger for a creature as powerful as Flail. But they maddened him, worried him, and forced him to make short defensive motions that exhausted his breath.

An angry growl ran from row to row. It was no longer surprise or disappointment. Fear was seizing on the crowd. For their money. For their understanding. There were shouts.

"The fiend is not playing the game."

"He is merely tiring Flail."

"This is not a fight any more."

"Let it be stopped . . ."

The chief of the district did not have to reflect on a difficult decision. Hayatal, not yielding an inch of his height or an ounce of his pride, bent his head to show the crowd he accepted their wishes. He thrust two fingers between his lips and whistled. This time the sound was savagely short and crisp. From that moment on the action was so fast and developed in so astonishing a fashion that even Uraz, in the front row, could scarcely follow it.

All at once Hayatal's ram stopped harassing Flail, drew back, gathered himself, and charged. Before his bewildered, flustered opponent had had time to collect himself, Hayatal's ram was on him. But instead of striking at chest or forehead, the little creature only grazed Flail's hock with the bare side of his head. Insults and protests were beginning to spread again, when a great terrified silence came upon the audience. A red flood was staining the black and white fleece, flowing from the hock. Flail gazed at the bloody spring with eyes whose rage was lost in stupor. And already the mangy little ram was confronting him again. With almost unbelievable speed, precision, and strength the little ram's forehead struck his enemy between the eyes, where the nose begins, the most vulnerable point of all. He sprang back like a ball and stopped abruptly, to watch with a kind of frigid curiosity how Flail behaved in his death throes.

The first cry came from Ayub. He roared, "Crime! Crime! Base, foul trickery! It cannot be otherwise!" He ran to the little ram, who was rubbing himself against his master's leg like a dog, passed one of his hands over the edge of the broken horn and held it high, facing the audience. It was deeply cut.

"The break has been sharpened like a dagger, a murderer's dagger," shouted Ayub.

The chief of the district allowed the crowd no time to show its anger. "What hast thou to answer, Hayatal?" he cried.

The man with the gun walked over to Flail's body, set the curved toe of his sandal on a white-gloved foot, and said, "Let Ayub answer thee, lord, and say whether this carrion here learned to use his foot as a bait the way he did—whether he learned it all alone." Hayatal paused just long enough for the audience to draw breath and went on, "And thou, Ayub, prince of breeders, wilt thou tell me why, instead of spitting on my beast, thou didst not look at the broken horn before the fight rather than afterwards? No man, above all myself, could have stopped thee."

A long silence followed these words. It was filled with stupor, spleen, bitterness, and anger. And with reflection too, painful inner arguments, struggles between sordid avarice and honest reason. But the men of Bamian had a sense of fair play. Justice won.

"If we have been blind," said they, sighing, "it was because Allah in His Omnipotence so willed it."

But Zaman Hajji was unable to overcome his agonizing pain and rage. He beat on Kohzad's bony knees and yapped, "Why didst thou not warn me, false seer?"

Kohzad went on skipping where he stood and singing, "The herb that dreams, the herb that laughs, the herb that sings . . ." The raven opened its scarlet beak and croaked gently.

"Courage has won the day, O horseman of the steppes," said Amjad Khan to Uraz. "And believe my heart, I am the happiest man here." He took his rosary from the list of bets and passed the paper to the district chief; and the chief said to Uraz, "In an hour's time, in thy room, thou shalt receive the whole of these from my hand."

"And from mine," said Amjad Khan, "whatever is lacking of the hundred thousand afghanis."

Uraz searched for his happiness: in vain. He felt nothing but a bottomless, infinite fatigue. "My horse," he said in a low voice.

Mukhi brought Jahil and set Uraz in the saddle. "Thou seest," said Uraz to the syce.

Without reply Mukhi looked at Uraz with unmoving, unmoved eyes. He did not forgive him: he never would forgive him. That was the single, fleeting pleasure Uraz felt after his victory.

When they reached the road with the great red cliff and the gigantic Buddhas rising over it, Zereh went by in her chadar, close to Mukhi.

"Dost thou remember thy words, untying the horse?" whispered her invisible mouth.

"I remember," breathed Mukhi.

"Everything."

"Everything."

"And about him, too?" whispered Zereh. The black tip of her cowl bent toward Uraz.

"About him too," said the syce.

"Then leave it to me," said Zereh. She melted away into the crowd of veiled women who were going home, a lusterless ghost like all the rest.

PART FOUR

The Last Card

1 6

The Bucket

A T URAZ'S SIDE ON THE CHARPOY stood the piles of notes duly counted, the hundred thousand afghanis that the district chief and Amjad Khan had left there. Uraz called Mukhi, jerked his head very slightly toward the heap, and said, speaking more with his lips than his voice, "Take a handful . . . No point in counting . . . Buy what is needed. Then we go."

"Zereh will come with me," said the syce. "She knows more."

Uraz was perfectly conscious of the new look in Mukhi's eyes—heavy, the simplicity all gone, and the light with it. He clearly heard that Mukhi's reply lacked the usual submissive tone. He tried to rejoice in it and he could not. Just then nothing mattered to him apart from the rest, silence, and solitude called for with such furious insistence by his exhausted nerves, his fainting muscles, and the hellish pain that his broken leg was giving him for having moved it in his passionate following of the game. His waxy face had a green tinge; his lips the color of ash. His eyes seemed sunk even deeper than their sockets; and from the wound an abominable stench spread.

"He will not last much longer," said Mukhi to himself. Once again the thought frightened him. Only now it was not the same kind of fear. He was not afraid of seeing Uraz die. He was afraid of having no hand in it.

Zereh, her chadar flung off, was back in the kitchen. There she sat in a corner, full of thought, doing nothing. Above her half-closed lids the eyebrows joined in a hard line right across her little face. When she heard the syce call her name from the courtyard she walked out unhurriedly, the hard line still there.

Mukhi said to her, "We are going to the market. Thou wilt choose what we need for the road."

"What with?" asked Zereh.

Mukhi unclenched his huge fist. At first Zereh maintained an unbelieving, superstitious silence. Then she whispered, "So much money! Allah! So much money! My whole tribe in its whole existence never owned the half of it . . . Come, come quickly." But when they were within sight of the shops she slowed down and said, "The merchants must never know that one is in a hurry, or they ask more at once, the thieves."

Zereh's brow joined again. Up to the very last purchase their slim black line continued to emphasize the obstinacy of her forehead and the watchfulness of her eyes. The syce followed her like a biddable child, and with wonder he saw a woman unknown to him make her appearance. What gravity! What a spirit of command! What a feeling for things, for people, for money!

In her mind's eye Zereh saw all the purchases she intended to make—those and nothing more. The deeply experienced traders tried to tempt her, lead her on, persuade her, in vain; in vain they tried to force a piece of embroidery or cloth or a jewel on her, or to seduce her into buying it. She was equally unyielding over prices. Before accepting the least object, Zereh searched through and through shelves, stalls, shops, and piled-up counters, arguing about where it came from, decrying its quality, throwing doubts on its lasting properties, jeering at its shape—in short, she bargained with such griping patience and crafty passion that she overcame the most gnarled and avid shopkeepers. Not one of them had learned as much as she in the school of destitution, not one had an equal knowledge of the worth of the most wretched object and the smallest coin.

In this way Zereh provided herself, at the lowest price, with what was needed for cooking and sleeping, with a tent, victuals, and warm clothes.

When all the sacks and bundles were assembled, Mukhi cried, "What are we going to do? Jahil will never be able to carry all that."

"Let us go and find a good mule," said Zereh. She sighed. "As for him, I shall certainly have to leave the buying to thee."

The draft and pack animals were sold at the far end of the village, on the road, opposite the tallest of the Buddhas. When Mukhi had fingered legs, sides, and withers, peered into mouths, raised hoofs, and examined eyes, he chose a mule among the beasts for sale, a high-standing mule with a gray coat.

"I like him, grandfather; truly I like him," he said to the dealer, an aged, wrinkled, shriveled, cunning Hazara who stood watching him in silence. "He is strong. He is well shaped. I have seen few like him. Thy price, grandfather?"

The Hazara named it and Mukhi paid without haggling. Then, stroking and gentling the mule with the affection he felt for every creature in his care, he led the mule to Zereh.

"See," he cried, beaming, "I too know how to choose."

"And even more how to have thyself robbed," retorted the young woman. "Thou hast given at least twice too much."

This touched Mukhi in his most innocent pride, and for the first time in speaking to Zereh his voice was vexed. "What does it matter?" he said. "Uraz will not call for accounts."

The young woman gave the syce a long, steady look. The line of her eyebrows was strangely hard. "That money does not belong to Uraz," she said. "It is ours . . . All of it."

Mukhi stopped running his fingers through the mule's mane. His jaw dropped as though it had received an unexpected blow. In a very low voice he said, "All of it? What . . . The hundred thousand afghanis?"

"The hundred thousand," said Zereh.

"It was he who won them," murmured Mukhi.

"Dost thou forget what he staked?" asked Zereh.

"I know," said the syce, "but . . ."

The girl broke in and asked again, "Dost thou want him dead? Still?"

"I do," said Mukhi.

They were approaching the shop in front of which they had

piled up their purchases. Zereh lowered her voice. In vain did she govern its violence; the savage note still frightened Mukhi. "Thou wouldst see him dead and I desire it too; and believe me, the thing is as good as done," whispered the young woman. "So tell me, what do the needs of a corpse amount to?"

The syce had no reply. Reason spoke in Zereh's mouth. And yet Mukhi did not, could not agree. In his deepest heart he felt that there was no possibility of overcoming his denial. Reason was speaking in Zereh's mouth. Reason. Not truth.

Uraz's death—Yes. Plain justice. He had betrayed his steppe, his blood, his people. Keep Jahil—Yes. Justice once again. Uraz had relinquished him. But the money—No. No.

The man who took the money profited by the crime and shared in it. In that case, why should he punish Uraz?

Zereh took Mukhi's silence for consent. "So, clearly," she said, "one would have to be out of one's mind to abandon that money."

A strange, muddled anger seized Mukhi. How could he find an argument against Zereh that she would be capable of understanding? The syce's eyes ran from the bundles of bedding to the cooking pots, to the stove and the tent, all lying at his feet and ready for him to divide into loads for the gray mule's pack. He kicked the nearest sack with his heel and asked, "Art thou not satisfied with all these goods?"

A contemptuous frown brought the girl's eyebrows together again. "Satisfied with what?" she cried. "Any family at all, unless it is as wretched as mine, owns more and better."

Suddenly Mukhi had the feeling that he had lost Zereh. The face confronting him was no longer hers. It expressed nothing but ugly greed and arrogant assurance. What, this ragged wench, but yesterday a hungry beggar, had the shameless effrontery to display scorn and disgust for the gifts of fate—gifts that she should have welcomed as treasures? And what a commanding, insulting voice expressed it! It was she who said what to do. She who gave orders. And he was no longer a man. Mukhi clung to the mule's mane to master his urge to strike this new, ignoble woman.

"If this animal fills all thy hopes to the full . . ." Zereh was crying.

The syce did not allow her to finish. In a voice brimming with fury he growled, "Stop! Stop fleering, giving orders. Or I shall wrench out that tongue which lays filth on everything. Thou shouldst praise Allah for His kindnesses and thou dost spit upon them. Thou art as grasping and thievish as the magpie of the steppes. There is not one single clean drop in the whole of thy blood."

Zereh flung herself toward Mukhi. Three paces at the most lay between them. That insignificant distance was enough for the transformation. The girl who seized the syce's hand had nothing in common with the one he loathed. Her forehead was smooth. Her eyebrows, back in their natural shape, made a supple bow over eyes that shone with the humblest emotion.

"Syce, tall syce," said she, and her voice trembled with supplication, "how thou art mistaken about thy servant. It is only of thee she thinks. She can no longer bear seeing thee in the state thou art. Look . . ." Zereh lifted Mukhi's arm and showed the frayed, ragged end of a sleeve that scarcely came lower than his elbow. And he was filled with shame. Not so much of the wretched material as of his hand, his muscles, and the thickness of his wrist, bared by the old, short chapan—too old, too short.

"Is it not lamentable, a foul injustice," went on Zereh with controlled passion, "that the wages of so much, so much work should be this ridiculous chapan? Thou dost deserve the finest of them all, thou so handsome. The broadest, thou so big. The softest, thou so kind. The noblest, thou the splendid horseman. Oh, how clearly I see thee dressed so, and wearing a magnificent turban!"

The girl had Mukhi by both hands now and drew him gently toward her. In her brilliant, swimming eyes he thought he saw the image of which she spoke that was himself.

Zereh's eyes grew wider and shone with an even greater fire, as though to welcome another vision. "And dost thou truly wish," she went on, "that I should always wear these rags, always go barefoot? Dost thou find me too misshapen, too ugly to wear silk from China, Indian cashmere, gold and silver necklaces, the scent of jasmin and roses, gems flashing the color of the sky and of blood, and to walk on carpets from Ispahan and Samarkand?"

And from the bottom of his heart Mukhi cried, "No woman, by the Prophet, is more truly born than thee for these delights."

With equal sincerity Zereh replied, "It is for thy happiness that I shall be adorned! For thy happiness, my syce!"

She repeated these words three times. Her face had taken on the expression of a waking dream and her voice the chanting rhythm of a legend. "And for thy honor," she went on, "thou in thy turn shall have syces and bachas, shepherds and camel drivers and splendid horses, flocks heavy with wool and deep in fat, and great Bactrian camels . . . And for thy honor also, thou shalt give me too, me at last, women to serve me, to spin and wash and embroider . . . Together they will make a tribe. Thou shalt be the prince of it. And we shall go to the great summer fair in the Hazarajat, thou on the tallest camel . . ."

But at that Mukhi protested, "I will only ride Jahil."

"He shall be dyed with henna," continued Zereh. "He will be magnificent . . . And thou shalt give me a gun: and by thy side I shall lead the caravan . . ."

The gray mule snorted. Mukhi soothed him with a caress whose kindness was merely automatic. A poor man's beast . . .

Beneath their half-closed lids Zereh's eyes no longer wore their veil of dreaming. She was watching Mukhi with a piercing gaze. "Syce, tall syce," she said so softly that he had to bend lower to hear her, "in my heart that is what all these afghanis are for. Only in my heart. Thou, thou art the thinking head, the master."

Images, thoughts, wishes, scruples, and the replies to those scruples clashed together and turned in Mukhi's head. He saw Uraz dead and the wads of notes in his belt. Take them? A vile theft . . . Leave them? Why? For whom? For the wind or the snow, or to let them rot? For the crows? For the robbers of the dead? Or else what? Carry the money to the only man who had any right to claim it—Tursen? Tursen . . . The father of the dead man . . . of the murdered man . . . murdered by Mukhi. To commit such an offense against Tursen, the great Tursen, his lord, his benefactor . . . And this girl at his feet, so small, so weak, poorer than the poorest since her birth cry, this girl to whom everything had been refused, always—he, Mukhi could fulfill her most impossible wishes, satisfy all her hopes at once.

Zereh rubbed her head against the syce's palm and whispered, "We will do as thou shalt decide."

Mukhi leaned against the big gray mule. His head was spinning. "We shall have the caravan," he said at last, in a dead voice.

After that they had nothing more to say to one another and they set about dividing the loads. Zereh hummed a lament of the roads. She only stopped for a moment to ask, "Art thou happy now, tall syce?"

"I am," said Mukhi. He was lying. His decision, however unavoidable it seemed to him, was forcing him to hate himself. Was it Zereh's fault? Or his own? Or the fault of someone he could not name?

BRINGING TEA, THE BACHA SAW THE HORSEMAN WHOSE WAGER ON the one-horned ram had made him as famous as a hero in the Bamian Valley lying there like a corpse, with his wound bare and open. He ran to him and poured a mouthful of the scalding liquid between his parted lips.

"More," said Uraz, his eyes still closed. Without stirring he emptied the whole pot. Then the bacha said, "Lord, I swear to thee by the Prophet that thou shalt see the Man that Heals as quickly as I can run."

Everything about the healer was round—face, belly, eyes, thick-glassed spectacles, and even his hands, which he held like cups. The only sharp feature he possessed was a big hooked nose. In the doorway he sniffed the room's pest-house stench, gazed like a thoughtful owl at Uraz's wound, and said to the bacha, "Very hot water, very clean cloths, and very smooth little boards. Hurry, child of my heart." The little round man's voice had a very curious gay, friendly, singing quality.

"Thanks be to thee, learned man of the valley," said Uraz faintly. "What canst thou do for me?"

"I shall ask thy hurt, my son, and it will tell me," said the healer. "And for my part I shall follow its advice."

He bent his round head with its round gold-embroidered velvet skullcap over Uraz's wound and set his two cupped hands round the leg where it was broken. Neither his palms nor his fingers touched the place. He seemed to be using them only as recipients for the confidences of broken bones and rotting flesh. Before taking them away he said in his singing voice, "O my son, O my son, why neglect this faithful servant so? What it needs now is great, great care and a very long rest."

"I must take to the road again this very day," said Uraz.

The owl's eyes, wide and friendly behind the thick glasses, settled on his bloodless face. "Thou art as much a gambler with thy leg as with the rams, I see," said the healer. "Take care. In this case the stake is worth more than all the money in the world."

"But so is the wager," said Uraz.

"Then let us say no more," cried the little round man cheerfully.

The bacha brought what the healer had asked for. He threw some herbs he had with him into the boiling water and washed the wound; then he dressed it with a bandage smeared with ointments and bound on the splints. "There thou art, at peace until tomorrow, my son, so long as the splints do not shift," said the healer. "After tomorrow, prepare for the worst."

"I thank thee for thy care of me, learned and skillful man," said Uraz, "and even more for the truth." He motioned toward the piles of notes at his bedside and went on, "Have the kindness to take a fee, which will never be worthy of the good thou hast done me."

The healer plucked a single note from the top of one heap, pushed it out of sight in the folds of his turban, and said, "Thy money spread abroad, is it another wager? On the nature of mankind?"

"Maybe," said Uraz. The round owl's eyes considered him for a long while. "What dost thou seek in my face?" asked the chapandaz.

"Well, my son, I have two herbals. The one for the sick comes from the fields, mountains, lakes, and woods. The other, which is for myself alone, I find growing only on the bed of suffering. Thou art a rare plant, my son, and dangerous . . ." Thus spoke the healer; and went silently away.

When Mukhi came back from the market he found Uraz sitting up very straight with his back against the wall. The syce's eyes darted to the empty place by the pillow.

"Rest easy, the money is in a safe place," said Uraz. He opened the top of his chapan and his shirt. On each side of the amulet hung a little tight, carefully knotted bag. "The will and the fortune," said Uraz. He buttoned his chapan and tightened his belt. As he did so Mukhi saw the dagger attached to it. "My own private purchase," said Uraz. "Hast thou finished thine?"

"Wholly," said Mukhi.

"Bring Jahil," said Uraz.

THE ROAD RAN ALONG THE FOOT OF A RED CLIFF, SO HOLLOWED OUT with thousands of caves cut by the Buddhist monks long ago that it looked like an enormous hive; and now the light of the setting sun made the whole face glow. They were traveling toward the west. Behind them the colossal statues were no more than gigantic shadows in their niches. Uraz rode in front. Mukhi walked near his stirrup. A few paces behind Zereh followed with the gray mule.

She walked with her head bowed toward the dust raised by her feet. Her lips moved silently. It might have been thought that she was praying. In fact she was concentrating the best, most active forces of her mind and her covetousness, her poverty and her love, to study, make ready, and ensure Uraz's murder with the smallest possible risk. At her disposal she had three days and three nights. The information gathered at Bamian, the recollection of tales heard in camps, and Mukhi's reckoning all agreed in giving her no more time than this. In her mind's eye the young woman held out the string of hours offered her, and just as she had done in the market she weighed, touched, measured, smelt each one of them with the same patient shrewdness before choosing the best adapted and the least costly for the death of the hated chapandaz.

"Violence will not answer the first day nor the last," reflected Zereh. "Violence leaves marks behind it—a broken neck, a hole in the belly. That would be dangerous in this valley, just as it would in the country near Meimana. There, everyone knows him. Here it is the same, from the rams onward. So not tonight, and not the last. The night of tomorrow, then . . . Unless . . ." Zereh stopped moving her lips. She no longer chose to whisper her thoughts, even to herself alone.

Unless the death should seem to be caused by an accident or a sudden bout of his illness . . . Uraz's condition would make either natural . . . Shelter his followers from suspicion. Who at Bamian, who at Meimana could accuse Mukhi? Or contest the legacy to the faithful, devoted, bitterly distressed syce who brought back his master's body? Yes, yes, she had three long days and three still longer nights. The young woman raised her head and smiled tenderly toward the heavens. She would set everything in train, and at once.

The mule she was leading suddenly stopped, preventing Zereh from carrying her plans any further. She then saw that Jahil had stopped too and that a curtain of dust was traveling toward them. "Another caravan," thought Zereh uneasily, remembering the ridge road.

A burst of flashes lit up the moving cloud and from it came the crackle of gunfire. Zereh had to exert all her strength to hold the mule. Once again jets of flame shot through the turbid screen. This time it seemed to Uraz that a swarm of furious hornets went past close to him. Splinters of stone, shot from the ground by the impact of the bullets, touched Jahil's flank. Uraz's fierce hand drove the bit into the corners of his mouth. In front of them people and animals on the road were taking refuge in the bushes and the fields, with a frightened bellowing.

"Go and see," said Uraz to Mukhi.

The syce ran along the side of the road in uneven leaps toward the clay-colored curtain of dust and disappeared into its whorls.

Another volley banged out. Zereh thought of nothing whatever but Mukhi's fate. Was he going to be involved in a quarrel between clans? A battle between tribes? Wounded . . . killed . . . ? And through the fault of that other one, the sick man glorying there on a horse to which he no longer had any right.

She breathed again. Mukhi was emerging from the reddish cloud. Out of breath he gasped, "Nothing wrong . . . A marriage. The bridegroom is going for his bride in one of those villages . . . Over there."

With narrowed eyes Uraz gazed at the noble buildings that showed at long intervals all along the valley between the river and the road. Their tall whitewashed outer walls, spotless, crenellated, studded with towers, scarcely allowed so much as a glimpse of the tops of the orchard trees and the roofs of the outbuildings, the quarters for the servants, gardeners, farm hands, and craftsmen that stood round the main house. These white islands in the middle of a lake of greenness were at once great houses, villages, and strongholds, and in this limpid twilight they were the homes of prosperity and well-being, order and pride.

And Uraz thought of the virgin one of these fortresses was still protecting and who tonight . . . For a fleeting moment that sheltered, innocent girl united in her person—fresh, shy smile, pure, blushing throat, the quick breath raising her bosom, her candid tender eyes—the features of all those he had come upon or made out at feasts, on the threshold of a yurt, the curb of a well, each one of whom had aroused a terrible desire in him to leap upon her, drag her down, rifle her, wound her cruelly in her shame and her virtue. And the fury of all these dreams concentrated on the unknown girl preparing for her hour of marriage in some remote village of the great valley of Bamian.

"Here they come! Here they come!" cried Mukhi.

The vision in Uraz's mind wavered and vanished. Nothing was left of his burning, intoxicating eagerness, of his overflowing, cruel delight but a weariness, an indifference that went to the edge of loathing.

Meanwhile, in the midst of the swirling cloud a procession had come into view. Its members, still without depth or solidity, made their appearance one after another against a powdery, mysterious background, with the marvelous secrecy of shadows. Their cries and the beat of the drum that marked their step seemed to come from the tawny fog flying up from their feet. First came a horseman. He rode his horse at the slowest walk, so as not to break or distort the ring of his friends dancing round him. There were a score of them, very young, lean-muscled, thin-faced. Their long thick wild black hair waved and floated below their shoulders. Loose coats, flaring at the knee and tied tight at the waist with a length of cloth, and wide trousers caught in at the ankle, left their limbs quite free. A tall man with a drum came after them. The dust of the dancing ring hid his face, but from his build and the dignity of his carriage it could be seen that he was by far the oldest of the band. Yet in his hands the huge drum seemed to have neither weight nor mass. He raised it over his head, threw it now on one shoulder and now on the other, held it at arm's length, or leaned it against one ear to hear it sing. And his complete control, the proud freedom his age required, did not prevent his tall body from following the rhythms his fingers beat out, or expressing them with a wonderful precision, happiness, and intensity, as though his blood flowed to their time. A bend of his neck, a swing of his shoulder, a stamp of his foot, and all manly gaiety blossomed under the sun. And the tight skin sang on and on, never pausing, with so rich, living, and inspired a rhythm that it made not only the legs leap but also the heart.

Borne, raised, and governed by it, the young men leaped, spun, fell back a pace, sprang forward another, bent a knee, and bounded again, spinning in whirlwinds that their long hair topped with great dark wings. So they made their way, a broken circle that danced and leaped. Every inch of spine, every joint, every floating piece of stuff, loose lock of hair, seemed to be inhabited by its own ardent life and to dance its own dance. And yet these bodies abandoned to utter freedom were bound one to another by a kind of inward spell and their wild ring obeyed a deeper order and harmony than that of its motions. They danced the happiness and glory of youth, of friendship among men, and of the bloody triumph in store for one of them that day.

Uraz heard and saw these shouts, songs, and leaps and the festive thunder of the drum with frigid indifference, just as he received the dust that had reached him now and was enveloping him. It would pass . . . These fools too . . . The road would be clear. Then his eye lit up. Where had she come from, this girl standing in front of Jahil? Her slim neck rose like the stalk of a flower above a cotton dress sprinkled with blossoms. Copper rings shone softly in the lobes of her tiny ears, and beneath the red shawl that drew her hair aside the back of her neck showed, smooth and chaste. There, within hand's reach. As it was in his most private, most fiery dreams. And then he made out the words. "Syce . . . tall syce. Just for a moment . . . The omen, to see him together."

Inwardly Uraz cursed himself for a fool. Because of a few new rags he had been unable to recognize the bastard gypsy, Mukhi's whore.

Zereh pressed herself against the syce. The wave of dust covered them. A few steps away the ring danced and spun. It was not an unknown young man on a commonplace mount that she was watching through the columns of tawny smoke: it was Mukhi, and he was riding on Jahil, coming to fetch her, Zereh, for their marriage.

A great uproar deafened her. "Make way! Make way!" shouted the young men. They were whirling so close to Uraz that beneath their hair he could see the brilliance of their possessed, intoxicated eyes. The drum seemed to be beating inside his skull.

A moment earlier he had been ready to go to the edge of the road in honor of the marriage custom. These shouts, these looks, forbade him to do so. Threat or insistence do away with all right to civility. Uraz did not stir.

"Make way! Make way!" repeated the dancers, in a louder, harsher tone. It would have been easy for them to pass around the single horseman. But their racing young blood, continually heated by the thundering rhythm of the drum, could not bear this challenge. The leading youth set himself in front of Jahil and said to Uraz, "Art thou deaf?"

The next in the ring did the same and asked, "Blind?"

Others came and stood at their side, and as Uraz did not open his mouth or make the slightest movement they shouted, "Into the ditch! Into the ditch!"

Not for a moment did their bewitched limbs cease jerking to the despotic orders of the drum. Jahil reared. Hands grasped at his bridle. Uraz raised his whip. He was about to hurl the stallion forward, overturn them, pass through, but a shoulder lurched into his injured leg. The anguish paralyzed him. "Now," thought he, "if Jahil leaps or goes wild, I shall fall . . . Dishonor in front of these beardless leapers." He thrust the whip between his teeth to take the dagger at his belt.

But at that moment the young men were struck motionless,

mouths open, arms stretched out, fists clenched, poised just as they had been standing when the astonishing silence fell on them. For the drum had stopped.

The man who wielded it set the drum carefully down at the side of the road, straightened himself to his full height, and stepped toward Uraz. The young men drew aside to let him pass, together with a little ram that lacked one horn and that followed him like a dog.

"Greetings, Hayatal," said Uraz, in an even voice.

"And peace be with thee, rider of my heart," said Hayatal. "Still dost thou chance thy stake alone against all, I see. I recognized thee by that, before I saw thy face."

"And thou hast made me win again. And I give thee thanks for that," said Uraz.

Hayatal gave so quick and slight a shrug that but for the movement of the long gun he carried on one shoulder Uraz would never have seen it. "Thou shalt do the same for me when I come to thy steppe and back thee in a great buzkashi."

At these words Uraz felt the full weight both of the pain and the uselessness of his broken leg. Harshly he asked, "Yet thou hast seen?"

"Seen what? Thy dragging leg?" cried Hayatal. He gave a short laugh. "Come, man. Thou art like my ram. Thou shalt turn blemish into excellence."

Because of his height Hayatal's forehead was almost on a level with Uraz's eyes, and for a moment Uraz saw the pitiless mockery and unforgiving pride light up with a hard, strong affection. It did him a good that he would not acknowledge. Yet with the most natural movement in the world, as though by chance he moved Jahil over to the side of the road.

"Thanks for the bridegroom, rider of my heart," cried Hayatal. "His blood must be boiling like the inside of a samovar fanned glowing red."

"Art thou a friend of his?" asked Uraz.

"No more than thou art," said Hayatal. "When I met these young men on my way, I was grieved for their pitiful drum. I made it sing as we do at feasts in my country, over by the eastern passes. Then the bridegroom swore that his happiness lay in my being at his marriage. And for my part I thought of the lambs roasted in their fat, the many-colored pilaws, the honey from the hives, the fruit from the orchards that rejoice, the mouth burned with spices, the singing and the dancing. Heï! Heï!" He thrust two fingers into the corners of his mouth and blew such a blast that Uraz seemed to hear the winter storms tearing across the dark steppe, when the devils breathe hurricane, snow, and night through their shrieking trumpets.

Jahil and the bridegroom's mount tried to rear. The riders managed to hold them in. But the big gray mule had no one to control him. Terrified, he flung straight forward, and with all his sacks and bundles ran into Hayatal, who was flourishing his drum, and the dancers, who were joining their ring again. The young men grasped him by the ears, the pack, the tail, and great shouting and laughter accompanied their capture. But in a voice hoarse with anger Hayatal cried to Mukhi, "Thou fool of a syce, why hast thou let thy beast disturb our pleasure with this disorder?"

"It was not he who was looking to it," said Uraz.

"Who then?" cried Hayatal.

"The servant-woman," said Uraz.

"That woman—and of so low a condition—she has failed in her duty?" asked Hayatal with even more astonishment than anger.

"Truly," replied Uraz.

In one stride Hayatal was in front of Zereh, towering over her with a height that seemed gigantic to the little nomad, and he growled, "If thou belonged to me, I should rip thy hide off."

In her fright Zereh turned her eyes to Uraz. Terror gave this look an artless, childlike expression. A strange warmth softened Uraz's loins. He threw his whip to Hayatal and said, "Do justice in my place."

From his full height and with all his strength Hayatal brought the thick, leaded thong down on Zereh's back. Under the violence of the blow she fell to her knees.

"Stop! Stop!" roared Mukhi. That was all he could do. Several young men had seized hold of him. Three times Hayatal lashed Zereh. The leather of the thong cut her thin cotton into rags. Uraz remained completely motionless. Only his eyelids and nostrils quivered slightly.

At last Hayatal gave him back the whip. And as the young woman got up it was not upon her executioner that she fixed her eyes, darkened and as it were burned with an undying hatred, but upon Uraz.

"Heï! Heï! My drum!" cried Hayatal. Once more his teeth were gleaming. A hoarse and rhythmic song poured from his chest. His shoulders danced. The bridegroom's horse curveted and moved on. The ring sprang into motion, like a whirlwind ruled by the thunder that growled, rolled, burst out, and laughed in the midst of its imprisoning circle. The dust raised its tawny veil behind the wedding train.

WHEN THERE WAS ABUNDANCE OF WOOD AND WATER—AND THE Bamian Valley was surpassingly rich in both—Uraz usually waited until the ash of twilight verged on the black of night before camping. On this particular evening the rule was not observed.

The sun was still making its way above the huge mountains that rose to the west when they crossed a stream and Zereh dropped down on the bank to cool the blood-red weals that Hayatal had drawn on her back and bosom. The syce stopped Jahil to wait for her. And all at once Uraz felt his entire body begging him not to push on farther. It was not the pain or the weariness. The effects of the healer's treatment and his salves were lasting still. But his innermost being was filled with so deep and so insidious a languor that it insisted on rest taken at leisure, in safety, and in warm, soft, total relaxation. Why force himself to delay the halt? There was no hurry. The place was wonderfully suitable—running water, a meadow below the road, bushes all round. And as for what was needed to make the camp luxurious, the mule had but to be unloaded for everything to be at hand.

"Pitch the tent," said Uraz to the syce. "And let my bed be deep and soft and well sheltered from the cold. I want a night like an amir's."

Mukhi strode over to the brook and helped Zereh to her feet. The top of her soaked and lacerated dress clung to her bosom like a tattered skin. "Didst thou hear Uraz?" asked Mukhi very softly.

"I heard him," replied Zereh with a whisper that made her dry lips twist with the force of hatred. "He will sleep well, I assure thee. None sleeps so deep as a dead man, as thou knowest."

These words did not surprise Mukhi at all. His whole being supported them. "What shall I do to help thee?" he murmured.

"Nothing," breathed Zereh. "He is mine. Mine alone." She drew breath and whispered, "He did not deign to dirty his hands on my skin. He made use of another man. And he took his pleasure in it, the crippled dog."

"How shalt thou do it?" whispered Mukhi.

"Thou shalt know when I utter the mourners' cry," said Zereh. A strange strength had come to her. She grasped the mule's bridle and led him over to the other side, where Uraz was waiting, deep in his saddle.

"O master," said Zereh, "before night falls thou shalt have a bed for thy back worthy of Ali, and for thy head a shelter worthy of the Prophet. Perhaps then thou wilt forgive my fault."

The girl's voice was clear and musical. Her face was humble— the most servile submission. "Whore's flesh and slave's heart," thought Uraz. "They are only to be won by the whip." He thought no more. He was too intent on the delight of idleness.

Zereh hurried Mukhi, pushed him, and urged him on with advice and orders. Herself she worked furiously. Since her early childhood her people, pitching innumerable camps for a single night, had taught her, with cuffs and blows, the great knowledge of the wanderers in every detail and particular. Each of her movements and orders was designed to get everything set up the best and quickest way possible. As she had promised, the tent was up and taut in the middle of the meadow, the bed ready under the felt roof, the fire lit, and the three hearthstones in position by the time the sun was setting—setting at the far end of the sky, where a granite trident pierced the round, showing the trembling of a fire as pink as heavenly flesh between its points.

Mukhi wiped his hands clean of the earth, grass, and twigs on his breeches, before coming to lift Uraz from the saddle. Looking at his face and eyes, Uraz thought, "He hates me for his bitch's whipping more than she does herself."

Now in the days when Mukhi still revered and cherished the

300 / THE LAST CARD

son of Tursen he had never shown such devoted attention, such skill in carrying him. The contrast between the hatred in the syce's face and the tenderness of his hands was so strange that it gave Uraz a feeling of indefinable discomfort. But Zereh ran up and enclosed the break with her hands, so as to prevent the slightest play in the bone, the slightest brushing against the wound, and Uraz said to himself, "She is trying at all costs to atone for the fault that earned her the whip. And as for him, he is dancing to her tune."

Zereh continued to hold Uraz's leg, tightly and gently, and he was carried to his bed without a single jar. Zereh had made use of all her finest purchases at Bamian to set up this bed and decorate the tent. When Uraz found himself lying on the easy, welcoming mattress, leaning on plump, downy cushions, warmed by feather quilts so light that he scarcely felt their weight, and when he saw the gentle lamp burning on a box covered with a golden scarf set at his bedside by way of a table, the unaccustomed luxury gave him a very deep pleasure, in spite of everything. His limbs and his back and his blood and his muscles stirred with a gratitude of which he himself was incapable. "By the Prophet," he murmured, with his eyes closed, "there has been good work done here."

At this Zereh bent very low to kiss the hand that hung down by the side of the bed. She was quite sure that in doing so she would increase whatever trust Uraz might have in her. This was an error. At the sudden, devout touch of her lips Uraz felt a kind of constraint enter to spoil his bliss. The instinct of self-preservation awoke. He opened his eyelids very slightly and through the invisible slit, saw the girl's face as she rose; and on it all the qualities he knew so well—cupidity, determination, cunning. He thought, "That thou shouldst double thy attentions, brought to it by the whip, bastardly whore—good. But that thou shouldst be brought to it by thy heart, capable only of fear, envy, or hatred—a mere lie." "I want Jahil by me," he said aloud. "And until morning."

Mukhi looked at Zereh. "Dost thou not hear our master?" cried the young woman with slavish zeal. This again was an error. "The stallion is not what they are after, this time," said Uraz to himself at once. "So it is the money . . . All their care is so that I should sleep the better." He stopped the grin that he felt forming at the corners of his mouth. Above all, not to warn Zereh. Deceive the deceiver. Give her the feeling of complete safety. Throw her on the wrong track.

"Has he drunk?" Uraz asked the syce as he led Jahil in through the high opening of the tent.

"His fill," said Mukhi. "And as for food, he had a double ration of oats at Bamian."

"Tether him right next to my bed," said Uraz. He appeared to watch Mukhi with the utmost attention and uneasiness, making him change the stake and alter the knots. The syce cheerfully obeyed all his requirements. "Prate on, prate on," thought he. "Take care of the stallion by all means. It will help Zereh take care of thee."

At last Uraz said it would do. Zereh brought the tray with tea, crying in a chanting tone, "The strongest, hottest, thickest with sugar."

Uraz watched every movement as she set the tray down on the little box that acted as a table and poured out the black liquid. He saw nothing suspicious. But she might have slipped a sleep-bringing drug into the tea outside. "Taste it first," ordered Uraz. "I do not want to burn my mouth."

"Thou dost me great honor," said Zereh, in the humblest and softest voice. She drank the full cup without hesitation. Then she rinsed it scrupulously and refilled it. "Wait a short moment and thy palate will be happy," she said. "I go to prepare thy food."

Leaving the tent, Zereh went and squatted by the fire, which Mukhi was tending. "May Allah protect us!" murmured the syce.

"Blessed be His name," said Zereh. "The fool, feeling sure of the horse, thinks of nothing but his comfort . . ." She began to groan like a child. Until then her fury, and the intensity of her work, her stratagems, and her fear, had kept her from thinking of her pain. But now as she let herself go, softened by the heat of the blaze, she felt as though she were flayed, burning all over. With the tips of her fingers she gently felt the furrows the whip had opened round her neck and down her back, weals that were now crusting over. As she felt, so she moaned, "It hurts, it hurts so . . . It hurts beyond bearing."

Instinctively Mukhi opened his arms to take Zereh in, but he dared not close them over a skin that was all wounds. "Thou must look after thyself," he said hoarsely, "thy salves . . . thy ointments."

"Yes, the salves . . . the powders," murmured the girl. Her eyebrows came together. In the dancing light of the flames it looked to Mukhi as though her forehead swelled.

"Put the rice on to cook first," Zereh said to him.

While he was doing so she made as if to take off the string holding the little packets she always wore round her neck. Her hand darted back as though it had touched something white-hot. The string had been driven into her naked flesh, and now it was stuck there in the bloody, clotting mass. Zereh tore a strip from her dress and soaked it in the water in which the rice was cooking.

"Let me, and I swear thou wilt feel no hurt," said Mukhi, taking the pad. And his big fingers were so clever, so accustomed to delicate manipulations that he kept his word. He waved the string as though it were a trophy. The little packets spun in the air.

"Shall I open this one? That one?" he asked. "For thy poor back? Thy poor neck?"

Zereh caught his wrist and whispered, "Do not, do not touch. Thou knowest nothing of these herbs. There is as much death as there is life here." She took the packets from the syce, held them toward the fire, and one by one studied the colored threads that marked each of them. She nodded. Just ajar, her lips moved in silent formulas. Mukhi did not move or take his eyes off her. Very low he said, "Thou hast spoken of death. Uraz's death is fast to that string, is it not?"

"Patience, tall syce; there is always too much talk," said Zereh slowly, with a quick glance toward the tent. As though she had an anxious, restless child to soothe, she began to sing a nomad lullaby in an undertone, thin, piercing, unutterably sad. As she sang she untied a packet bound with red, took out a pinch of herbs, mixed with them a little hot water, tore off another strip of dress, and soaked it in the preparation. "Press the rag on all my wounds," she said to Mukhi.

When he had done so she put on a very heavy, very thick postin with wide pockets. Into the pocket on the right she put all the packets except for one marked with a bister star; and that she put in the pocket on the left. The warmth of the sheep's wool lining made her sigh with bodily contentment. She thrust a wooden spoon into the steaming rice, tasted it, and began to add the seasoning.

INSIDE THE TENT NOTHING STIRRED. NOT JAHIL, LYING ON HIS SIDE asleep, nor the lamp flame behind its smoky glass. Nor the shadows stenciled on the felt walls. Nor Uraz, leaning against the cushions. Even his mind and his senses were torpid. He allowed them total rest. He knew that he could count on their help in time of danger. And he knew that the danger would come in the course of the night.

"Is this the moment?" Uraz asked himself. He had just heard a confused whispering behind the flap covering the opening of the tent. It opened abruptly and Uraz saw Mukhi's dark shape outlined against the red background of the fire. He was carrying a saucepan that gave out a strong, warm smell of food. The curtain fell behind him. The syce came as far as the box, set the steaming pot down, and stepped back.

"Stay," said Uraz.

Was this indeed the moment of that unknown danger he was certain he would have to face sooner or later?

"Stay," said Uraz again. Through his half-closed eyes he considered Mukhi. Apart from direct, undisguised attack he had nothing to fear from him. "A mere tool of the nomad whore," thought Uraz. And immediately afterwards, "Yet in clever hands a tool can grow mortally dangerous."

Uraz turned his head toward the pot, sniffed the odors that came from it, and said again, "The pilaw smells good—excellent. What a pity I have no appetite to eat alone." He let his eyes drift back to Mukhi and went on mildly, "I invite thee, thee and thy splendid hunger, to share this dish."

"Me?" exclaimed Mukhi. Zereh's packet . . . The one with the bister star . . . He did not think the girl had poured the powder into the rice. But was he certain that he had followed every one of her movements? "Me, at table?" he went on.

"On a journey there is no master and syce any more," said Uraz. "There are only traveling companions." Suddenly his face hardened. "Sit down opposite me," he commanded. Mukhi squatted on his heels, on the other side of the box. "And begin!" said Uraz.

Mukhi remembered Zereh's ferocious whisper, just as he was about to go into the tent, "Do what he wants . . . Everything he wants." He reached out his right hand toward the pot . . . And let it hang there above it. In spite of her measureless cunning, had Zereh foreseen that Uraz would insist on . . . ?

"Thou art very shy this evening," said Uraz. His eyes, black with unconcealed distrust, searched Mukhi's face. The syce understood: if he were to hesitate a second longer suspicion would grow into certainty. The plot would be discovered and through his fault . . . His fear of Zereh overcame his fear of the poison. Mukhi thrust three fingers into the hot, rich food, kneaded it, rolled it, slipped the ball into his mouth, and swallowed it at once.

They both of them let some moments go by without either moving or speaking. At last Uraz said, "Is it good?"

"To enchant the Prophet," murmured Mukhi. He could feel the drops of icy sweat dripping down the back of his neck. They seemed to him like the dew of Paradise. He had tasted the pilaw and he was alive. Now he felt a blissful hunger and, plunging his whole hand deep into the pot, drew out an immense bolus and devoured it noisily. Then another, and another. He never even noticed that between each mouthful Uraz gently turned the pot about. When the gorged Mukhi began to lick his fingers one by one there was not a single part of the dish that he had not touched.

"My turn," said Uraz. He ate without any real hunger, merely to keep up his strength. The pungency of the dish helped him on. Wonderfully swimming in fat. Rich with the bones and marrow of mutton. And above all so seasoned as to ravish the mouth and set it in a delightful blaze—even a mouth most dulled to the enchanting fire of spices.

Uraz pushed the pot away, gave a prolonged belch, and dismissed Mukhi with a wave. The flap opened again. Mukhi came back with Zereh just behind him. He with a half-filled bucket, she with a leather bottle all dripping with water.

"Forgive us if thy rest is disturbed for a moment, O master," said Zereh. "The syce thought of Jahil and I of thee."

Mukhi set the bucket by the sleeping horse and the girl hung the waterskin on the corner of the box next to Uraz. The flap of the tent fell back into place. The two shapes, large and small, vanished, and with them the light of the fire.

"They want me to sleep," thought Uraz. "They count on weariness, safety, a full meal . . ."

Uraz drew out the dagger at his belt and thrust it into the boot that covered his sound leg. His watch began . . .

THE FIRE DIED DOWN. MUKHI RESTORED THE BLAZE WITH A HANDFUL of branches. "The third time," he murmured. Zereh signed to him to be quiet. She was at the end of her patience. They had been waiting for hours. They were waiting in the flow of time and the darkness of the night for the sound of a cry, a moan, a loud unnatural breathing, a groaning from the depths of the tent. In vain. As she had already done before, Zereh flattened herself on the ground, crept, light and pliable as a snake, to the flap of the tent, and opened the edge of it a crack. The faintest breeze would have made more noise. Uraz, stretched out there, seemed to be wrapped in an overwhelming sleep. The girl crawled back to Mukhi.

The syce whispered into her ear, "And what if he sleeps until we leave?"

With the same caution she asked, "The pilaw . . . he did eat enough? Thou didst say that for sure?" Mukhi nodded violently several times. "The thirst will overcome the sleep," said Zereh.

At about this same time Uraz felt such a burning along his lips, his palate, and his throat that in spite of his wish to remain motionless in order to deceive the enemy, he decided to drink. He unhooked the still dripping waterskin, held it up with its spout pointing toward his mouth, and grasped its bottom with greedy fingers. A single squeeze would send a jet of delicious coolness to soothe and enchant his raging thirst. Uraz's fingers did not stir: it was as though a sudden palsy had struck them. On the other hand, the thoughts darted through his mind much as one flash of lightning follows another.

The mortal danger was in the goatskin . . . Mukhi's dread of the pilaw? Feigned. To avert suspicion. And the spices . . . Unfavorable to sleep . . . designed to make one drink. Drink what? Poison.

Blood flowed in Uraz's fingers once more. He laid his hand on his heart, which was beating too fast.

As they squatted by the campfire, Mukhi and Zereh heard a piercing cry from the tent. They darted in. Uraz was waiting for them, sitting upright against the cushions. "Water!" he said.

"But . . . but . . . the goatskin . . . Was there not enough water?"

"It is Jahil," said Uraz.

Only then did they see that the stallion was up, standing there wide awake.

"He was strangely thirsty," said Uraz again. "He finished his water. I have given him mine."

"He drank it?" cried Mukhi savagely.

"Maybe," said Uraz.

In a single bound the syce reached Jahil, thrust him back, and upset the bucket.

Uraz gazed unwinkingly at Zereh. "When they are woken suddenly, these stupid great fellows are as awkward as bulls," said the young woman.

Her eyes had not avoided Uraz's gaze. And he saw that she at least was not deceived. She knew. He had beaten her. And on the ground she herself had chosen. She accepted the defeat without weakening. Until the next encounter. And Uraz rejoiced in his heart: it would be a splendid match.

"Excuse me an instant, O master," said the nomad.

She came back with a full pitcher. Uraz did not oblige her to taste this water. He took the pot and drank in long, marvelous gulps. He felt that as far as Zereh and this night were concerned he had become immortal.

17

The Mastiffs

THE SLOPE climbed steeply. The track rose and rose out of sight between the great walls that touched the sky. Uraz turned in his saddle toward the stony headland that rose at the mouth of the gorge. The great Bamian Valley had suddenly vanished behind it. The silvery river, the green poplars, the white splendor of the fortified houses, the crimson cliffs were still close . . . So close . . . And yet already Uraz doubted their existence. Only a few moments earlier the first beams of the sun had danced on the surface of running water and bright orchards; it had shone back from the windows in the villages. Here the narrow cleft was a river of deep shadow, and on its sheer banks nothing grew, nothing sprang except loneliness and time that knew no seasons.

"It was all dream and illusion, no more . . ." said Uraz to himself. "The oasis. The tent . . . The happiness of victory. What victory? And over whom?"

Over the half-wit with a flabby neck who was walking there in front, bulging with muscle, ruled not by courage or honor . . . but by a whore? And as for that bastard gypsy, very great worth and merit to be sure, for having foreseen that she would make use of every possible means of stealing the fortune hidden under his shirt! Uraz spat—a thick, bitter spittle. At the ram fight he had thought himself possessed of a divine power, just because one animal with a shortened, cheating horn had bled another. Pitiful, pitiful. And last night he had felt that he was immortal because he had overcome a wench of no account.

"What then? The danger over—no more joy . . . So am I to begin again . . . Begin again forever?" wondered Uraz. He felt a terrible weariness. Its leaden weight pressed down on every muscle. His blood was turning into ice. The Bamian Valley was ten thousand feet up. And this narrow defile climbed perpetually. The sun never touched it. Along its dark bed flowed a wind laden with the cold of everlasting snow.

And the pain had come back, a thick, inflamed, and rotting liquid that oozed and spread from his knee to the sole of his foot. Uraz remembered the healer at Bamian. "The virtue of the ointments and the treatment cannot last," the little round man had said. "Afterwards, thou wilt be in danger of death." And it was death indeed, that horrible worm, that Uraz could feel rotting his flesh, gnawing away his bones, and changing his fine red blood into loathsome matter. "I can no longer even sit my horse decently," he reflected, hunched and sunk on his saddle.

Mukhi stopped, climbed onto a boulder that had fallen into the middle of the track, and turned, crying, "The end of the defile is near."

The echo repeated his words, and it seemed to Uraz that they passed above him, through him, going to Zereh alone. Inwardly he said, "For them I am carrion already. They look on themselves as masters of the stallion and the money."

As he shortened the reins he felt that the worm was drawing out, endlessly drawing out its horrible coils, and that it was crushing all the nerves in his body, tearing them to pieces. Nevertheless he managed to straighten himself. After that a flow of burning, crackling fever came to his help. He emerged from the narrow pass with his head high. From that moment on, he was no longer fully himself.

Before him lay a plateau, stretching out forever. There was a powdering on its surface, as of a coarse, hard kind of ash. Over it all reigned the resplendent death of ice-cold suns. This plain, lying here at fifteen thousand feet, so dazzling that it made all light seem thick and sightless, this plain more barren than the nakedness of black lava flows, sadder than angels' tears and lovelier than beauty, was no longer part of man's universe.

The world of this lunar steppe was rimmed with mountains. It was so close to the sky that only the very highest crests rose beyond it. For this reason it seemed as though gods, gods of shapes and names unimagined, unguessed by any religion, had reared up a wall against the icy firmament—a wall built of rock and light, on the same scale as this sublime and terrifying plain, and similar to it. From this same substance they had forged landmarks, instruments, and symbols intended for legendary travelers. Huge porphyry ships anchored in the everlasting snow. Coral rafts hung in the sky. Sharp peaks like immeasurable lighthouses, whose beams, meant for the use of the voyaging planets, were the rays of the sun. And sometimes vast dragons and monstrous idols rose up from a petrified rose-pink foam.

His face raised to the sky, Uraz never took his eyes from the huge, splendid, and mysterious structures that had the mountain tops as their base. He felt that he himself had no more weight or substance than a shadow.

Mukhi was afraid. And Zereh even more so. She desperately searched on every side for a sign of life, a trace of man's existence. At last, on her right, very far away, at the foot of the distant mountain that bordered the plateau, she discovered a faint wisp of smoke. Then another. She made a sign to Mukhi. He looked questioningly at Uraz. Uraz did not see him. Mukhi gradually changed his line of march to aim for the smoke, and Jahil followed him. Uraz did not notice anything. It took the appearance of the dogs to draw him from his remoteness, weariness, fever, pain, and from the ecstasy into which these high solitudes and their supernatural rocks had plunged him.

As the little caravan came nearer to the northern mountain chain, a strange noise rose over toward the wafts of smoke. It was reminiscent of the savage blast of cruel winter weather: but here there was no movement in the air. The sun was shining brilliantly. The distant sound had neither the voice nor the wings of the wind. Hoarse, rough, and choking, it stayed on the level of the ground and its gritty ash. It increased, swelled, ran toward them. The height, immensity, and nakedness of the plateau, its granite walls, and the mineral silence that hung over its limitless space, gave this relentless, unceasing ululation a quality that went beyond nature's most mysterious powers. It seemed as though the rock, the clouds, the sand, and the light were all weeping, laughing, and jeering at the same time. And that their fiends, let loose, were announcing the heavens' fall in an appalling, hideous, raving delirium.

Uraz felt no fear or surprise. This road could only lead to the end of all roads. Nor was he any more surprised to see Mukhi stop, and Jahil beside him: the stallion and the syce were waiting for the rock to burst, shatter under their feet. And when at last Uraz made out the furious baying he thought, "So here it is, the infernal pack shut up in the depths of the earth: the pack they say will only come out on the last day of mankind and the stars."

The three beasts appeared on the stony plain all at the same moment. Uraz recognized them as those he had expected. They were knotted, thickset, all great solid bone and quivering muscle. They were covered with short, sulfur-colored hair, all on end with rage. Their foam-whitened muzzles had huge jaws and gleaming teeth. Their eyes blazed with crimson hatred. And their enormous heads had no ears.

The dogs, solid and yet at the same time light on their feet, came on as fast as wild animals, scarcely rising from the ground in their immense long bounds. The dog a few strides ahead of the others flung itself at Uraz's broken leg, which hung loose against Jahil's side. Uraz raised his whip. He knew that any kind of defense was useless and ridiculous against a supernatural beast, a demon beast: yet instinct impelled him to bring the loaded thong down on the foam of the open mouth, the red fire of the eyes. Then he let his arm hang, resigned to death. But the dog uttered a roar of pain and fury and leaped back. At the same moment Jahil raised his foot for a kick. The dog darted to one side. "By the Prophet, the whip bites, a hoof frightens it . . . like a real beast," said Uraz to himself.

The mastiff came in to attack again. With all his strength Uraz flailed on the side of its head, where its ears were lacking. The animal flattened itself with an endless bawling. "A fine demon," thought Uraz, filled with shame. "Yes indeed, a fine demon, this shepherd's guard dog, cropped by its master to give the wolves of the hills and the steppes no hold."

Now the two other dogs both leaped at Uraz together, on the side of his injured leg. "The smell of open flesh, the blood, the carrion," thought Uraz. His mind was fully awake and running free. His spirit delighted in this sudden battle. His strength returned: he made Jahil spin, rear, lash out, and he struck and struck again with his whip with all his might and all his heart.

Mukhi came toward the fight, his hands full of heavy, sharp-edged stones. Zereh ran to the syce and ordered, "No stones. It will only make the dogs wilder. They are nomads' beasts . . . I know them." She fell silent, to get back her breath. Uraz continued to flog the three furious mastiffs, dodging and spinning about them. "And he—he will not fall from his horse," went on Zereh. "He gets his strength back, fighting. I know him too, now."

"The stallion could be maimed," said Mukhi.

"That must not be," said Zereh.

"What can we do?" cried the syce.

"Above all," said Zereh, "take care not to follow me."

The terrified Mukhi saw the girl walk toward the whirlwind of baying, kicks, neighing, and whip strokes. The dogs were harrying Uraz without a moment's pause. Wholly engrossed in their rage, they took no notice of Zereh. She came nearer. One of the mastiffs, avoiding Jahil's hoof, rolled over and over, leaped up, and there before Zereh was this terrible, earless head, its lips drawn back over a mass of foam and its eyes swimming with blood. She did not make the slightest motion to avoid it. The dog growled, gathered its shoulders, crouched for the leap . . .

In spite of her prohibition the syce was on the point of running to Zereh. A harsh, rough cry with the strangest modulation stopped him short. It was impossible that Zereh, so slim and frail, should have uttered it. Who then? Mukhi's muscles contracted to fling him forward and then at once relaxed. The mastiff had flattened itself just in front of the little nomad. The cry rang out again and the two other dogs left Uraz and came to set themselves by their companion. The three of them, calm all at once, questioned the young woman with an attentive, exceedingly intelligent look.

"They are waiting for her orders. So it was she?" wondered Mukhi. As though to answer him, Zereh stretched her arm in the direction of the smoke.

The dogs' savage eyes blinked several times. Then in long leaping bounds the three earless fiends raced away toward the north from which they had come.

"That cry, that master cry, where didst thou get it?" asked the wondering syce.

"Were they not tent dogs?" replied the girl. "I should be a poor thing, truly, if I had already forgotten their language."

Uraz went by close to Mukhi and Zereh as though he did not see them at all. The rage of the fight and the happiness of the challenge had already exhausted their power. The jerks and wrenching they had forced on his leg meant a renewal of his torture. Uraz knew only one way of dealing with that—to thrust straight on, making his horse's step harmonize with the to-and-fro of the saw that tore his flesh, to reach the very edge of unconsciousness and make the whole of life flow back into that refuge of a man aware neither of joy nor pain, accessible only to their play of thought and dreams. The fever with its ever-louder bells, and the sun climbing to its height in a blaze as white as molten metal, came to Uraz's help. Gradually the pain shifted, moving as it were toward the outside. It was still there, but it no longer dwelt in him. It clung to a horseman attached to Uraz, a horseman who sat in Uraz's saddle and yet was no longer Uraz. This wretched double to whom he had abandoned his rag of a body went on, jolt after jolt, hunched, crushed, racked. In the meantime Uraz, the real Uraz, rode high, flying at the level of the tallest peaks. He was that astonishing rock and the rock was Uraz. He sailed upon enormous rafts that wore the sky for their wings. He stroked the gigantic dragons that had the pointed mountains for their teeth. And in the temples of which the great ranges themselves were but the foundations he discovered prayers unknown to the most pious of the faithful and the most learned of mullahs, prayers that surpassed all their orisons in truth, virtue, and light.

The barking of the earless dogs had died away long ago. Over the whole great plain the only sound was the ring of Jahil's hoofs on the stony ash. Mukhi's and Zereh's feet made no noise. The syce kept behind the stallion, close to Zereh. He no longer had to serve as scout, to preserve Uraz from jerk or fall. He hoped for nothing better. "Fall, fall, thou sack of filth, fall," repeated Mukhi within himself, filled with disgust for that hunched body, indecent in a saddle. "Fall, and may the sun parch the corpse and the night freeze it."

He looked at Zereh. What was she thinking? Her face expressed nothing. Ask her? How? The holy silence of rock, sky, and sun left no room for the sound of a voice. Nevertheless Zereh spoke: she knew how to move her lips in speech like a dumb person. And she said, "If he slips, we finish him off."

"Yes, yes," whispered Mukhi.

Then again the young woman said, only moving her lips, "And we take the nomads to witness that we are innocent."

"Yes, yes," whispered Mukhi.

These words had been no more than the exchange of breaths. But the air was so sensitive to the slightest quivering that the vibration of the sound reached Uraz. At least it reached his double, whom pain held down on earth in the man's skin. And while the other Uraz, quite out of reach, voyaged on from peak to peak, this one felt the warning, like a very sick wolf that scents the carrion eaters on its trail.

And it was indeed with as greedy a hope that Mukhi and Zereh, side by side, without a word, without a sound, followed the exhausted rider . . . A fall. A blow on the temple. Another. Death. And all the look of an accident. Quick . . . The will, the money. The nomads' tents. Tears. The burial. And freedom at last. And wealth. To fulfill this all-devouring longing all that was necessary was a dizziness, a jerk, a sudden sideways movement.

Meanwhile the sun climbed, climbed . . . The shadows grew shorter and shorter and then vanished. The slumped, tottering, sagging body still held up in the saddle. And the plain stretched on out of sight, without a rough place, without a fold in the ground. Mukhi lacked the patience of the jackals and hyenas. He set his mouth against Zereh's ear and said, "I am going to throw him down."

The girl nodded her round forehead.

Mukhi chose a heavy pebble that fitted his hand and began to run. Jahil was going at his slowest walk. The syce had no difficulty in catching him up. Another moment and he would thrust Uraz and bring him to the ground. But at that moment the stallion turned his head toward Mukhi and suddenly lengthened his stride. Mukhi stood there, wavering on one leg. In those great moist eyes he had seen an expression that he could not believe . . . That harshness, that enmity for him, the syce, the man who had looked after him, who fed him, his brother . . .

"Impossible . . . not Jahil . . . not me. I saw badly . . . the light of noon deceives. . . so high," thought Mukhi. He stamped violently with the foot he had held poised in the air, hurried, and caught up the stallion again; and again he met his look. This time no doubt was possible. Jahil would not allow himself to be approached. Why? Mukhi asked himself. Why?

He felt frozen, paralyzed. He could not bear to see himself suddenly denied by the one being on earth he had always understood, protected, cosseted, and cherished, and from whom he had never received anything but gratitude and happiness. This interchange was as natural to him and as necessary as the sun. So why, why? Mukhi asked himself.

"The stone in my hand, perhaps," he said to himself. He opened his fingers, let the pebble fall, and, as though he were before a judge, showed Jahil his empty palm. The stallion remained on his guard. Mukhi made as if to approach. Jahil stepped quickly aside—a movement brisk enough to take him out of the syce's reach and yet so careful that it did not endanger Uraz's balance. Then he paced on with long, even, springy stride. Mukhi watched him go, standing there incapable of movement or thought until Zereh, clinging to his shoulder, asked, "What art thou waiting for?"

"Nothing," said Mukhi in a very low voice. "The horse will not let me touch him."

"Didst speak to him?" asked Zereh.

"No," said Mukhi.

"Call him. He always obeys thy voice," said Zereh.

"He will never listen to me," said the syce.

"What is the matter, then?" asked Zereh.

A strange, heartbroken pride showed in the syce's face. He said gravely, "A great buzkashi horse defends his rider to the death, against the man who means him harm."

"But how can this horse know?" said Zereh.

"He knows," said Mukhi. There was such strength and faith in his eyes and voice that the girl had no reply. She reflected, "As for me, I know the language of the dogs who guard our tents—know it well. Why should this tall syce not understand what the horses from his country say?"

Jahil had gone ahead of Mukhi and Zereh far enough to protect Uraz from the throw of a stone. He slackened his pace. But from time to time he turned his head. His watchful eyes showed that he meant to keep his distance undiminished.

Each time Mukhi uttered a heavy sigh. And each time Zereh whispered, "He will surely stop in the end."

So they traveled on over the enormous plain, the half-fainting horseman protected by his horse's instinct. Far behind him the tall syce, shattered by the loss of his only friend, and beside him the little nomad, entirely given up to her covetous dream.

Long, long was their road. Neither exhaustion nor hunger nor thirst seemed to have any hold on Uraz, nor on his stallion. The sun set out on the second half of its everlasting path and moved smoothly toward the mountain tops. Jahil went on and on. The shadows came into being again. The three travelers saw the birth and growth of strange companions under their feet, fluid and transparent, made in their likeness, and floating, gliding over the surface of the bare stone plain. Jahil went on and on. Now only a narrow strip of sky separated the red sun from the highest mountains. Twilight was giving the peaks colors as wildly strange as their monsters and their monuments. Over the whole surface of the plain from one end to the other the air had taken on the color of the ground so exactly that it seemed to be made from its dismal ash. Jahil went on and on.

Was he impelled by his own motion? Was it Uraz who was pushing him on by the automatic thrust of his muscles? In the gloom of the evening and at the distance that separated them from the horseman it was impossible for Mukhi and Zereh to make it out.

"Maybe he is dead," said Zereh.

Throughout the whole interminable pursuit, without halt, without food, without water, she had remained silent, to husband her strength. Her voice was constrained, held in to the utmost. The syce thought it was a bat brushing against his cheek in its velvet flight.

"Yes, he is dead . . ." whispered the nomad girl again. Instead of the joy that this thought should have filled her with, she felt a singular anguish. Presently the sun would touch the peaks. And then would come the icy darkness with all the kinds of evil begotten by a desert built by fiends high above the world.

Zereh's hand touched Mukhi's. She was asking for help. "If their masters die in the saddle, what do the steppe horses do?" she asked in a plaintive murmur.

Mukhi shivered and said heavily, the words coming hard, "In our country they stop, their manes hanging low . . . Here, I do not know . . . I know nothing."

"So we shall have to follow him, then?" whispered Zereh. "Follow in the darkness and the cold? And lose him . . . and ourselves?"

"There is everything we need for camping when we choose," said Mukhi, pulling the exhausted mule's headrope.

"And the stallion? And the money? Dost thou give them up?" asked Zereh.

"Never," said Mukhi.

He no longer hoped for the booty, but he felt that now he too was incapable of stopping. What was it that was dragging them along behind Uraz, then? Mukhi stared at the celestial line drawn out between the setting sun and the ridge. The sky's path was narrowing to the merest strip. The darkness was beginning to blur the horse's outline. Mukhi closed his eyes with horror. He had just realized the truth. The shape traveling in front of him was not Uraz, dead or alive: it was . . . Mukhi tried to stop his thoughts but he could not. It was the ghostly horseman . . . The ghostly horseman . . .

Zereh was still holding Mukhi's wrist. She felt its pulse beat so wildly, so unevenly, that she asked, "Art thou sick?"

Mukhi did not seem to hear. Zereh's fingers were wet with a

sticky liquid. It was a sweat that she recognized, and she murmured, "Now thy dread is greater than mine. Why?"

Mukhi sought in vain for the proper words. How could he explain the long evenings when little children in the darkest corner of the yurt, hidden and forgotten, listened to the old shepherds, the passing pedlars, and the wandering storytellers, squatting around the samovar? Their tales were always terrifying. They wrung the belly. They forced the child to thrust his fist into his mouth to stifle the shriek. Bloody, murderous kings, appalling wizards . . . And most terrible of all, the faceless horseman who rides day and night, day and night, through waste and sand and thorns and stones, through time and through time again, going nowhere. And those he meets he draws after him without remedy, without any turning back, until the death of the stars. Once more Mukhi felt the terror of his childhood. His sweat flowed thicker. His teeth began to chatter. He pointed to the shadow of the man bound to the shadow of the horse vanishing in the evening mist and stammered, "Thou dost not know . . . Thou dost not know . . . The ghostly horseman."

With a fierce gesture Zereh threw Mukhi's arm from her. The excess of this panic fear made her forget her own. When she took the syce's hand again it was not for support. It was to lead him. "Thou speakest like an old woman," said Zereh.

She had given up whispering. In the enormous silence of those high frozen places, of mineral ash and solitude, her voice rang out, vibrated in all its rich fullness. Mukhi stopped, awaiting the punishment of heaven and earth. The sky sent no lightning. The ground remained firm beneath his feet.

Zereh began to run. With one hand she led Mukhi, with the other she dragged the mule. The clatter of hoofs and the noise of the jolting load gave the syce back his strength and courage. He recognized the earth's solidity, its firmness. With every stride he was surer of his right place in it. In so true and sound a world there could be no room for a ghostly rider. As the distance between them lessened so the spell diminished. The dim form he was chasing was no longer magnified or transformed by the darkening shades. It had the size and shape of ordinary men. Its mount was a fine and powerful creature, but no more. A man on a horse, that was all. A few moments more and the horse was Jahil and the man Uraz. And Uraz powerless, at his mercy. He would show the impostor, the liar, the traitor, so he would!

Zereh clung to the syce's arm with all her weight. "No!" she cried, "No! Thou wilt send the stallion off again. And look . . . It seems as though he means to stop at last."

Although there was no obstacle in front of him Jahil had slowed down and was veering away to the right. Mukhi and Zereh could vaguely make out a hill in that direction. Until then the false light of the evening had apparently attached it to the mountain wall behind it. It looked like a headland running out, a cape jutting from the main range. In fact an immense distance separated the two.

It was a pyramidal hill. The sun, already pierced by the fanglike peaks, now touched no more than its topmost point. Beneath this sharp, fire-reddened point everything was in the spreading shade. Yet the shadow was still light enough to allow them to see little squat buildings set in rising steps, along narrow lanes.

"A village! Here!" cried Mukhi.

He no longer held in his voice. But Zereh took to whispering again. "By all the spirits of the road and night, be silent!" She dug her nails into Mukhi's palm and whispered, "All the nomads who come and go between the pastures of the Hazarajat and the High Passes talk about this hill . . . It is their burial place."

"So . . . so those houses . . ." said Mukhi even more softly than the girl.

"Tombs," said Zereh. "Those who are overtaken by death on the journey are not buried by the side of the road: they are brought here."

"Since . . ." stammered Mukhi. "Since when?"

"Since the beginning of time," said the girl.

And the syce understood: the buildings that covered the whole height of the hill and all its sides were sepulchers, made of piled-up blocks. Beneath them the everlasting caravans, each time they went by, left their human remains in continually spreading circles.

At the very top glowed the red signal lit by the last rays of the sun. The funeral pyramid was the gray of lead and the stones of the graves the gray of iron. All about them rippled the ground and the twilight, the color of ash.

"Listen," whispered Zereh.

The night wind of the highest plateaus was rising. Was it that which howled, quivered, and groaned in a lament so very nearly human? Or was it the bones of those who had traveled the road from their first day to their last and were camping forever amid the stones of these solitudes? "Man's end, soul's end," thought Mukhi. He was cold. Cold to the very roots of his life. In an almost imperceptible voice he said, "Zereh . . . We cannot stay like this—we cannot."

"Wait and see what the stallion wants," said the little nomad.

Jahil had just stopped at the foot of the hill. He was sniffing the air with a look of astonishment. His ears quivered. He swung his head from left to right and right to left, undecided, uneasy. He had been so delighted in his hide and his legs and his wind at having found the village at last after such a day's journey—the village that like all the rest would provide rest, warmth, water, food, safety. And now here, on the threshold, he found nothing of what was promised, what was owing. Not a single light. Not a sound. No scent of man or beast. And on the evening wind no trace of that excellent smell of cowdung burning on the hearth. Throughout the whole length of the day Jahil had acted by himself, but now he felt that this was a difficulty he could not resolve alone. It called for decision, for guidance from the motionless horseman who weighed so heavy in the saddle.

A shrill neigh, a fierce shake, a dart of fire in the broken bones. Uraz opened his eyes. Before him the tip of the hill was no more than a spark that flared up and vanished. "Night is here," thought Uraz. His last memory was of the full sun. He wondered what he had done with all those hours. Slept? Fainted? It did not matter. Although he was very weak he felt well. His head was clear. His refreshed body obeyed his commands. The frost of the evening counterbalanced the burning of his fever and delighted it. The whole of his being—like his skin in this—lay at a kind of strange and exact frontier at which two conflicting elements joined in his favor. He was in the clearest, most direct contact with reality, and yet at the same time it was perfectly easy for him to accept, with dreamlike lack of all dread or uneasiness, circumstances and images that reason could not possibly allow.

When he perceived—and this he did very quickly—the purpose of the seeming houses that rose before him, he was neither afraid nor astonished. The day before, or even that morning, he would have had nothing to do with such an encampment for anything on earth. Now he merely observed that the sepulchers were a protection against the wind that was sweeping the naked plain.

With his sound knee Uraz gently pushed Jahil's flank and began to make his way along the bottom of the hill. Because of the dim light the tombs seemed to touch one another. Yet seen near at hand it appeared that they were not all of the same shape. They varied according to the size and the shape of the blocks from which they were made, and in the intention or chance that had governed their making. In some the walls were almost smooth. In others the roughnesses formed strange designs. On some were broad eaves. Others had deep niches. Uraz went very slowly. He was looking for the ramp that would lead up to the inside of the pyramidal cemetery.

It was then that a voice arose from among the stones of the tombs. Frail, broken, spent, yet nonetheless extraordinarily clear. In its worn purity its ring was reminiscent of the sound of flawed crystal. The words came one by one in the silence, as though filtered through the layers of time. "Is it thou that comest, son of Tursen, O Uraz?"

Surprise made Jahil stagger. A few steps behind, two mingled cries rang out, a shriek and a wail in one.

"Mukhi . . . Zereh . . ." said Uraz to himself. "They too, they heard a grave call out to me."

At all other times he would have lashed Jahil with his whip and galloped into the darkness, the cold, the desert . . . On this night he could not be afraid of anything, since everything was natural to him. He cried, "Whoever thou mayst be, thou art not mistaken. Tursen is indeed my father, and my name is Uraz."

"Go straight before thee," said the flawed crystal voice. "Thou wilt find me easily."

Uraz reined in. It was not that he hesitated. It was only that he had the feeling that this voice was not unknown to him. Where, when could he have heard it? He could not bring it to memory; he pushed the stallion on.

Never yet had Jahil been put to such an exact, constrained pace. As he went past in front of the sepulchers Uraz peered at every gap between the stones, and sometimes he searched them with his whip. Maybe a ghostly hand would seize the lash. He moved as though feeling his way. Night had fallen. Then in spite of his tight rein Jahil began to walk faster. And Uraz saw why. In front of them, at the level of the ground but how far off he could not tell, the darkness was threaded by a broken golden line, like a motionless lightning flash. "The reflection of the flame that rings ghosts round, taking the place of shadows for them," thought Uraz. He loosened the reins.

Jahil was almost trotting. "Poor simpleton," thought Uraz, "he believes it is a real fire." The brilliant line did not shift. "The spirit is making game of me," thought Uraz again. All at once he found himself in front of a fire. A real fire. A little campfire of dry branches. It was burning in the hollow of the cell that stood before a roughly built tomb. There, behind the flames, a man was sitting. No skeleton. No ghost. A living man. He wore a long cloak. A knapsack lay at his feet. To the light of the fire he held out an ageless face. He said, "May the great peace of this place be with thee, O Uraz."

And Uraz bowed as low as he could in his saddle and replied, "Peace and honor to thee, Ancestor of All the World. I am strangely fortunate to meet thee here."

"I was waiting for thee," said Gardi Gaj.

*****

18

The Mourners

T HE STONES OF THE TOP of the tomb stood out much farther than those that supported them. A kind of short covered gallery ran along the lower part of the front. At each end broken pieces and pebbles formed a low wall. The stone cell had only one opening—a very slender one—that opened onto the plateau.

Gardi Gaj's fire made this slit into a window of flame. Mukhi and Zereh saw the silhouette of Uraz and his stallion, outlined against it as though drawn in Indian ink. Zereh whispered, "It is not he, but his ghost."

"No," said Mukhi. "No!" He had already been caught. Once was enough. With his rounded hand to his mouth he cried, "Uraz, O Uraz, I am here."

"Well," replied the ghost, "what art thou waiting for to lift me off the horse?"

Zereh clung to Mukhi's shoulder. "Do not go," she begged. "Never, never listen to that spirit."

"Would a spirit have that smell of pus that is coming on the wind?" said the syce.

The north wind shook and parted the veil of flame. In the opening, an extraordinarily emaciated man appeared, leaning against the wall of the tomb.

"See, see," whispered the nomad girl, "the ghost of the sepulcher is out to lure us."

Now Mukhi hesitated. As for this specter, he knew nothing of it. The fiery hanging spread across the crack once more and hid everything in the cell. "Uraz, O Uraz," called Mukhi in an uncertain voice, "the one behind the fire there, is he a traveler like other men?"

Before Uraz could reply, a weak voice with the ring of flawed crystal carried far out into the night. "Come to my fire without fear," it said. "A spirit has no old bones to warm."

"A living man," said Mukhi to Zereh. "And I believe . . . I believe . . ." Without finishing, the syce ran to the opening of the cell and there, looking over the fire by the light of its dancing flames, he saw the ageless face of Gardi Gaj, so wrinkled with countless, deep, crisscrossing lines that his cheeks might have been parchment covered with mysterious writing. Mukhi bent double, touched the frozen ground with his hands, and cried, "I knew it, Ancestor of All the World, I knew it, O Memory of All Time . . . The man who hears thy voice, if only once, never forgets it again. By the Prophet, it is so with all the gardeners, craftsmen, cooks, shepherds, and syces on our estate to whom thou didst tell the glory of Attila, the great warrior. He was born, thou saidst, in our province of Meimana, and it was from his town of Akcha that he set out to conquer half the world."

Was it the play of the flames? A shadow of a smile seemed to float on Gardi Gaj's white lips. In him age, experience, and weariness had dried up and exhausted all the springs of joy. But the old storyteller still loved his tales. And it pleased him that a very young man should remember one, for that meant the sons of his sons would hand it on, still living, in spite of the flight of time and the scythe of death.

Uraz spoke to the syce between his clenched teeth. He was suffering terribly. "Carry me behind the fire," he said. "Tether Jahil at my side. I do not need the tent."

"A little farther off," said Gardi Gaj to Mukhi, "thou wilt find a well and dry wood beside it. Every caravan that passes leaves a supply for the next."

Mukhi set Uraz with his back to the wall of the sepulcher, close to Gardi Gaj, and said, "I will bring Jahil back when he has drunk."

"And tea," said Uraz. The marrow of his bones was colder than the night, colder than stone. He leaned his lower jaw on both his hands to prevent it from chattering.

"It was indeed thus that I expected to see thee again," said Gardi Gaj. "At the uttermost end of thy strength."

Speaking with difficulty, Uraz asked, "How didst . . . thou know . . . thou shouldst find me . . . in this high graveyard?"

"For the man who will not take the common road, the only way is written in the lie of the land. The way runs across this plateau and on this plateau the only halting place is that of the tombs."

With his palms against his chin Uraz asked again, "Where didst thou learn of my defeat, Ancestor of All Men?"

"On the track that runs from Kalakchikan to the stables of Osman Bey," said Gardi Gaj.

Both men thought of Tursen with such intensity that they had the feeling of being separated by his image, sitting there between them at that moment. Yet his name was not uttered. Each waited for the other to speak of him first. Pride prevented Uraz from doing so. And Gardi Gaj was silent out of wisdom.

The fire died down. The old storyteller revived its zeal with dry branches. A flame, leaping up again, lit his fingers, his wrist, and then his face. They were all so frail, so transparent, that it was almost unbearable to look at them. Bone and skin alone, without a trace of flesh.

"How didst thou come from the steppe so fast, Ancestor of All the World?" murmured Uraz.

"Is it not the old goats," said Gardi Gaj, "that have the surest foot and go by the shortest way?"

Mukhi brought Jahil to the cell and tethered him close to Uraz. Behind the syce came Zereh with a teapot, a bag of sugar, two cups. She served the two men, beginning with Gardi Gaj, then, small and fragile, she slipped into the darkness of the stones. Mukhi followed her with his eyes, and then spoke to Gardi Gaj. "O Memory of All Time and of All Places, enlighten me. This terrible plateau, where does it lead? And which way must one go then?"

Gardi Gaj sucked in his dark tea and said, "The very high plain on which we stand ends against a mountain wall. There is only one cleft in it, and that so steep that its name is the Ladder. Above, there is a flat land once more, sprinkled with small black and gray stones. Then thou goest down to the Band-i-Amir."

"By the Prophet! The lakes of the Band-i-Amir!" cried Mukhi. "Truly?"

"Truly," said Gardi Gaj. "And the finest tales thou mayst have heard of them are nothing, compared with those enchanted waters."

Uraz did not speak. He was shivering. Mukhi went to fetch coverings for him, and having done so offered to spread a quilt over Gardi Gaj. The storyteller said, "It is not worth the trouble. On my bones there is nothing left for the frost."

"Zereh's pilaw will rejoice thee soon, Ancestor of All the World," said Mukhi.

The ancient man spread his two hands over the fire. They were translucent. "Thanks to thee, O syce," said Gardi Gaj, "but what indeed have I to nourish?"

Uraz felt a strong gratitude for the old man's words. The mere thought of that thick and greasy dish nauseated him. "Go," he said to the syce, "go fill thyself and leave us in peace!"

Mukhi took off the mule's packs and saddle and set about pitching the tent; neither he nor Zereh chose to pass the night in the shelter of a tomb. The stony ground made the task difficult. He put all his heart into it and the work brought warmth back into his muscles. The strong smell of highly spiced rice cooking slowly on the three hearthstones filled his belly with happiness.

In the cell Gardi Gaj looked steadily at Uraz's face. It was a mask in which everything, even the eyelids, was tense with anguish. "Thou art suffering," said the old storyteller, "suffering cruelly."

Usually Uraz looked on compassion as an insult. No one on earth had the right to display pity for a man who made game of his own flesh. But in this voice he heard neither commiseration nor anxiety. The ancient man was merely stating a fact.

"This heap of blankets weighs too heavy on the broken bones," said Uraz. "If I push them aside the cold gnaws at the wound and tears it."

"I have an ally for thee," said Gardi Gaj. From his cloak he drew a little brownish stick and held it close to the fire for a few moments. When the substance had grown softer he pulled off a very little piece, rolled it between his transparent fingers, and said, "Swallow this pellet with a mouthful of tea. And wait."

Uraz obeyed. Then he asked the ancient man, "Is thy remedy magic, O Ancestor of All the World?"

"It could be called so," said Gardi Gaj. "It is a gift from the wisest and oldest of witches."

"What is she called?" asked Uraz.

"Earth," said Gardi Gaj.

"A plant—an herb?" murmured Uraz.

"The poppy's juice," said Gardi Gaj.

"What!" cried Uraz. He leaned abruptly toward the ancient man and went on fiercely, "Thou, thou, so wise and aged, why hast thou given me a poison that takes away a man's strength and dignity, just as wine does, accursed by the Koran?"

"Nothing that the earth gives is accursed," said Gardi Gaj. And when Uraz made as though to answer, he stopped him with a wave of his hand. "Do not distress thyself, O chapandaz," he said. "Motion and loud cries are opposed to the good actions of the medicine. To help thee to patience I shall tell thee of the birth of wine. Come, set thy head back against the stone that shelters the remnants of a man of the roads, open thy bosom to calmness, and listen to me."

And Gardi Gaj began his tale. "In that very distant time Shah Shamiran reigned in Herat the Magnificent, a wise and powerful sovereign. And in the fierce heat of the afternoons it was his delight to walk among his hanging gardens, rich in shade, in rare flowers, fountains, and sculptured kiosks. His court followed him— dignitaries, priests, soothsayers, commanders, poets, and princes.

"And one day he saw, perched on a screen of trees, an unknown bird so beautiful that he stopped to admire it. At that very moment a serpent reared up, just by the splendid plumage. 'Is there no one to prevent it from striking?' cried Shah Shamiran. With an arrow his eldest son shot the serpent down. The bird flew, vanishing far into the sky. It was forgotten.

"Now a year later, day for day and at the same hour, it returned and wheeled above the royal garden; and before it disappeared, it dropped certain seeds from its beak. 'What dost thou say to that?' asked Shah Shamiran of his chief soothsayer. And the soothsayer replied, 'The wonderful bird has brought thee thy reward.' The Shah thereupon gave orders that the place where the seeds had fallen should be watched. A plant as yet unseen by any man began to grow there. It did not rise very high, but on its slender branches appeared bunches of small round fruits. No one dared touch them. Their juice might be deadly. Slowly the bunches grew overripe. The Shah had a tall vase set there to receive them. When they had fallen they fermented and a red liquid came from them. Was this the reward? Or was it a deadly poison?

"They took from his prison a man condemned to be impaled. The Shah ordered him to drink a goblet of the unknown liquid. The whole court stood there at the sovereign's side. The wretched man drank and closed his eyes. A whisper ran among the courtiers—'O fatal draft. He is about to die.'

"The prisoner raised his eyelids. Joy danced deep in his gaze. He smiled. Then—and his voice was no longer that of a slave wearing irons but that of a master who inflicts them—then he cried, 'Let them give me another goblet!'

"The Shah signed to his cupbearer, and the cupbearer poured a ruby-colored liquid into the highly wrought gold cup that the ruler alone honored with his lips. After him the others tasted the mysterious drink. And joy and strength sang in their persons . . ." Gardi Gaj paused a moment and finished, "It was thus that wine fell from the skies for the pleasure of men on the Afghan land."

Uraz had followed the tale with a bowed head, and now he said thoughtfully, "Ancestor of All the World, the truth and nothing but the truth falls from thy venerated mouth. But in the days of thy tale, had the Prophet yet enlightened the blind world and named in the Book of Books those things that are forbidden?"

As he often did, Gardi Gaj replied to this question by another, "Hast thou heard, O pious chapandaz, of the Emperor Baber?"

"Baber, the Afghan with the invincible arm," cried Uraz, "he who was the Great Mogul in India?"

The old storyteller gave a slight nod and went on, "According to thee, was that Emperor a true believer?"

"Who would presume to doubt it?" said Uraz. "Did he not convert the idolatrous Hindus to the One Faith?"

"Very well," said Gardi Gaj. "And dost thou believe that this conqueror in the name of Allah, the Sword of the Prophet, was capable of disobeying the teaching of the Book?"

"I should have to be mad to do so," replied Uraz simply.

The ancient man's voice grew very slow. "How then did it come about," he said, "that in the reign of the great Baber there was enough wine made in the Afghan land to fill skins and barrels without number?"

"That was because the Sword of Islam did not know that it was done!" said Uraz.

"Thou art mistaken, pious chapandaz," replied Gardi Gaj. "That Emperor went from village to village, where the finest grapes in the world were grown, and followed by his ministers, his generals, his singers, and his poets, he tasted the young wines. And one day he saw a tulip so beautiful that to honor it to the highest possible degree he caused it to be filled with the most exquisite wine and drank from the flower goblet."

"What art thou saying? What art thou saying?" murmured Uraz.

"And again I say," went on Gardi Gaj with the same gentleness, "that on a hill from which the whole of Kabul, the capital, may be seen spread out, Baber ordered a broad pool to be dug. And when the Great Mogul entertained especially beloved friends, he caused that pool, which is still there, to be filled to the brim with the most precious wine . . . And his guests and he himself drew deeply from it."

"Ancestor of All the World! Ancestor of All the World!" cried Uraz, "if it were not from thy mouth that I heard this . . ."

"If every one of my words is not the truth, may the tongue in this mouth so dry up that never, never again may I tell legend, fable, or tale," said Gardi Gaj.

Uraz turned away his head, and as though asking them for a reply he set his anxious gaze on the flames. "The Book of Books was indeed the same in Baber's time as it is now, in ours?" he asked.

"In every line, word, and comma," said Gardi Gaj.

"What has changed, then, is the spirit of those who teach it?" said Uraz.

"Or their opinions," said Gardi Gaj.

"Who then, as between the masters of those days and of our time," said Uraz again, "who then perceived the truth?"

"Neither these nor those," said the ancient man.

Uraz turned his eyes from the fire and looked at Gardi Gaj. They were lit by an inner fire that gave them a greater brilliance than the blaze of dried grass and branches. There was a profound serenity on Uraz's face—a face like hollow wax. "So it is for me alone to decide," he said. "And according to my own reason alone and my own heart."

"As in all things."

A smile that had nothing in common with his usual wolf's grin appeared on Uraz's bloodless lips. "So that is where thou didst intend to lead me?" he asked. The old storyteller's reply was a scarcely perceptible motion that stirred all his innumerable wrinkles. "Truly, truly," said Uraz. He leaned back against the wall of the tomb, carefully arranged his blankets, and went on, "I feel no more pain at all. My body is full of sober prudence. My mind floats above it, and is amazed at nothing."

Gardi Gaj rolled a pellet of brown paste and gave it to Uraz. When Uraz had swallowed it he felt his blood flowing in his lightened, nourished body like an enchanted tide. The coarse fur and harsh cloth that covered him were deeper and softer to the touch than silk and velvet. And from this blissful clay his thinking mind rose, escaping, to judge the world, men, and himself without haste or passion, judge them from a great height.

"How came it that my life meant nothing to me unless I was before all other men and above them?" murmured Uraz. He remembered the first caravanserai and his harmony with the exhausted animals, the wretched travelers . . . He said, "This horseman who flogged, flogged his horse to be perpetually in the lead . . . The poor fool . . ."

"There is a good proverb," said Gardi Gaj. " 'If luck is with thee, why hurry? If luck is against thee, why hurry?' " Uraz's head nodded. The smile of peace lay on his mouth. He was very sleepy. "May the gods be with the rest," said Gardi Gaj.

"Why the *gods?*" murmured Uraz. "There is but one."

"When a man has traveled far through the world and through years, he finds that hard to believe," said Gardi Gaj.

From the night sky an even, muffled roar came down to them. They did not look up. They were used to this noise. For several years now, two or three times a week, flying machines crossed and re-crossed the air above the Afghan valleys, mountains, steppes.

Uraz went to sleep. The old storyteller added a few twigs to the fire.

THE BAYING STARTED WITH THE DAY. IT HAD A DESPERATE, HEART-breaking ring.

In the rocky cell, where Gardi Gaj slept squatting and Uraz stretched out, the little fire was still alight. But it no longer had its fiery color. Through the eastward slit the sun was already pouring in, and although this was only the first moment of its course, the flame of the sky ate up the flame of men.

The baying came closer.

The countless wrinkles on Gardi Gaj's cheeks—innumerable cracks in an ancient parchment—began to stir, and as he did not hear sounds so well as he had in earlier times he automatically thrust his face toward the place from which it came to make out what it was. Then he revived the fire with a handful of twigs thrown onto the white embers and leaned his head back against the wall of the tomb.

The baying grew louder.

Uraz heard it too. Yet for all that his sleep did not leave him. It was the most astonishing sleep he had ever known in his life. It gave out calmness, peace, a pillowy annihilation. And at the same time it turned his body into a kind of shell that took in all the scents of the night, all the sighing and breathing of the darkness, and with them it fed a great welling of images, ruled sometimes by the laws of reason and sometimes by the wild dartings of delirium. They did not belong to the world of dreams and Uraz knew it. A strange power allowed him to follow them, to judge them, and yet at the same time to give himself up to them entirely and to believe in their wonderful chaos. When the sound of baying vibrated in the hollow of the sounding conch that covered and contained his skin, Uraz was pierced, filled through and through, dwelt in by earless sulfur-yellow beasts, hellish dogs that raced over the stony plain. It was inside his head that the slavering jaws opened wide, in his own mouth that the long teeth clashed together. Uraz did not stir a finger or raise an eyelid. He was at once the field of battle and the watcher of the field, the matter of the game and its controller. The pack ran flowing through his body itself.

ZEREH THREW BACK THE ARM THAT HELD HER PRESSED AGAINST A broad, warm chest and raised herself on one knee. "Where art thou going?" murmured Mukhi in a sleep-laden voice. He opened his eyes and closed them again for a moment: the close-woven canvas of the tent was like a sponge soaked in light. "The sun is up before me," thought Mukhi with remorseful astonishment. "How can it have happened . . . ?" Carnal memory came back to him and his feeling of culpability faded away. He stretched out his arm and with his hand entirely covered the slim, soft belly that had so filled him with delight. Zereh's skin slid beneath his fingers.

"Listen!" said the girl. She stood upright, off the mattress on which they had slept so little, and leaned toward the baying.

"The dogs?" asked Mukhi lazily. "Like yesterday?"

"Yesterday's are far away," cried Zereh.

Mukhi scratched his close-clipped head and observed, "That is true . . . They are already driving their herd toward Bamian."

"These dogs, the dogs here," said Zereh, "dost thou not hear why they are howling?"

Mukhi listened attentively and said in a whisper, "A dead body . . ."

"The caravan is coming to bury it," said the nomad girl. "Come."

Zereh's eyes were wider, more strongly marked, and her bosom rose faster and higher. The syce picked up the filthy length of stuff that served him as a turban and tied it, reflecting, "Women are like that . . . They like burials even more than birth or marriage feasts." He said to Zereh, "Thou art not afraid any more?"

"Why should I be?" she asked, astonished. "It is broad daylight. This is a real dead man and his tribe are here to bury him. Come!"

She darted from the tent but stood there, caught motionless between the opened sides of the flap. Dawn on the high plain was unbearably brilliant. Everything shone, sparkled, shimmered, dazzling and blinding the eyes. The stony ash, the bare mountain walls, their snowy icy peaks. The points and the edges of innumerable swords appeared to be dancing, trembling, and scintillating in air brilliant as diamonds.

Standing there behind Zereh, topping her by half his height, Mukhi felt as though a heavenly blade had slashed his eyes. He said to himself, "The prayer . . . The prayer. I had forgotten it . . . Allah will punish me." He picked Zereh up by the shoulders, turned her to the holy quarter, bent her, and almost threw her down. There she was, bowed to the ground at his side, and she heard him murmur, "Beg the Almighty to forgive us for having let the hour go by because of each other."

Mukhi plunged deep into his supplication. The girl could not follow him. With her forehead to the earth she dreamed of the funeral caravan.

When they stood up again they found themselves facing the hill of tombs. In this icy light the graves inspired no dread. Thickset, solid, regular, they comforted the eye. They were the only things on that cyclopean plain that were within human reach, on a human scale. The nearest of them gave forth a very thin smoke.

"They need us," said Mukhi.

"Be quiet . . . Listen," whispered Zereh.

Above the cry of the dogs a more piercing lament rose, so infectious that Zereh clasped both hands to her heart and the same wail poured from her throat. With this harsh, rhythmic, broken, inexhaustible cry flying before her she ran to join the mourning women as they came.

Mukhi followed her with his eyes. When she had vanished round a spur of the hill he turned toward the cell from which the smoke rose. He leaned halfway in through the narrow gap. Uraz and Gardi Gaj were resting, their eyes closed. Jahil's were wide open, and they questioned the syce.

"He is thirsty," thought Mukhi. And he whispered, "Patience, patience, my beauty. As soon as they are awake thou shalt have fine cool water, enough to plunge thy nose in deep."

Then he waited to see the stallion twitch his ears, flutter his eyelids, or move his lips in something like a smile, giving him his usual answer of friendship. Jahil did nothing of the kind. Mukhi clicked his tongue, whistled in an undertone. Jahil knew these calls and had loved them since the time he was a foal, uncertain on thin, feeble legs, learning to run on the steppe. Between him and his syce they were a simpler, truer means of communication than words for men. But this morning the stallion did not seem to hear them. His unmoving eyes remained watchful and severe. "Just as yesterday, when I meant to fling Uraz down," thought Mukhi with immense respect. "This horse forgets nothing."

He withdrew his body from between the walls of rock, and as he did so the brilliance of the plateau dazzled him, an extreme clarity so harsh and incisive in its flintlike brightness that it seemed to him as though the great cry of mourning and the baying that spread beneath the sky were the very utterance of the light. He shook his head to be rid of the illusion, and as Zereh had done he turned to walk along the foot of the hill toward the place behind, from which the wild lament of the mourning women was coming.

The farther he went from the eastward side, the darker and longer grew the shadows thrown by the graves that lined the path. Mukhi took care to step outside this uneven line of darkness. After a while he saw that the black, ill-omened ring drawn between him and the tall burial mound was gradually diminishing in width. He looked up toward the graves: they no longer came more than half-way down the slope.

"Truly," said Mukhi to himself, "it was on the side of the rising sun that they began the cemetery. On the west there is still room for a great many dead."

He walked faster along the barer hill. When he had made half the circuit he came to a fold in the ground that had no tombs at all; and at the end of it he saw the caravan coming toward him.

It was a clan of some fifty or sixty Pathans. They were traveling on foot. As usual, the men carried guns of the traditional kind, inlaid and damascened. But against all ordinary custom it was not they who led the long, slow procession that wound toward the graveyard. There were women walking in front and other women surrounding them. Women of every age and condition, and they walked with their eyes closed. They were guided, pulled, thrust on by their chant, a wail of frantic harshness and suffering, continually broken off, taken up, lost, found, a chant that never ceased and that held their mouths wide open, like those of sightless masks. They beat their breasts, scratched their cheeks, tore their hair. At the same time there was a strange, indwelling happiness in their distress, their trance . . .

Mukhi could not find Zereh among the mourners. His eyes left them, searching farther off. Behind the first group he saw a human form—the only one in the caravan not to tread the hard ash of the plain—on top of the load on the largest of the three camels belonging to the band. She was quite drowned in the black folds of her veils, shawls, and wrappings, and to begin with it was hard to make out the very small bundle from which protruded a head scarcely larger than a pomegranate and which she hugged passionately to her bosom. The only woman who did not walk. The only woman to remain silent. The dead child's mother.

And gazing at her unopened lips Mukhi could not understand the outcry that surrounded her and went along with her, louder, stronger, and more frenzied than the rest, even more loaded with anguish and passion. Then he saw a woman pressed to the camel's side, her head leaning against the mother's knee. The frantic lament, more powerful than all the other mourning voices, came from her throat. At first Mukhi had no notion who this woman was. When she went by in front of him, and only then, he saw that it was Zereh.

At her heels came two earless mastiffs, baying to the dead in time with her cries, while the herds in their charge straggled in a shapeless mob behind the procession.

Without moving Mukhi watched the caravan reach the foot of the hill and form a ring around a flat place where the remains of

many encampments could be seen. The mourners went on shrieking, wailing, and beating themselves. The men unloaded a few
packs, set up a tent, and made the camel carrying the mother and
her sorrow kneel on the ground. Stiff, mute, with her arms tight
round the little bundle, she stepped toward the tent, her clothes
spreading like an enormous bat. And although the thing seemed
impossible, the mourning took on fresh strength and soared up
louder, terrible and wild, until the black-veiled woman with the
cold, motionless bundle pressed to her heart had vanished between
the wings of felt. Then, at once, there was silence.

The mourners, as though drained by their frenzy, sank to the
ground, their clothes in tatters, their faces bleeding. Yet the oldest
remained standing. She tucked up the white locks that hung to her
deeply wrinkled bosom, ran her tongue over her bare gums, and
said, "Come, women: to work. The children have a right to their
food. The men must have strength for their work, and we for fresh
tears."

Zereh stayed there alone by the tent, squatting with her cheek
against its harsh stuff. When Mukhi leaned over her shoulder and
called she turned toward him so violently that he was afraid he had
sent her back into her wailing trance. Instead of the terrible mask
and voice of the mourning woman possessed by her devils he saw
eyes filled with supplication, and heard a frail, humble murmur,
"Tall syce, tall syce, I want children," said Zereh. "My womb has
held some, no doubt, but by worthless men who beat me, who did
not belong to me . . . With herbs I stopped everything. Only
every time, what sadness afterward, what pain in my heart!"

She glanced toward the tent, from which came a muffled lament, something between a lullaby and a sob. Then she looked at
the children, boys and girls running, playing, quarreling, and laughing. The sun shone on the brown of their cheeks, the blackness of
their eyes. She clasped her hands round Mukhi's neck and spoke
with a passion that bound her whole being, "By thee . . . Yes . . .
Without fail . . ." She let his neck go and unconsciously her arms
crossed on her chest as though they were holding a baby. "They
will be beautiful, so beautiful," she chanted. "Yes, the most beautiful of them all."

Not far off came the sound of metal biting into stone. "They are breaking off pieces of the hill for the grave," said Mukhi. "Dost thou choose to stay until the end?"

"Truly," said Zereh. "And I shall weep for the dead child louder than all the others . . . and fate will protect mine."

Under his turban Mukhi scratched his cropped head and said, "I must go back. Time is running by."

"Go," said Zereh. "I shall not be long. They only need a little grave." Once more she clung to the syce's neck, bringing his eyes close to hers. "They will be beautiful, they will be strong," she said. Her eyebrows joined in a single line. With ferocious gravity she added, "And rich, I swear to thee."

URAZ WAS NO LONGER IN THAT STATE IN WHICH IMAGES POSSESSED their own life, their own volition, outside and beyond reason, yet at the same time having reason's assent, that state in which dream and reality possessed the same meaning and the same laws; that magic state was over. His mind was clear. He did not move. In spite of the thirst that parched his mouth and throat he did not call for tea to be brought; and this was because he dreaded the slightest damage to the tranquility, smooth and soft as though woven from the finest silk, in which both his body and mind were lapped.

The dogs could be heard no more. The silence had the same taste as the sun which was now darting into the stony cell. Its warmth and its brilliance made it impossible to see whether the fire was still burning. Gardi Gaj threw a pinch of dried grass onto the ashes. There was a slight crackling.

To speak to the ancient man it was not necessary either to stir or open his eyes. "Where dost thou intend to go now, Ancestor of All the World?" asked Uraz in a murmur.

The ancient man, equally motionless and also with closed eyes, replied, "Usually it is not I who choose my road. A lorry comes by—it takes me with it . . . A caravan passes—I follow it . . . The wind blows and wafts me along . . ." Gardi Gaj let the fire crackle for a moment and added, "Usually . . ."

"And this time?" asked Uraz.

The old man seemed to listen attentively to the song from the hearth. Then he said, "This time I know. Last night I saw my road." Gardi Gaj spread his hands toward the invisible flames, and their parchment-colored skin became transparent. He went on, "A few days ago, at Kalakchikan with the great Tursen, I was close to tears because of a tune played on the dambura. A few hours ago I spoke for myself alone."

"Well?" asked Uraz again.

"I thought I had grown older than old age itself," said Gardi Gaj, "that I had gone beyond the true, the only death, forever. Well now, here they are, both of them, they have caught me up . . . I want to carry them away to the valleys where my cradle lay."

"With thy gods?" asked Uraz.

"Those who were not burned are held in captivity, kept as a spectacle, at Kabul," said Gardi Gaj. "It matters little. At my age there is no longer any need."

A great din of leather soles on the stony ground and the clatter of crockery came into the cell. Mukhi brought the tea. Its smell and the sound of the cups showed Uraz the full extent of his thirst. His lips and nostrils quivered. He had to exert a great effort to wait while Mukhi offered his tray to the storyteller first.

"Welcome to thee, O syce, coming at the best of moments to quench our thirst," said Gardi Gaj.

Mukhi, still panting from his hurry, cried, "You heard them, the mourners? I went . . . to greet the nomads."

"That was fitting," said Gardi Gaj. "We are the host of their dead."

When he had emptied three cups Uraz asked, "Whom were they burying?"

"A new-born child," said Mukhi.

"Another cup," said Uraz. Then, "Such bellowing for a little puling bladder filled with woman's milk and filth."

"Is that all thou dost think of children?" asked Gardi Gaj.

"And that they are stupider, dirtier, noisier, more demanding, and harder to rear than a horse," said Uraz.

"Hast thou had any?" asked Gardi Gaj.

"My wife died bearing the first," said Uraz.

"Wast thou sorry for it?" asked the ancient man again.

Uraz shook his head and replied, "That same spring I won my chapandaz cap at the Three Provinces buzkashi."

Gardi Gaj gave his cup back to Mukhi, relaxed against the wall, and said to Uraz, "So thou lovest none but thyself?"

"That is not true," replied Uraz. "Only I love the others even less."

Mukhi took away the tray, came back with an overflowing pail for Jahil, and went out very quickly. He was afraid that Uraz might ask about Zereh.

As the sun rose higher, so its rays left the cell. When it was directly overhead and so fiery that the gravel of the plain seemed to spit with the heat, Uraz's and Gardi Gaj's shelter had long since been filled with shade. It was a gentle shade, warmed and gilded by the embers of the dying fire, embers that could be counted one by one in the hollow of the ash.

Jahil had lain down again after having drunk; now he rose suddenly and came to sniff at Uraz's face. Uraz said to Gardi Gaj, "The stallion has had all the rest he wants." He stroked Jahil and added, "So have I . . . I shall call the syce." He did nothing of the kind. He could still feel a kind of grace just touching him, and he wanted to keep it, to experience its very last delights. "In a moment," he said to Jahil, gently pushing the moist nose away. The stallion would not obey and whinnied. When the silence returned Uraz could just make out, very faint and far off, the barking of the dogs. He raised himself on one elbow. At this Jahil agreed to move back.

The barking grew louder, more distinct. It took on a meaning. And Uraz heard that it was now no longer the same as it had been at dawn. Then the baying had expressed woe and distress. Now it conveyed nothing but merciless rage.

Yet it approached in a strange, unusual way. It had nothing of the speed of chase or running in to the kill. It was as though the dogs were holding themselves in, reducing their pace to that of a human step. And from time to time they were silent, as though they meant to keep their course unknown.

This stealthy advance . . . These moments of silence . . . The wolf's grin appeared and settled firmly upon Uraz's face. There was no hint of languor left in him. Among the stones that littered the ground he chose the heaviest, sharpest edged; he fixed it to the lash of his whip; he tried the strength and suppleness of this new weapon, a short whip and club at the same time. With the stock between his teeth he began to crawl toward the entrance, dragging his broken leg behind him. The stones hitting the break and their rubbing against the wound were shockingly painful. Red sparks danced in front of his eyes. The wolf's grin widened, grew sharper. It was excellent that pain should restore him to himself. Measured in paces, the distance he had to cover was trifling. With the burden of flesh to draw along and his torment to undergo, the journey took a considerable time. When he reached the point he had set himself, halfway between the opening and the remains of the fire, Uraz lay flat on his belly and recovered his breath.

Mukhi, still holding the greasy wheatcake he had just fried, ran toward the sound of the mastiffs. He saw them a great way off, one on each side of Zereh. She was guiding them, with her fingers on the back of their necks.

As soon as he was within calling distance Mukhi cried, "Why these dogs?"

Zereh remained silent until the moment her path brought her in front of Mukhi. "So that our children shall be rich," she said. And passed the syce at a light-footed run, with the two earless monsters hard at her side.

Mukhi caught her up and cried, "But the Ancestor of All the World?" She made no answer, not even looking at the syce. "Allah Omnipotent . . . He is no more than skin and bones . . . Do so order it that the dogs may scorn him!" prayed Mukhi.

What else could he do? Stop Zereh? The dogs would be at his throat the same instant and Zereh would not hold them back . . .

They came opposite the cleft that opened onto the cell. There Zereh dug her nails into the mastiffs' necks, held them motionless, then suddenly launched them straight forward with a harsh long cry not unlike a bay.

URAZ HAD RECOVERED HIS BREATH. AT ZEREH'S CRY HE LEANED HIS weight on his sound knee. He felt the broken bone pierce flesh and skin. His grin spread right across his face. The furious voices of the dogs came into the stone cell, and echoing from walls, ceiling, and ground they filled it with a hellish roar. Uraz took the flint-loaded whip from his mouth. The broad chest and gaping jaws of the first mastiff appeared in the opening. Uraz plunged his left hand into the embers, grasped a handful, and flung them into the open mouth. The dog stiffened, turned its head away. Uraz raised his whip and the sharpened stone came racing down on the end of the thong: it struck a terrible blow right on the naked place under the hole of the mastiff's ear. The dog staggered. Uraz had no time to strike again. The second monster hurtled in through the cleft in the rock. Its speed and bulk flung down and crushed the first. The shock threw the mastiff off its balance. It fell, its legs apart. Uraz flattened himself on it, belly to belly, and slit its throat with the knife he had drawn from his belt.

The beast's death throes were so violent that they threw Uraz to the ground again. He was on the brink of fainting. Gardi Gaj's voice prevented him. "What dost thou expect, what dost thou still ask of thyself, O chapandaz?" the old storyteller was saying.

A warm breath wafted over Uraz's face. He opened his eyes. Jahil's head was next to his own. "Lie down," whispered Uraz.

The stallion stretched out, his back to the man on the ground. Uraz seized him round the neck with both arms, dragged himself, raised himself, and fell on the stallion. With the utmost slowness and caution, Jahil rose up. And his load rose at the same time. Since there was no saddle, it seemed to Uraz that he and his horse shared the same skin.

He untied the tether, turned Jahil toward the opening. "May peace be with thee, Ancestor of All the World," he said to Gardi Gaj.

"I always go with my guest as far as the threshold," said the ancient man.

The stallion strode over the bodies of the dogs and stood

framed in the cleft. Uraz, with his clothes, face, and hands covered with clotting blood, saw Mukhi and Zereh a few paces off. "Do not forget the saddle," he said to the syce. Then to Gardi Gaj, who stood close by him, holding all his wrinkles up to the midday sun, "May the gods watch over thee, O Ancestor of All Men."

"O chapandaz, beware of thine!" said Gardi Gaj.

And Uraz rode off toward the west.

*****

1 9

The Five Lakes

ONCE HE HAD GONE beyond the grave-laden hill, Uraz found that the end of the plateau was not far off. The two mountain ranges that had enclosed it hitherto were rapidly converging, and a high slope, stretching from the one to the other, closed the horizon.

Jahil went fast. He no longer had to accommodate his pace to those who came on foot. He had only his rider to consider. And although Uraz was riding bareback, and although his broken leg (dragged, struck, and distorted during his struggle with the mastiffs) hurt him atrociously, he did not hold Jahil in. He too delighted in this solitude and freedom. And even in his torment. They were the continuation, the price of the battle in which he, brought down to a fragment of himself, had crushed and stabbed the ferocious dogs. The cutting stone still swung at the end of his whip and he had not wiped his knife. He felt that he was stronger than all obstacles, all traps, all cut-throat ambuscades. He began to sing a traveling song, as spreading, as old, as monotonous as the steppe and its people.

They were soon at the edge of the plain. Jahil stopped. Uraz fell silent.

Before them rose an enormous slope, so steep that only a wild goat could go straight at it. Winding up sideways was a track the caravans had gradually worn into the mountain side. Steep, slippery, crumbling, it rose from stage to stage, continually narrower and more nearly vertical. "A ladder," Gardi Gaj had said. "Well named," thought Uraz. Sure-footed animals and men could climb it. And on a good horse a good horseman could do the same, provided he had all his faculties. But without the help of his calves and knees? Without the support of a saddle?

Jahil pawed the ground, rocking gently to and fro. "He is hesitating," thought Uraz. The stallion half-turned his head toward him. In that long, powerful face seen sideways, the single eye had an expression that Uraz understood with no difficulty at all. "I know," he said between his clenched teeth, "I know very well: alone, thou wouldst have no hesitation. Nor with a sound man on thy back. And thou art afraid . . . Not for thee—for me. Why then . . ." What Uraz refused was not help—every horse owed that to its rider. It was the unbearable expression in Jahil's eye, the almost human expression of anxious concern.

"Why then!" continued Uraz. He raised his whip, saw the jagged stone, and turned the blow aside. Yet not enough to prevent Jahil from hearing the whistle of the lash or seeing the gleam of the flint. The stallion shook his mane. All his muscles tautened to send him leaping up the dangerous slope. But then his gathered strength made him feel the weakness and uncertainty of his load, the rider in his charge. He lowered his head, looked attentively at the slope, and began to climb it with the utmost care and prudence.

However he set about it, the angle of the track forced him into something more like a climb than a walk. His back was in itself a slope. In vain Uraz tightened his thighs on the stallion's flanks; at every fresh jolt he felt them slide ineluctably back, along the horse's sweating coat. "I shall not be able to hold on," he said to himself. "Mukhi and his whore will find me broken. I shall be no great trouble to them . . . If indeed there is anything left for them to do . . ."

Uraz thought of the pain that he had summoned and desired, the stratagems he had imagined, the deadly plots he had managed to baffle . . . So much will power, fertility of mind, and courage: and then to fall and sag like an empty waterskin just as the end of the ordeal was at hand.

In order to reach the first of the platforms that stood at the angles of the winding track, Jahil had to rise almost straight up. Uraz saw himself falling, sliding off. The most primitive of instincts made him fling his arms around the horse's neck and cling with his hands to the warm, moist hide. In this position he let himself be hoisted up.

With his hoofs all on the flat stone Jahil stood breathing for a long while. During this time of even balance Uraz did not try to regain his seat. On the contrary, he took advantage of it to settle himself closer to the stallion and link his fingers in an even firmer grip around his neck. The attitude was shameful. He did not care in the least. No one could know apart from Jahil. And Jahil knew what it was caused by. And approved of it. And returned to his climb.

Stage after stage they rose up and up. The track ran from one turning place to the next, now on their right and now on their left, following the least ferocious slope. At each platform Jahil stopped to recover his breath and Uraz tried to arrange his wounded leg for the best. Then once more they began their climb up the ladder cut into the mountain wall. Once, in full climb and at the risk of falling to the ground, Uraz straightened himself abruptly. Higher up he had heard the sound of falling stones. A late-traveling caravan was coming down to meet him. He must not be surprised in that state of disgraceful collapse . . . A few endless moments went by. He felt his own weight pulling, heaving him backward. He was on the point of seizing Jahil's mane when at last he saw a family of ibexes come dancing down the slope.

There was no other alarm or incident until the end of the track. There, in an effort that reared him almost upright on his hind legs, Jahil scrambled up the last incline and reached level ground. For a long time he stood without moving a step. His legs trembled like reeds in a breeze. Uraz let go of the horse's neck, all soaked with sweat and foam, hung down his legs, and slowly raised his body. Behind his horse's hoofs the track they had just climbed fell away and away. A giddiness seized him and he turned his head. Before him he saw an immense flat stretch of country, scattered with dry tufts of grass and dwarf bushes. This kind of savanna ran east and west. On the north side it ended against a mountain range so deep

and lofty that in mass and height it surpassed all Uraz had seen up
until that time. Faced with this wall, rising at such an altitude, he
felt an even more powerful, more exhausting vertigo than that of
the abyss. Here the dizziness affected not his eyes but his soul.
These enormous barriers grew continually higher . . . How far
were they going to go? Would they not reach the sky in the end,
and bar it out? Uraz looked up. The clouds were as remote from
him as though he had been on the steppe. Another thing astonished
him: the sun rode far higher over this savanna than he had thought
it would. Was it possible that that ascent should have taken up so
little of the world's time?

Everything humiliated Uraz and made game of him—the slope,
the mountain peaks, the sun. He brought his eyes down to the
earth and felt more at his ease. The flat land, the harsh, stubborn
vegetation, belonged to any man who could still rule a horse.

His own was flinching. His legs had not yet recovered all their
firmness and his body was steaming like a damp fire. "Thou hast
found it heavy going, thou too," thought Uraz; and he was
tempted to grant Jahil some respite. But he remembered how he
had traveled up the slope and he said to himself, "If I do not make
myself obeyed directly, of the two of us he will be the master."

Uraz struck his good heel into the sweat-black side. Jahil moved
forward. Without zeal. His head low. No spring in his hocks. Uraz
made no attempt to correct this. Jahil had obeyed. He asked no
more. As for him, he was destroyed with weariness and racked with
pain. The binding on his broken leg had become so loose that it no
longer accomplished anything. Beneath the filthy cloth and rotting
flesh the lower half of the bone shifted with every jar. Uraz never
looked at this revolting mess. He turned from it in disgust. Yet he
felt a curious kind of gratitude to it. He felt that it prevented him
from yielding to unconsciousness. He held out thanks to his pain
alone.

Jahil's pace had strengthened. From time to time he lowered
his muzzle, sniffed the harsh tufts of grass, snatched a mouthful,
and chewed it, slavering heavily. "He must be very hungry to take
such forage," thought Uraz. How many days had he been without
real food?

Uraz thought of how the buzkashi horses went through their

qantar fasting at the end of the summer. But they remained all day long without moving, in the sun, reflected Uraz, and at night they were bedded down on litter as fresh, soft, and clean as the beds of princes. As for Jahil, he had been sleeping in any sort of place and any sort of way, with an empty belly in the appalling cold, having labored enormously from dawn until nightfall. He ran his hand over the stallion. It discovered limp folds round his neck. The ribs were beginning to protrude. "I am destroying him," said Uraz to himself. "Will he keep on until the end? This is the most terrible mountain of them all." Then Uraz remembered the words of Gardi Gaj. The last barrier, the final wall of the Hindu Kush. Beyond it, the steppe . . . Jahil was powerful enough, hardy enough, to drag himself that far, even if he were foundered, even if he were utterly exhausted . . . And he, Uraz, could certainly do it, however maimed and crippled. Once more he urged Jahil on with his heel. Jahil moved faster through the dried grass and the thorns.

Uraz felt a great weight on his eyelids. His neck bent and wavered to the rhythm of Jahil's pace. Was it that long regular stride that was rocking him to sleep? Was it the poppy juice still mixed with his blood that gave him this torpor, this fluid lead spreading throughout his body? Before he could make up his mind he fell asleep, his fingers holding Jahil's mane.

He was equally uncertain what it was that woke him up. The sudden cold? The horse stopping? The first thing he did was to look up at the sky. The passage of time was as much out of order now as it had been when he reached the top of the slope. But in the opposite direction. He thought he had only dozed for a moment. Yet his eyes could already bear the glare of a sun that was reaching the edge of its heavenly vale. Uraz gazed at his surroundings—a landscape he no longer recognized. A scree had taken the place of the savanna. On his right a very tall rise of clay and red boulders cut off the view. In front of him was the beginning of a slope. It was not so great as to alarm a good horse, properly harnessed and mounted by a fit man. But Jahil had to carry half a rider down to the bottom, without stirrups or saddle. At least the rider had to be awake. There, just where the ground began to plunge, Jahil was waiting for that moment.

Uraz leaned back, supported himself with his two arms on the

stallion's loins, and grasped his flanks as hard as he could. "I am
not sleeping any longer," he said. "Go on . . ."

They went down the length of the natural wall that served as
their guide and protecting barrier. Corners, curves, bends, clefts,
wanderings . . . A never-ending descent. It seemed to Uraz that
he was voyaging upon a nightmare torrent. His boat kept pitching,
continually plunging its bows deep down; and all the time he had
to put out a huge effort to cling to his place, to hold on behind and
not overturn. The flow of blood darkened his sight and thundered
in his ears. Cramp ripped and tore the muscles of his arms and
thighs. He could not hold out against it and collapsed onto Jahil,
clinging to his neck as he had done before. The first time he had
thought he was experiencing the ultimate depth of shame. This
time it was even worse. He was no longer even stretched out, held
by his hands. He had slipped, sitting, as far as the stallion's neck,
and the shapeless, powerless, grotesque mass of his body hung and
wavered there. It pressed heavily on the horse, and at every jolt it
ran the risk of sliding over the sweat-soaked mane. The moment
came when this weight, thrusting him forward, made the slope impossible for Jahil. He had to lean his shoulder against an outcrop-
ping rock and wait for his breath and strength to come back.

Held there a prisoner, crippled, destroyed, Uraz thought,
"Why put up with such dishonor? I have never been afraid to
die."

Jahil's breath came more evenly. His legs trembled less.

"I have only to open my arms and it is over," thought Uraz. He
saw himself on the ground, rotting on himself, a rag, filth, a dead
dog at the bottom of the wall. He squeezed Jahil's neck. Die—Yes.
Like that—Never. Shameful things in life could be corrected,
atoned for. Dishonor in the manner of one's death could never be
wiped out.

Jahil left his support. Uraz clenched his fingers, jaws, and eyelids, and let himself be carried off like a rag doll. The cold was
stronger, the pain more searing, the torrent steeper. The boat
pitched and plunged, pitched and plunged . . . Suddenly it
steadied and came to rest. Uraz's body returned to its usual place
of its own motion. Without yet letting go of the stallion's neck he
stared hard at the ground under his hoofs. It was a flat place, cov-

ered with sand. Uraz unclasped his arms, filled his unconstricted chest with air, and raised his head. The rise of ground had vanished. There was nothing to interrupt his view any more. And there was the Band-i-Amir, opening before him.

In spite of the softness of the evening light Uraz closed his eyes, like a miser who comes suddenly on a heap of gold and at once plunges his hands into it to be sure of a handful at least, whatever may happen. "Even if this is the most fleeting mirage, I shall keep what I have seen," said Uraz to himself, his eyelids tight.

They opened timidly and stayed open wide, without blinking. It had not been a mirage.

From the gray shore on which Jahil had stopped rose an enormous cleft, guarded on either side by red cliffs: it mounted, widening and soaring continually toward the vague, remote frontier of the sky. This huge rift belonged in its entirety to the kingdom of the water. And so strange was that kingdom that reason could not encompass its existence. For the flood that ran down from the high ridge, instead of racing by in foam on the slope as it should have done, suddenly stopped—why, and against what barrier?—and became a peaceful, unmoving mirror. Yet it did not remain sluggish. Beneath its smooth and motionless surface it overflowed, made its way along underground channels, and just at the foot of the first lake it made another, this too held back by an invisible dyke. Here there was no rest at all. The marvelous, invisible current became apparent again. The stream of the Band-i-Amir flooded into overflowing pools set one after another like so many steps. As its threshold the last of them had the shore on which Uraz and Jahil were standing.

And Uraz, so trifling and insignificant before this tremendous mystery, felt no dread or even astonishment. All his fanatical belief in legends and wonders came to his aid. What could be simpler? Giants, demons, dragons, jinns, those who piled up mountains or disemboweled them, had hacked and split this one before him. Uraz could hear their lightning axes split and strike. He saw the

Masters of the Waters take possession of these depths hollowed out to their desire.

Who, apart from them, could have piled up and commanded these waters, defying all the laws of flow and level, and have kept them thus through all recorded time?

"They call them lakes," thought Uraz. "But a lake is a thing to itself. It does not run and overflow and beget others without end . . . A waterfall? But in falls the water comes down foaming and leaping in sprays. These have never a hollow, never so much as a ripple. Truly, truly, here nature is outdone, put down and turned about by the Workers of Earth and Sky."

And as Uraz said this within himself, a fresh miracle took place. A glow that had both the shining brilliance of glaciers and the delicacy of springtime flowers rose from the chasm with its liquid terraces. The sun had reached their level. Its rays, skimming the ground, set the motionless silk on fire. And to add to the enchantment not one of these huge unmoving blazes had the same shade. Muted blue, deep green, sky-blue, pink, black—each pool drew from its depths the color of its fire.

In a single moment, and from all its lakes, the water vanished. Uraz was not in the least surprised. He thought of the underground giant in the Kirghiz tales. His name was Kol Tavisar and he drank up lakes and rivers in a single draft. "He, no doubt . . . or one of his brothers," thought Uraz. And forgot it. When magical acts take place, thought is quite forbidden.

Now, instead of the Band-i-Amir, a rainbow like no other rainbow on earth appeared, and the shades of its spectrum had each the width of the colossal steps. In its turn the rainbow vanished, and a majestic, supernatural flight of steps rose up, its treads onyx, jade, sapphire, coral, and lapis lazuli. It rose, framed by the red rocks, mounting forever until it reached the very edge of the sky.

The sun was reaching its farthest limit. A fire began to blaze at the level of the horizon and its final rays made each step send forth its most brilliant color, its purest, most jewel-like splendor.

This light had arisen with the speed of a gust of wind. With the same speed its glow went out. And carried with it the rainbow and the steps made of precious stones. Once again water flowed in the pools. But in all it was the same color: that of shadow. At last Uraz was afraid. "O Allah, the True, the One! Of all these miracles, thou alone art the master," he cried.

Uraz turned away from the dark, motionless fall. In the play of light and shade on the other side of the first lake, nestling in the side of the mountain, showed a building topped with a meager dome and a little minaret. "Thou hast heard me, O Allah! The One, the True!" said Uraz.

Jahil set out toward the mosque of the Band-i-Amir. The path between the water and the rock was wide and flat. It steadied Uraz's balance. This easiness took away all his defense. No more effort, no more danger, no more ecstasy . . . In his head earless dogs, their throats slit, ran through the rainbow of the lakes. He himself was being hurried down a hurtling stream that flung him against slabs of precious stones. One last shock threw him out of his boat. Jahil, who had just stopped, uttered a neigh of distress. Before Uraz's body touched the ground, arms whose strength seemed to him miraculous seized it. He lost consciousness.

THE SWOON LASTED ONLY A FEW MOMENTS. THE ARMS THAT HAD saved Uraz from his fall were still carrying him when he began to think and feel once more. He saw that he was in a long, low, narrow room. The warm air smelled of mutton fat. There were lines of empty charpoys against the wall. Uraz was set down on the nearest.

He heard quick, heavy footsteps ring on the tamped earth floor. The hard light of a hurricane lamp moved away, vanishing. The gallery was lit only by the muffled glow of a jar full of embers.

"That is where the warmth comes from," thought Uraz.

The gleam of the hurricane lamp suddenly reappeared. The stocky man walking in its light had powerful great limbs and a barrel-shaped chest. No neck. Smooth yellow cheeks with a line across—the mouth. A beak—his nose. A shining thread—his eyes. Apart from the lamp the man was carrying a steaming cup of tea. Before speaking a word he helped Uraz to drink it all. Then—and his voice was young, deep, and cheerful—he said, "Thy leg has a terrible reek. Thou canst not sleep with it like that."

"Where am I?" asked Uraz.

"In the house of Allah and of the passing traveler," replied the man.

"My horse?" asked Uraz.

"He will have all he needs," said the man. "Upon Qutabay's word."

"The stallion first," said Uraz.

"It is but right," said Qutabay, laughing. "Thou owest more to him than he to thee."

The hurricane lamp went away. The glow of the embers was kind to the eyes. Uraz felt himself filled through and through with that strange numbness, half velvet and half lead, that he owed to the poppy juice . . . Qutabay reappeared, the light in his hand. He set down a jug of boiling water and rags of very clean linen at the foot of the charpoy, and bared the wound. Its color and stench were hideous. He cleaned it scrupulously, pitilessly, set the broken bones in order and fixed them as well as he could. Each one of these motions sent a wave through Uraz's flesh and nerves—a wave whose crest seemed to be made of all the fire and all the darting spray of pain. He suffered them without a quiver and without a groan. The call of honor helped him. Even more the shame of having accepted this care. To hand over his mutilation, his rotting flesh to a healer, to Mukhi, to Zereh—well enough. It was their trade, their calling, to look after such things. But this stranger handling his vileness, breathing it in . . .

Qutabay raised the hurricane lamp, throwing its full light on Uraz's face, and said, "Thou hast not fainted. Thou hast not stirred. Praised be the strength of thy heart!"

"I am used to my carrion," said Uraz roughly. "But thou?"

A simple laugh stretched the line of Qutabay's mouth and the slit of his eyes. "Thy wound!" he cried. "It is attar of roses after all those I see on the lepers."

For a moment that terrible word spurred Uraz's mind. He wanted to ask questions, to know more; and he did nothing. The pain was ebbing away. The peace of exhaustion took hold of him. Why go on speaking? What was there to be concerned about? Apart from the glare that was stabbing his eyes . . . "Take that lamp away," murmured Uraz.

His sleeping breath was as faint as that of the embers in the glowing jar.

"TAKE AWAY THAT ACCURSED LAMP," MUTTERED URAZ.

The white glare, the heat, grew stronger. Uraz opened his eyes in anger. The sun was raking the whole gallery, and at the far end it faintly showed a round, windowless room. Uraz remembered. The mosque . . . Qutabay . . . He must have slept twelve hours at least. Yet he still felt exhausted. He wanted tea and food. Out of habit he was on the point of calling for Mukhi. But where was the syce? Uraz felt an anxious distress not far from panic. What if Mukhi were to lose his track . . . ? All that effort, that whole deadly game—all for nothing, for emptiness. Infinitely better to have died from the poison, to have perished under the teeth of the mastiffs, even to be a corpse parching among the thorns and rocks . . .

Two voices began talking outside. Uraz heard them very clearly through the thin and porous wall of the mosque. One was Quta-bay's: the other . . .

"Mukhi! Mukhi!" called Uraz with a strength and joy he did not realize.

The door opened at the syce's thrust with such force as almost to fly from its hinges. A single stride brought him to Uraz's bed. "Alive!" he cried. "Truly alive! Allah be praised!"

Each looked into the other's eyes. Both faces were lit with the same delight.

"Two brothers would not be happier to see one another again," said a deep voice. Uraz and Mukhi saw Qutabay smiling at them from the threshold of the gallery. "Truly," he went on, "truly, two brothers who meant everything to each other."

Uraz and Mukhi exchanged another look. This was devoid of expression. Both men now remembered why they had been so afraid of missing one another.

"How didst thou follow me?" asked Uraz.

"There was only the one track as far as the Band-i-Amir," said

Mukhi. "Then I saw Jahil's prints in the sand. Only thy setting out was earlier and thy pace faster. We had to camp for the night."

"I am very thirsty and hungry," said Uraz.

"The tea must be ready," said Mukhi. "Zereh is seeing to it. Then she will make thee wheatcakes and pilaw."

Mukhi was near the door when Qutabay leaned over Uraz to prop him against the wall.

"Not thee, with thy bear's arms," cried the syce violently. He came back to the charpoy, raised Uraz, and as he did so felt at his bosom, where the bundles of afghanis lay hidden.

"Thanks to thee," said Uraz. It was sincere gratitude: everything was falling back into place.

"Thou art a good syce, truly!" said Qutabay, nodding his broad head. "When my father was ill, I should not have allowed a stranger to take care of him, either." He let a sigh escape him. His huge chest had the resonance of a gong. "After his death," he went on, "my mother went back to their village. And I took their place here, as guardian."

Mukhi brought the ritual tray. "Never wilt thou have had such good tea!" he cried to Uraz.

"Taste it," said Uraz. He had not forgotten the nomad's herbs; and when it was time for the pilaw he invited both the men to share it with him. As they plunged their hands into the greasy rice, Uraz asked Qutabay whether he knew the road that led to the northern steppes.

"Travelers who have crossed the mountain—and very few of them there are—have told me of a terrible narrow gorge," replied the guardian of the mosque. "It is not fit for horses."

"Mine will go through," said Uraz.

"I will take thee there," said Qutabay. He carefully licked his oily palm and continued, "It is already too late for today. Before you had passed through the defile the darkness would have come, and death with it. So thou must make up thy mind: either camp this evening before the gorge or else leave at dawn tomorrow, after a night beneath this roof."

Uraz was still very weak and Jahil needed a real rest. "It is thy hospitality that I choose, O open-handed guardian," he said.

The jet-black thread of Qutabay's eyes sparkled as though with an inner fire. His voice boomed out, deeper and more sonorous than usual. "It will be a great rejoicing for me," he said. "Loneliness weighs on the heart, even in a holy place."

"Dost thou not see many men go by?" asked Uraz.

"What men?" cried Qutabay. "Foreigners from unbelieving lands, with their noisy cars? They do not understand our language! Eat unclean food! Swallow drinks accursed by the Prophet!" Qutabay drew breath and then finished more gently, "Or then again the lepers."

"The lepers!" cried Mukhi in horror.

Uraz remembered that the day before Qutabay had uttered that dreadful word. "What brings them here?" he asked.

"It has always been said," replied Qutabay, "that the waters of the Band-i-Amir have a healing power for their disease."

"Hast seen them cured?" asked Uraz eagerly.

"No, truly," said Qutabay. "They pass and come back no more."

Uraz leaned over the edge of his charpoy, grasped the square shoulders of the man squatting in front of him, and whispered, "Tell me, tell me, on the Koran . . . Dost thou think . . . for my wound . . . ?"

Qutabay turned his eyes toward the ground and said timidly, "Everything is in the hands of Allah, the Omnipotent."

"The Omnipotent," said Mukhi.

"The Omnipotent," repeated Uraz.

The three men turned their gaze toward the end of the gallery where the round building began, decorated with a few indifferent prayer rugs. And Uraz said to Qutabay, "Carry me outside."

It was about noon. Before the sun cast the spell of its declining fires on the terraced lakes of the Band-i-Amir again it would have half the sky to cross. Yet in the hard, direct light these mysterious waters preserved all their splendor and magic. The green, the pink, the azure, the deep blue, the inky black owed nothing to the enchantment of the twilight. There was only one difference—the substance of the liquid steps was no longer precious stones but flower petals. The celestial stair now had hanging gardens for its treads, as wide as parks; and the real plants that lined their sides

and over which the little falls poured seemed all part of that miraculous flowering.

As Qutabay slowly approached the water with Uraz in his arms,
his booming gonglike voice pronounced the names that the five
marvelous lakes of the Band-i-Amir have borne for century after
century.

"Zulfikar," said Qutabay.

Then, "Pudina."

And then, "Panir."

"Haibat."

"Ghulaman."

Qutabay set Uraz down quite close to the water, as though in
the court of a temple. This one had enormous lakes for steps, inaccessible mountains for walls, and, for dome, the sky itself. Uraz
murmured, "In all the unending world, there are no waters like
these."

"And how could there be?" cried Qutabay. "It was Hazrat-i-
Ali the Martyr who, with a single word, hung the current of an
unbridled river here and brought about the miracle of the lakes."

"Hazrat-i-Ali," said Uraz in an undertone. "Himself . . . It
does not surprise me."

Mukhi, squatting on his heels, listened to their conversation.
From time to time he gazed at the wisps of smoke that rose above a
hollow rock. Zereh was over there. "Tell us, O Qutabay," said the
syce, "is there any village in the Band-i-Amir?"

"One alone," said the young guardian of the mosque. "At the
very top. When the lakes are frozen the people come as far as this
place on the ice. My mother belongs to their clan. And one day I
shall take a wife from among them. If Allah grants me the money
that is needed."

"One who serves Him as well as thou is always rewarded," said
Uraz.

"May He hear thee," cried Qutabay.

The noonday sun beat furiously down. And within himself
Uraz was eaten up with fever. Sweat gathered in all the folds and
hollows of his skull-like face.

"May He hear me too," he murmured. A gust of air ruffled the
surface of the lake, bringing its coolness to his skin. And it brought

with it so clear, light, and benign a scent that it seemed as though all the herbs of the fields, the flowers of the meadows, and the barks and leaves of the woods had been steeped in it. "Didst thou smell that?" cried Uraz with wonder in his voice.

"It is the breath of the roots and plants that grow everywhere in the waters," said Qutabay. "The Five Lakes are all scented with them."

"The omen is good," said Uraz. "It is time to make the trial."

Qutabay knelt at the edge of the lake, picked up Uraz as though he had been a child, held him over the surface of the water, and let him plunge his broken leg into it, saying, "The Prophet be with thee!"

The cry that burst out against his chest did not astonish Qutabay at all. But the syce knew the full extent of Uraz's pride. He said, "What is the matter?"

"Nothing . . . nothing . . ." gasped Uraz between clenched teeth.

"The cold," said Qutabay to Mukhi. "Try."

The syce dipped his fingers into the lake and plucked them out directly.

"This water never grows warm," said Qutabay.

Uraz's jaws chattered. "How . . . how long?" he muttered.

"As long as thou canst," said Qutabay.

One shuddering breath . . . another . . . a third. Uraz felt that his bowels were freezing.

"Enough," he said.

When the blood began to flow again through his body under the burning sun he asked, "Do the lepers stay longer?"

"It is not the same thing," said Qutabay. "They feel nothing. Their bad flesh is dead. In the end it drops of itself."

Again Uraz asked, "They never . . . disgust thee?"

Qutabay paused before answering. He wished to speak in all honesty. Then he said, "No . . . Truly, no. No . . . They are so very much more unfortunate than all my misfortunes." Uraz began to shiver so violently that his blue lips could no longer manage to utter a word. "Thou must be taken in, wrapped up, and made to drink boiling tea," said Qutabay with authority. He carried Uraz off.

Mukhi joined the nomad, who was in front of the tent. "We leave tomorrow at dawn," he said. "A very difficult gorge. Then, by the evening, the steppe."

Zereh made as though to speak. Before she could do so Mukhi said exactly what she was about to say: "Uraz shall never see it."

*****

20

The Vise

THE FIVE LAKES OF BAND-I-AMIR stood out one after the other in
the dim light. All their waters were the color of pearl. Mukhi
brought Jahil, harnessed, to the door. A little way behind was
Zereh, holding the big pack mule's bridle. Qutabay came out of
the mosque with two blankets. He folded them, put them under
the stallion's saddle, and said to the syce, "Thy master will need
them. He had a bad night. The ankle has no shape any more . . .
A bag of putrid matter . . ."

Qutabay and Mukhi set Uraz on the horse. They could not
make out his face in the darkness, but through his clothes they
could feel the burning of his skin.

The travelers set out toward the little beach. The light came
quickly. The liquid steps began to regain their colors—gray pearl,
pink pearl, black pearl. And the top of the red wall to one side of
the track that ran between the rock and the water glowed with fire.
Its highest points had been formed into shapes by natural forces.
And these untouched standing, leaning, prostrate sculptures, the
work of the elements, had human bodies and faces.

"Have these magic stones grown in the night?" asked Uraz,
speaking to Qutabay, who was walking at his side.

"They have been there since the beginning of time," said the guardian of the mosque. "Thou didst not see them yesterday evening. It was too dark."

After the little beach Qutabay took a path that led away to the right. Still, all along the skyline were the naturally formed statues. The last was that of a girl. Her body was completely separated from the rock wall. Stretched high and almost flying in the blue air she seemed to be watching over the travelers from a great height as they passed under her sheer cliff. Immediately beneath her there was a sudden split in the mountain. This was the beginning of the gorge that pierced the last rampart of the Hindu Kush.

"Allah be with you all!" said Qutabay.

"I thank thee, brother," said Uraz. His voice had a ring of something very like tenderness. He thrust his hand beneath his shirt, brought out a thick wad of notes, slipped them into Qutabay's belt, and said, "Take a wife quickly and be alone no more."

Unbelief, trust, and happiness softened Qutabay's powerful features and threw them into confusion. Uraz felt ill at ease. He turned from Qutabay and fixed his eyes on Mukhi and Zereh. And came back to himself immediately. Those faces expressed the most savage rage: they were being robbed—robbed of their due. The familiar grin cut into Uraz's fleshless cheeks. He forgot Qutabay's existence, no longer heard his cries of gratitude; he motioned to the syce to walk ahead. Following on Mukhi's heels Jahil made his way into the defile.

They were barely into it before they were obliged to stop. They could see nothing ahead. The twilight was as thick as at the end of a murky evening. They raised their heads to find the light again. All that could be seen at the remote top of the soaring walls was a faint blue thread. After that the corridor seemed even narrower than before.

Eventually their eyes grew accustomed to the half-darkness. Mukhi took a pace forward, then another, and went on more confidently. The ground was even, with smooth rock underfoot. Jahil's hoofs echoed as though they were deep in a cave, and behind him the mule's did the same. The syce called out, "Wait . . . wait."

Uraz could make out an inner wall that blocked the gorge from one side to the other. The invisible Mukhi called out again, "There is a gap . . . Just enough for . . ." At that instant his voice was cut off, swept away. At the spot from which it had come was a kind of tunnel; it was so low that Uraz had to lie flat over Jahil's neck to get under it, and so narrow that the stallion scraped his shoulders. No longer hidden by the screen of rock, the light burst suddenly upon them. And at the same moment Uraz received the whole rush of air in all its force.

He had never known a wind of this nature. Its blast had the strength of a hurricane and the thrusting rhythm of a river in full spate. It wrung an astonishing music from the cliffs. The whole gorge sang and wailed like a vast flute made of rock. This furious, impalpable flood—from what source could it spring? From what abyss, these long wavering cries, these appalling laments, this endless sobbing? "The souls of all dead shepherds—the depths of the world," thought Uraz.

Neither he nor Jahil, buffeted, deafened, blinded, dared make the slightest movement. In a straight line from their feet a steep shining slope ran down and down as far as the eye could see.

Mukhi left the rock against which the blast had flattened him and passed in front of Uraz. Zereh, bent in two at the mouth of the tunnel, could no longer move forward at all. The syce dragged her along the ledge that overhung the slope. With all his strength he shouted to Uraz, "What now?"

Uraz stretched his whip straight out in front of him. Its lash was still loaded with the piece of flint that had stunned one of the mastiffs. Mukhi turned away his flat face, distorted by the fury of the air and convulsed with hatred, and with his eyes sought for the nomad's advice. Uraz no longer heard the clamor of the wind. The instinct of danger shouted louder still. He could not let Zereh draw breath or allow time for her eyes to send the syce an order.

Uraz brought his whip down between their heads. The cutting stone on the thong flashed before their eyes. Mukhi and Zereh moved away from one another. Uraz gripped Mukhi by the back of the neck and flung him forward down the steep slope. Carried on by his own weight, Mukhi was unable to stop until he was well below the high ledge. In the intervening space Uraz rode Jahil forward, straight toward Mukhi. Mukhi hesitated, his hands hot with the urge to kill. But being lower down and hemmed in by a gully scarcely wider than Jahil's chest, there was nothing he could do against the stallion's mass and the sharp-edged stone at the end of the whip. Between Jahil's legs Mukhi could see first the mule, then Zereh, leave the ledge and begin the descent. He turned his back on Uraz and let his body follow the downward slope.

Jahil could only follow him with great difficulty. The gully was paved with long slabs, and centuries of wear had smoothed and polished them until they were as slippery as a path of ice. This meant the stallion must choose a place for each hoof at every stride. He had to search for the slightest folds, rises, and cracks, to use them as footholds. Even so, he slid and skidded.

"Neither he nor I can get up without Mukhi," said Uraz to himself. "And then . . ."

Nevertheless, they did have one ally—the enormous wind. The strength of its thrust compensated for the pull of gravity, lessened the danger of the slope. Jahil quickly learned to make use of its help and lean on the air as he might have leaned on supporting water, and to watch for the highest pitch of the blast before he moved forward.

Behind him, in spite of the weight and encumbrance of its load, the big mule walked easily along. When it so happened that Uraz turned his head he found himself envying the sureness, ease, and delicacy of that pace. With this he reflected, "Here a stupid, unworthy creature is handsomer than the finest buzkashi charger. That is because it is fulfilling the destiny for which it was born."

And Uraz returned to his watch over Mukhi. The wind made the prodigious stone flute sing and the slanting rays of light came down and down along the cliff on the travelers' left hand. At last the sun itself appeared high up in the middle of the blue crack which was the sky. From top to bottom the whole defile burst into flames: skyline, enormous cliffs, paving underfoot. Beasts and men all stopped. They seemed to be walking on fire.

Mukhi tried to slip between Jahil and one of the walls. Uraz wheeled the stallion across the corridor.

"Let me see Zereh," cried Mukhi.

"No," said Uraz.

"Only for a moment," cried Mukhi again.

"No," said Uraz.

The instinct of obedience was dead in the syce. Rebellion, hatred, and rage showed naked in his face. His hand moved toward the stirrup that held Uraz's sound foot. Before it reached it, the flint on the whiplash struck him full on the forehead with such force that his whole body was thrown backward. He rocked on his heels, lost his balance, and rolled down the slope. Uraz's eyes did not follow his fall. Instantly he whipped round toward the nomad girl. Just in time: Zereh was stabbing into the big mule's thigh with the scissors she had at her belt. The beast shot forward. Its size and load plunging down that slope made it a deadly missile. If it struck Jahil's side the stallion, torn from his hold, could not but slide, fall, and break his bones on the slabs that shone like mirrors reflecting the sun. Uraz shifted the whip to his left hand and struck with a sideways hook. The blow ripped the mule's nose. It reared. The staggering, wavering, lashing in the air were like a dance for life. At last the mule recovered its balance.

Uraz pushed Jahil on up to the syce, who was leaning against one of the walls. Blood poured from the hole in his forehead, covering his face and running down onto his chapan. The handle of the whip between his ribs thrust him forward. He slipped, staggered, caught a protruding edge, and with bent knees followed the slope.

The march continued, interrupted by halts and glissades. The sun left the thread of sky. The cliff on the west had no more sun. On the other side, the shadow began to climb the rock. The gorge kept to the same slope and went on straight ahead, now widening, now narrowing. The more the sides drew in, the stronger blew the roaring wind.

Suddenly its voice doubled in power. The travelers knew that they were about to engage in the narrowest pass of all. Mukhi, making his way into it first, automatically reached out his arms. Before they were extended he was touching both sides. Jahil, with his shoulders narrowed and his sides drawn in, scraped the wall. Uraz's broken leg, which the morbid swelling had turned into a loathsome mess, was caught, squeezed, and crushed. Under the shattering agony of the pain—he had never known any like it— Uraz shrieked aloud. It was the howling roar of a beast out of its senses, but he himself could not hear it at all. However unrestrained and shameless it was, the bellowing of the wind swallowed it up and smothered it. At this he no longer tried to hold it in. The unheard shriek followed him until the moment the taut skin of his leg yielded and split, letting the pus squirt out and run down. The pain grew bearable. Uraz fell silent.

At the end of this gully the gorge took on an unexpected width. When Jahil made his way out Mukhi was resting there, leaning against the left-hand wall in a sheltered corner. Jahil did the same, on the other side. He breathed freely, blowing out his flanks; impatiently he shook the blankets that Qutabay had put under his saddle when they left. Friction against the rock wall had so pulled them that now they were almost touching the ground, and they flapped against the stallion's hind legs.

At this moment Zereh, wild-haired and crouching against the rush of air, came through the pass and ran to Uraz. "The narrow place . . ." she cried. "The mule cannot get through . . . Because of the packs."

"Cut the girths," said Uraz.

"All that wealth!" cried Zereh. "All that wealth!"

Uraz shrugged his shoulders.

"It is easy for thee . . ." cried the nomad again. Her eyes were fixed on Uraz's chest, where the afghanis lay. Uraz waved his whip. Zereh vanished into the narrow opening.

Mukhi took a step toward her. Jahil's chest rose in front of him. Mukhi did not resist, but the muscles and tendons of his flat face stood out and set, as though it were a mask carved out of very hard wood.

Uraz smiled into this homicidal face and pushed Jahil on.

The gorge lost its width and once again became a strongly sloping, smoothly paved corridor, filled with the fury and sobbing of the wind. This great howling prevented the travelers from hearing the noise of a waterfall. And as it flowed down that side of the dark wall they could not see it either.

But Mukhi's feet gave way under him. He felt himself soaked by an icy flood that carried him down the slope. Jahil made a convulsive backward movement. Even dry, the slabs were so slippery that he could barely keep his balance. Wet, they could not be crossed.

Now Uraz knew that he had never been in such mortal danger.

From above, Zereh and the big gray mule were coming down. Below, Mukhi, having been swept against the wall, was getting to his feet. And he, Uraz, blocked where he stood, could move neither forward nor back. There was no way out of the trap: no remedy. With his eye Uraz measured the distance the water flooded before it ran off into the channels at the foot of the cliffs. Three hundred, perhaps four hundred feet. He had to get through, or die.

A recollection came into his mind. After the very heavy rains in spring there was not a single carter who did not provide himself with planks to free his wheels when the steppe turned into a sticky swamp. Against the mud of the plains, certainly . . . but what here? Uraz grasped one of the blankets hanging from the saddle and threw it in front of the stallion. Jahil understood and set himself on the cloth. The other blanket spread beneath him. He took another step, waited a moment, then turned his long head toward Uraz. And Uraz saw that by himself he could do no more. Mukhi was climbing up the slope on his hands and knees. Zereh was coming down it, protected by the mule, her scissors in her hand. Uraz gripped his whip with barren rage. What could it do? The syce was coming on all fours, out of his reach. And Zereh was out of it too. Uraz thought of her eyes alight with cupidity. How they must be blazing at this moment! Was not the treasure hers at last?

"No it is not, whore of a gypsy," said Uraz in an undertone. "By the Prophet, no!" He plucked the bundles of afghanis from their hiding place, swung toward Zereh, and flourished them in his left hand, the notes shivering in the raging, tearing wind. She seized the mule's bridle and stood motionless. As loud as he could he roared, "Submit, both of you . . . instantly."

With his right hand he took a fistful of notes, opened his fingers . . . A pain, a nameless horror appeared on the young woman's face: above her, high above her, the pitiless blast carried away those scraps, that fortune, forever. Her gaze followed their flight. To Uraz her watching seemed to last forever. In every hair on the back of his neck he felt Mukhi's approach. At any second the syce might seize the powerless Jahil by the hocks and throw him down. The last bank note vanished in the depths and shadows of the gorge. Zereh's eyes were on Uraz once more. He took another layer from the diminished bundle. She flung herself on her knees and clasped her hands. Uraz jerked his thumb in the direction of Mukhi. The nomad slid along past Jahil's side. At last Uraz could turn. One step away from the stallion Zereh was dragging back like an animal crouching for the kill, its muzzle all daubed with black clotted blood.

Very slowly Mukhi stood up; very slowly he went to fetch the blanket that lay behind Jahil; very slowly he spread it out before him. Jahil stepped from one to the other. And Mukhi repeated his motions until Jahil had thus crossed the whole flooded part. During all this Zereh never ceased gazing with anguish and supplication at the notes Uraz held high at the mercy of the wind. And Uraz thought that the world did not hold a finer song of victory than its prodigious howl.

After this Zereh traveled beside the syce. Uraz no longer set himself against it. He contrived to hold the treasure well in sight —notes that his slightest movement could send flying away forever, never to be regained.

The slope grew gentler, the paving slabs less smooth and less close-fitting. Streaks of clay, tufts of dry and spiny grass stood between them. The little caravan moved faster. It was high time. Only the topmost fragment of the eastern wall was still lit by the sun. Suddenly Jahil raised his head, flared his nostrils in the racing air, quickened his stride almost to a trot, thrust Zereh and the syce aside, and left them far behind him. In his turn Uraz caught the bitter scent that was coming on the wind. Moving faster than his thought, his blood thundered and his heart was filled with a poignant emotion which was that of happiness. Between the cliffs standing on each side like the pillars of a mighty gate an endless stretch of land was visible.

Uraz rode out of the Hindu Kush. And the steppe offered itself to him, the steppe where all day long a man might watch the passage of the sun and see it, before it vanished, settle on the earth's rim for a long embrace.

MUKHI LEFT THE THRESHOLD OF THE GORGE WITH A GREAT LEAP AND ran on and on until his breath was gone. When he stopped he had to rub his eyes, for their sight was blurred. He did not realize he was wiping tears away.

"The steppe . . ." he murmured. He could not believe it. He turned round, saw the gigantic barrier of the Hindu Kush, and smiled blissfully.

"Why didst thou leave me?" cried Zereh. "And why this joy?"

Mukhi had not seen the girl coming. He shivered, and with the light of ecstasy still shining on his flat face answered softly, "The steppe, Zereh, the steppe . . ."

"Yes," cried Zereh. "Yes: the steppe: with no money, no stallion, and nothing left on the mule!"

"That is true," said Mukhi, in a scarcely audible voice. His happiness had taken on the taste of gall. He turned his back to the mountain and looked for Uraz. He saw him there, a few steps away, motionless in his saddle, facing the west: he seemed to be praying.

The stallion snorted and pawed the ground. Strident cries from the north stabbed the quiet air and reached the travelers.

"What is that?" asked Zereh.

"Mounted shepherds," said Mukhi. "In this faint light they cannot be seen. They are bringing the herds that graze on the steppe all day back to their tents."

The word "steppe" had evoked no tenderness in his voice. Like the nomad he was thinking of the difficulty of killing, now that there were these witnesses.

On either side of Jahil Uraz saw a human shadow on the ground. "Mukhi and Zereh," he said to himself. Jahil was already moving off with his longest stride. And already Uraz had hidden the bundle of afghanis beneath his shirt. The action gave him an unbearable feeling of pointlessness, of emptiness. He let himself be carried where his horse thought fit.

21

The Thread Must Be Cut

THE CAMP had the simplicity of the steppes. By night a huge
rectangle made of wire on wooden posts held the flocks and
their dogs. The horses and the pack camel were tethered to the
same posts, on the outside. For the men two tents were enough. In
the larger camped five young shepherds. Their leader shared the
other with his youngest son—a child still—and it was as bare and
empty as the first. The earth was their bed and a saddle their pillow.

They had just brought in the animals. A high-leaping fire
burned between the two tents. Although they were under his father's orders, the shepherds, squatting in a circle round the flames,
were waiting for the bacha to serve them tea and food.

Uraz halted Jahil so that only his head went beyond the line of
darkness. The barking of the dogs that had accompanied his approach for a long while now grew twice as loud. The shepherds did
not stir.

"Honorable people. They know how to keep a rein on their
curiosity."

From the bend of their necks, the shape of their turbans, the
cloth of their chapans, the nature of their silence, he felt that they

were as familiar as his own skin. To speak to them he once more used the language of the steppes, unknown in the valleys of the Hindu Kush and beyond.

"Peace upon you and prosperity to your flocks," said Uraz in Turkoman.

And in Turkoman the shepherds cried all together with a single voice, "Welcome, welcome to thee and thy horse!"

Jahil stepped into the ring of light. At last the shepherds turned their faces toward Uraz. Without knowing them he recognized them all. They were of his own clan, his own blood. When he realized this fully he was very near to reining the stallion back into the shelter of darkness. Here he was no longer an ordinary passerby. This was where the land of the buzkashi began, and the passion for the game. The fame of the great chapandaz shone throughout the Three Provinces. What was more, the province he had reached was his own, Meimana. These shepherds had seen him play—and win—at least once. One of them at least would remember him . . . And when he did so, turmoil, anxious care . . . The news brought to Tursen . . . And the pitiful return of the beaten man, the cripple. No one, ever, would be able to know what he had braved, endured, overcome . . .

Like a thief seized with panic because about to be unmasked, Uraz leaned over Jahil's neck, to hide his face as long as possible. His check brushed the stallion's mane and it felt hairy and foul. Unconsciously he put his hand to his face, and for the first time thought of the state to which he had been reduced. A prickling, sticky beard: sunken cheeks: sharp bones jutting out: hollow, bleary eyes . . . Uraz imagined his cadaverous, awkward body, shameful under the rags that covered it. And he straightened his back; for who could detect the proud Uraz, son of Tursen, in this wretched horseman on a foundered mount?

One of the shepherds, without so much as touching the ground to thrust himself up, rose to his feet, uncoiling like a spring. He was the oldest of them. Lean, sharp. All sinew. White hair and mustache. But his eyebrows, which joined over his hooked nose, had not a gray hair in them—a smooth, shining line that might have been drawn in indelible ink. This peculiarity gave the eyes a most uncommon, piercing liveliness. "Sit by our fire," he began..

And stopped, because he had seen Uraz's broken leg. He took Jahil by the bridle, led him to the smaller tent, his own, lifted Uraz off, and laid him on the ground.

"My syce is following me . . . With a servant-woman," said Uraz in a very weak voice. "I do not want them. They are too tired."

"Rest easy. We shall look after them, and thy horse," said the head shepherd.

"And thou shalt have my son, Qadir, the last-born, for thy bacha."

"Whom must I thank for all these kindnesses, O my first host on the steppe?" asked Uraz.

"My name is Mizrar, and I am entrusted with the care of part of the flocks of Behram Khan," said the chief of the shepherds.

He brought Jahil's saddle, took away his own, and went to find a hurricane lamp. When he came back the nostrils of his great hooked nose wrinkled. A smell of corruption was spreading through the tent. The man with white hair and ink-black eyebrows was on the edge of giving Uraz advice. He confined himself to turning the wick lower and went out wishing Uraz an easy night.

The tent flaps fell into place.

The tent flaps opened.

Mizrar's son offered Uraz tea, wheatcakes, rice. Uraz pushed the food away and drank eagerly. The boy's intelligent, cheerful, impatient eyes never left him. But the bacha behaved as discreetly as his father. When Uraz had slaked his thirst the child sat with his legs crossed, close to the hurricane lamp, and remained there without a word. It was Uraz who broke the silence. "Hast seen my followers?" he asked.

"Truly," said Qadir. He tried to leave it at that but could not manage it; he suddenly leaned his face toward Uraz and all the gravity he had forced on it until then was rendered vain by his smile. "And I saw the mule, too," he exclaimed. "It is tall and strong. But by the Prophet, it is thy stallion I should like to have. What a horse! Although he is filthy enough to make one tremble, everybody can see . . ." The words hung in the air. Qadir bowed his head. He had promised Mizrar not to talk to the sick man. But Uraz asked again, "What did they say?"

"That they were perishing of weariness and hunger," said the child. "That is all. They must be asleep in the big tent by now."

"Good," said Uraz. Hunters and quarry were in agreement on keeping silent. "Very good," murmured Uraz. But which was the hunter and which the hunted? Uraz was no longer sure. His mind was growing heavy and numb . . . The air was thick; it stank. The drowsiness that was coming over him with all this weight, this smell . . . His neck stiffened on the supporting saddle and he opened his eyes. The strongest, most certain of his instincts forbade him to give way to this lethargy. It had nothing of the good open kindness of sleep. It was as deceitful and slimy as the mud of a deadly marsh. Instead of rest, a mortal sinking down.

"The poison of the wound is spreading, spreading," thought Uraz. "If it sends me to sleep it will rot me through entirely . . ."

Already whatever he did his eyelids were continually drooping. Already everything was beginning to seem indifferent to him—life, death, defeat, fame . . . Once more he raised the overwhelming burden of his eyelids. He had used up all his strength in doing so. He could never start all over again. "Qadir," whispered Uraz, "turn the lamp up high, set it on my belly, and let your father come."

Mizrar appeared shortly afterward. A vague outline was all Uraz could see of him. His red, burning eyes, covered with a deep film of tears, were almost blind from having stared unwaveringly into the glaring light.

"What can I do to serve thee?" asked Mizrar.

"Look into my wound," said Uraz.

"I know it . . . There is nothing hiding it any more," said Mizrar.

"What then?" said Uraz.

The head shepherd's eyes wandered toward the hideous mess that hung at the end of the broken leg—burst, swollen blue and blackened flesh; shreds of cloth stuck in the open ragged wound; and showing through the skin, piercing it, points and edges of bone.

"Long-rotten carrion and source of foulness," said Mizrar.

"What then?" said Uraz again.

"If thou wouldst live still," said Mizrar, "thou must be rid of it this very night."

"Thou wilt undertake it?" asked Uraz.

The head shepherd wrinkled his forehead so deeply that his black eyebrows were only separated from his white hair by a thin line of skin. He answered, "I have succeeded with so many beasts that I believe I can do it for a man."

"Without anyone knowing," said Uraz.

"Only my son, and I am his warrant," said Mizrar.

"Wilt thou start now?" asked Uraz.

"No," said Mizrar. "I must be sure that everyone in the camp is sleeping, and sleeping well."

"Take that light away from me," said Uraz.

HIDDEN BEHIND THE SADDLE THE LAMP WAS BURNING AT ITS LOWEST point. A soft and gentle light whose source Uraz could not see filled the tent. Now nothing, whether from the outside or from within himself, defended him from the torpor he had resisted till then. He let himself sink down into it as though to the bottom of a muddy pool.

From time to time some impression pierced through the mire and touched his consciousness—the clink of metal, a strange warmth, the smell of fat . . . And then a dart of fire against his eyelids and in his face an icy jet.

Sitting straight up, whip and dagger in his clenched hands, Uraz stared uncomprehendingly at the blazing lamp and the aquiline nose above it. He wiped his forehead with one hand, and found it wet.

"I had to sprinkle thee," said Mizrar. "Thou couldst not come out of thy sleep."

Uraz closed his eyes: opened them again. At the side of his bed Qadir was tearing a clean shirt to pieces. At his feet a round-bellied pot was smoking on a red-hot brazier. Close to the brazier lay a small axe and a long, broad-bladed knife. Uraz's gaze settled on the polish of steel, the glittering light on keen edges. He dropped his weapons and covered his wound with his hands; they moving faster than his thought. He withdrew them with equal speed. It was this reaction of shame that at last brought him back to himself.

His head fell back into the hollow of the saddle. He crossed his arms over his chest and said, "In the name of the Prophet, I am ready."

"Not yet," said the chief shepherd. He felt in the pocket of his chapan and drew out a long, thin, strong line. "Sit up," said Mizrar. "I must tie thee."

Uraz did indeed sit up, but armed again and saying in a voice that hissed between his clenched teeth, "No one . . . ever . . . I swear on my blood."

Placidly Mizrar asked his son, "Qadir, how many strong shepherds do we usually have to hold a ram whose leg is to be cut off?"

"Two at least," replied the child.

"I am not an animal," said Uraz.

"That is the very reason that I cannot take risks," said Mizrar. He spoke in a tone of utter detachment. His eyes, usually so lively under the black arch of his eyebrows, expressed nothing.

"There is no shaking his determination," thought Uraz.

He gazed at the rope. He gazed at the swollen, putrid flesh above his ankle . . . He whispered, "I shall never forgive thee for this." And held out his bare hands to Mizrar, the one clasping the other.

"Not like that," said the chief of the shepherds. He took hold of Uraz's forearms, crossed them behind the back of his neck, tied his wrists so tight that the skin was cut, bound him round the waist, fixed his good leg at the knee joint and then at the ankle, and so tied the cord under the sole of his foot in one last knot, tightened beyond all chance of slipping. Then he turned Uraz over, flat as a board on his back, took off his turban, rolled it into a gag, and stuffed it in his mouth.

Uraz made not the least resistance. Now all his pride lay in putting up with the worst without wincing. But everything happened, everything ran in so precise and rapid a sequence that he had no time to be aware, to suffer.

Mizrar had dropped to his knees. The cheekbones stood out on his lean cheeks like the heads of great nails. His left hand grasped Uraz's thigh and flattened it with all its strength against the ground. Qadir held the hurricane lamp high and passed Mizrar the axe. In the harsh, violent light the shining iron rose, fell; rose, fell. In shadow play against the canvas wall Uraz saw these executioner's motions. He felt no more than a vague, muffled pain. While the violence of the blow still kept Uraz numb to the torture of the severed bone, the head shepherd changed the axe for the knife. Before Uraz had quite understood the significance of his movements Mizrar, having cut through flesh and skin, thrust a lump of vile carrion aside with his foot.

"It is done already? Then why the gag? The rope? So much humiliation? Why?" In the same second he lost the power of thought.

For Mizrar, with one knee thrust into Uraz's belly, lifted up the mutilated leg, and Qadir leaned the smoking cauldron over it. Then the shadows that peopled the canvas of the tent and the ghastly sun of the hurricane lamp and the red glow of the brazier suddenly uncovered and the spitting of burned skin and the revolting waft of boiling tallow and the still more horrible stench of burning meat— all was veiled, confused, carried away in the onrush of unbearable agony. Uraz's courage and pride had been prepared for the ordeal of the striking iron, the cutting iron. They were of no help whatever to him when the boiling fat poured over his naked, bleeding stump.

A purely animal revolt flung his entire body into furious, convulsive action. All it did was to tighten his bonds, making them more rigid. The knee grinding into his belly pressed harder still, while the pitiless hands did not allow what was left of his leg to escape the torment for a second. A flood of liquid fire . . . another . . . another. Uraz was no longer in control of his muscles and they stretched and jerked with raving power, fighting vainly against the rope and its knots. His wild teeth ripped into the gag. His mouth flooded with spittle. And he shrieked and shrieked, silent behind the muffling cloth.

The pot was empty. Qadir carefully wiped the bottom and sides with a piece of the clean shirt he had torn earlier on. He tied the bandage, heavy with scalding fat, to the blackened stump, which bled no more.

Uraz's convulsive heaving died away. By the time the child had finished his task the body was limp. Mizrar gently let down the thigh he was holding and freed Uraz from the gag and rope. Uraz never stirred. Mizrar took the piece of leg lying on the ground by the end of its toes and left the tent. A little later the sound of a galloping horse drummed in the silent darkness over the steppe.

"He will come back, be certain of that," said Qadir to Uraz. "He is only going to carry thy ill-fortune far from the camp." Uraz did not hear. He had lost consciousness. "He will soon come back, I swear to thee, I swear," cried Qadir. It was for himself that he was talking now. His father had left him alone with their unconscious guest. Alone! What a trust! What an honor! But what could he do for a man who never moved, never spoke, a man without sight or thought? And what if death took him while he was in Qadir's charge? What would his father's beloved eyes under their black brows say to him then?

Qadir squatted close to Uraz, the better to listen to his choked breathing. It whistled, weakened, stopped . . . No, not yet . . . Then choked again. The beating of the child's heart followed the rhythm of that wavering breath. His anxiety grew intolerable. He could not bear to look at that waxy yellow face any more or to watch over the gasping breath . . . He stood up and stared around the tent. "What a mess!" he said to himself with happy relief: "My father would blame me."

He began by wiping off the clotted blood on the tools and the axe, which he put in order beside the brazier. Then very carefully, one by one, he picked up what the amputation had left behind it—scraps of cloth, splinters of bone, pieces of soft flesh—and burned them. Then he put a half-filled kettle on the glowing embers. "He will need very hot tea," said Qadir to himself, "very hot." This reflection brought him back to Uraz, who was still in his swoon. His skin was crisscrossed with shivering. "How cold he is," thought Qadir. He took off his little chapan and spread it over Uraz.

The thud of a quick gallop rumbled in the tent. "Here he is! Here he is!" said Qadir half aloud.

The angel of death had not come. And everything was tidy . . . No, not everything—there was the rope and the gag. The unconscious man had one hand over them. Qadir tried to take them. At this the limp fingers closed with a strange power over the damp rag and the slimy cord and the unconscious man whispered, "Leave it . . . I shall cry no more . . . By the Prophet."

It was the faintest of breaths and so plaintive and humble that a shout would have frightened Qadir less. He let go. The tightly closed lips were a thin white line on the ashy, waxen mask. So who was it who had spoken?

The drumming of hoofs stopped before the tent. Qadir darted toward the opening, then stopped short. A boy to whom a father like his had given such great trust could not behave like a frightened child.

Mizrar at once saw the tent's orderliness, the kettle on the brazier, and Qadir's chapan half covering Uraz. He took his son by the shoulder and said, "Well, boy? All well?"

The friendliness of the horny great hand . . . The tone of the gruff voice, speaking as to another man . . . Qadir did not answer at once; when he was sure of himself he replied steadily, "I am not sure, Father. His soul has not yet returned to him."

"That is as it should be," said Mizrar. "It rests better far from the body." He stretched out at Uraz's side, opened the sides of his chapan, and put his ear to his heart. And heard nothing. The black arch of his eyebrows puckered. The patient was breathing: so his heart must be beating. Mizrar pushed his cheek harder against the shirt and heard a curious rustle. He felt under the stuff and his fingers met a mass of big bank notes. For a moment surprise kept him from moving. Then he gently shook his head, pushed the bundle of afghanis to the right of the bared chest, set his hand where they had been, and found the beat at once. He carefully buttoned the shirt, closed Uraz's chapan, and turned up Qadir's to look at the shortened leg. The thigh was still blotched with dark crimson patches, but the swelling had gone down. Mizrar felt the skin: hot, to be sure, but not burning . . . Lastly he took the damaged stump and raised it to his nose. Qadir watched his movements with religious attention. Mizrar said to him, "There is no telling. The bandage smells too strongly of the fat. Undo it. Thy fingers are lighter than mine."

Uraz did not move when the seared wound was uncovered. Mizrar smelled close to it, winked at his son, and said, "Boy, we have won. Put back the dressing."

Was it tiredness, the cold and the night, or delight in praise? Qadir's hands trembled a little and his nail touched the bare flesh. Uraz quivered: his head was pressed back flat against the ground and his opening eyes saw Mizrar's face right above him. The head shepherd said to him, "Be comforted. Now thy carrion concerns none but the vultures."

"What vultures? Why?" murmured Uraz. His fingers clenched. He felt cloth crumple under them. And remembered everything. Of itself his left hand darted toward the place of the break—the place it knew so well. It felt nothing but the ground: felt farther down—still ground and nothing else. The hand hesitated and began to move slowly, timidly up . . . It found the stump, grew brisker, ran to the knee, then back to the cut, measuring . . . "Shall I . . . shall I . . . ?" whispered Uraz.

"Upon my honor," said Mizrar, and his voice was grave, almost solemn. "Upon my honor, thou wilt soon be able to hold the wildest stallion between thy legs, and hold him as strongly as before."

"May Allah hear thee!" said Uraz. There was strength in his voice. And in his eyes, brilliance. A quick, exact movement brought him against his saddle. He leaned on it, wound one arm round the pommel, the other round the cantle, and held himself upright, his chest high.

"Thou art a man," said Mizrar. "Truly."

Uraz opened his right hand, which was holding the spittle-soaked gag and the sweat-soaked rope. He watched them drop, while his bloodless lips came together and narrowed to form a long, curving line on his haggard face, a line that gave it an expression of inhuman sarcasm and contempt.

"Truly, truly," said Uraz, in a voice that could scarcely be heard.

Qadir smoothed out the torn cloth and said solemnly, "It is no longer any good."

"Into the fire!" said Uraz. He took off the length of cloth that was his belt and made a turban of it. Around his waist he tied the rope.

To do these things Uraz had had to let go the saddle. His body collapsed. He made no attempt at hoisting it up again but let his head lie there in the hollow of the leather. He was shivering. Qadir helped him to drink boiling tea. Mizrar said to his son, "He needs a great deal of warmth. Go and fetch our blankets."

"At once! In a moment!" cried Qadir. At last he could give way to the violent needs of his age. He was out of the tent in two skips.

When the boy, wearing only his thin shirt, had vanished into the glacial night of the steppe, Uraz felt an odd sensation of something lacking, of emptiness. "Why have I no son like that?" he said to himself. The regret astonished him exceedingly. He had no feeling for children other than impatience and disgust . . . Yet this one . . . He had borne a hand in the bloodiest, most disgusting task without flinching. Had watched over him with intelligence and courage . . . And there was this very small chapan over his leg. "The real man here," he observed suddenly, "is thy son."

And Mizrar replied, "One day he will be proud of having looked after Uraz of the hundred victories."

At first Uraz could not speak. Then he murmured, "So thou didst recognize me?"

"At the first glance," said Mizrar. "But be easy in thy mind. The others are too young. I am the only one with enough years on my back to have seen thee play and win more than once. And as thou knowest it is said that black hair over an aged eye means a sound memory."

Qadir came running in with the blankets, his face all pink with the cold.

THAT NIGHT BROUGHT URAZ LITTLE SLEEP. PAIN KEPT HIM AWAKE. The sharpest, most rousing, did not come from the fresh wound. It lay in its old lair, there where there was now emptiness, deep in that piece of leg that had been thrown to the carrion eaters. More than once that strange pain was so vivid, so real, and so like that which had made him suffer so much and so often that his hand ran beyond the stump to touch the place of the break and to its astonishment found nothing there—emptiness. At these moments, by the light of the dimmed hurricane lamp behind his saddle, he saw Qadir squatting by his bedside, anxiety and a desire to help on his little face, made still smaller by his weariness. And Uraz pretended to be asleep so that the child might doze. At last, at dawn, they both fell deeply asleep.

The barking of the dogs, the cries of the shepherds, and the bleating of the flocks they were assembling woke both Uraz and Qadir at the same moment.

"How dost thou feel?" asked the child.

"I am hungry," said Uraz. Then, with an astonishment that was directed to himself, "Terribly hungry."

There was only a faint glow in the brazier. "I go for charcoal to heat the pilaw," cried Qadir.

"No," said Uraz. "Cold, but at once."

He was licking his fingers over the empty dish when Mizrar came in, booted, whip in his belt. "Thou hast found thy best medicine," said the head shepherd. "I shall go about my work in peace."

"No one in the camp must know," said Uraz, looking at his mutilated leg.

"Nor thy syce either?" asked Mizrar.

"No one," said Uraz.

"I will ride off to the grazing with him behind me," said Mizrar. "We have none too many hands."

Like a slow wave that surges past and dies away on the sand, so little by little the noise of the flocks lessened and vanished. Qadir listened to its farthest, faintest murmur. His inner eye saw the columns of wool that mingled, took on orderly shape, and traveled across the steppe according to his father's will. At last he said, "They are grazing at the foot of the great mountain . . . The grass lasts until late in the season there. Because of the springs. The well in the camp—it is one of those springs that feeds it." That word brought him back to a sense of his duty. "I will run and fetch the shepherd's samovar," he cried. "With that thou shalt have piping hot tea until nightfall."

He had barely closed the flap of the tent behind him before Uraz saw his gold-sewn cap thrust in again through the folds of felt. "Thy servant-woman is not far off," said Qadir.

With an instinctive movement Uraz ruffled up the blanket that covered his stump and said slowly, "Let her come . . . But if she speaks to thee about me, thou shalt reply . . ."

The little round face jerked strongly from left to right and right to left and then replied, "I have nothing to answer. She is only a nomad woman of no account and I am the son of the head shepherd."

"Thou speakest like a man. Go . . ." said Uraz.

Scarcely had Qadir's head vanished before Uraz changed his posture completely. He stretched out on the ground, doubled the thickness of the blanket over his maimed leg, thrust his chin into the collar of his chapan, and hid his cheeks under the folds of his turban. When Zereh came in all that could be seen of Uraz was the sockets of his eyes, deep and hollow as those of a skull, and the corpselike ridge of his nose. He did not give the young woman time to utter a word or make the first beginning of a greeting.

"I wish to die in peace," he said to her. "And if thou art found prowling round my tent once more, just once more, Mizrar shall flay thee with the whip."

Although Uraz's voice was extraordinarily weak, it was pitiless. Without meaning to, Zereh shrunk her shoulders where a frail skin was growing to replace that which Hayatal had lashed off her. She went out backward.

A little later Qadir brought in the big copper samovar. Uraz drank cup after cup of steaming tea. And he ate again. And so it went all through the day. Qadir was filled with amazement at this insatiable hunger. Rice, wheatcakes, ewe's cheese—Uraz devoured everything the child brought him, finishing the last crumb, the last grain. For the first time since his fall he felt the pleasure, the goodness, the kindness of food.

Evening came. The flocks returned. Mizrar changed Uraz's bandage. There were no more blotches on his thigh, no more swelling at the knee. His fever had gone down. The two men spoke little. They had nothing to say: all was going well.

Uraz slept without waking all that night and all the next morning. The air was very hot when he woke. He recognized the burning heat of the steppe at noon. Yet his skin was cool and his mind alive. Qadir was not in the tent. At the well, or perhaps at the storehouse, or else at the open hearth that was the kitchen . . . Uraz threw back his blanket and rubbed the greasy cloth that covered his wound. He rubbed it hard: pain shot up, a fierce, open, healthy, proper pain. Uraz bent his knee. Above the stump the joint moved awkwardly. He went on with the movement until it became supple and easy. Then he set his two hands to the ground, thrust with the muscles of his arms, and raised his body, his two legs held out at right angles. For a moment he gazed at the amputated shin, which only reached halfway along the other, and then, with a strong, sudden jerk of his loins he threw himself forward, landed neatly, and raised himself again. In this way he moved right round the tent, going faster and faster, his motion nimbler and more exact. He was filled with a sensation of power and independence such as he had never known before. Once more he could manage his own body, and by himself.

The sound of Qadir humming a chant of the steppes outside stopped Uraz's crippled progress. He was afraid of mockery and he went back to his saddle. There he squatted on his crossed legs, the stump sheltered by the sound calf.

Qadir's obvious astonishment at the sight did him great good. "No one, I swear it, would ever know about thy leg," cried the boy. "Thou art a new man."

"May Allah hear thee!" said Uraz gently.

Qadir turned to put the skewers of meat he had brought onto the fire and went on, "Thou must be strangely happy. Now thou wilt finish thy journey in peace."

"Allah . . ." Uraz could not utter the rest of the wish. Suddenly his throat and tongue were dry. He could—he must—go on with his crossing of the friendly steppe. It would lead him to the end without hindrance or difficulty, in total safety. A mere question of time. And all the chapandaz would be there. And Tursen. And there he would be, after a huge detour, a foolish detour—there he would be back again, thanks to his syce's help: beaten and mutilated.

Uraz remembered the effort that had filled him with such pride and joy only a moment earlier. A splendid feat indeed, a fine triumph to hop like a toad, hidden, skulking, out of sight. In his mind's eye Uraz saw his stump strike Jahil's flank while Tursen watched, and he longed to die.

Then a kind of hope came to him, a most base and ignoble hope and one that he clung to. Jahil . . . He knew nothing about him. What if the stallion had not regained his strength . . . Or if he were sick . . . Or lame . . . ?

Qadir took the skewers off the fire and waved them under Uraz's nose. They gave off a strong, succulent smell of grilled meat and fat. "Dost thou smell it?" cried Qadir. "Dost thou smell it?"

"I am not hungry," said Uraz.

"Thou hast eaten too much." said the child. "I have not." He gulped down the plump rounds, licked his fingers, and rubbed his belly.

"Now that thou art full," said Uraz impatiently, "go and fetch my horse."

"Thy horse . . ." said Qadir. "Oh, yes, to be sure. Thou wouldst judge his strength before the journey."

"Go on," growled Uraz.

At the first glance he saw that his hope had been as futile as it was base. Had he forgotten how little rest and care a great buzkashi horse needed to recover its strength? Jahil's vigor seemed to fill the whole tent. Uraz ran his hands over the stallion's belly, chest, thighs, pasterns; felt his muscles, sinews, and joints. "As for him, he really is new," reflected Uraz.

"None of the shepherds has had time to clean him," said Qadir. "Nor has thy syce. He is watching over the flocks. With thy permission I could . . . And what an honor . . . Such a splendid horse!"

"No!" said Uraz. "No."

That ultimate shame was all that was lacking—Jahil groomed, currycombed, gleaming; and mounted on him a filthy, unshaven horseman, ragged and crippled.

"No," growled Uraz.

The child gazed at him with astonishment and sorrow. Why this grim, muffled voice? He had no time to think it over. Uraz made Jahil bend his neck, grasped his mane, and holding on by it, raised himself on his uninjured leg. A heave carried him onto the stallion's back. In spite of himself, in spite of everything, he felt a moment's happiness. His knees gripped, held on. But Jahil felt that half of one leg was missing. He stared at the empty place. Uraz let himself slide to the ground, tossed the headrope to Qadir, and said to him, "Tether him in front of the tent and do not come back here until thy father returns: I have to think."

"Until this evening?" asked Qadir artlessly. He received no answer.

THE FLOCKS WERE PENNED. GRADUALLY THEIR BLEATING AND THE barking of the dogs died away. The cold, harsh night of the steppe wrapped Uraz about. A hurricane lamp appeared, held head high by Qadir. Higher, and as it were cut out by the light, Mizrar's face—eagle nose, white mustache, black eyebrows.

Uraz was by the saddle, squatting on his crossed legs. There was no longer any bitter humor on his face.

"I congratulate thee, O my guest," said Mizrar. "Thou art quick at coming to life again. Allow me to see thy wound for the last time. Then thou wilt be safe for a great while."

Uraz stretched out his stump. Mizrar wrapped it in a fresh bandage, thick with another kind of ointment. Uraz thanked the head shepherd with irreproachable politeness.

"Qadir will bring thee thy meal and heap up the fire," said Mizrar. "Thou wilt have a a good night, I trust."

"The best of nights, be sure of that," said Uraz.

When the child finished his tasks Uraz said to him, "I shall have no further need of thee. Do no more, but send me my syce."

"He is strong, kind, and open," cried Qadir. "Everyone has come to like him. Thou hast great luck with him."

"Very great, truly," said Uraz.

THE LAMP WAS BURNING LOW BEHIND THE SADDLE THAT SUPPORTED Uraz's head. The blankets hid the whole of his outstretched body and the lower half of his face. Under the low-swagging turban

Mukhi could see nothing but his eyes. They had such brilliance in the dimness of the tent that it seemed as though they were the real source of the light.

"Eaten up by fever," thought Mukhi.

He had to bend down to make out the meaning of the breath whispering through the rug. "Cannot go on . . . journey . . . Death . . . in me . . . Tursen . . . must tell him . . . Take Jahil . . . Go . . ."

"What, tonight, thou sayst?" stammered the syce. His chin was trembling.

"At once," whispered Uraz. To prevent Mukhi from speaking he waved a hand that seemed scarcely under his control, and in a dying voice he said, "At once . . . Already too late . . . Maybe." His hand went back under the rug, searched clumsily, jerkily all along his chest, rustling as it did so. And at last he put a big crumpled bank note at Mukhi's feet. "For . . . the road," murmured Uraz.

His hand went limp and flat on the ground. Mukhi closed his eyes and tried to pick out the one idea he ought to follow, to choose it among all those that surged up in his mind, confusing and astounding it. All the money belonged to him . . . He had only to reach out. But the camp was not yet asleep. And if the dying man summoned up enough strength for a cry . . . Smother him . . . But the child was going to come back. Mizrar, too, no doubt. Instant alarm, pursuit. No . . . Ask Zereh first.

Mukhi felt blindly for the note, picked it up, and only opened his eyes to get out of the tent. Beneath the rug Uraz relaxed the gripping fingers from the handle of his knife.

THE MOON—IT WAS IN ITS FIRST QUARTER—GLIDED FROM THE SKY. All at once the ground under their feet seemed colder. Jahil shivered.

"It is time to go back," said Zereh in Mukhi's ear.

"More than time," said he.

Silently they crossed the stretch of steppe that lay between their halting place and the shepherds' camp. Mukhi went along close by the great pen so that the dogs should recognize him. This was successful. A few scattered, lazy barks hardly disturbed the night at all. He skirted very widely round the larger tent. No doubt it was carrying caution too far. From his own experience he knew the depth and deafness of healthy men's sleep when they have worked hard from dawn until after sunset. And Jahil's hoofs had been muffled with cloth. But the syce needed all the odds on his side—even the slightest. Nothing that depended on him could be left to chance. He had to kill Uraz. Greed for money no longer had any part in this imperative need. Mukhi had murdered Uraz so many times in his mind and wishes and had tried so many times in vain that now his blood, his entire being refused to let his victim escape again.

The tent that housed Uraz took shape in the starlight. Zereh set foot on the ground as softly as any night bird. Mukhi took off his sandals and dismounted barefoot. He hobbled the stallion. Listened. No movement . . . no sound. The only waking thing in the whole steppe was the line of light that made its way from under the felt sides—the light from Uraz's bedside . . . Mukhi's naked feet no longer felt the frost on the grass. He went with long, silent strides, gliding toward the golden thread running along the bottom of the tent—he opened the flap a very little. Zereh's hand touched him. "We must look and look," whispered the nomad.

Everything was in order. The fire of the brazier. The hurricane lamp turned low, on the other side of the saddle. The body stretched out and the blanket pulled right up to the hump made by the head . . . An unbearable thought came into Mukhi's mind. "And what if he is already . . . ?" He could not pursue it. A single leap flung him on Uraz. Zereh followed.

Only she never managed to get farther than the doorway. There her ankles were seized and crushed. She fell instantly. The back of her neck hit the ground. She called, "Syce, tall . . ." And her breath was cut off.

Mukhi turned. His face still expressed nothing but stupidity. Under the blanket he had found a chapan instead of the body and a boot instead of the head. And there was Zereh lying on the ground and a man in a ragged shirt on one knee holding her by the throat. And the man looked like Uraz, that sick, dying creature

. . . And in Uraz's voice the man said, "Move a finger and I choke thy whore."

"I do not move, I do not move," whispered Mukhi. Terror began to show in his eyes. Uraz had deceived him: Uraz was restored to his full strength. And the softest, most fragile neck in the world was at the mercy of a squeeze of those fingers, the iron fingers of a chapandaz.

"Thy orders," whispered Mukhi.

"First the horse, here, close to me," said Uraz. "And keep out of reach all the time. Otherwise . . ." He narrowed the ring of his fingers. Zereh's face darkened, went blue.

"By the Prophet, I will try nothing, nothing, nothing," cried the syce.

Uraz loosened his grip. A rattle came from the tortured throat. Mukhi darted out, came back with Jahil.

"Come to within a step of me and hold out thy wrists," ordered Uraz. He untied the rope he had round him as a belt, thrust a knee into Zereh's chest ("the knee of the dead leg," said Mukhi to himself with horror), tied the hands held out and the ankles too. Then he unhitched Jahil's tether, made a noose in it, put the noose round Zereh's neck, wound the end of the rope round his hand, and said to the nomad girl, "Get up!"

She stood, tottering. When she was upright such a dizziness overcame her that she leaned against the stallion.

"Hold her up, good Jahil," whispered Mukhi. "Hold her up!"

Uraz bent his legs again, squatted on them, and looked at the bound syce. "The horse," he said, "was no longer enough for thee, truly . . . Or rather, not enough for this woman here." He turned his head toward the nomad. Her senses had hardly yet come back to her but her gaze had a striking intensity. It was fixed on Uraz's chest. Unconsciously he put his hand to it, and through the holes in his shirt he touched pieces of paper, stuck right against his skin . . . The afghanis.

At this an astonishing hatred made him tremble throughout his body. His fury confounded the woman and the money. The woman, still half-dead and already restored to her passion of greed. The money, capable of inspiring so base a madness. Both had to be destroyed. The one by the other. A red mist of blood troubled his sight. He thought it was the reflection of the glowing charcoal. His hands on the ground carried him toward the brazier like springs. The noose round Zereh's neck dragged her behind him. He grasped a handful of bank notes, thrust them between her fingers, and growled, "Into the fire!"

An appalling, insane agony distorted the young woman's face. She hesitated. The noose cut into her flesh. The afghanis blazed on the embers. Another handful of paper. Another jerk of the rope . . . Another blaze. Zereh wanted to close her eyes. She could not. A fiend within forced her to watch this fortune, this treasure, take fire, curl up, and blacken.

When there was not a single note left in his bosom, Uraz put on his chapan and untied Mukhi's hands so that he could harness Jahil. Then he hoisted himself into the saddle, picked up Zereh and put her in front of him, and tied Mukhi to the saddle by his neck. Once out of the tent he uttered his ululation, his galloping shriek. Mizrar and his shepherds came running, and to them he said, "This man and this woman came back to murder me. Do not forget it on the day you have to bear witness." And plunged into the darkness and the steppe.

PART FIVE

The Circle of Justice

22

The Judgment of Uraz

EVERYTHING was in its usual place. The early sun in its youthful bloom at the rim of the sky. The first morning shadows on the still cool earth. Osman Bey's splendid horse against the baked-clay walls. The litter boys, the feed boys, the grooms, the chapandaz. And, greeted by their very low bows, Tursen.

He had just appeared in the courtyards as he did every day with the regularity of the sun and the shadows—and, it seemed, their everlasting quality.

As usual the heaviness of his tread was a demonstration of his strength; and the stick on which he leaned, the symbol of his power. He stood upright in his chapan, and although the garment was wide and spreading his massive chest and arms quite filled it; he held his head high under the turban with its sculptured folds and showed the day his square, seamed, battered face, plowed with glorious scars and wounds, a face whose cheeks, jaws, and temples bore a kind of spiny, whitish moss, carved by the wind and the rain, such as that which grows on certain isolated rocks.

And nothing in all this proud severity gave a hint of the accumulated effort and torment by which Tursen had once again succeeded in raising, dressing the body and head of an old, stiff-jointed, bed-fast man, and turning him into what he ought to be—the Head of the Stables, the Master of the Horse.

389

One courtyard . . . another. One horse . . . the next. The same examination: motionless, silent. The same speed, the same hardness, the same justice in his eye. Tursen's movements followed one another like those of a rite. They had the same economy, precision, sureness.

Yet there was one that did not obey this austere law. Tursen's hand—sometimes the right, sometimes the left—brushed his belt where the whip ought to have been, and the fingers closed on emptiness. "How hard it is to give up the tool, the ornament of a lifetime," he thought. But then he remembered the young stallion he had murdered and he acknowledged that his belt should remain bare forever.

Tursen had inspected the last horse in the last court. And Taganbai, the oldest of the chapandaz, took him aside and said, "I have received a message from Kabul, the capital, sent by Osman Bey, our master and the best master under the sun."

"So he is, truly," said Tursen.

"Thy rank calls for the letter to be addressed to thee in person," went on Taganbai. "But out of the friendship and esteem he has for thee, Osman Bey desires to show thee that he requires nothing, commands nothing; and he thinks that if thou shouldst choose to answer with a refusal, it would be easier for thee to let it be known to me than to him."

"Truly," said Tursen. He leaned more heavily on his stick.

Taganbai coughed to clear his voice and continued, "The feasts at Kabul arranged for the winner of the great buzkashi are coming to their end. Salih will soon be here, with the master. He must be given a banquet." Taganbai coughed again. He waited for a question from Tursen. It did not come. Taganbai spoke faster. "The master," he said, "is in doubt whether it would suit thee to share the place of honor with Salih, in spite of . . . in spite of thy misfortune."

"Nothing," said Tursen, "should or shall prevent me from paying honor to a chapandaz of my stable when he has won the first royal buzkashi and has brought the king's pennon back to my province."

"And on thy horse," said Taganbai.

"That is true," said Tursen. This hurt him even more. He had

forgotten. It was on Jahil that Uraz had suffered his most terrible
defeat. It was Jahil who had given Salih the victory . . . What
was astonishing about that? At the point where he gave Uraz the
wonderful stallion his old man's jealousy was setting ill-fortune up
there behind him on the saddle.

One courtyard . . . another. Tursen passed through them in
reverse order. The sun was higher, the shadows less long . . .
Where had the ill-fortune carried Uraz, to what country?

He was alive; Tursen was certain of that. Otherwise Mukhi
would have come back to tell of his death. Yes, the syce had followed his master . . . Over toward the rising sun? Toward its
going down? India? Persia? What did the country matter! Not in
one or the other was Uraz a famous man. Not in one or the other
were there any witnesses of his fall. No Salih to be feasted . . .
"He has done well; he has done well . . ." thought Tursen,
with a despair devoid of compassion.

He was back at the first courtyard. On the right was a door
toward the stables. On the left another that led to the open country. In front of it, standing as though to bar the passage, Tursen
saw Rahim, his bacha. "Here? Without my orders?" he cried.

Rahim did not look away. On his small, thin face, tense with
alarm, the ridges left by Tursen's wickedness—the first—trembled
a little. And Tursen thought, "If I had my whip, I should give thee
more to add to them." He raised his stick.

"Strike, master, strike . . . But first let me say . . ." cried
Rahim. He had not lowered his head. His fear-troubled eyes
showed that he meant to sacrifice everything to carry out an essential duty; they showed it with so grave an obstinacy, a steadiness so
far from childhood that Tursen let his cane drop to the ground.

"Listen," begged Rahim. "I must . . ."

In turning aside the blow, Tursen had exhausted his patience.
He took the bacha by the collar of his chapan, tossed him to one
side as he would have done an importunate puppy, and thrust open
the door.

Outside began the tree-shaded road that led to the living quarters. Tursen observed that it was blocked by a strange gathering of
people. All the men on that broad and wealthy estate, the gardeners,
sweepers, farm hands, masons, carpenters, cooks, servants, kitchen

bachas, table bachas and laundry bachas were standing in a deep-packed silent ring, a circle incomplete on the side toward Tursen. In its center, and separate from the gazers by a space wide enough to set him fully, shockingly in sight, stood a horseman, like a statue, covered with filth.

From the rag on his head to the hoofs of his mount he seemed molded of some nameless substance that shared the qualities of mud, dirt, filth, muck, and glue. The outside covering of man and horse was not made up of tail, mane, hair, and beard but of a slimy moss stuck onto the crust that took the place of their coat and skin.

At the sight of this horseman Tursen's only feelings were disgust and anger. This did not arise from the grime that soiled both man and beast. Better than any, Tursen knew how shattered and exhausted a traveler might be after a difficult journey with dangerous obstacles, forced marches, and wretched places to lie. But he also knew that a horseman worthy of the name would cut short his rest, however brief and precarious, and find time to look after his horse. And in any case, even the idlest and most unworthy would do this before anything else, when at last his journey led him to a decent halting place.

What spirit of challenge, what perversity, had made this traveler refuse his duty, bringing him to the richest, most hospitable estate to parade his ignominy? Proudly throwing back his head as though he were riding on glory rather than on a horse that had, through his fault, lost all its honor?

The door opened behind Tursen. The stable boys, syces, chapandaz came out one by one and stood in a line against the wall of the courtyard. Not a sound, not a whisper came from them. They, like the other servants on the estate, seemed to be holding their breaths. Why were all these men, usually so eager to be amazed, to hold forth, to argue, why were they remaining silent like this? wondered Tursen. Had they some information about the unknown man that called for this strange muteness? Nothing stirred on Tursen's face. Yet the scars and weals, the planes, the battered bony edges, took on that expression which usually frightened the most fearless. He took a long stride toward the insolent, worthless horseman. And stopped all at once. He felt a strange mounting distress. The stick on which he leaned began to tremble. Beneath the vile squalor covering the horse he recognized that splendid chest, the curve of that neck. And now, although the rider was sawing the bit in his mouth to hold him in, the horse came toward Tursen with a gentle whinny.

Jahil.

So . . . so . . . The horseman . . . the horseman . . . Tursen's heavy lips struggled to open over his yellow teeth. "Uraz . . . my son . . ."

And none of those who heard that voice in the silence could at first believe, so tender and gentle was it, that it belonged to Tursen.

The reins dropped, the stallion set his muzzle against the old chapandaz's neck, and the horseman said, "Peace on thee, my revered father. It was long before thou couldst tell who I was. And indeed I expected it, the Prophet be my witness!"

And those who in the still heavier silence, a silence filled with anxious concern, heard Uraz, stated afterward that never, in spite of his revolting state, had his words held so much pride and satisfaction.

What could their tone or meaning signify to Tursen? Uraz was there. But what kind of Uraz? Now that he was within touching distance of his saddle Tursen saw, beneath the shell of filth and foul beard, the fleshless limbs, the skull-like face. And Tursen's heart swelled and grew warmer. A wonderful strength came into his arms, which longed to pick up and carry off this light, frail body, as they had done in earlier days for a child that already knew how to sit a horse but who could not yet manage to get off. But in front of him, behind, and on either side were a hundred witnesses following his every movement. Tursen remained motionless—only his stick thrust into the ground under the push of his enormous hands—both for his own dignity and for his son's. And in his usual voice he asked, "My son, what happened?"

Uraz made Jahil retreat a little. Then Tursen saw Mukhi, and some way behind him a young woman. The one and the other had their wrists tied by ropes that ran to the saddle. And Uraz cried,

"O revered Father, I bring thee back a criminal syce who desired my death. The nomad woman helped him. I deliver them to thee, as is right, the chief of our blood."

At these words a hoarse uproar deafened Tursen. It came equally from the workers on the land, the craftsmen and house servants who were opposite him, and from the men who worked with the horses, lining the wall behind. The secret of the drama had been opened to them. At last they could let their emotions run.

The silence of Mukhi and the unknown woman was an overwhelming confession to all of them. And to all the ancient, implacable custom was law. Fine, prison, or death—it was for the eldest of the clan, for Tursen to decide and see that the sentence was carried out on the guilty. Gradually the hubbub died away. The master of the two lives was about to speak.

Tursen's stick trembled no more under his hands. No hint of his enormous joy, compassion, and tenderness remained to him. He felt calm, wholly, desperately calm. He in his turn had detected that accent of pride in Uraz, that challenge. Nothing else. Nothing uttered from the bottom of the heart, nothing from a son to his father. And Tursen said, "No man should appear before a judge in thy condition, O Uraz. Bathe thyself, send for a barber, and change thy clothes. Then I shall hear thee, beneath my roof." He called Taganbai. "Let those two over there be shut up and carefully guarded."

In spite of himself Tursen turned his eyes toward Uraz. It was then that he saw the mutilated leg. He yearned to call out an appeal, a question. Too late. Uraz, rid of his prisoners, was riding toward the bathhouse.

THE HEAD SYCE AND ONE OF HIS MEN, PICKED FROM THE STRONGEST, thrust Mukhi and Zereh into an underground room where the spare harness was kept. The thick, low door slammed behind them. A key groaned in the huge rusty padlock. To light the bridles, saddles, and reins ranged along the rough walls was a thin, sad, miserly gleam that came in through the airhole, nothing more. The smell of leather was stupefying.

Zereh seized Mukhi by the shoulders and cried, "Is it in this ditch, this hole that they are going to keep us?"

"It will not be long," said Mukhi in a low voice. "Tursen makes his mind up quickly."

A shiver rising from her deepest being made Zereh's teeth chatter. She moaned, "He will have our lives. He is a terrible old man."

"He is just," said Mukhi.

"They are coming, they are coming," whispered Zereh. "Already!"

The head syce came in, leaned his back against the door, set a pitcher on the ground with a few cold wheatcakes, and said to Mukhi, "It is not by order. It is in memory of Baitas, thy father. He was a friend of my early years."

"O good Aqqul, may Allah reward thee," said Mukhi. Both his tone and his shoulders had a wretched humility.

Hesitantly the head syce asked, "Uraz . . . What he accuses thee of . . . Is it true? Is it possible?"

Mukhi's chin touched his chest. He murmured, "A demon in my heart, no doubt . . ."

Aqqul sighed and made as if to go. Zereh stopped him. She flung herself against his knees, seized his hands, kissed them, and cried hysterically, "Tell, oh tell, I beg thee, tell our venerable judge that Mukhi alone is guilty. I, I am no more than a poor weak servant girl. And tell him too . . ."

Aqqul thrust Zereh from him. The door banged. The key shrieked.

"I shall take all the fault on myself, be easy," said Mukhi to the nomad.

"Thou hadst better," she cried. "What can I be accused of? The poison? The earth drank it long ago. The dogs? They attacked by themselves because of the smell of matter and blood."

Muhki let his body sink on his crossed legs. His chin touched his chest once more. Above him Zereh went on talking. Her hissing, rancorous voice said, "It is all thy fault. Thou hast wavered . . . waited . . . always. Every time I had to give thee courage.

If I had thy strength I should be far away, free, rich, beautiful . . . And instead of that . . ." Convulsively Zereh ran her hand over her filthy rags, her face all sticky with dirt, and with all her strength she spat at Mukhi's feet. He did not seem to notice. Zereh seized the pitcher and the bread, squatted as far as she could from the syce, and ate and drank greedily.

ONE OF THE COUNTLESS CANALS THAT IRRIGATED THE FIELDS PASSED in front of Tursen's house. The happy water, brought from the springs on the estate, sang its morning song. The petals of the autumn flowers danced on the gentle wind.

Sitting bowed on the charpoy, which he had pushed as near as possible to the open window, Tursen felt an obscure gratitude for the shimmer of the dance and the ripple of the song. They helped him to be patient. When, too hastily, he asked himself, "Why this journey that has exhausted and worn him to this degree? And Mukhi, so good, so faithful—how could he turn himself into a murderer?" and was about to leave the charpoy and pace up and down the room like a caged animal, Tursen made himself watch the movement of the flowers with greater attention and listen more closely to the murmur of the water. Time ran by with the stream, waved with the petals.

Hoofs sounded on the path outside. Tursen leaned against the wall, to see without being seen.

Uraz, riding Jahil and accompanied by two young mounted chapandaz, stopped in front of the porch. His beard was cut short in a sharp point and his cheeks were smooth; he was wearing a new turban and a new chapan. The stallion's beautifully groomed coat gleamed in the sun. His combed and plaited tail and mane delighted in the wind.

"They have worked well in the stables," thought Tursen automatically. His head thrust a little beyond the edge of the window. It was now that he must not lose even a glimpse of his mutilated son. Uraz leaped from the saddle as any healthy man might have done and landed lightly on his right leg. The two young horsemen dismounted and each gave Uraz an arm to lean on. He used them as crutches to reach the baked-clay porch in a few hops. He disappeared into the house.

Tursen thought of the crippled, tortured movements that Uraz would have to make to reach the gallery of the privileged guests, of those that would allow him to sit down, and he shook his head sadly. By the Prophet, he had done well to leave Uraz free to manage his first tentative movements as a cripple out of his sight.

The main gallery opened onto a little inner court through dark wooden arches. In this court were a few bushes, growing round a fountain. Along the three walls lay mattresses covered with carpets and strewn with cushions.

When Tursen appeared in the gallery Uraz was sitting there alone, leaning against the far wall near a corner, with his legs crossed so that his injury could not be seen. Tursen settled heavily opposite him, against the other wall. Scarcely had he done so before Rahim set a great tray between the two men, with not only tea things but also white cheeses, sweetmeats, marzipan, and mutton-fat preserves. He filled the cups and went away. Tursen and Uraz ate and drank, their heads lowered. Sometimes under its bushy eyebrows Tursen's eye darted a glance at his son's face, then looked away directly. Now that Uraz's features were stripped of their hideous mask, their color, their thinness, and the jutting bones made them look like a smaller wax version of those Tursen had known. They caused him a pain that was all the harder to bear in that he could find no name for it. Fear for Uraz's life? Pity? Tender affection? How could he tell? In the course of his long life he had never come across these feelings. He knew one thing only, but he knew that with heartbreaking strength—Uraz was his son. His son; truly his son.

Oh, how he yearned to rise and cover those emaciated shoulders with the power of his arms—cover the fleshless throat with its great pointed Adam's apple jerking every time Uraz swallowed or drank.

The sun was high, the courtyard hot. The shadow of a bird, a hunter of the steppes—falcon, eagle, or kite—passed over the ground. All at once Uraz said, "They fly close at hand over there—over there on the plateau of the nomad tombs."

Tursen felt a chill in the marrow of his bones. That was not the voice of a man sound in his mind. For the first time since they had been alone together Tursen looked openly straight into Uraz's eyes. Lying there at the bottom of holes so deep that they were no longer fully in touch with life, they looked as though they were faded, blinded by an infinite grief.

"The Ancestor of All the World and his gods were waiting for me there," Uraz continued. He was speaking very softly and Tursen had to lean over to hear him. "He saw me kill the earless demons . . . In spite of the carrion I had to drag with me . . ." The dull eyes lit up, black embers deep in their sockets, and stared at Tursen as though they had never seen him until that moment. "I escaped from the hospital," cried Uraz, "because there they had given me over to the care of a foreign woman, with no veil, an unbeliever, who had the right to see and touch my nakedness."

"Dost thou swear that by the Prophet?" asked Tursen. The deep bushes of his eyebrows had risen straight up.

"By the Prophet," said Uraz.

Tursen's face returned to its customary indifference. He said, "Very well, my son . . . Go on."

But Uraz was silent. It seemed to Tursen that his cheeks were even more hollow, even ashier. "Didst not hear me?" he asked.

Uraz nodded. Oh yes, he had heard Tursen. And he would never, never forget that tone of pride and satisfaction underlying the simple words. It had been the same in Mizrar's voice when his youngest son Qadir had done him honor. And that tone—the same, the same!—gave Uraz such tranquility, fullness, and blessed contentment that he had no wish to speak any more. What was the point? He had reached the goal of his journey. A journey that was not limited to the terrible crossing of the mountains; a journey that had lasted the whole breadth and duration of his life.

"Tursen is on my side . . . He has pride in me . . . Friendship . . . There is no need for me to speak any more," thought Uraz with a wonderful calm happiness. Then the silence frightened him. He could not let the approval and admiration that Tursen was granting him at last weaken and die away in his mind. He was to feed, enrich, and enhance those feelings, drive them deep into that proud old bosom forever. "The hospital, that was nothing," thought Uraz. "When he knows the rest . . . Why then, truly . . ." Living color came into his cheeks. "Hear, O great Tursen, hear what thy son has lived through and overcome."

Uraz's voice was rough and hoarse; in its violence and strength it was like those torrents that raced down the bottom of the rocky gorges. And like those fierce waters too, sometimes it died to a harsh murmur and sometimes it rose to a thundering sound as he spoke of all that he had confronted alone, sick, and often at the point of death.

So as to give the enmity of the land, the ferocity of the weather, the torment of the pain, and the ceaseless watch against sudden attack and treacherous death their true meaning and their full value, Uraz would have liked to spread all his ordeals out before Tursen in one single picture. To appease this desire he began to talk with no order, no thought, just as the memories came. His tale took no account of time or distance. He skipped whole days, cut back, leaped forward again, returned to what was past. Not a word to explain or to connect. The pus in his blood, the poison in the bucket, the lightless tunnels, the high plain of ashes, the closing jaws of the chasms, the caravan of the great Pathans, the lake that cured leprosy, the earless dogs, the guile of the murderers and their attacks, the boiling fat on the stump of his leg—there was nothing to link them except the furious and almost supernatural energy that had brought back this body which had so often been more than half a corpse, had brought it back living and triumphant, had brought it back along the terrifying stages and their wild alternation from valley to mountain top, from prostration to frenzied activity, from trap to ambush.

Uraz spoke without a single movement, his eyes closed. He only opened them at widely spaced intervals, just long enough to dart a glance at Tursen. As he did so he experienced a kind of emotion, a stirring sacred beyond all else. For it was given to him to detect what no one until then, including himself, had had the right to see—his father's face stripped of that impressive majesty that no pain or anger, however furious, had ever been able to change or bring down. Now it might have been said that under the thrust and heave of unseen forces within, the hard-grained wood from which Tursen's face was made was cracking and splitting apart.

The heavy eyelids flickered. The thick lips relaxed. The deep lines of the cheeks all stirred. The high skin over his cheekbones quivered and the thick tufts of his eyebrows trembled. And the dull blue vein, almost bare on the scarred temple, throbbed, throbbed, throbbed.

No man on earth knew the true value of this disarray better than Uraz. It rewarded his pains, torments, humiliations, appalling bouts of delirium, and even his fall, his defeat, far beyond anything he had hoped.

"Even if I had brought the king's pennant back from Kabul, this face would not have been opened to me so," said Uraz to himself. And he would happily have submitted to other trials beyond those he was recounting, far more savage ordeals, to keep Tursen's features in their fluid disorder and prevent them from returning to that proud, unbending dignity that was all anyone had ever known—all he himself had ever known.

But the moment came when he had no more to say. And he felt weak, exhausted, and empty, just as he had so often felt on those hellish tracks and paths. His body sank against the cushions lining the wall behind him. His head was spinning. A rhythmic murmur filled his ears. The bells of fever? The drum of victory? He could not tell. Tursen's voice reached him through the vague roaring. "Drink," it commanded. "Drink, now . . ."

Uraz pushed himself up from the cushions, gazed at his father, and at first could not believe what he saw. Tursen, the great Tursen, the eldest of his blood, was holding out a cup of tea that he himself had poured and sugared, to him, Uraz, the son, the servant . . . Uraz almost snatched the cup from Tursen, and without presuming to look up, began to drink . . .

Tursen let his shoulders move back and slowly straightened himself. He could see from Uraz how deeply he had offended against custom. In its turn this offense made him realize how strongly the tale of his son's torments had moved him; making him wish to come to his help at last, even if it were by an action contrary to decency. He looked at the turban bowed humbly before him and suddenly observed in his harshest voice, "No victory in any buzkashi whatever comes up to thy return."

Word for word the praise was that which Uraz had sought and desired with fanatical persistency the whole length of his journey. To gain it he had undergone tortures and fought battles. At last it rang out and wiped away his defeat. More than that; because of it, he had conquered the winner of the royal game. And now, hearing it, he felt nothing.

No joy or pride or even appeasement. Nothing. As though his body were dead and his mind empty. This state lasted as long as the flicker of an eye; to Uraz it seemed to go on time out of mind. Rage restored him to a sense of life. Rage of which he himself was the only object. What was there, rotten and accursed, in the marrow of his being to deprive him of his reward, to steal what was owing to him, his most essential possession? This gift that his father, the great Tursen, was making him. The father, who understood him, supported him, honored him, and suffered for him. His father—his friend, his only friend.

A wholly instinctive impulse—distress, appeal—bowed Uraz over the tray toward Tursen, and their heads were separated by no more than the breadth of a hand. Tursen's face filled the whole of Uraz's field of vision and the whole world at the same time. And now he saw that there was no call to be surprised by his own mortal indifference. The mask had come down again over Tursen's features, sealing him up within himself, hidden and inaccessible. Where was that man, wondered Uraz, who had followed his adventure with passion and suffering? Who had given him tea like a bacha?

"That was where it all broke," thought Uraz with the unfailing certainty of intuition. "He felt that I was confused, ashamed for him and for me. He will never forgive either of us."

Tursen, looking at him steadily, said, "I know thy achievement through and through, O Uraz, and I honor thee for it. The time has come to tell me as much about Mukhi. He awaits my judgment."

"Thou knowest everything concerning him," said Uraz.

"That he sought thy death, no doubt," said Tursen. "But why did he do so?"

In the same instant Uraz remembered that in fact he had not

put forward any reason that could explain the syce's conduct. Was this carelessness? Was it on purpose? He said, "Mukhi wanted the horse, that is all."

Smoothing the folds of his turban Tursen reflected. "A poverty-stricken syce . . . A stallion like that . . . The occasion. Yes. But Mukhi? The simplest and most biddable and most attached ever since his childhood?" He said to Uraz, "What need to kill thee? It was easy for him to run away on Jahil."

"He was afraid of living as a thief," said Uraz. "With me dead, the horse was his by law. I had dictated a paper to a scribe."

"Ah?" said Tursen. "And didst thou give Mukhi that paper?"

"No," said Uraz. "I kept it under my shirt."

"Ah?" said Tursen. "And Mukhi knew that?"

"Yes," said Uraz.

"And was it straightaway," asked Tursen, "that he tried to kill thee to take it?"

"No," said Uraz. He was determined not to say another word. Yet he added, "He was urged on by the nomad."

"Ah?" said Tursen. "And as for her, thou didst pick her up on the road, I believe? Didst need her to serve thee?"

"No," said Uraz. "The syce wanted her . . ."

"Enough," said Tursen. "I know what I ought to know." He pushed his elbows between his crossed legs and thrust the lower part of his face between his enormous horny palms. All this was not an attempt to meditate in peace. He only wished to hide the convulsive hardening of the muscles and sinews of his jaw and throat. As for reflecting, weighing, gauging, he was incapable of it. All that Tursen wished or hoped for from his intelligence was that it should help him control the furious, animal rage that was setting his bowels, blood, and skin on fire. Yet his thinking did nothing but feed and increase the blaze. "As for the hospital—Yes. Decency and honor were with him," said Tursen to himself. "After that he did nothing but gamble and cheat with his life, his soul, and fate. He picked an insane route . . . He tempted and corrupted the most artless heart . . . And as his accomplice he took a whore. He threw his leg away . . ."

Tursen's hands still hid the gripping of his jaws, but he was no longer master of his breathing, which grew shorter and harsher every moment, making the cloth of his chapal rise and fall. "And I," he said to himself again, "I, during that time . . . I was mere pain and remorse . . . all my blood wept for a lost son, lost through my fault . . . And he, vain, foolish and criminal, sought nothing but the obliteration of his defeat."

Tursen's hands had clenched into fists that crushed his lower face. He was no longer thinking. He was shouting inside himself, "Like a child, an ill-conditioned child eaten up with vanity—a child that must be put in the right path, corrected." Tursen plucked at his empty belt, pointed a finger at Uraz's whip, and, almost without opening his lips, ordered, "Give!"

Uraz did so. He was incapable of doing otherwise and he knew it. And knew too that his father was about to strike him without mercy.

Tursen gripped the handle of the whip greedily, happily. At last! What power, what confidence flowed into him from the smooth wood clasped in his hand, from the plaited thong waving at its end! He waited for it to stop swinging. He was no longer ruled by fury and pain. He was no longer a man in a rage but one who was strong, wise, and just, one whose duty it was to lash his son's face . . .

Suddenly that face which ought to have turned away, bowed, drawn back from the blow, thrust forward, hurried to meet the stroke. And on it Tursen saw a ravenous, unbearable impatience. "Strike," said the eyes buried in the skull-like face. "Strike quickly! So that I may know what I shall do afterwards!"

The whip scarcely stirred in Tursen's fist. He thought, "Either he will try to kill me or else he will force himself to undergo it . . . In any case, if I touch him that is the end between him and me. I thought him lost—he has come back . . . From this, there could be no return." He took the thong between two fingers and looked closely at the tip. "The leather still shows where it was rubbed by the stone that killed the earless dog," he said.

Uraz put both hands to his face. To draw it back? To wipe out the traces of distress? He could no longer tell at all.

The silence lasted a great while. Tursen slowly raised himself, moved close to Uraz, set his heavy hand on his shoulder, threw the whip onto his son's knees, and said, "I have given up mine, didst thou see?"

"It was not for me to ask thee why," said Uraz.

"Truly," said Tursen. "But the time has come for me to tell thee." His powerful hand weighed heavier on the gaunt, sharp-edged shoulderbones, and a growling breath wafted across Uraz's forehead. "I no longer have any right to my whip," said Tursen's voice above his head, "because I, Head of the Stables and Master of the Horse, I used it in the murder of a faultless young stallion, the best among the horses of Osman Bey, whom I serve."

Tursen felt Uraz quiver and heard him whisper, "Thou?"

"I," said Tursen. "To take vengeance on him for my own great crime." Tursen leaned his hands so heavily on Uraz's shoulders that in spite of all resistance he made him bend his back. Measuring each word, he went on, "Listen, O Uraz, listen well! A man who deserves that name may, with his head held high, remember even the most terrible iniquity, if it was committed in a blind rush of passion, once he has acknowledged it before Allah the Magnanimous and above all before himself. But he who persists in the wrongdoing that he has calculated, thought out, and carried through in cold blood shall forever be forbidden to look into his own heart and soul."

Painfully Tursen straightened himself. His old joints cracked. "As they do on the charpoy at break of day," he thought, and spoke again, "Now, O Uraz, collect thy mind. It is for thee to exercise the justice of the clan."

"Me!" cried Uraz.

"Yes," said Tursen. "It is on thee I lay my burden."

"Why break the custom?" asked Uraz.

"Because," said Tursen, "were I to listen to thy words for a whole day and those of Mukhi for the whole of another, it is thou who wouldst for all that remain the only master of the truth."

"The truth," said Uraz in an undertone.

"When thou hast heard it, tell me," said Tursen. His thick, scarred eyelids dropped over his eyes. His breathing seemed to have stopped.

Uraz filled a cup, but drank only a mouthful. Cold tea . . .

tasteless . . . tray littered with the remains of the meal . . . "I have had what I longed for," thought Uraz. "Even more. What can justice matter to me? In the first place, what justice?" He listened to the steady music of the fountain. For a long while. The wound on his stump hurt. He straightened the mutilated leg, waited for the pain to stop, and tucked it back again. He said to Tursen, "Let him be brought."

He had made no decision.

THE TONGUE OF THE LOCK GRATED. A BREATH OF AIR FRESHENED THE reek of leather. Standing on the threshold, Aqqul, the head syce, cried, "The hour of judgment has come!"

Mukhi felt so weak that he had to push himself up from the ground with both hands. His head turned as though an abyss had suddenly opened before him. The dizziness vanished when his eyes met Zereh's. She was quite crushed by the weight of terror. Mukhi's strength returned to help her. "Thou hast nothing to fear," he said to her. "It is only I who am summoned."

"Do you not come near, do not come near me!" cried Zereh. "Keep thy ill-luck for thyself. Thou hast given me only too much of it. Oh why, why cannot the day I met thee be wiped out of time?"

"I thought," said Mukhi in a low and gentle voice, "thou hadst great liking and friendship for me."

"When I thought thee another man," said the nomad.

Outside, the kindly sun. Fruit ripening on the walls. The singing rills. For Mukhi everything smelled of death. But not the death that Tursen's judgment would pronounce on him. That which he bore within.

TURSEN AND URAZ WERE IN THE SAME PLACE. BETWEEN THEM LAY a tray that Rahim had laid with fresh tea, clean cups, more delicacies. Aqqul and three syces brought Mukhi by way of the inner court to the edge of the gallery, opposite Tursen. "The people have followed us, O Tursen," said Aqqul. "Dost thou wish them to come in?"

"No," said Tursen. "It is a family matter. But you shall stay, as witnesses."

Tursen filled his mouth with tea and spat it out noisily, to clear his throat. Then, with grave solemnity, he said, "Bear witness of this to all men: to Uraz, my only son, I hand over the right of the head of the clan. His law shall be my law." Having spoken, Tursen lowered his eyes to the carpet spread at his feet and stirred no more. The syces turned toward Uraz.

Uraz looked at Mukhi; he was astonished to see him so ragged and foul. He forgot that a few hours earlier he had himself worn those tattered clothes, had been covered with that same dirt. With one finger he stroked his smooth cheek, the new stuff of his chapan. He had always taken great care of his body and his clothes. He felt not the slightest pity for Mukhi. That bowed, hopeless head . . . Those weak, drooping arms . . . "A scarecrow . . . or something from the gallows," thought Uraz with disgust.

The silence—and the murmur of the fountain made part of it—seemed to have settled for all eternity. One syce could not bear it any longer and shifted his feet. The shuffling noise made his neighbor jump and he gasped in the hot air with a kind of hiccup. Uraz felt himself as it were pierced, searched, and spurred by the tension of the men guarding the prisoner. Even more, throughout his being, he was aware of the dominating impatience of that motionless block that was Tursen. He felt that he could no longer delay his judgment. But what judgment? He knew no more about it than the rest of them.

Uraz stared fixedly at Mukhi and thought, "All these people are holding their breath, waiting to know thy fate. And thou, thou . . ." He was seized with a violent hatred for this man whose life and death he held in his hand and who seemed utterly indifferent. "We shall see whether thou art quite so calm when thou knowest," said Uraz to himself. "Raise thy head!" he ordered.

The silence had taken on a subtler, more intense quality. The voice of the fountain no longer belonged to it. The water rippled and sang according to its own private life, its own fate alone.

Mukhi's face could be seen now; a dirty mask, without the least expression. It looked as though the mud had seeped right in, even to the point of filling his eyes. They had assumed the color of mud and even something like its substance. These two little flecks of earth, fixed on Uraz, seemed not to recognize him or even see him. And all at once Uraz remembered the youth, the innocence, the trust and friendship that had made Mukhi's eyes so beautiful. And he hated and feared life, which could destroy a man to that degree. Then he said to himself, "It was not life; it was I alone." The murmur of the fountain sounded in his ears like the roar of a torrent. He was incapable of carrying his thought any further. His voice echoed in the silence, loud, expressionless, dull, as though it had been obliged to hand on the words by some compelling force other than itself. "I declare thee exonerated from thy crimes," said Uraz to his former syce. "Thou art free."

Not one of Mukhi's muscles stirred, face or body. His even breath remained unchanged. On the other hand all those who witnessed the sentence uttered a long, deep sigh. In this united expiration Uraz heard only one sound, and one that appeared to him triumphant—Tursen's sigh. And the first feelings that he was aware of after having given his judgment were those of bitterness and humiliation. Once again he had yielded to his father's purpose. Once again he had been no more than the reflection, the inferior. And that as the crown of an ordeal that he had devised and for which he had paid a terrible price. By the Prophet, he could not leave it there. He must, by the Prophet, he must make a gesture that should be his own, that should belong wholly to Uraz and go beyond the will and authority of Tursen—an action that should challenge him and at the same time dazzle him with admiration. What? What?

Suddenly Uraz was on the edge of crying out with joy. As Tursen saw it, Mukhi was not a guilty man, but the victim of a lure, a trap . . . The stallion, yes, the stallion . . . Ah, Tursen called for full justice! By the Prophet, he should have it!

The silence was still unbroken when Uraz spoke again. And now his voice was filled with a strange warmth and intensity. He cried, "Yes, thou art free, O Mukhi. And from now on Jahil is thy horse."

At these words the syces and their leader were unable to contain themselves any longer. Stupefaction, disbelief, and envy burst out in their cries. These merely irritated Uraz. But from Tursen's face he harvested his reward. Anger had turned his scars crimson: it was twitching the tufted eyebrows, the deeply furrowed lines, the massive lips. "He remembers how he bred Jahil and trained him," thought Uraz. "He will speak. He will forbid it."

Tursen waited until his face had returned to its rough serenity. "Silence," he said to the syces. "What you have heard is the law of my clan." Then to Mukhi, "Truly, Jahil is thine."

"Truly," replied Mukhi. Neither his limbs nor his face had changed their expression. "And Zereh?" he asked.

In spite of all their control, Tursen and Uraz exchanged a disconcerted look; they were utterly taken aback. Pardon, freedom, a matchless horse—all these miracles left Mukhi unmoved. All that counted for him was the nomad whore.

"Let no trace of her be found here tomorrow," said Uraz, without looking up at Mukhi.

When Tursen was alone with Uraz once more he called Rahim and ordered, "My whip." And when the bacha had brought it Tursen said to his son, "Set it in my belt, O Uraz, since thou hast returned to give it back to me."

23

Zereh's Marriage

A FEW YURTS belonging to the far-off days were still to be found on the estate. Osman Bey's ancestors had brought them with their flocks and had lived in them until gradually, generation after generation, the master's house had taken root there. They were set in the middle of clearings and dells where the purest water ran, and they were used to house guests of outstanding wealth or rank for whom there was no room in the main building.

After Uraz had given his verdict, Osman Bey's old steward in person led him—a most unusual honor—to one of these half-settled, half-nomadic dwellings. It was surrounded by thickets, and between them flowed the icy ribbon of a stream.

Although he had two syces following him, the steward himself helped Uraz to dismount and make his way into the Mongol tent. As he did so he explained, "Of all the yurts it is the best shielded from the wind. I have had three new carpets spread beneath the mattress . . . Outside, there will always be a man and a horse at thy service."

Uraz returned thanks, without knowing what he said, replying to words that he had not understood. A strange, vast weariness, of a kind that he had never known during the worst stages of his journey, bound his mind as much as it did his limbs. Tursen's shady gallery, the song of the fountain, the soft cushions, the pleasant things to eat—no day's journey, no trail had exhausted and emptied him as much as they. As soon as he was alone he dropped onto the bed and sleep took hold of him. Because of the shape of the roof over his head and the way he had been traveling without pause, he still imagined that his journey was not yet done.

And although he slept like a man drowned, deprived of soul and feeling, the illusion followed him so close behind, with such insistence, that it was in his mind as soon as he swam up to the surface. "Time to go," thought Uraz. He stretched his arms and legs, cracked his joints with pleasure. Not for a long, long time had his body felt such suppleness, power, and fullness of strength. It called for instant movement and activity. "Time to go," said Uraz to himself again. He rose to his knees, and there, lying close to his bedside, he saw a pair of crutches.

All the happenings of the day before, in their precise succession, instantly lined up in his memory. He was bewildered by it all. The yurt? A lie. It was as heavy and unmoving as a stone-built house. His recovered body? A lie. To make use of it he had to have these wooden things. Uraz took the crutches, settled them under his armpits, felt a vague surprise at the way they fitted and at their kindliness, and then in a moment, carried and pushed along by them, he was out of the yurt.

A groom was squatting on his heels against the basketwork wall, humming. He was a little thin frail old man reminiscent of a molting sparrow. His running eyes had much candor in them.

"The crutches?" Uraz asked him.

"Thou wast so deeply asleep," said the man, "that thou didst not hear me lay them down. By the orders of the great Tursen."

"Where is he?" asked Uraz.

"At the inspection of the horses," said the groom. He pointed toward the nearest thicket and added, "Thou hast a saddled horse there. Dost want him?"

"No," said Uraz.

"Tea, then?" said the man. "The samovar is boiling by the spring."

"No," said Uraz. He wheeled round and propelled himself into the yurt, rolled onto his bed, and threw the crutches over his head, out of sight. "My father's first present," he said to himself; and without being aware of it he gave a sneering laugh. His mind's eye saw Tursen going from courtyard to courtyard in all his majesty, always the same, everlasting . . . Head of the Stables, Master of the Horse since time began, as long as time should last.

Outside the little old man's voice had gone back to its tune, one of the oldest of the steppes. Poets, storytellers, caravan men, shepherds, and beggars had improvised words that freed their hearts against the background of that melody forever. Maybe the groom was practicing that game, satisfying that need. What did it matter to Uraz? He thought about the life his father led. Arranged, set for every day, every hour . . . By the Prophet, it was fitting for his age and his fame. But he, he, Uraz . . . Who had never owned his own house, nor even his own horse . . . Who lived from buzkashi to buzkashi, and in the dead season from bazaar to caravanserai, there to use the money from his victories in dog fights, contests between quails, rams, camels . . .

Where was the great spreading joy he had known yesterday, when he laid out his tale for Tursen? In its place was black gloom, revulsion. The same, the very same that had come after each of his achievements. Only then he had the resource of raising up a fresh trap, the power of bringing a new, deadly peril into existence. "The arrival means nothing; all that counts is the road . . . and mine stops here," thought Uraz. He measured the depth of his despair by the insane wish that formed in his mind; his other leg, yes, his sound leg—he would give it for the hellish journey to go on and on and have no end.

He breathed deeply, powerfully. The blood ran through his body, full and lively. Fifteen hours of sleep had entirely renewed his strength. And its bloom, its spur, made Uraz feel like shrieking. What good could it be to him now? He swept a look full of hatred round the yurt that had so thoroughly deceived him. And saw a frail human shape come into it.

For the moment the light came from behind and the floating headdress prevented Uraz from making out who it was. Irritated, he thought, "The old man," and was on the point of shouting at him to go away. But it could not be he . . . The tune, sung by his thin, broken voice, was still quavering along on the other side of the wall.

The outline took two hesitant paces. A woman . . . Two more steps. Zereh.

Uraz's first movement was to tuck his maimed leg under him. Then he said, "Hast thou not had my orders?"

Zereh had kept her head bowed since she first appeared, and without raising it she whispered, "I have indeed received them, master. I was ready to leave at first light. But I could not take to the road before saluting thee." The nomad's voice, timid and fearful as all the rest of her attitude, had nevertheless a determination that Uraz knew very well.

"Why?" he asked harshly.

"I had to kiss thy hands for the great pardon thou hast granted me," replied Zereh. With a single movement that had the speed, smoothness, and harmony of an animal's spring, she darted from the middle of the yurt to the side of the bed made of carpets and cushions and there set her lips on Uraz's hand. Then she dared raise her face and she cried, "With thee as judge, I ought to have lost my life. For thou knewest."

Never had Uraz seen such an expression on the girl's face. Her features were as one might say scraped, scoured clean of all avarice, cunning, greed, and vileness. And with this base film removed, a wholly pure and humble gratitude was revealed.

"For once she is not lying at all; she was too frightened of death," said Uraz to himself. That was of little importance to him. But two words of hers had touched him to the depths, the most secret part of his being. "Thou knewest," the girl had said. And Uraz remembered their strange battles on the edge of destiny. The water poisoned by her; the earless fiends set on by her; Mukhi thrust forward, pushed, spurred to murder by her . . . And after each of these attempts, their naked exchange of looks. Zereh's saying, "I missed thee today; I shall succeed tomorrow," and his replying, "We shall see."

That was what Uraz searched for in the nomad's eyes. He found nothing but dazzled admiration.

And for Zereh what could there be in common between the filthy, hairy, sick horseman with corpse's eyes and the reek of carrion, and this shaved, clean, handsome man who smelled so pleasantly of the bathhouse and its scents beneath the heavy precious silk of his chapan?

"A prince has given me back my life," thought Zereh. "And I am troubling him." And speaking very quickly she murmured, "I shall never forget thy goodness, lord. Every day I shall say the master words of the road for thee."

Zereh moved backward toward the door. When she reached the far end of the yurt Uraz, to his own surprise, called, "Stay!"

She stopped. And Uraz, still as it were in spite of himself, ordered, "Come back."

With her light step Zereh crossed the space between them, and as he saw her coming Uraz knew why he needed her presence. So long as she was there he also had in the yurt the lofty burial place of the nomads, the gorge paved with slippery stones and the huge voice of the wind thundering in it, and the rainbow of the waters of the Band-i-Amir.

To keep Zereh there without losing face, Uraz asked the first question that came into his head. "Mukhi? Hast thou seen him?"

"I have seen him," said the nomad.

"How is he?" asked Uraz.

"I hate him," said Zereh. "He has not yet cleaned himself. He lets his big arms hang from his shoulders like broken sticks. His eyes are empty . . . Thy pardon—thy gift of the horse. Not a word of delight, not a smile. I hate him."

"Then why," said Uraz, "didst thou want him so much?"

The nomad's attitude changed in the strangest way. She drew herself in, moved back with one hand in front of her eyes, as though to protect herself from unbearable images. Those of her failed, abortive loves. Those loves that were made horrible to her, base and vile, by Uraz's proud beauty, the richness of his clothes, and the splendor of his ancient Mongol tent.

"There was an evil fate," she said in a barely audible voice. "I do not know . . ." She was unable to go on. Her bosom heaved with her troubled breathing. And from its smooth hollow to the lobes of her ears her bronze skin took on a pinkness, a blush that adorned her neck against the light-colored, coarsely embroidered cloth, adorned it with grace and innocence.

Her new dress, bought out of secret reserves, her sudden

shamefacedness, the tenderness of her newly washed person, her ardent, timid eyes made Uraz say to himself, "She might be a bride." And before he was aware of it, Saadi's lines were shimmering in his mind.

Then the sexual hunger of a restored body, the dream of recovering and possessing with the nomad the heart of his great adventure, the secret and obsessive urge to wound and sully inaccessible maidens, all joined in Uraz in one enormous desire. He plucked Zereh to the ground.

A moment later she was lying on his bed. Another moment and the new dress was in rags. Through one of the tears Uraz pierced the nomad with the violence of a murderer striking his knife deep into his victim's belly.

Zereh uttered a shrill cry of surprise and pain. The wolf's grin widened Uraz's face. "Scream, scream!" said he, between his tight, rigid lips. "Scream? Thou art scarcely at the beginning of thy torment."

And now he set on his chapandaz's hands and loins, his teeth that could crush great muttonbones, and his nailed fingers that like talons could grasp the headless bodies of goats—he set them to the service of an insane, forbidden yearning and a passion that he could at last assuage. He was no more than an executioner, a torturer intoxicated with the torments he discovers and pours out. He was omnipotent in evil. He was granted boundless license to rifle and tear modesty, purity, and shame, to trample them under him as he chose. To compel a body to every kind of suffering, every kind of dishonor. And thus to delight the fibers, cells, vessels, and essences in him that yielded pleasure and from which, by an ever-increasing ferocity, he sought to draw an ecstasy that should go beyond all human bounds.

Zereh never stopped screaming. At each of her cries Uraz felt a still more furious, more delightful wave pass through him, and he sought and found a crueller torment. So he let himself be carried from crest to crest, from hollow to hollow, his eyelids convulsively shut to lose nothing of the flames and shadows that peopled his hellish paradise.

And, by dint of using these dark and burning spells, Uraz blunted their edge. It was no longer enough for him merely to hear pain and humiliation. He had to feast his eyes on it. He opened them and brought them close to Zereh's face. And at first he was gratified beyond all measure. That mouth, stretched, torn, racked by its own shrieking, was indeed the mouth of his hopes. But his satisfaction lasted only a second. Why, on that face tilted back beneath him and so taking on a strange new dimension, why did nothing agree, nothing harmonize with the torment of the mouth? Why did this shining light from within transfigure cheeks, temples, forehead? Why this richer, tauter, vibrant happy skin? Why this look of holy rapture? These eyes dazzled by the agony of bliss?

For Uraz Zereh's unceasing cry suddenly changed, both in sound and meaning. He recognized the frenzy of that voice; it was the same, only more intense and wilder, the same as that Mukhi had wrung from Zereh, close to a night fire, at the encampment of the little nomads.

Now Uraz's feelings were wholly unbearable. Never, by any living soul, had he been deceived, made game of, mocked to that degree. He had mistaken the song of lust for the shrieking of pain. He had desired to torture a virgin; he had thought he was doing so; he had only provided a shameless whore with the agonies of delight.

Foam whitened the corners of his mouth; he searched for the tenderest place on the body at his mercy. He found the weal that Hayatal the drummer had drawn along her bosom with his whiplash. A very young and delicate skin was beginning to cover it. Uraz hooked his nails in and dragged them down to the end of the scar. Zereh's belly gave such a leap that it raised Uraz high, and the nomad's mouth became an open, tortured hole. But although the shriek she uttered went beyond all others in strength and piercing shrillness, it also surpassed them in its frenzy of joy.

At this Uraz seized Zereh's hair with one hand and her throat with the other, beat her head on the earth, growling, "Does that not hurt thee?"

"I am dying," stammered the nomad girl. And by the ecstatic smile that closed her lips for a moment she tried—but how could it be done?—to say to Uraz, "O horseman made of mud and fever and pus, conqueror of the poison, the mastiffs, and the terrifying mountains, O silk-clad prince of this palace, O prince of my life, strike, bite, flay me, unworthy that I am! The more pleasure thou takest in it, the greater mine shall be."

And because she had had that thought the nomad, drunk with total submission, abandoned herself even more deeply to the fathomless delight of her demigod. Uraz, who could not understand that he and she, so closely interwoven, belonged to contrary signs, redoubled his barbarity. And only succeeded in stimulating, inflaming, satisfying the flesh he tormented even more. And he thought, "She is taking her revenge for all her defeats. To put an end to her victory there is nothing left but death."

Uraz's fingers were already round the nomad's throat when he felt a kind of flaming dart transfix his neck and loins. His body, appeased, softened, broke away from Zereh. He lay a few moments neither thinking nor feeling. Then he heard an even, profoundly happy breathing. He did not move but said in a whisper that contained both prayer and furious threat, "Go away! At once!"

Zereh left the yurt, still moving backward. But above her stripped, ravaged body she carried her head like a queen.

*****

24

Jahil's Revenge

THE OLD GROOM was still squatting on his heels when Zereh went
by. He did not look up and his plaintive voice went on chanting the verses of his endless song. From under a tree whose
branches shaded the yurt stepped Mukhi.

He had washed. His bared face bore witness to the trials and
fatigues he had suffered during their journey. His round cheeks no
longer hid the underlying skull. All his features hung from his
cheekbones as from a couple of nails. His skin had an earthy tinge.
In their slits, his eyes were devoid of expression. He was wearing
the same skimpy chapan and the wrists of his thinner arms protruded. He reminded Zereh of an overgrown boy, at the height of
his awkwardness. "What dost thou want with me?" she asked.

Had Mukhi understood? He gazed with shocked, wretched eyes
at the wounds, the bleeding scratches, tears, and toothmarks on the
girl's face and body. She drew herself up, broadening her shoulders
to show her scars the better. She seemed bigger; she cried, "It was
Uraz."

"I know," said Mukhi. "I heard."

Strong, tranquil pride glowed in Zereh's eyes, one of which had
been half-closed by the blows. She repeated her question. "What
dost thou want, then?"

"To leave with thee," said Mukhi.

Zereh began to move on. Mukhi tried to hold her back by her dress. The rag he seized came away in his hand. He stood in front of her and begged, "Listen, listen, in the name of the Prophet. I will work . . . And we have Jahil. We will do anything thou sayest with him."

Zereh made no reply. A poor shred of hope came to Mukhi. The nomad's eyebrows had joined. Her face was marked with its habitual expression of grasping cunning. Because of her bruises it showed with a most naked shamelessness, particularly in her half-closed eye. "I make him sell the horse, I take the money, and that same night I vanish," thought the nomad girl. Mukhi no longer dared to stir or breathe. In the silence Zereh heard the words the old groom was chanting. They were artless and clumsy. They ran:

> As soon as he was home,
> Uraz judged them, our Uraz.
> May Allah raise him high
> Above all chapandaz!

At the first words Zereh threw back her head. The sun, right above her, lit up her forehead. Her eyebrows relaxed. The avid wariness vanished from her features. They no longer expressed anything but a tranquil, proud assurance.

The old man had fallen quiet. His lips were moving silently as they searched for a new verse. Zereh brought her eyes down from the sky and to her astonishment she saw Mukhi. "Wilt thou take me with thee?" he asked humbly.

"I cannot," said Zereh, with simplicity and gentleness. She had neither meant nor foreseen this reply. It was not she, the lying, thieving, venal, common little nomad girl, who had uttered it. It was the answer of the young woman who had the right to hope that her womb held the prince's, the hero's first child. How could she possibly admit this tear-stained bumpkin, this beggar ready to put up with anything at all? And how could she deceive and rob him, thereby falling back to the very same abject level?

Mukhi had no means—nor had Zereh—of naming that power unknown to either that had suddenly turned a face destroyed by the joys and ravages of unbridled lust into something clean and austere. But when he saw dignity spread its virtue over her, his knees yielded under him and he stood aside from her path. She vanished between the thickets and bushes with their autumn flowers. Mukhi went in the other direction without purpose. His arms hung from his shoulders like long-dead branches.

A LANGUOR FROM WHICH HE THOUGHT HE NEITHER COULD NOR would arise held Uraz to his bed; he raised his head, leaning on his elbow. A thin voice was singing,

> *Uraz, flower and fame,*
> *Uraz, pride of our land . . .*

He craned up, his brows wrinkled with attention. He recognized the customary tune for singing about the splendid deeds and fables of the steppe. What was his name doing in it?

The voice quavered on,

> *Thy fame flies afar*
> *Over peak, vale, and plain,*
> *Uraz, son of Tursen,*
> *More swift than the gale.*

The chant stopped. Uraz lay back. It was indeed in his honor that they were sung, these lines running to the beat of legends. They would spread through the estate and reach the nearby bazaars. Storytellers and poets more gifted than the old groom would embellish them with finer verses, and they would travel out in the mouths of horsemen and riders swaying to the rhythm of their camels. Village by village they would cross the steppes. It was fame, the fame he had so longed for . . . The fame of dead men turned to dust . . . Uraz had the feeling that the princely yurt was a grave, a monument raised up over his crumbling bones.

THE OLD MAN HAD NO TIME TO GO ON WITH HIS SONG OF PRAISE. He heard several horses trotting toward the clearing. A little later

Rahim came into the yurt to tell Uraz that Tursen invited him to come to the edge of the stream, under the trees.

"Bring the horse that is waiting for me," said Uraz.

He stood up as soon as Rahim was outside, hopped to the door, leaped into the saddle, and followed the bacha to a mossy rotunda whose roof was a tracery of leaves and branches and which was divided by a little brook. Two syces had spread brilliant carpets on the soft turf and had lit the samovar: they were taking pots and food out of their saddlebags. Uraz waited until the preparations were over before he dismounted and sat down opposite his father. They exchanged the proper greetings. The syces led their horses away. Tursen said to Uraz, "Hast thou received thy crutches?"

"I have them," said Uraz.

"Hast tried them?" asked Tursen.

"I have done so," said Uraz.

"Do they suit thee?" asked Tursen.

"Perfectly," said Uraz.

"Why didst thou not come on them?" asked Tursen.

"For a reason of my own," said Uraz.

From a son to a father, and above all to Tursen, this answer was a flagrant insult. Tursen seemed unaware of it. When he sent those cripple's tools to Uraz he had known that they would arouse his fury. He also knew that Uraz had to be broken to the requirements of his new condition without delay. "When a child is not at once compelled to remount the horse that has thrown him, he will never have a sure seat," reflected Tursen. He said mildly, "Truly I did not know that in my son respect and courtesy could depend on no more than a leg."

Uraz remained silent. Tursen thrust his hand into a pot full of saffron-colored pilaw, shining with grease, hot with spices, and studded with pieces of mutton, ate what he had drawn out, licked his fingers and the palm of his hand, and asked, "Those crutches, thou didst not recognize them? Mine."

Uraz was just about to put his hand into the pilaw. His arm hung motionless above it. "What?" he said, "They were . . ."

"The same that I used when my right knee was split and my left thigh broken," said Tursen.

Uraz's hand went to the bottom of the pot and came up full of saffron-flavored rice. He did not taste it. He was throwing his mind back thirty years, and once more he saw Tursen at the height of his fame, skipping about on those crutches in the paddocks and stables and through the bazaar at Daolatabad.

"That was only for a while," said Uraz.

"What did I know of that?" said Tursen. He picked a muttonbone out of the pilaw and cracked it between his yellow teeth. Then he said, "Didst thou ever see me lose face at that time?"

"The opposite, truly," said Uraz in spite of himself. In his memory he could see the faces of the people in those days; whether on the estate or in the town, they expressed a livelier friendship and admiration for Tursen than usual. He said, "At that age, things are easier to bear."

Tursen slowly relaxed his shoulders, and with his yellow eyes fixed heavily on Uraz replied, "In those days my life was shorter than thine is now. Reckon it up."

Uraz counted. And refused the answer. And counted again. And was forced to believe it. The aged man that had been Tursen for Uraz as a child was in fact younger than Uraz at the present moment.

To avoid the gaze of those yellow eyes Uraz began to eat with particular greed. The unusual tone of Tursen's voice stopped him.

"I have no merit in knowing that time well, O Uraz," Tursen was saying. "I was not then the Head of the Stables on this estate." He bent his head, half-closed his eyes, and asked Rahim for tea.

"For me too," ordered Uraz.

And again Tursen said, "And now it is twenty years that I hold this office . . . Truly, it is too long. But I can see no man to take my place . . . Apart from thee."

Uraz's cup clashed against its saucer. He set it down close at hand. The movement gave him time to collect himself and answer without showing his horror of the resignation, the withdrawal that Tursen was offering him.

"I return great thanks," he said, "but the honor is too great for me."

"Reflect on it until tomorrow, for tomorrow Osman Bey will be home," said Tursen. Then he touched on the last question he meant to discuss with Uraz, the hardest of them all. "Home with Salih," he said.

"Salih . . ." repeated Uraz, his lips whitening. "Salih."

"In a week's time," said Tursen, "there will be a very great feast to celebrate his victory. There Salih will sit at the master's right hand. I should be proud to have thee at mine."

"With my crutches?" asked Uraz. He desperately longed to hear anger in Tursen's reply. It held nothing but unaffected sincerity.

"That would be better still," said Tursen.

Now Uraz felt himself caught, taken, bound. Here fate left no possible way out, no sort of chance. Appear at Salih's triumph? Unbearable degradation. Fail to appear? Low, cowardly escape. Whatever he chose—dishonor. Disgust for himself that would last to the end of his days.

How, by what road, could he escape once more from men and men's rights, from nature and its laws, and by a gesture universally considered insane force and remold fate? Who and what could he make use of? When he escaped from the hospital he had Mukhi and Jahil . . . As far as he was concerned, the syce was dead. But the stallion? Uraz drove his nails into the scarlet wool of the carpet under him and said, "I shall give my answer tomorrow. Only today I want to have the use of Jahil."

Tursen's eyes, sharper and steadier than ever, examined the set face that submitted to their gaze. He could detect nothing in it. He said, "Why not?" He has been cared for as was right and fitting. As for Mukhi, he has not even been seen at the stables.

AQQUL, THE HEAD SYCE, HAD INSISTED ON BRINGING JAHIL HIMSELF. When the stallion came into the path Tursen had the impression that beneath its leafy roof the whole shade-filled rotunda lit up. He felt warmth in his bowels and delight in his blood. Deep in his yellow eyes rose the reflection of an inner sun.

Stripped of all useless fat and flesh, Jahil had been brought down to his finest shape, his most exact dimensions. The care and skill of the syces had given his coat the shine of a wild animal's skin

and the ripple of s...
after gleam running a...
brushed, combed, smooth...
in the province, waved over t...
up a long, high-bred head whose...
the color of an open pomegranate.

Truly, Jahil had never been so han...
honor his beauty in all its aspects and re...
tience and rebellion against the man who h...
opening of the rotunda. He pawed the ground, h...
ing all the delicacy of his hocks, the solidity of...
breadth of his chest. His mane waved high. And in h...
there flashed and laughed a crimson flower.

"Bring him near," said Tursen to the head syce.

And the syce, raising one of Jahil's feet, cried, "Truly, he m...
come onto the richest of carpets. His feet are cleaner than ours."

"Truly, truly," said Tursen in a very gentle voice.

The two old men exchanged a look full of pride and complicity; shells washed and re-washed by the tide since the beginning of time were no cleaner than Jahil's hoofs. Voluptuously he set them on the deep pile, one after the other. And as he came forward over it with a dancing pace, he bent and arched and swayed his neck like a swan.

"See, O Uraz, see how he comes to thy hand," cried the head syce.

"It was not for his pretty ways that I sent for him," said Uraz.

His abrupt, harsh tone hurt Tursen deeply. "He is not fine enough for thee, no doubt," he said.

Uraz replied, "When thou hadst need of crutches, didst thou require them to be beautiful?"

The head syce had no time to move before Uraz was up on one leg: he got a purchase on the pommel and the cantle, swung right up, and fell into the saddle. He rode off between the trees, slim, collected, and proud.

The two old men exchanged another look full of deep understanding. They had never seen a rider and his mount so perfectly matched.

k. The splendid play of his muscles sent gleam
long the precious surface. And his mane,
, and stroked by the most artful hands
e tall, pure curve of a crest that held
immense eyes shone with a glow

dsome. He knew it. And to
ources he feigned impa-
d him there at the
lf-reared, display-
his flanks, the
great eyes

FOR
ough
ot an

. Age
there
place.
t him
olt he
picture
Tursen
rying a
l chest

e years
gth. As
m that

day on," he said to himself, y heart
for any horse? No one but myself ever has had or ever will have power or hold over my torment or my pleasure. A horse still less than a man."

A horse? A man chose a horse for his own sake, not for the horse's sake. And he took care of it not for the horse's sake but his own. If the animal decayed in strength, it was replaced.

Suddenly Uraz said aloud, "Jahil or no Jahil, thou art there for my saddle, my whip, my wishes. As for the rest . . ."

He aimed at a long branch and cut it in two with his whiplash as cleanly as with a knife. Once they were out of the trees they took a path that led to the steppe. Jahil raised his head and sniffed deeply. It was no longer the undergrowth he smelled now—bark, moss, dead leaves, gentle decay—but the wafting of hot earth covered with dry grass; it was the breadth of limitless space and boundless freedom that filled his nostrils. He rippled his mane and whinnied. Uraz reined him in savagely. "Wait until I want to," he said between his teeth. "There is no hurry."

He remembered the cage of his princely yurt, his crutches, and the banquet in honor of Salih, and he thought, "Why should a man run, a man for whom there is no return?"

Uraz narrowed his eyes . . . No coming back; that, at all events, was certain. And the goal? The Russian frontier was near. Beyond that, Tashkent, Samarkand. Long ago, in the days of the great white Czar when he was very young, Tursen had known their mosques and bazaars. It was easy to cross the frontier then. Now police and soldiers kept watch on either side. Uraz shook his head scornfully. If he really wished . . . But did he?

Uraz let Jahil go at a walk. Samarkand . . . yes. Over toward Persia, too, there were those pitiless, unknown deserts. He could plunge into them, lose himself . . . And there was the side of the rising sun. Beyond the province of Mazar, beyond Qataghan, beyond Badakhshan, at the far end of the Afghan land, was the Qal'a-i Panja, that mysterious chasm, so high, so high that it touched the Roof of the World . . . There men traveled on white buffaloes. The abominable snowman dwelt in those parts . . . Musing, dreaming, Uraz left the estate. And then none of it had any meaning, none of his thoughts, plans, or dreams. Nothing but the steppe. Before him. Open to him. His own.

It was not the ashy, diminished steppe, hemmed in by rising shadows, which he had found that evening as he came out of the Hindu Kush an exhausted, destroyed, rotting man, ready to weep from weakness and emotion—a man the present Uraz could not recognize as himself. It was the steppe in all its limitless sweep, its sea of grass rolling away as far as the eye could see, its sun larger and prouder in a higher, wider sky than anywhere else in the world, and its winged clouds sailing before the wind; and its scent, above all its scent—essence of bitter wormwood and wild, splendid liberty.

The steppe in its entirety. Before him. For him.

For him, and he born once again for it. Fair and free in his fine clothes, strong and easy in his saddle. And he too was free, freer than any man on earth could be or ever had been, a horseman whose ride had no goal or return.

And his mount was no longer an animal deep in filth, sweat, and mud, starved and flayed. Between his legs was a stallion that had no equal for beauty or for strength. And like himself, a son of the steppe. Like himself filled with a consuming instinct to tear, plunge into that shimmering openness. Jahil no longer tried to show off his splendor. His neck was tense, his nostrils flared, and his ears lay back as though the wind of his speed were already whistling past them. The sun and his impatience made stars sparkle in his coat.

Uraz was one with Jahil in every desire of his skin, bones, sinews, and blood—a single creature. Every moment fired him more. The waiting became an agony, a torture. But also, in its fever and piercing sting, an ineffable delight. He must not yield. Hold out, hold out to the point at which pain and extreme pleasure reach so high a pitch that going beyond would give birth to a joy as intoxicating as either.

Leaning forward over Jahil's neck, his slit eyes almost closed, his cheekbones jutting sharp above his hollow jaws, Uraz shortened and shortened his rein, listening to the sound of the steel against Jahil's teeth; and he whispered, "No . . . Wait . . ."

Thus, in harmony and simultaneously in conflict, Uraz and the stallion stood poised at the edge of the steppe. And Uraz felt such an ardent pent-up fury accumulating in Jahil's body that he wondered whether, crippled as he was, he would be able to stay in the saddle when it burst forth. "I shall soon see," he said to himself. Loosening the rein, he thrust his knees into Jahil's sides. And at the same moment he shrieked out the barbarous ululation with which horsemen, age after age from the depths of Mongolia to the banks of the Volga, have called on the devils of the tall, bitter-scented grass and defied them.

He had held on. In spite of the strength of the rush. The shock of the leap. The fury of the gallop from the very first stride. He had held on.

Once again Uraz experienced the delight of pride. But only for a fleeting moment. At once another happiness filled him, a happiness of such a kind that any other feeling whatever was mean and empty. As spreading as the steppe. As lofty as the sky. Open-handed as the sun. Pure as the wormwood-scented wind.

As for the stallion, his pace was less a racing gallop than flight itself. Stretched in the air, he touched the ground only to leave it again in a single strike of his hoofs. And Uraz, his face against the flowing mane, his body light, unconstrained, and almost fluid, had no other wish than to float like this over the steppe so close to it that the earth, grass, and his own being seemed mingled.

Every fold of the wild carpet that glided racing by under his horse's belly had been so familiar to him that he could name its warp and weft as he flew by. And the little rodents, the dwellers in the dry tufts, he knew their kinds from their muzzle and their fur as they ran for their burrows or flattened themselves in the hollows, terrified by the thunder coming down on them. In his mind's eye Uraz saw their tiny nation on the watch, whispering, rustling, as far as the hammering gallop could be heard.

He thought of the winter that would presently spread its snow on the more uneven ground, of the white tempests beneath the black sky, the needles of frost on the bushes, the horses' breath turned to thick steam, the ring of ice at every step.

And then the sky lifted high, the horizon drew far back, the snow melted, the ice cracked, and springs, brooks, streams, short-lived torrents all burst out, surged up, and ran singing. All at once the whole steppe in its vastness was one mass of brilliant flowers, their thousand-colored heads dancing in the spring breeze. Everything was covered with them. The poor huts, the tumbledown shelters for shepherds and their flocks, bore marvelous gardens on their roofs and among their ruins. Then the grass grew so high that a mounted man could scarcely see through it and the scent of the fresh-sprung wormwood was enough to make his head spin.

So Uraz raced flying over the steppe in all its majesty and silence and through all its seasons. And if ever in his life he had been at peace, happy in the world and in himself, it was then indeed. But he was so made that he always called for more, both from fate and from himself. A smooth, even-flowing happiness ended by being happiness no more. Uraz lifted his head from Jahil's mane and looked about him to find food for his insatiable demands.

The day was almost at its end. Already the evening blaze was in the sky. Clouds traveled across it, edged and rimmed with crimson like legendary birds. Lower, planing on their outstretched wings, flew the steppe eagles, searching for a last quarry before the fall of night. Uraz desperately envied the fire-winged clouds and the smooth flight of the great birds. How fast! How light! And Jahil, how heavy and slow!

The whip came hissing down.

But the blow acted as a break. Jahil slowed and turned his head toward his rider. Between the strands of the mane Uraz saw a great eye, lit by the pink and liquid sun, that said to him, "Why this injustice? Thou knowest very well that I was giving myself without reserve. And we were so happy."

To Uraz it seemed that his blood caught fire. His horse no longer obeyed. His horse was preaching to him! With all his strength and so fast that Jahil had no time to escape the lash, Uraz struck him over the muzzle three times.

Jahil reared, uttered an insane neighing shriek, and in a single movement, a single leap, charged straight forward.

Uraz was certain that every one of the stallion's movements was his own. His knees, shoulder, loins all moved in advance of them and in harmony with them. Nothing could surprise him. His breathing followed the rhythm of the hoofs.

Jahil neighed continuously. His ears were laid flat back and in them rang the continuous ululation that Uraz shrieked out against the wind of the steppe. And this wind carried away both the raving howl of the horseman and the furious cry of the horse, carried them away in snatches, like spindrift, like the foam that this mad pace brought pouring from Jahil's mouth and sides.

When first it wetted Uraz's face he let the whip that had been ceaselessly flogging Jahil stream in the wind. The oldest horseman's instinct made itself heard in spite of everything. "I am destroying him," thought Uraz. Then at once he said to himself, "And why spare him? For us there is no halt, no goal, no return."

His shriek burst out louder still. He struck faster and harder. It was not cruelty. All he was trying to do was to go beyond what was possible. For a moment he succeeded. Jahil and he surpassed their own limits. And in his trance Uraz thought, "The swans in the sky and the eagles in the wind have an easy task. They have the air on their side. Wings. I—I have nothing but my desire alone; my will and nothing more."

Now, on his left hand, skimming the ground and going before him, he saw a huge black ill-omened bird—his shadow, which the dying rays of the sun welded to Jahil's. And that bird, whatever he did he could never outrun it, nor even reach its level. He let his whip fly loose and slackened the grip of his knees a little.

Jahil stopped so short that his hoofs might have plunged straight down into the earth and he kicked up behind so that he was almost upright. Uraz lost his one stirrup, left the saddle, and, flung as though from a sling, joined his own shadow, suddenly diminished to his own human size—quite small.

Any ordinary horsemen would have been killed by such a fall. Uraz landed on the roll, his injured leg tucked under the other, his mind clear. "The horse tricked me," he thought. "It was not the whip that made him gallop so. He did it only so as to throw me at the first mistake . . . And the shadow bird has come . . ."

Uraz leaned his ear to the ground and pushed it down so that under the thickness of the grass he could feel the hard earth . . . There was the distinct reverberation of galloping hoofs. They were going off in the direction of the estate.

Over the steppe everything was silent; not a single bird's cry, no animal's call, no insect's stridulation, not a breath of air. Over the horizon shimmered a blazing embroidery. Uraz's eyes, flat against the grass, were at the same level. He watched and watched, seeing how that fiery lace grew thinner and thinner until it reached its slimmest fine-drawn glow, its final spark!

And he saw all the rest happening simultaneously—the stallion, lightened of his burden, spurred by the coolness of the evening and the lure of the stable—his arrival—the empty saddle—astonishment, anxiety—Tursen warned—help setting out—torches, hurricane lamps—and then, in their beams, a vainglorious fellow whose mount had dealt with him as he deserved, a chapandaz unable to keep his seat, a cripple whose pride and fame were all no more than bladders pricked and burst. "Myself . . . myself!" whispered Uraz.

In order not to groan or shriek he bit the ground, filling his mouth with mingled grass and earth. Then he spat out the dirty paste, flung himself on his back, and saw the first stars in the night sky. What could he do, O Allah, what could he do? Where could he bury himself to hide from the searchers? Where could he die alone in the darkness, in his honor and his legend? Oh why had he not let his half-dead body drop and rot in any of those places so well suited to the everlasting loneliness of a corpse? Why had he so clung to life—to Jahil's mane?

With unbounded hatred Uraz repeated the stallion's name . . . Jahil. It was through him that all the misfortune had come. From the king's buzkashi to this last insult. Uraz raised his eyes to the sky where, among the thicker studded stars, the moon slid the slim, tender bow of its first quarter, and he made a solemn oath. "In the name of the Prophet, I swear that whatever happens I shall cut the throat of that accursed horse."

He thought of the slit carotid, the hot red frothing stream jetting from it, the stallion collapsing, a sacrifice . . . He felt better.

The crescent moon climbed the heavenly slope. A very faint and misty light floated over the dark face of the steppe. Uraz set his hand on his left side. What sudden illness was causing these strokes, this irregular beating? It did not take him long to understand. It was not his heart. It was the sound of hoofs. He no longer had to put his ear to the ground. The gallop rent the silence, filling it. And it was coming nearer . . . Nearer.

The black tide of panic smothered his wits and his power of thought. "The syces! Tursen! They are here! They are here!" said Uraz to himself. He raised himself on his good leg and dropped again at once. His alarm faded. It could not be anyone from the estate. Going his fastest, Jahil could only just have arrived. And then there would have been lights . . . A belated horseman's going back to his yurt. A traveler in a hurry riding by night. Nothing more. Even if the man were to pass close by him, no one who was not looking out could ever notice a shadow flattened in the dark grass.

But all the comfort that his mind poured out was not enough to soothe Uraz's anxiety. His upper half rose straight and stiff, as though stretched up from the ground, and his eyes stared out over the grassy space, over which wavered the faint gleam of the crescent moon, like half-lit water. In it he saw a riderless horse come into being, take on breadth, depth, and substance. "Escaped from its herd," thought Uraz. The horse was no more than a dozen strides away. It did not slacken its pace. And from the carriage of its neck and the breadth of its chest Uraz recognized Jahil.

Yet he had to hear Jahil's great neigh to believe it. He thought, "He is lost; he is turning in circles over the steppe. No . . . I drove him mad . . . He has come back to finish me off—crush me. If only I had a knife."

Jahil was on him. Uraz crouched and folded in on himself, his knees to his stomach and his head sheltered under his arms. Jahil, just as he had done to throw his rider, stopped short, instantly, out of a full gallop, right against the human ball. The earth trembled at the impact. Uraz felt the grass waving. "With a knife I would have had time to hock him," he thought. And he waited for the furious kick that was to break his ribs, stave in his chest, batter his face. Nothing happened. The stallion did not move . . . He was recovering his wind. The warmth of his deep, rather hoarse breathing wafted over Uraz's skin. Slowly, Jahil lay down by him. "He is resting, getting ready . . . In a moment . . ." said Uraz to himself. A knife, oh for a knife . . . The carotid was within his reach.

Suddenly Uraz began to tremble in all his muscles, bones, joints, and inward parts. Jahil's head, hot and moist, had settled with the utmost possible gentleness on his shoulder. Uraz unfolded his arms, straightened his body, and leaned back—the stallion's eyes were like liquid mirrors filled with moonlight. Never, in his worst bouts of fever, had Uraz trembled so violently. Beneath him the earth was wavering. In the sky the stars staggered and swung. Jahil drew away from Uraz. "Is he going to strike? Have I frightened him?" wondered Uraz. No . . . There was neither fury nor dread in the stallion. He had merely settled on his knees. Uraz thrust his fingers into the grass so deeply and fiercely that his nails broke against the hard, rough earth. All he was capable of understanding, knowing, or feeling were these sobbing gasps that made his trembling body resound like an empty wineskin. He whispered, or thought he whispered, "What hast thou come for?" Jahil's head with its huge moon-filled eyes bowed, rose again to be certain of Uraz's attention, and slowly, clearly, turned toward the saddle.

Deep in the ground, high in the sky, all movement had ceased. In Uraz too. Jahil's eyes fixed on him again. Then, with an impulse that did not belong to him at all, that denied and blasphemed his entire code and faith, Uraz wrapped his arms round Jahil's neck and pressed, flattened his cheek against it. By the Prophet, there was not on earth so noble a being as this horse . . . He had not borne the injustice; he had revenged his honor. But with his anger exhausted he had forgiven . . . The buzkashi training? No; oh no! Uraz pressed himself closer to Jahil, against his foam-wet coat. That smell of sweat and weariness . . . The stifling gorges, the deadly slopes, the high plain of the nomads' burying place, the Band-i-Amir . . . How Jahil had spared him, cradled him, protected him, saved him . . . He was doing it once again.

Uraz loosened his grasp a little. A wonderful peace was spreading all through him. In his silence he felt the beating of the arteries in Jahil's neck. He remembered that he had taken an oath to slit it . . . Softly, religiously, he ran his lips along them. And as he did so he saw himself, as it were, from without. And felt no kind of surprise. And knew that never, never, would he, Uraz, feel shame, embarrassment, or regret for the gesture.

He mounted. Jahil took the homeward path, trotting to begin with, and then in an easy gallop. Uraz noticed that he was not holding the reins and he smiled with enchantment. Round his fingers he rolled a wisp of Jahil's mane. A little later he had another surprise. He heard a voice singing softly. It was his own, and to the traditional tune it was chanting Saadi's verses.

At last the words had the same meaning for Uraz as they had for other men.

THE TEXTURE OF THE NIGHT WAS A LITTLE LESS THICK WHEN URAZ reached his clearing. A man was waiting in front of the yurt, squatting on his heels. Uraz thought he distinguished the old syce who was looking after him. The man stood up, and from his height Uraz saw that he had been mistaken.

"Peace be with thee, O Uraz," said Mukhi's voice. It had no expression, no resonance.

In his turn and in the same manner Uraz said, "Peace be with thee . . ."

Each could see the vague outlines of the other's face, and from time to time, like dim flashes, the gleam of teeth, the shine of the eyes. That was all.

But Uraz had no need to see the meaning on the face the night hid from him. He knew what it was showing; Mukhi had come to claim Jahil. *His* horse. *His* property. Property that he, Uraz, had made him the master of by means of a solemn, public declaration that could not be undone.

Only then—because he was losing him—did Uraz understand what Jahil had become for him. His heart, his soul, his life. He could no longer accept his existence if he were not free to stroke Jahil's mane as he chose, hear his whinny, see the color changing in his eyes, and laughter, affection, wisdom, and courage passing through them. On the one hand were all the horses in the world. On the other, Jahil, unique. His friend, brother, savior, child. From now on what worth and what meaning could there be in a day that did not begin with that long, noble head resting on his shoulder, and on his cheek the moist caress of those great soft lips?

Uraz had the feeling that Mukhi's mouth, darkness and the white gleam, had an insolent smile upon it. He thought, "Tomorrow it will be *his* shoulder, *his* cheek, that Jahil will love." At the same moment and with the same strength he felt a passionate yearning to die and to kill.

"Dost thou want the stallion?" he asked Mukhi.

"No," said Mukhi.

Uraz grasped Mukhi by the arm and cried, "What, friend, dost thou mean to give him back to me?"

"To sell him to thee," said Mukhi. Suddenly it seemed to Uraz that the vague shadow in front of him took on firm, clear lines. Its voice had a determined, obstinate will behind it. "Now that I know what women taste like I want one," said Mukhi. "And not like Zereh. A woman of my own, that I marry. As thou knowest, they are costly, beautiful fresh girls their father can answer for."

Uraz dropped Mukhi with a sort of religious horror. A woman, a woman was worth more to him than Jahil! He said, "Thy price?"

"Thou art the best judge," said Mukhi. (His tone was a curious mixture of greed, mockery, and slavishness.) "Remember Bamian."

The ram fight—the sum against which he had staked the stallion—Uraz shivered. How, how could he have done such a thing; how had he dared . . . ? The tall shadow came closer. "O Allah

the Just," thought Uraz. "In this base groom I see Thy punishment."

His silence frightened Mukhi; he had been mad to think of all
those afghanis. Uraz would break off the deal. To keep him there
and at the same time soothe him Mukhi touched Uraz's knee before
he cried, "Do not imagine for an instant, O Uraz, that I dream of so
vast a sum. I know too well that thou art neither bey nor khan,
but . . ."

"How much?" asked Uraz.

"Oh, not a fortune," replied Mukhi with a false-sounding
laugh. "Just enough . . ." Uraz could see that he had raised his
hand and knew that he would bend one finger for each of his requirements. ". . . Enough to pay the dowry, have a house, keep
the household at the beginning. Dost thou see?"

"How much?" repeated Uraz.

"I shall give thee the reckoning tomorrow," said Mukhi.

"Then get out of the way!" said Uraz. He rode Jahil so straight
at Mukhi that his former syce had to jump to avoid him.

Yet Mukhi cried, "I have given thee the first refusal of Jahil
because he was thy stallion . . . If thou dost not like the price, I
shall easily find a buyer in the bazaar of Daolatabad."

Uraz rode into the middle of the great yurt and slid to the
ground. Balancing on one leg he took off all Jahil's harness. The
stallion lay down at once. Uraz stroked his forehead, turned down
the hurricane lamp as far as he could, and reached his bed by a
series of hops. He could not bear the smell that rose from it—
Zereh, her skin, her sweat, her torments, her rapture. Uraz went
and stretched out by the stallion with his saddle as a pillow. Jahil
was asleep already.

"I have worn him out," thought Uraz. There were wet, dark
patches along the flank that extreme weariness made rise and fall
too fast. The nostrils trembled with a choked, jerky breathing.
Uraz leaned over them. The wounds, the drops of clotted
blood . . . It was he himself—his whip. He whispered, "Sleep,
sleep, my beauty. Tomorrow thou shalt have the care worthy of a
prince, worthy of thee . . . Tomorrow thou shalt have . . ."

Uraz closed his eyes and thrust his head down into the saddle.
Tomorrow. Mukhi—the money. What money? He did not possess

a single afghani. He was living on his father's kindness. A contract
for the buzkashi season? No contracts for a cripple. Uraz ground
his teeth. He had just thought of the packets of notes he had made
Zereh burn to ashes. What then? Jahil put up for auction? That
could not be! Sooner stab Mukhi. Yes, stab the vile dog. But what
then? Himself in prison . . . And Jahil . . . Jahil . . . Alone in
the world.

Uraz pushed himself against the stallion's belly and curled up
between his legs. But even in this position he could not win a moment's sleep.

AT THE USUAL TIME TURSEN SET IN MOTION THE SERIES OF TORMENTS
that one by one turned a broken, knotted old man into the majestic Head of the Stables. He was still at one of the earliest stages—
legs out of the charpoy, feet on the ground, hands leaning on the
sticks to hoist the rest of his body from the bed—when a strange
tumult burst out the other side of the door. First was Rahim's cry,
"Do not go in, I conjure thee! No, not even thee. No one. No
one."

Then the angry voice of Uraz, "Stop clinging to my caftan,
bacha. Stop, or by the Prophet . . ."

Tursen felt that his face was no longer obeying him, was losing
control, falling to pieces under the thrust of panic terror. O Allah!
O the Magnanimous! To be surprised in that most carefully
guarded, most precious, most shameful secrecy! Found, worse
than naked, in this long shirt, with no turban, hair awry, palsied on
the edge of a charpoy with rumpled sheets all rolled back and mingled with the blankets like a heap of dirty linen, his hands gripping
a sick man's sticks! O the Merciful! To make a show of his old age
and his impotence and his ugliness and his abasement! And before
whom? Before the one man among all others to whom it was forbidden to see them! Before Uraz, his son!

From the antechamber came the sound of blows and Rahim's
cry, "My hands! Oh, my hands!" And the door handle grated.

"O Omnipotent," begged Tursen. By an enormous effort he
tried to heave the mass of his body from the loathsome bed and

fling it, roll it as far as the wooden leaf that was his protection, his shield, his salvation. His body refused to obey. The door opened wide. Uraz appeared.

The violet blood of shame mantled Tursen's cheeks and forehead, beat in his swollen temples, and colored the veins of his neck. He made as though to cover his face with his hands. But did not. The hot blood ebbed as quickly as it had risen. His bosom was light again. His heart beat once more. "Why, O Highest Wisdom, why?" Tursen asked himself. The answer came to him from the antechamber as the door swung back, borne on Rahim's voice. "Forgive thy bacha, master. He destroyed my hands with his crutches."

Tursen's mind then grasped what his blood already knew. Uraz was there, to be sure, but on crutches. The proudest of men had lain aside arrogance, show, and pride. He was coming to him without a thought for the wood tucked under his arms, the way his breeches flapped over his mutilated leg, or the pitiful clatter of his props on the ground.

"Between him and me and me and him, what indeed have we to do with empty pretense?" thought Tursen with a surprise so happy and open that he did not realize it.

Uraz, coming to the charpoy, cried, "I had, I had to speak to thee before thou shouldst leave for the stables."

Very mildly Tursen said, "I hear thee . . ."

"Mukhi wants to marry," cried Uraz louder still.

"I know it," said Tursen. "Yesterday, while thou wast riding upon the steppe, Aqqul told me. Mukhi thinks of his daughter."

"He has chosen already," said Uraz in a heavy voice. "And apart from the wife there is her housing and feeding. And for that the dog, the swine, puts Jahil up for sale."

"Jahil is his," said Tursen quietly. "He does what he chooses with him."

"No, by the Prophet! No! Jahil shall not go," replied Uraz. At each of these exclamations he struck the ground with a crutch.

"Take care," said Tursen. "Thou wilt fall." He had seen Uraz sway dangerously on his one leg. He put out a hand to support him. The stick it held dropped and rolled on the ground. "Two cripples," thought Tursen and forgot it at once, as he had forgotten that he was sitting on an unmade bed in his shirt. That unhidden, unashamed pain in Uraz . . . Those unaffected movements of a mutilated man . . . "Sit down," said Tursen. In spite of his wildly disordered hair, his wrinkled neck rising from his gray and flaccid flesh, Tursen's face once more possessed its customary strength and dignity. Uraz dropped to the edge of the charpoy, with his crutches beside him.

"What then?" said Tursen.

"I must have the stallion," said Uraz with savage violence.

"There are other horses in the world," said Tursen gently.

"There is only one Jahil," said Uraz. "Only one."

Without replying, Tursen nodded his head. He had known hundreds and hundreds of horsemen and each one of them who loved his horse was filled with the same certainty. If his mount were not as fast as another man's, then it was either hardier, or quicker on the turn, or more intelligent, or gayer or more faithful. Yes, to be sure, horsemen were all alike when they loved their horses. But Uraz?

Uraz said, "Thou sayest nothing? Why not? Thou knowest better than any man on earth that Jahil is the fastest, most skillful, bravest, and most generous of all. And the most beautiful."

Tursen went on nodding. "Thou didst not seem to see all that yesterday, under the trees, when the stallion was brought to thee," he said.

"I did not know him," said Uraz. And he told Tursen what he had done to Jahil the day before and what Jahil had done for him. As he listened Tursen remembered the colt he had killed and he bowed, bowed his forehead under the weight of a pity that seemed to him heavier than the burden of all his years. Pity for his son? For himself? For horses? For men? For the difficulty, the unhappiness of living?

Uraz fell silent. Tursen raised his head and asked, "Mukhi's price . . . How much?"

Without remembering that this repeated the motions of his former groom, Uraz crooked one finger and said, "The dowry." Another, "The house." Still another, "The couple's livelihood."

Then he gazed anxiously at Tursen, who sat there with his two hands resting on the one stick left to him, his huge back bowed under his old shirt, staring steadily at his deformed and horny feet.

"Good," said Tursen at last. "Good . . . As for the dowry, I shall give Aqqul my word for that. The house? There is Kalakchikan. And as for the stock—the land I own there."

For the first time since he had forced his way into the room Uraz felt a thrust of extreme embarrassment. Not in his pride at all. That he no longer cared about. But in his sense of justice; he was receiving too much. "Kalakchikan?" he said hesitantly. "Didst thou not intend . . . One day . . ."

"That day, my son, is not yet near to its dawning," cried Tursen. He had never been more sincere. Thoughts of retiring? Tursen? When Uraz was so in need of his help? And would need it again. Until the end of time. He had but to press very lightly on his stick and his shoulders were straight; beneath the soft linen his chest resumed all its old powerful line.

"How young his eyes are," thought Uraz.

A kind of shadow veiled their sudden brilliance. "At Kalakchikan, dost thou see," said Tursen thoughtfully, "it is the house that . . ." He stopped. Uraz supposed his mother was still alive. What indecent carelessness had made him, Tursen, forget . . . The number, speed, importance of the happenings that had piled up since Uraz's return, no doubt. "I must tell thee," he went on. "Thy mother is dead . . ."

"I learned it from the Ancestor of All the World, far back, among the nomad tombs," said Uraz shortly. "Peace upon her shade."

"Peace upon her shade," said Tursen with deliberation. "She was a good woman. Yes . . . Better, truly, than I thought in my indifference."

He would have liked to go on speaking of the dead woman. In an impatient voice Uraz repeated, "Peace upon her shade." And rose on his crutches.

"Well, my son?" asked Tursen gently.

"I should like . . . to give Mukhi thy word . . . at once," said Uraz.

"Go along then," said Tursen, "go along."

Uraz jerked violently to go as fast as he could. But the next moment he pivoted on his crutches and set his lips on his father's right shoulder. And nothing, ever, had seemed so good to him, so precious to breathe in, as that sharp, sour smell of night sweat and old age. With a few long swings of his crutches he was on the threshold of the room.

"Close, close the door," cried Tursen in alarm. "Close it well; and let Rahim wait—as usual."

25

Halal

THE SOLEMN BANQUET given by Osman Bey in honor of Salih, his chapandaz who had won the trophy of the royal buzkashi for Meimana, their province, took place a week later.

The delay was necessary. It was a question of sending invitations by the hundred, some of them a great distance. Of bringing together sheep by the flock, mountains of fruit and vegetables for all those mouths. Of summoning butchers, cooks, sweetmeatmakers, kitchen hands. Of bringing out the stored carpets, mattresses, utensils beyond counting . . .

On the morning of the great day Tursen set out on his horse for the place where the feast was to be held as soon as he had finished his usual inspection.

On the estate this spot was called the Lake of Honors. It was said that the name came down from Osman Bey's grandfather. At all events it was he who had caused the great rectangular pool to be dug out, lined with bricks, and fed by streams and canals. At the same time he had given orders for the planting of the birches, poplars, and beeches that now formed thick, tall hedges, exactly parallel to the edges of the pool. For the last three generations all the most important feasts of the estate and even of the province had

taken place on the beautifully kept lawns between the water
the trees.

When Tursen arrived, hosts of servants were still busy dec
ing the scene. Some brought armfuls of flowers, which they
tered over the grass. Others filled the ewers for the washin
hands. Others saw that everything was perfectly laid and arran
And then others, up to their shoulders in the water, cleared le
and twigs from the surface of the pool. Apart from these
touches the stage was set. And it was of such a splendor that
sen, used as he was to these ceremonies, could not prevent him
from clicking his tongue in approval several times over.

All round the great rectangular pool ran a continuous r
without an inch left bare, of the finest carpets of the provinc
Meimana, famous for its weavers. On this smooth path spraw
heaps of mattresses, eiderdowns, quilts, and cushions, all touchi
their covers blazing like beacons. That was not all. At the feet
the greaty leafy trees could be seen an equal profusion of se
divans, and materials. There, under the shelter of the branches
long as the burning heat should last, Osman Bey's guests could
before the meal itself, enjoying the pleasures of the shade, the
light of fruits, curds, and whey, and the cool smoke of the narg
talking or musing as they chose.

"Never was there such magnificence," said Tursen to hims
"And it is but justice. Never has the estate known such glory. T
king's pennant!"

A heavy burden of weariness pressed on his shoulders. A bitt
taste was in his mouth. He had thought, "Why, oh why is it n
Uraz that they feast today?" And then he heard the voice of trut
"If Uraz had been the winner," it said, "thou wouldst be dyi
under the lash of jealousy, as the young stallion died under thine
Tursen groaned in his heart. "But I am no longer that man, ar
Allah sees it clearly!" And the voice of truth answered him, "C
not attempt to be cunning, O chapandaz too old for thy tim
Thou hast only become another man—and Allah knows it well—
because of the defeat of Uraz, granted at thy wish."

At this moment, to make sure that nothing was lacking in th
arrangements, Osman Bey's steward arrived at a canter. He wa

white-haired, pink-skinned, fat, and a very good horseman. There was deep, long-established affection and esteem between him and Tursen. As soon as he was within calling distance he cried, "Peace be with thee, friend of ancient times."

"Peace be with thee, friend of every day," said Tursen. And because this meeting took a haunting care from his shoulders he added, in a warmer voice than usual, "And praise, praise to thy handiwork. Thanks to thee, the Lake of Honors has never worn its name with better grace."

Everyone knew Tursen's blunt frankness and the severity of his judgment. At so rare a eulogy in such a mouth, the steward's eyes, narrow and deeply buried in fat, lit with joy like glowworms. But his reply, as usual, was pure simplicity and good nature. "Thy friendship goes far beyond my deserts," he said. "When one loves all that delights the body and rejoices the eye as much as I do, it is enough to work for one's own satisfaction to please others."

The two old horsemen rode round the pool side by side, skirting the edge of the trees. Everything was in order.

"Now thou art at peace," said Tursen.

"Not yet," said the steward. "The hardest has still to be done . . ." He drew a very narrow, long piece of paper, written on from top to bottom, from the folds of his turban, and added with a sigh, "Setting each of these in the place that is his due."

"Truly, truly," growled Tursen. "Peace be with thee."

With a remarkably brisk, firm movement in one so fat, the steward grasped the bridle of Tursen's horse. "O friend," he cried, "add thy kindness to that of the fate that set thee in my path. Help me with thy advice."

"I am not clever at that game," said Tursen.

"It is not being clever that matters here," said the steward. "It is understanding the worth of each man's station."

"Give it," said Tursen. He took the ribbon of paper, held it out as far as his arm would reach, and set about deciphering the names that blackened it. Having done so he read them aloud in a mutter. And scratched the back of his neck. Read them again. And scratched his beard.

Indeed it was an uncommonly difficult task. Not so much for

the men of the first rank. Their places were settled by ancient custom and on this occasion by the nature of the place in which the feast was to be held. Thus Osman Bey's seat stood just in the middle of one of the long sides of the rectangular pool. Opposite him, on the other side, the governor of Meimana. On his left Osman Bey would have the three chiefs of the royal buzkashi. On his right Salih, then Tursen, then Uraz. For his part the governor would have Osman Bey's eldest son, already the head of a family, and the two richest and most influential landowners after their host, on his left; on his right the general commanding the troops of the province, the chief of the mounted police, and then the chief of a Pathan tribe that had been settled on the steppe at the time of its conquest by the mountain warriors.

It was not too difficult either to place those who owed their invitations solely to their length of service on the estate or to remote ties of blood. These cousins of cousins by marriage, these nephews of the uncle's brother-in-law (so long as their wealth was as slight as their relationship), and the head of the gardeners and the syce who commanded the others and the chief shepherd and the most learned of the scribes and the musicians and singers summoned for the pleasure of the guests—they would all crowd together at the two ends of the pool, along its short sides. For them, as for the great men, their place at the banquet was self-evident. As it was in life.

But between them were the others, the crowd of others, the people of the middle range, decently well-to-do, with unremarkable offices, of honorable family. There were the landowners of the second rank, the subordinate civil servants, the wealthy merchants of Daolatabad, the real members of the family. Not one of these men really outweighed the next. There was nothing that made his precedence clear. In order to seat him properly it was necessary to take the most scrupulous measurements. To weigh all the factors that made up the man. Appraise all his qualities. To calculate the sum of his wealth, birth, power, friendship, influence, and true worth.

Sometimes standing still, sometimes riding very slowly, with the list passing from one to the other, Tursen and the steward balanced the scales of their wisdom—on the one side, the public value of a life; on the other, the precise rank that counterbalanced it. In most cases their judgments were the same. When they disagreed, the disagreement did not last long. Yet sometimes Tursen remained silent and thoughtful longer than seemed necessary to his friend; and at these moments the steward admired the old chapandaz's meticulous attention to justice.

But the guest who was then in fact filling Tursen's mind had no need of careful placing. His seat had been laid down these many days past. On Tursen's right—Uraz. But as Tursen's horse carried him along past the carpets and the cushions, and as in imagination he saw the guests all seated there in their rightful order, so he was seized by a haunting anxiety. He could see them all, even those he scarcely knew; he could see them all in their places as though they were present in the flesh. Every one, except for Uraz—and this in spite of all his efforts. In that row, Uraz's place alone was empty.

"Is it an omen?" wondered Tursen. And while he weighed up, gauged, and measured the real or apparent merits of the other guests, his anxiety never left him. He remembered that since Jahil had been ransomed Uraz had as it were vanished from the life of the estate. He rode off into the steppe at dawn. He did not come back until after nightfall, worn out, soaked with sweat and foam. He took Jahil to the stables himself and there slept on the horse's litter. And began again the next day. And the next. That very morning too, he had disappeared . . .

"There now, it is done, and well done," cried the steward. He spoke to the scribe who had been following to write the names of the guests and the numbers of their order. Then he turned to Tursen. "It was high time, friend. Look."

Along the passages through the screens of tall trees the first guests were making their way onto the lawn. As was fitting, these were the humblest, who wished to show by their eagerness how conscious they were of being invited and how grateful.

"Good," said Tursen. "I must go and see what has been done for the horses." He looked at the shining cream-colored silk chapan with green stripes tight over his friend's belly and added, "And change my working clothes."

As usual, Tursen's men had done their work well. Behind the rows of trees and for some length stood rows of pickets. Within reach of the tethered horses were heaps of forage, neatly in line, and huge tubs filled with water.

"Good," said Tursen to the head syce. "Go and dress thyself for the feast, Aqqul. The old servants of the estate are already here."

"May I beg a favor, O great Tursen?" asked Aqqul with downcast eyes.

"Do it quickly," said Tursen.

"Allow me, I conjure thee, to bring Mukhi, soon to be my son-in-law, so that my family may acquire great face," said the head syce.

Tursen reflected: "One more or less in the crowd at the end of the pool . . ." And he said, "Thou mayest." He gathered his reins and in the most offhand tone asked, "Uraz, hast seen him?"

"He took Jahil again this morning," said Aqqul. "Rather later than usual."

Tursen found Rahim before the door of his house. The bacha held his stirrup as he always did, but with a contracted, unnatural motion, and he straightened himself at once, stiff as an image. He scarcely dared move because of his new clothes—a flowered caftan and a pair of shoes with turned-up toes that he was wearing for the first time. What is more, a brilliant piece of cloth, a present from his master, was wrapped turbanwise around his meager little everyday skullcap.

Tursen handed the horse to the bacha and went to his room. Rahim had smoothed the blankets on the charpoy until they were as flat as a polished board, and on them, brushed, ironed, and arranged according to its natural folds, lay Tursen's banqueting robe in all its splendor and simplicity. The wild silk of the chapan was at once soft and modest, thick and light; there was not the slightest ornament on it, and its only color was the warmest, richest shade of autumn-gilded leaves.

"The prize that my last buzkashi won me. Five years ago already," thought Tursen in spite of himself. That was in the neighboring province, and in spite of his great age he had wrenched the goat from the hands of Maqsud the Terrible right by the Circle of Justice, just as the young giant of Mazar-i-Sharif was about to roar out the triumphant halal.

Wrapped in his broad wild silk chapan, Tursen mounted again and took Rahim up behind. Without turning his head he asked, "Uraz did not come?"

"Oh, I should have told thee, master," cried Rahim. "Didst thou expect him?"

"Hold tight to the saddle," said Tursen. And he pushed the horse to a gallop.

Galloping still, he passed in front of the place prepared for the horses—full and busy now—and plunged into one of the alleys that led through the high walls of trees to the lawn of the Lake of Honors. He stopped only at the edge of the carpets that lay all along the edge of the pool. Rahim jumped down, helped his master to dismount. And stood motionless.

"Dost not know where to lead the horse?" growled Tursen.

"Surely . . . At once . . . I go," stammered the bacha. He began to move, walking slowly, uncertainly, as though the ground were shifting beneath him. Every other moment he closed his eyes and opened them again to try to believe in what he saw. So many splendid things, such luxury, so many men of high degree!

For during Tursen's absence guests had been continually arriving, guests of ever-rising importance. They did not leave their horses at the picket lines, as the earlier arrivals had done, but rode onto the lawn, where their own grooms or the estate syces took charge of their horses. The coming and going of the chargers, their strength, their grace, the richness of their saddles, and the polish of their bits filled the great stretches of turf between the water and the trees with wonderful life and movement. As for the masters, they walked with conscious majesty to the divans and cushions scattered in the shade of the trees and rested nonchalantly on them. The landowners and the famous wealthy merchants had put on their finest chapans and turbans; the high officials were dressed in European clothes, but the kulahs they wore on their heads were made of choicest, softest astrakhan. And on the chapandaz, who had just appeared, were seen for the first time in the province the jackets and breeches they had worn at the royal buzkashi.

"And Uraz?" said Tursen to himself continually. "Yet he gave me his word." As more and more new horsemen rode in, and the crowd along the trees increased, so his anxiety grew harder and harder to control. When it was going too far, reaching his heart, Tursen said angrily to himself, "Come, come, old man; be calm! Uraz's leg excuses him entirely. There is still time for him to come. He will not, he cannot, put such an insult on decency and right conduct. There is time still . . ."

But time was fleeting past. Already the brothers, Osman Bey's sons, were dismounting to welcome the guests in the name of the master of the estate, who was waiting at the boundary of his land, as civility required, to greet those of the very highest rank, who would naturally come last of all.

Time ran by. The men who were privileged to appear later than the rest were all in their places. Now, from behind one of the lines of trees, came the sound of a car, hooting three times. A long, broad, fiery-red open machine emerged from the trees. On the back seat, Osman Bey and the governor of the province, one on each side of Salih, the guest of honor. In front, next to the chauffeur, a very thin old man, almost blind and almost in rags—the most revered holy man in the whole of Meimana. And next to him the chief of the Pathan tribe that the great amir Abdurrahman had settled on the steppe after the conquest. He had a powerful chest and neck, his hair grew thick, and he carried a gun, inlaid and damascened; lines of cartridge pouches crisscrossed his black caftan. A group of horsemen followed close behind the motorcar: two of Osman's Bey's personal servants, the governor's secretary, and another Pathan, very tall, very thin, also armed with a rifle—a man whose eyes, bold to the pitch of impudence, seemed to be amused by all they saw and to make game of the world at large. Although he appeared to be a servingman, he let the others dart to open the car doors, and he threw his reins to a waiting syce.

Osman Bey, dressed and turbaned in Chinese cream-colored silk with a gold filigree thread, stepped majestically out of his car. The dignified governor of Meimana, in a dark suit, gray tie, and broadtail kulah, did the same. But as soon as Salih had room he jumped onto the seat and stood on it. Everyone saw him there, upright in his wolfskin hat, and on his back, spread out to make a star, the white skin of a new-born lamb. A murmur of praise greeted him, and it grew almost to an uproar when Salih waved the pennant he had won at the royal tournament over his head. He leaped over the edge of the car and landed on the ground, the high heels of his short boots driving some way into the turf.

Tursen felt like spitting. Shameless exhibition . . . Circus buffoon . . . Bazaar mountebank . . . Tursen was in pain for his calling. For the great game of his life. For his province. He thought of Uraz and of his silent pride, and it did him a great deal of good. And immediately after it hurt him violently. Uraz had not condescended to appear even though the guest was there.

Affectionately, deferentially, Osman Bey said to Tursen, "Stay with us, worthy Head of the Stables and most famous of the chapandaz . . . Let us all go into the coolness of the shade, and taste the kickshaws that lead on to the banquet."

He sat down with the governor, the holy man, and the Pathan chief on the cushions that were waiting for them in the very middle of the row of trees on the east side of the pool. Tursen sat by them. And the tall thin stranger with the cheerful mocking eye leaned against a trunk behind the warrior laced with cartridges. The running servants brought them milk in all its forms, cakes, and fruit. And while, one after another, the important men came to kiss Osman Bey's shoulder, Tursen's piercing eyes, to which age had given great carrying power, desperately searched the ranks of the guests, even the farthest off.

Right at the back he recognized Mukhi, in new clothes. With one arm over his future father-in-law's shoulder and a great laugh splitting his face in two. "He dreamed of being a chapandaz, and by the Prophet he might have become one," reflected Tursen. "He tried to murder his master to have a fine stallion and wander through the perilous world at a wench's heels . . . and he nearly succeeded. And there he is, settled, a family man already, happy . . . Freed from all his devils by one single adventure, and forever . . . Whereas Uraz . . ." The faces at which Tursen was staring were no more than a blurred mass. It was not that his eyes were troubled, but his mind. "What?" said Tursen to himself. "What? Have I reached such a point that I want Uraz to have a little house, a scrap of land, a wife in the kitchen, children to wipe, and that happy simpleton's foolish laugh?" He remembered the wolf's grin on his son's pitiless, insatiable lips and he felt the balm of pride revive his old blood once more. For Uraz there would never be any refuge, shelter, burrow, security.

Tursen leaned his forehead on his fist. Was it because of that furious eagerness for life that he had hated Uraz? Was it because of it that he loved him so? Or had he always loved him? Without choosing to acknowledge it? Loathing him because he was secretly afraid for himself—afraid of suffering too much from his love? Suffering as he did at this moment.

Where could Uraz be? What could he be doing?

"Here he is!" Tursen very nearly shouted. He straightened on his cushions to see quicker and then let the mass of his body fall heavily back. The rider was not Uraz . . . only a messenger. He belonged to one of Osman Bey's relations and he had come at full speed to say that his master, struck down by a malignant fever at the last moment, begged to be excused.

Tursen looked at the shadows of the tall trees. They were lengthening, reaching out toward the artificial lake. But the banquet would not begin before they had covered its edges and cooled them. Between this time and that perhaps . . . "Let no one, no one at all, speak of Uraz until then," prayed Tursen.

As though in answer to this prayer—was it the helping hand of chance or a wave from Osman Bey?—at that moment the musicians began to play. The lament of the bandura, the rumbling drum, the caress of the flute . . . An enchanted silence fell at once. In this country every man, whatever his station or his origins, had a passionate love of music. And on that day the music's servants were men famous in their art, men who had played for years and years on the sunlit terraces of chaikhanas, in the covered alleys of the bazaars, in great houses and in poor, for funerals and feasts. And as a companion they had an old man, once a shepherd in this province, well known for the trueness of his song and his unfailing memory.

It was above all to the shepherd that Tursen listened. In his voice he heard the whispering of the passing wind and the tall stems rustling, the songs of the encampments, sad as their own smoke rising in the evening air. And Tursen knew peace of the senses, mind, and heart when the old old tune began to well up—

flute first, then dambura, then drum, and lastly the human voice—
the oldest melody of all, perhaps, the one that from age to age had
sung endless adventures to countless horsemen, innumerable cara-
vaneers, along their endless trails.

Once again the old shepherd took its frail thread and on it he
strung ballads, legends, fables, and tales. Tursen's massive head,
his lined, battered face, followed the rhythm gently, heavily.

Suddenly he felt his neck go rigid, stiff and hard as a piece of
wood. In the song he had heard Uraz's name. And that could not
be. By Allah, that could not be. The name of Uraz among those of
the great deeds, the legends? Uraz in the fame of ages? To have
heard that, Tursen's mind must have wavered; his brain must have
been touched, struck by a malignant spell . . .

For he heard it again, his son's name . . . And recognized the
deeds the verses sang. Uraz's return—his adventure—his high justice. This was the raving illness of madness, the sacred malady . . .

But in that case why did the governor, leaning toward Osman
Bey, say quietly, "The rumor of it has reached the town." And
Osman Bey's reply, "That, I swear, is just how it happened."

And the people of the estate and the chapandaz of the region
displayed no surprise whatever. Some even recited the lines before
the singer chanted them!

Tursen's eyes sought Salih, and it was only the look on his face
—the look of a robbed and cheated man—that forced him to believe in his son's astonishing fate. And inwardly he cried, "Uraz!
Why art thou not here, O Uraz? Thou art losing thy finest day,
and thou art dishonoring it!"

The shadows had reached the banks of the pool. Osman Bey
took Salih by the shoulder to lead him to the feasting place.

WHEN THEY WERE ALL SEATED, CROSS-LEGGED ON THE CUSHIONS THAT
had fallen to their lot, every man, from the humblest guest to Osman Bey himself—every man forgot his rights, ambitions, and
cares for the space of an instant to relish the sight offered his eyes
by the beauty of the place, its marvelous arrangement and decora-
tion, and, against this background, the other guests. On whatever

side they sat they all looked out over the lake, an iridescent mirror under the slanting rays of the sun, and saw the spreading, brilliant carpets, cushions that lay thick upon the ground, turning it into a path from Paradise and forming divans, couches, and resting places worthy of the companions of the Prophet. The garments, in their richness, harmonized with all this splendor. Gleaming flowered silks from Persia. Wool from the steppes, wonderful in its depth and weave. Indian cloth worked in gold and silver. Materials in such prodigal abundance that their puffed-out, overflowing width might without any skimping have clothed several men in addition to the one who wore them. Materials so varied and so rich in shades, patterns, ornament, and cut that out of the hundreds of chapans there assembled no two were the same. Jade green or the green of a new shoot, rose pink or strawberry or the color of dawn, azure or lapis lazuli, dead leaf and topaz, purple, crimson, scarlet, amaranth, ivory white, dove gray. Single-colored, banded, striped. Gold and silver threads. Proliferating foliage. And this flowering of clothes was crowned by the immense petals of the turbans. And amid all the splendid, luxuriant softness stood out, like harsh lichen-topped trunks, the rough jerkins of the chapandaz and their wolfskin caps.

The poorest, meanest, ugliest of the guests was delivered from the burden of his poverty and his shortcomings by the feeling that he formed part of all this wealth and strength, and by the illusion of seeing in them his own reflection. And those men to whom fate had been kindest felt that their wealth, power, and success were borne up and extended by all the other fortunes there—carried to a height they had never reached before.

No one round the Lake of Honors rejoiced in this intoxication of self-esteem as much as Salih. The feast provided his vanity with a matchless opportunity for coming into full bloom. Why all this splendor? Why all this pomp? Because of him, Salih. What star had brought together this crowd of lords and chiefs—a greater assembly than the province had ever known? The king's pennant, standing on a brocade cushion, blue and gold, immediately in front of him, within reach of his hand. The hand of Salih, the triumphant, invincible, nonpareil conqueror! Salih!

While the guests settled the folds of their chapans, tucked up their sleeves, and held out their open hands to the water that the bachas poured from precious ewers, Salih perpetually rearranged the cushion that bore his trophy, pushing it a finger's breadth or a hair's breadth backward or forward or sideways, so that it should always be full in the breeze and the cloth should never cease flapping to his greater glory.

Sitting there close to Salih, Tursen stared straight ahead, over the pool, over the heads, over the tops of the trees, not moving or blinking. Salih and his cushion—he saw nothing of them. Just as he saw no person there. Just as he was aware of no sensation. Except that his whole suffering body felt that empty place, that blank on his right side, that open wound. Uraz was not there! Uraz was no longer alive!

All at once Tursen was so convinced of this death that he would have sworn to it on the Book of Books. How could a man famous in song bear to do no more than listen to it for the rest of his days, a cripple at the fireside? And in that moment Tursen understood and felt for him so intensely that he was Uraz himself. And rode his beloved stallion out into the steppe to sleep there forever like those great chiefs of former days whose bones lay mingled with those of their chargers beneath the ruined mounds.

On either side of the pool appeared a cloud of servingmen. They came from the open-air kitchens hidden behind the trees and they bore vast pyramids of yellow, green, pink, and violet rice, pilaws made in twenty different ways, saddles of roast lamb, skewers loaded with mutton, dishes of chicken, sweet and burning sauces. The men and the bachas stood in a line, their arms held out, waiting for Osman Bey's sign to run to serve the guests.

Salih could no longer contain himself. He turned abruptly to Tursen and said to him, "Is thy son so sick that he cannot come to salute the king's pennant? Yet I have been told . . ."

At that moment Osman Bey began his signal to the servingmen. He could not finish the gesture, nor Salih his remark. An ululation cut them short. All the guests there had heard the same kind of cry on the steppe. But this was so prodigious in its violence and harsh yelling madness that it rang to the very marrow of their bones. The air quivered and the water trembled. And the horse burst out of the leafy shade, stretched out low over the grass in the fury of his gallop.

"Jahil . . ." murmured Tursen. The saddle was empty. "Uraz has taken pity on his stallion," thought Tursen. "Not on himself."

Between the trees and pool the space was perilously narrow for such a shattering charge. "The Mad Horse," cried the men belonging to the stables and the courtyards. "Bolting. Riderless."

Some among the guests took fright. These were the merchants of the town. Their hennaed beards, their sleeves, their turbans darted to and fro. They made as if to rise.

"Remain seated," said the people used to horses. "Leave the animal to the chapandaz."

The three chapandaz nearest to Jahil were on their feet, ready to leap for the bridle, for the stallion's muzzle. As he reached them they jumped back, in spite of all their experience and their courage. The shriek rang out again and it seemed to come from Jahil's chest. Meanwhile the stallion wheeled, spun round in a single movement, and without slackening his speed raced along the side of the pool. And the guests sitting the length of the bank saw a man stretched under his belly.

They had just time to utter here a groan, there a dull gasp, and there again a sigh. Then the man was no longer to be seen. But from the swiftness and ease of the motion that had whipped him over onto the far side of his mount his comrades and his opponents knew who he was.

"Uraz," said the horsemen of Meimana, Qataghan, and Mazar-i-Sharif.

"Uraz," repeated the owners of the great stables.

"Uraz," whispered Osman Bey's people.

"Uraz . . . Uraz . . . Uraz . . ."

From within and without the name beat and hammered on Tursen's ears. By the Prophet, Uraz was alive . . . And with what fury he was living! This was what they had been working at in secret, he and Jahil on the steppe, from the sun's rising to its going down. To show that though maimed, a great chapandaz remained a great chapandaz, when his name was Uraz. In his mind's eye, in a single vision, Tursen saw the learning day by day, hour by hour, the training, the marriage of crippled rider and marvelous horse. The devil! He had foreseen, arranged, calculated, worked everything out to appear at the supreme moment, like a specter, like a thunderbolt. Was he right or wrong to interrupt a ceremonial feast, to make game of the guests and their host, and to throw custom, decency, dignity, and modesty beneath his stallion's hoofs? Tursen shook his dazed head violently. He no longer knew. He had been mistaken about so many things, so mistaken . . .

Now the thunder of the charge was coming behind him. "He is on this side of the pool," thought Tursen. "I will not look." But for all his resolution the clamor around obliged him to do so. He saw Uraz, his wolfskin on his head, a thin shirt over his chest, his whip between his teeth, leap out of his saddle, drop onto his single foot, and with one hand on the saddlebow follow Jahil's stride. Anguish and fury tore Tursen apart with equal force. "Wretched fool! Mad dog!" he cried inwardly, "Maniac who is going to break his other leg—who would rather have a plank on wheels than a pair of crutches." Uraz was already on his stallion's back, tearing round the lake. "How many falls on the steppe? How many times has Jahil picked him up?" thought Tursen.

Once again the barbarous shriek shook the air. Uraz waved his cap, flung it full pitch ahead of him, dived from the saddle, and reappeared with the cap on his head. And many people cheered him.

After this he seemed to be at the end of his resources. Flattened against Jahil's neck, his face buried in the mane, he galloped along the pool without attempting any other feat. Right round. Round again . . . And again.

"Stop, stop!" thought Tursen. "Thou hast done all that man could do. There is nothing left to prove, nothing to try. Go as thou didst come. This is spoiling it, wrecking it all . . ."

And indeed one after another the guests, left to themselves, were no longer bound by the spell. Their eyes wandered away from Uraz. Whispering broke out. Osman Bey leaned toward Tursen behind Salih and asked in an undertone, "Is thy son about to present us with yet another noble surprise?"

Tursen meant to say, "I do not think so at all," and heard himself replying, "The very finest . . . Certainly."

On this Salih said to him, "Where then is this great wisdom, O great Tursen? As thou knowest better than we, Uraz has reached the bottom of his purse."

"Wait and thou shalt see," growled Tursen.

As he could hear himself, his answer lacked confidence and truth. He could no longer understand, no longer feel what it was his son wanted. Salih shrugged, stroked the brocade of the cushion that bore the royal pennant, and turned toward Osman Bey with a curt laugh.

Meanwhile the guests' irritation against Uraz was growing every moment. Some felt themselves offended in their dignity. Others were impatient to taste the exquisite dishes whose odor they could smell. And then others were afraid. Uraz was now making his round so close to the seats into which they had shrunk that the galloping Jahil brushed against them. One false step and they might be struck and wounded. They said so, more and more loudly.

Behind Salih Osman Bey leaned once more toward Tursen. He no longer attempted to smile. He said rapidly, "Uraz is no longer himself. It is the effect of his misfortune. And thou must . . ."

"Wait, wait; thou wilt see," cried Tursen. He had uttered the same words to Salih a moment earlier; but this time they had the strength of sincerity and conviction. And of remorse. How, oh how had he, Tursen, been capable of believing that Uraz was exhausted, at a loss, spending himself in vain? Old fool, old idiot, how had he not sensed that Uraz was very gradually lessening the width of his turn, as the hawks and kites of the steppe circle in smaller rings before they stop and strike?

Osman Bey shook his head with regret and said firmly, "It is too late, my friend. If thou dost not stop him I shall be forced . . ."

The master of the estate could not continue. All the guests gave a sudden start. Above the murmuring and the recriminations came the breath, the humming, and the roaring of a drum. Osman Bey frowned. At whose orders had the musician . . . ? But the musician was not guilty. His drum was in another's hands—those of the tall thin unknown who, with his gun over his shoulder and mockery in his eye, had hitherto been acting as the Pathan chief's companion. His touch had nothing in common with the rhythms of the drummer of the steppes. In his hands, and struck by him, the drum became a wild voice whose deep, burning cry entered the blood like a song of gaiety and challenge. Suddenly a rhythmic, strident, trumpeting, intoxicating, intoxicated cry leaped out toward Uraz.

> *Haya! Haya!*
> *Remember*
> *Haya!*
> *The one-horned ram*
> *Haya! Haya!*
> *Hayatal is with thee!*
> *Haya!*

Now Uraz, still galloping, lifted his face from the mane that hid it and raised his body from the stallion's neck. Tursen saw the wolf's grin on his son's mouth. He knew that the game was reaching its climax. And had but one desire, one agony—to help Uraz. For his memory was filled with that moment among all others when, on the roof of a hut that his horse had reached in an amazing leap, he had heard Uraz cry out, begging, "Father! What can I do for thee?" And in his heart Tursen cried out, he begged, "Son, my son, what can I do for thee?"

At this moment Uraz was racing like a gale along the stretch of lawn that lay behind the long row which had Osman Bey, Salih, and Tursen in the middle of it. And as though he had heard his father's call Uraz shouted with all his strength, "Draw over, O great Tursen. To thy right side, draw over!"

Without stopping to think, Tursen leaned his hands against the carpet, raised his body from the cushions just as it was, legs crossed, and with a single thrust set it down in the empty place on his right.

He had scarcely done so before Jahil's breath warmed the back of his rigid neck and a huge man-shaped liana plunged uncoiling down into the slit that he had made between Salih's body and his own and stretched darting toward the brocade cushion.

Tursen had the feeling that all around him time and motion were suspended for eternity, and at the same moment exploding thoughts raced crowding into his head. So this was what Uraz had planned! The hardest and most dangerous of all acrobatic feats.

The movement in which the chapandaz, holding by one stirrup alone, throws himself forward, stretches out, hangs floating in the air, wrenches the goat from his opponent, and flies up, back into the saddle, in an almost miraculous recovery. "He crippled himself doing it at the great buzkashi," said Tursen to himself. "And there, as a counterweight to balance him, he had a whole leg. Now—impossible—he is going to sacrifice the other . . . The fool! The vainglorious fool! The mountebank!" But however Tursen repeated his insults he could not succeed in raising his anger. It was not for the sake of the watchers, he knew, that Uraz was taking this terrible risk. It was still this perpetual need to go beyond his limits. And Tursen began to pray, "Demon, O demon of fire that dost possess my son, may the Prophet be at one with thee today."

The liana waved, quivered, cracked against Tursen's side. He thought, "A bone broken." And then on his left there was emptiness—a wonderful emptiness. And behind him galloping—a wonderful galloping. His eyes moved to the brocade cushion. It was bare. Tursen flung himself back. Uraz was racing off at full speed with the king's pennant waving over his cap.

The silence that settled now—was it admiration, unbelief, rage, or the shock of the insult? wondered Tursen—was so heavy, so intense, that it seemed to him that no thing or person could ever break it. On what side, by what corridor cut through the trees was Uraz going to vanish? In what lost corner, what hidden fold of steppe did he mean to hide the trophy, burying it out of sight? Salih began to rise. He did not finish the movement.

At the end of the lake Uraz, far from escaping, spun round. And launched Jahil once more. And the wind of his furious gallop filled the cloth he waved with triumphant life.

"O Allah, what does he mean to do?" whispered Tursen. A moment later he, with all the others, knew.

When he reached the place he had left empty, Jahil reared. Uraz's body rose up along the length of his mane. The pennant quivered at the height of his upstretched arm, shot down from it like a javelin, and the sharpened point of its staff pierced the heart of the cushion.

Then for the first time in his life Tursen lost all self-control. He raised his enormous hands toward the sky and in a broken, thundering voice he himself had never heard before he began roaring, "Halal! Halal!"

All the chapandaz took up the cry. Then the other guests. And in Hayatal's hands the drum leaped and rolled and danced. And the Pathan chief fired his gun at the sky.

Uraz let himself slide to the ground, pushed Tursen gently toward the left, and sat there in the place that had been waiting for him so long.

*****

26

Tursen's Waking

D AY BEGAN TO DAWN over the province of Meimana. Flat on his
   back—a back so broad that it reached from one side of the
charpoy to the other—Tursen lay like a roughly hewn block of
wood.

When he opened his eyes the pale murky grayish light that met
them was exactly the same shade as that which had greeted his gaze
dawn after dawn. "Not a moment too early, not a moment too
late," his eyes told him. In the dim waking, his awareness floated
over his physical perceptions as vague as the half-light in his room.

As for the room, all that he could see of it was the ceiling, a
brown waving surface. As usual. The two sticks upright at his bedside drew dark lines across his world. As they always did. The door
leading to the courtyard made a slight noise. Rahim was fetching
water for his washing from the fountain. In the customary way.
And once again he, Tursen, was there in the viselike grip of his
body and was going to wait, wait a great while for the bolts to
unscrew one by one. Everything was the same as every other morning.

And yet in the depths of his half-sleep, in the confused light
and darkness that still bathed his mind, he was conscious of a
vague uneasiness. He had the feeling that around him and within
him was a trap, a falseness. The lights, the objects, the bacha, and

459

his own body were in their invariable time and place, certainly; but they were not the same. Steadiness, balance, and security were lacking . . . Suddenly Tursen's mind was wholly clear. Uraz was not there . . .

With all his strength, all his will, Tursen tried to sit up. Not a limb, not a single muscle obeyed him. As the only answer to this terrible effort, he heard the uproar of his heart. At this he felt himself as it were soaked through with disgust. Not because of his powerlessness; he had learned to put up with that without whining or complaint. The shame lay in the fact that, knowing his body so well, he had yielded to an impulse that he must have known, that he did know, to be useless. Anger, pain, and bewilderment had overcome patience and the courage to undergo what had to be undergone like a real man.

Tursen held his breath until his head spun, until he was on the edge of losing consciousness. In this way he managed to suppress thought and feeling. When he breathed again, serenity, wisdom, and the lofty pride that was their fruit dwelt in him once more. "Henceforward this is forever, and in spite of everything," said Tursen to himself.

He remembered the furious emotions that had tossed him to and fro the day before. All those errors, terrors . . . bouts of despair and madness . . . "I no longer belonged to myself," he reflected. "My life had passed into Uraz." Yes . . . Maybe there was an excuse there. So strong and new a feeling at the height of old age . . . But now he had uncovered it and recognized it. He no longer had any right to allow himself to be taken by surprise by the indecency of inward chaos.

"A man is a real man," said Tursen to himself, "only if he accepts what he cannot change with an unshaken mind and heart. It is a much harder task, I find, when it is a question of a being one loves. But it does not matter. The happiness and the torment of affection cannot escape the law. They form part of all that the sun shines upon and the darkness covers."

Tursen swore to accept, bear, and overcome the wild terrors of his heart, whatever should follow. He swore it to himself. And to the Master of the World. Then he allowed himself to think of Uraz. And from the prison of his body he followed his son's motions with as quiet a mind as he would have done had he been looking down at a stranger from a very high tower.

The banquet had been nearing its end. Everything had fallen back into its due order. Everyone had eaten enormously. Mouths and beards, and in some cases lapels of chapans, all shone with grease. Over the lake and the heads of the guests floated the smells of spice, grilled mutton, and curds and whey. The governor of Meimana had spoken of Salih's glory. Then Osman Bey. Then from the hands of the winning chapandaz the head of the buzkashi for the province had solemnly received the royal pennant. He was to keep it until the next year and then carry it to Kabul for a fresh tournament.

Apart from Tursen no one paid attention to Uraz any more. And he sat very straight on his cushion, his head so far back that his face could not be seen, held up toward the sky, where gold-fringed clouds surrounded with coral and foam were beginning to sail by, first celestial barques of the sunset.

Tursen wondered why his memory gave this moment such great power, such vivid life. Had he then supposed that Uraz, after his feat, had at last attained serenity, and that the two of them would live serenely together for the rest of his days? "Can it indeed be true that even at my age a man will still hope for the impossible when he needs that impossibility more than anything else?" wondered Tursen.

The shadows were lightening. He could make out the ceiling more clearly. He closed his eyes to leave his inner sight complete freedom . . . Uraz was still gazing up at the sky. He did not notice the approach of the Pathan chief's companion, the stranger whose hands were so skillful at making a drum dance and sing.

This man displeased Tursen exceedingly. It was impossible to assign him calling, rank, condition. Strolling musician? No. He carried a warrior's gun. Bodyguard? Not that either. He was too easy with the master of the tribe. A lord himself? Lord of what? He had the freedom of movement, the carelessness, the clothes of those men who have neither house nor hearth. A vagabond? In that case how did he live? The easy freedom of his tall person, the proud carriage of his head, and the bold cut of his face were not those of a parasite, a beggar. Still less his eyes—merry eyes that angered Tursen because their laughter respected nothing and nobody. And when Uraz was galloping round the lake, what made this fellow think he had the right to utter that war cry, that call as from one confederate to another? And why did the sight of him suddenly make Uraz's face, until then so tense and hard, immediately loosen and look gay?

Tursen remembered the anxiety he had felt at that moment. A forewarning? But after all what did it matter?

The man squatted on his heels. Uraz put an arm around his neck and said, "What a happy chance, Hayatal, what a happy chance!"

And the stranger replied, "I told thee, chapandaz—wherever there was good food, good entertainment, and good money to be had, there thou shouldst always find me."

They began to talk about a ram fight, a one-horned beast, a marriage procession. Then Hayatal's voice sank so low that Tursen could not catch his words. When he had finished Uraz's eyes gleamed in the evening light like two glowworms and the wolf's grin was on his lips. "By the Prophet," he said, "count on me!"

Hayatal walked round the pool and returned to the Pathan chief sitting on the other side of the water, immediately opposite Tursen. He spoke into his ear for a moment. And the chief waved to Uraz with a wide, cheerful gesture. Then he rose, as did the other guests, to come and take leave of Osman Bey.

Osmen Bey, before confronting the multitude, said to Tursen, "When they have all gone, we will end the feast under my roof, all of us who belong to the household."

Tursen returned thanks, as civility required. Uraz remained dumb. In an undertone Tursen asked him, "Why this silence?"

Uraz fixed an unmoving, unfathomable look on his father, the look of a man gazing at his future, and answered, "I shall no longer be here. I am leaving directly with that chief with the cartridge belts. The buzkashi season is about to start throughout the Three Provinces; I shall win them for him. Princely salary. All the prizes for me. He has never had a team before . . . He leaves everything to me. In spite of my crippled leg . . . Because of it."

The Pathan chief, coming up to Osman Bey, passed in front of Uraz and smiled at him beneath his greasy beard. Uraz did not notice him. He said to Tursen, "There have been famous chapan-daz forever. Thou art among the greatest of them all. But hast thou ever heard of a conqueror who lacked a leg? Well, there will be one from now on and his name will be Uraz. And next year, by the Prophet, riding Jahil, he will carry away the king's pennant as he did today." Uraz stopped, his breath coming somewhat short. Another voice took the place of his. It was that of Hayatal, suddenly standing there beside him, one hand on his shoulder. "And in the hot season when the horses rest," said he, "we shall go from bazaar to bazaar, from ram fight to camel fight, and from feast to feast—marriages, births, or burials."

The Pathan chief came back riding on his horse. A syce brought Jahil for Uraz. They set off side by side. Hayatal followed them on his long lean legs, accustomed to unending roads.

The dawn was cold. Under the heap of blankets and quilts Tursen's body remained icy. But a damp unhealthy heat spread over his face. Shame seized on him again, there in his bed, with the same violence and cruelty as it had done at the moment Uraz went away. That abrupt, furtive departure . . . That chief who sat his horse like a sack. And above all that stilt-legged companion, a dubious beggar, an armed vagabond . . . Player of what games? Go-between in what unsavory trafficking? What an indignity for Uraz and all those of his blood!

Tursen felt that he had to disperse these pictures, and he opened his eyes. The room was light. Above him stretched the ceiling, cracked all over, stained here and there. And now, after all these countless wakings with nothing but this scaling plaster as his horizon, he found that it was a mirror—in the wrinkles and dark patches before his eyes he saw his own old age. This reflection began to speak, and it said to Tursen, "What is the cause of all thy care? And what is its object? Is it in fact Uraz? What crime has he committed? Whom does he wrong? Himself alone. And art thou sure even of that? Dost truly believe that it would be better for him to stay in these parts, after what he presumed to do yesterday? A great feat, that is certain. A great scandal too. The master of the estate will never forget it. Nor the other beys and khans, his fellows."

Tursen was no longer gazing at the ceiling to seek the advice of his double up there. He was thinking on his own. The Pathan chief was the only man who had stretched out a hand to Uraz, giving him a chance . . . And it was not really the chief, but the other one . . . the long-legged fellow, the drummer. The tramp with the damascened gun . . . Hayatal, who had suggested, whispered the astonishing offer to the chief.

"And who can tell?" reflected Tursen. "Perhaps, because of that, in a hundred years' time there will be tales of a matchless chapandaz who lacked a leg. And as for me, what did I produce for my son? A pair of crutches and a post in the stables!"

All around Tursen the light had taken on the quivering of dawn. He thought of Uraz's awakening among the Pathans, that tribe implanted in the province with the customs, language, and features of the other side of the Hindu Kush—people of the deep valley and the soaring peaks. They had managed to take root in the flat country, the country of immense plains of grass. Whereas Uraz, as much a child of the steppe as the bitter wormwood, had neither house nor hearth on it . . . Strange, strange destiny!

Tursen raised his bushy eyebrows, pursed his thick lips . . . Was this fate in fact so very new for Uraz? When and where had he ever been seen to come to a halt, establish himself? He had always competed in the buzkashi as a lone wolf, playing for the bey who paid him best. During the close season he wandered across the Three Provinces, betting, following the fighting animals. He had never possessed anything of his own. Not even a horse . . .

"So is nothing really changed for him or in him?" wondered Tursen. "And does a man's true fate sleep thus within him?" There was not a trace of darkness left in the room. Or in Tursen's mind. "So it is with Mukhi," he reflected. And again he thought, "I shall go to his marriage because his wife is my head syce's daughter. And I shall go to the buzkashis in which Uraz plays because I am his father. And every morning I shall go on with the inspection of the horses because . . . because that is how I am made."

All at once Tursen's meditation was cut short. The time had come and gone—he could tell from the nature of the light—when the usual warmth should have oiled and eased his joints, unstiffening his limbs and giving them back the power of movement. He tried to stir them. In vain. "All that emotion . . . All that food

. . . Not enough sleep," he said to himself. Yes indeed; he had stayed up very late that night without yielding an inch; he had paid honor to the dishes; he had kept up the conversation. The guests had praised his resistance. And what a price he now had to pay for that praise!

Wisdom, peace, and clarity of mind abandoned Tursen. With fury, terror, and bewilderment he tried, tried, and tried to raise his upper half, to move it at all. Only his arms obeyed him. He grasped the sticks hanging by his bedside . . . and could do nothing with them. And thought, "I shall not be seen in the stables or courts this morning; this one morning above all others when I must appear."

He could see the smiles, hear the remarks—one night of feasting and the Master of the Horse had to stay in bed. No more respect; no more dread . . . he was done for, the great Tursen.

From the antechamber the sound of pouring water reached his ears. Rahim was filling the ewer at the customary time. A hoarse, tormented call burst of itself from Tursen's throat. "Bacha! Here! Bacha!"

Frightened, unbelieving, and therefore more childish than usual, Rahim's voice came back. "Dost thou really mean . . . ? Thou dost permit . . . ?" it said.

"Thou hast heard me, sow's bastard," growled Tursen.

The latch lifted slowly, fearfully. The door opened inch by inch; stopped halfway. First Rahim pushed his little flat face topped with an old rag through the gap, then his skinny shoulders in their ragged chapan. Finally he came bodily in and stood petrified on the threshold.

The shame of having to lay his weakness and his old age bare, the furious impatience to be done with the dishonor they forcibly reduced him to, filled Tursen with every kind of raging insult, every sort of blasphemy. He was on the point of bursting out when he met Rahim's eyes. And the look in them filled Tursen with a curious certainty. It was not of him that the bacha was so afraid. It was fear of suddenly being allowed to open the door of the sanctuary that stretched his eyes, making them look hollower and older with an amazed and holy dread.

"Nothing, ever, can diminish such respect," Tursen found himself thinking. He said mildly, "Come near." Rahim came to the charpoy, his head bowed very low. "Strip off the blankets," said Tursen. The bacha obeyed. "Rub my ankles, knees, wrists, and shoulders with all thy strength," said Tursen again.

When Rahim had done so he said to him again, "All the quilts behind my back. Good. Now take my hands and raise me up."

Taking a firm stand against the wooden frame, the bacha began to pull his master's bulk toward him. Gradually Tursen felt the back of his neck and his spine hauled free. With a heave that seemed to break his loins he hoisted himself upright. His muscles were growing warm, his joints more free. Yet not enough for him to be able to set his legs to the ground. Rahim brought them round one after the other, while Tursen, leaning his weight on his hands, pivoted on the charpoy.

The old chapandaz painfully regained his breath. He was now to undergo the last, the worst indignity—that of being dressed like a helpless child.

"The clothes," he said between his teeth.

Rahim took the breeches from their massive nail on the door. They were broad, and Tursen's legs went into them easily. The difficulty began when they had to be drawn over his thighs. Leaning on his two sticks, Tursen vainly tried to raise himself from the charpoy even by so much as the breadth of a fingernail.

Then a voice, so faintly piping and frail that it seemed to come from a great way off, said to him, "Lean over to the right a little . . . Just a very little." He obeyed. The cloth slipped up over his thigh, covered his flank. "Now to thy left, I beg thee," said the faint whisper. Tursen obeyed again and returned to his sitting position. He felt marvelously nimble fingers pulling and tightening the cord that fixed the breeches around his waist and the other that closed the codpiece. He would have stopped them. That he could do for himself. He had no time. Rahim's hands were too quick, too skillful. Never in the whole of his long life had Tursen felt so degraded. "If Uraz saw me like this . . ." said Tursen to himself. "O my son, how I envy thee, all crippled as thou art!"

With the chapan there was no difficulty. As Rahim was closing its sides, neatening them over Tursen's chest, their heads were at the same height. Tursen drew his back the better to see his bacha.

It was a face he found hard to recognize. Humble still, no doubt, but strengthened by an intense, secret confidence; weakly and poor-looking still, yet full of delighted gratitude, lit up with happiness. "In his eyes I am still greater, still more venerable, for having allowed him to be necessary to me," thought Tursen. He tried to find a name for the instinct that lay behind Rahim's state of mind, but could not hit on one. But he felt a wonderful appeasement. Someone existed who could look after his body and its wretchedness without Tursen's shame for himself and hatred for the witness filling him with the urge to kill and die.

The first sunbeam came into the room, settling on Tursen's face. To the depths of its wrinkles, his skin delighted in it. He closed his eyes and gently moved his head and shoulders. "Like an old horse," he thought. And did not mind it.

Abruptly the sense of well-being came to an end. Rahim brought the length of white linen that was Tursen's headdress. He held it stretched out over his forearms as though it were the most precious silk. Tursen snatched it violently away. "Myself," he growled.

He set about tying the turban. In his dressing this was the longest, hardest, and most painful operation. But his muscles and joints had recovered enough suppleness and flexibility for him to be able to try it. With his first turns, his first torments, Tursen felt his anger melting away and he thought, "What fiend seized on my spirit all at once? I let the bacha look after the whole of my body, and I hate him for wanting to touch my head."

Tursen's shoulders were stretched as though on the rack. He gritted his teeth and went on with his task. A voice like the ring of a flawed bell sounded in his memory. "Grow old quickly, O Tursen, grow old in thyself quickly—that is my advice and my wish for thee." Tursen's lips remained closed. And he alone heard himself reply, "I am coming to it, O Ancestor of All the World. I am coming to it. But, by Allah, how sad it is! And hard!"

His arms, powerless and broken with pain, fell and rested on his knees. The wood of the charpoy creaked. Rahim moved toward his master. "No . . . What has been begun must be finished," said Tursen to his bacha. He spoke mildly, with friendship. He said again, "Watch, watch carefully and see how I work. Who knows?

Perhaps tomorrow thou mayest be charged with the doing of it."

Tursen's arms heaved up once more. His fingers returned to their building up, rolling, smoothing, perfecting the folds and even sides of his tall headdress. And all the time Gardi Gaj was in his mind. He remembered what the ageless storyteller had told him about men's need to give protection and receive it. All men. Even those who had no notion of it and did not want it. Tursen thought of Uraz; he thought of Rahim . . . and he murmured, "O Ancestor of All the World! Truly, truly, great and deep is thy wisdom."

Tursen slowly lowered his arms. His turban had its customary regularity and magnificence. Tursen breathed deeply, took a purchase on his sticks, and rose without too much difficulty. His strength was flowing through him once more. He took a step toward the door.

"One moment," cried Rahim. "A single instant, master." He ran to the charpoy where the whip lay by the pillow in its usual place, came back to Tursen, and tucked it into his belt.

"I had forgotten it," said Tursen, in an undertone. With vague surprise he gazed at the dirty, blissful little face his bacha held up to him. Under the layer of grime and ecstatic expression the weals of badly healed stripes were visible. "Thou wilt bear those scars until the end of thy days," said Tursen, without changing his tone.

For a moment Rahim was no longer either timid or humble. He raised his little face boldly. He looked into his master's yellow eyes without flinching and cried, "Thanks be to Allah for that. When I am old, old, as old as the Ancestor of All the World, people will know from the marks on my cheek that I served the great Tursen. And they will count it to me for glory. And because of them my son's grandsons will be respected."

On his two canes Tursen took another step. He reflected, "It will not be the finest of my matches that will give my fame a few more years in the steppe's memory before it is forgotten forever. It will perhaps be the injustice that slashed a child's face open."

Rahim darted past Tursen as though he were dancing. When Tursen reached the antechamber the bacha was holding the earthenware ewer ready to pour. Tursen put his sticks in a corner, leaned against the wall, and performed his ablutions. After this he felt stronger on his legs. "One stick, as usual, will be enough," he said

to himself and it gave him the pleasure of a great victory. He had
been sure that his body was refusing to observe the rules of the
game, but now it was obeying them once more . . . Outside the
sun welcomed him more heartily than it had ever done before. Its
light clothed his skin with a garment warm beyond anything else in
existence. For his joints and the marrow of his bones its rays were a
miraculous elixir. No more stiffness in his neck, shoulders, loins,
wrists, knees, ankles. "What is happening today, then?" wondered
Tursen. The answer came to him at once: the sun was warmer
because it was higher than usual.

"And the morning prayer—I have missed it . . ." thought
Tursen. His remorse did not last. It could not last. His feeling of
happiness was too full and lively to allow itself to be spoiled. Tursen remembered one of Gardi Gaj's observations, "The best, the
truest prayer is to fulfill the destiny for which a man has been
tossed onto the earth as well as he possibly can."

Had he not done this very thing, he, Tursen, when this morning he had begged the help of a child?

He moved off toward the courtyards. His stick was an emblem
of majesty. His turban a crown. On this day, as on all other days,
the syces and the chapandaz would see, true to himself, the Head
of the Stables, the Master of the Horse . . . Life was still beautiful and good and straightforward. For how long? Once again Tursen thought of the ageless storyteller. Had he reached the valleys
of his birth? Had he died there as he had foreseen?

Tursen smiled gently. Who could tell the hour of his death,
indeed? He straightened his back, held his head still higher and
made the dry ground ring louder beneath his tread. He could feel
that Rahim, with dazzled eyes, was following the old man who had
been raised, washed, dressed by his care and help, but who was
nevertheless formidable, indestructible, everlasting. The great
Tursen.

Le Four à Chaux
Avernes
16 October 1966

Psychology

Eighth Edition

Lester A. Lefton
TULANE UNIVERSITY

Linda Brannon
McNEESE STATE UNIVERSITY

BOSTON   NEW YORK   SAN FRANCISCO

MEXICO CITY   MONTREAL   TORONTO   LONDON   MADRID   MUNICH   PARIS

HONG KONG   SINGAPORE   TOKYO   CAPE TOWN   SYDNEY

Executive Editor: Carolyn Merrill
Editorial Assistant: Kate Edwards
Marketing Manager: Wendy Gordon
Developmental Editor: Kelly Perkins
Senior Editorial Production Administrator: Deborah Brown
Composition Buyer: Linda Cox
Manufacturing Buyer: Megan Cochran
Cover Administrator: Linda Knowles
Text Design and Electronic Composition: Deborah Schneck
Editorial Production Service: Susan McNally
Photo Researcher: Laurie Frankenthaler
Copy Editor: Susanna Brougham

For related titles and support materials, visit our online catalog at
www.ablongman.com

Between the time Website information is gathered and then published, it is not unusual
for some sites to have closed. Also, the transcription of URLs can result in unintended
typographical errors. The publisher would appreciate notification where these errors
occur so that they may be corrected in subsequent editions.

Library of Congress Cataloging-in-Publication Data

Lefton, Lester A.
    Psychology / Lester A. Lefton, Linda Brannon. – 8th ed.
    p. cm.
    Includes bibliographical references and index.
    ISN 0-205-34643-X
    1. Psychology. I. Brannon, Linda II. Title

BF121.L424 2002
150–dc21

Printed in the United States of America

10 9 8 7 6 5 4 3   VH‖ 08 07 06 05 04 03

Photo credits appear on page 739, which should be considered an extension of the
copyright page.

Brief Contents

Contents

Preface

The **completely revised** eighth edition of *Psychology* is the result of a new and exciting partnership between Linda Brannon—the author of *Gender* (third edition, Allyn & Bacon) and co-author of a textbook on health psychology—and me, Lester Lefton. Linda's expertise in the fields of diversity and gender studies has been essential to the substantial integration of these issues in the eighth edition. Moreover, her engaging writing style and fresh approach to the field of general psychology have greatly enhanced every subject covered in the book. Together, we **thoroughly updated and rewrote** every chapter in order to bring the eighth edition of *Psychology* into the 21st century and to address the most recent topics and concerns in the field today.

Why This Book Was Written

The goal of this book is to help students appreciate the exciting field of psychology, to increase their knowledge, and to stimulate their interest and understanding of human behavior and mental processes. The complexity of psychology makes the task hard, but our love for this discipline makes the task a joy. To share our enthusiasm and appreciation for psychology, we have chosen to focus on four themes that help explain and present psychology.

Four Major Themes

The 21st-century world is diverse and increasingly more connected. Issues of diversity crop up everywhere in the field of psychology and help make it the varied, complicated, and challenging field that it is. We use the following themes to organize our presentation of diversity and interconnection in psychology:

- the complex relationship between nature and nurture
- the changing impact and definition of diversity
- the importance of evolutionary and biological topics within the field of psychology
- the relevance of psychology in students' everyday life and the importance of critical thinking

Because it is so important to keep current with new directions in psychology, we have **totally rewritten** the book based on our colleagues' reviews of the previous edition as well as reviews of our competitors. Though the seventh edition of *Psychology* was very well received by both students and the instructors, we felt that the eighth edition needed substantial revision in order to stay attuned to the needs of students and professors in the upcoming years. To achieve this goal, we wrote completely new opening stories that focus on current news events, updated or completely rewrote all the boxed features, and stayed up-to-date on new research and theories—making the eighth edition as current as possible.

Our Goals: Be an Active Learner

Because Linda and I both teach introductory psychology, we remain engaged with the course material and have, for years, experimented with various presentation methods. We share a mutual goal: to encourage the student to *be an active learner*. To accomplish this in the eighth edition, we did the following:

- Used a personal voice in our writing and shared our own points of view on various aspects of the field

- Added a new text feature called Be an Active Learner to encourage students to become actively involved in the learning process, to be responsible for their own learning, and to make psychology meaningful by linking information they are learning to their own life experiences, which is a theme of our text

- Emphasized and expanded upon aspects of psychology that might be particularly relevant to students' lives in a new feature called Psychology in Action

- Added a new Point/Counterpoint feature to each chapter, encouraging students to actively consider psychological controversies on their own

- Included interactive figures, labeled For the Active Learner

- Let real-life students and recent grads tell how they use psychology in their own lives in a new feature called Student Voices

New Features to the Eighth Edition

We also updated **all** the features in the book and added several brand-new features for the eighth edition.

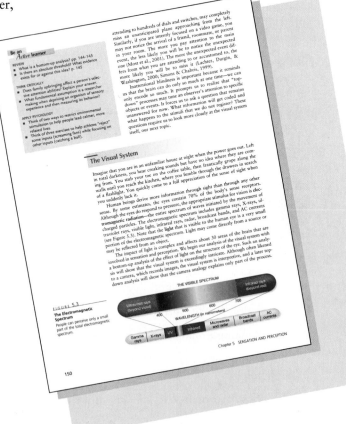

Point/Counterpoint

The new *Point/Counterpoint* feature
focuses on controversial issues in
psychology, such as ethics in animal
research, whether men are naturally
promiscuous, whether homosexuality
is biologically based or learned, and
whether Ritalin really helps people with
ADHD. We discuss both sides of the issue
and present the latest research results.

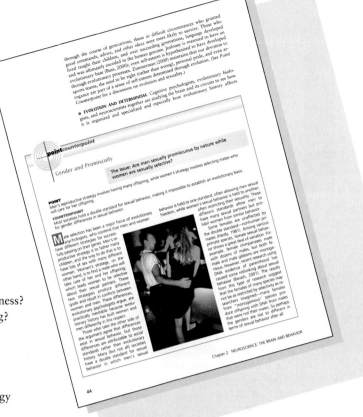

Be an Active Learner

Be an Active Learner reminds students
to pause, answer questions, and think
about what they have just learned. Some
questions review material the students
have just read, others encourage
students to think critically, yet others
ask students to apply what they have
learned to their own lives.

Introduction to Research Basics

We believe that research is a cornerstone of psychology, and the eighth edition of *Psychology* reflects an increased emphasis on its role. We reviewed every citation from the seventh edition and revised and updated all citations that correspond to the latest research in the field. We kept citations of classic studies from the history of psychological research.

We also believe that the research method should be contextualized within a book and that it is more important to focus on the analysis process rather than on actual data. To accomplish this, Linda Brannon has updated and rewritten the research information that appeared in Chapter 1. It now appears as a series of research lessons—one per chapter—called Introduction to Research Basics. Each box highlights a different research method used in psychological research, and connects it with chapter-related content. These boxes, as a group, stand as a series of lessons in research methodology.

Psychology in Action

Psychology in Action boxes focus on how psychology can be applied to everyday life. We want students to leave their general psychology class with more than just memorized facts; we want them to gain a pronounced appreciation for the relationship between the theory they have learned and the lives they are leading.

Student Voices

Student Voices is a new feature, found in the margins of the text. Current college students and recent graduates discuss why studying psychology is important to them and how they actively apply it in their own lives.

Features That Have Stood the Test of Time

Brain and Behavior

The *Brain and Behavior* box reinforces one of the main themes of the text: the important role of biological and evolutionary topics within the rapidly changing field of psychology. The box introduces students to the role of recent research and touches upon topics such as geography and dyslexia, the aging brain and Alzheimer's disease, and neuroimaging and mental disorders.

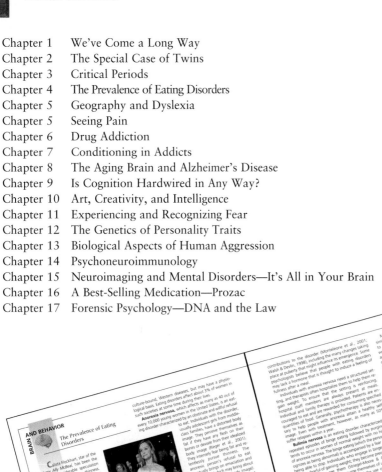

Building Tables

This feature, popular in previous editions, synthesizes the information presented in each chapter in a chart that provides a review at a glance. Aptly named, *Building Tables* build fact upon fact to ensure that students retain the most important concepts from each chapter.

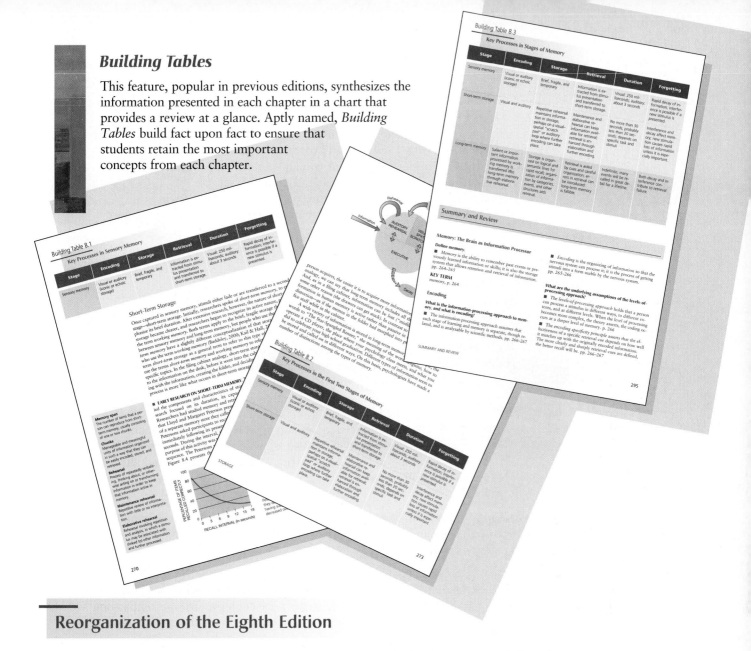

Reorganization of the Eighth Edition

The chapters on child development and on adolescent and adult development now follow the chapter on brain and behavior, in order to underscore the importance of development in the study of psychology and to introduce the complex relationship between nature and nurture. However, every chapter in the book has been written so that it can either stand alone or be read in sequence with others. Also, every chapter has been rewritten with the aim of providing a more structured approach, with a smoother, more cohesive flow of information. We have attempted to match the internal structure of each chapter with the way teachers present material.

Twentieth-Century American Artwork

Art and psychology can both be viewed as windows to the soul. The eighth edition capitalizes on this connection by drawing students into each chapter through the visual language of the 20th-century American artist. A carefully chosen piece of art appears at the beginning of each chapter, representing the glorious diversity of modern psychology. The art selections span the portfolios of a varied group of 20th-century artists. Both men and women are represented, as well as artists of various ethnicities and those who are famous as well as less well known. The idea is this: When students view the works of artists such as Jonathan Greene, Ruby Pearl, Andy Warhol, Margarett Sargent, and Jacob Lawrence, we want them to *feel* psychology as it moves through our modern age.

Supplements for Instructors

The *Instructor's Resource Manual,* written by Melvyn B. King of State University of New York–Cortland and Debra E. Clark, has been completely revamped for this edition. Each chapter begins with a valuable grid correlating the text to every print and media supplement available. King and Clark continue to correlate ancillary materials and instructor resources throughout their detailed lecture outlines. In addition, the *Instructor's Resource Manual* contains a wealth of activities, handouts, and numerous additional teaching aids.

Margaret Condon and Therese Scheupfer of Northeastern Illinois University have developed a lengthy *Test Bank*. Many of the items have been classroom-tested. More than 2,000 multiple-choice questions are available; to make the items more challenging to students, the authors have added a fifth answer option to each question. In addition, they have crafted numerous true/false, short answer, and longer essay questions to flesh out this robust *Test Bank,* which is also available on a dual platform CD-ROM. This computerized version is available with Tamarack's easy-to-use TestGen software, which lets you prepare tests for printing as well for network and online testing and has full editing capability for Windows and Macintosh.

The Allyn & Bacon Introduction to Psychology Transparency Set contains 200 full-color transparencies and is available upon adoption of the text from your local Allyn & Bacon sales representative.

The Allyn & Bacon Interactive Video, a 90-minute tape with on-screen critical thinking questions, has been developed to accompany Psychology. The accompanying video user's guide offers suggestions for using the video in class and contains a summary of each video segment.

Course Compass, BlackBoard, WebCT—Allyn & Bacon's course management systems—combine premium online content with enhanced class management tools such as quizzing and grading, syllabus building, and results reporting. See *www.abinteractive.com* for more information.

The *Digital Media Archive* 3.0 is a CD-ROM that contains hundreds of full-color digitized images, as well as video clips, audio clips, web links, activities, and lecture outlines to enhance introductory psychology lectures.

A *PowerPoint CD-ROM* presentation for Windows, which includes an electronic copy of the *Instructor's Resource Manual,* as well as a link to the book's companion website, was prepared by Albert M. Bugaj of University of Wisconsin–Marinette and is available to adopters of the book.

A *Companion Website* was designed to accompany this eighth edition. Access is available with the purchase of a new textbook; available on this free site is an on-line study guide, which includes chapter learning objectives and multiple-choice questions. The site also contains video, interactive activities, and web links. See *www. ablongman.com/lefton8e* for a sample of the site.

Mind Matters CD-ROM was developed by James Hilton of the University of Michigan and Charles Perdue of West Virginia University, this CD-ROM is available to be packaged with your text. A unique learning tool, the CD-ROM helps students explore psychology by combining interactivity with clear explanation, fostering active learning and reinforcing core concepts. Visit *www.abacon.com/mindmatters* for sample activities. Both a print copy and a downloadable copy of a *Faculty Guide* are available.

Allyn & Bacon Video Library makes available to instructors an extensive videotape library. Please see your local Allyn & Bacon sales representative for details regarding the video policy.

Supplements for Students

Grade Aid, a workbook by Andy Ryan, a police psychologist who teaches at the University of South Carolina, actively involves students in the learning process. For each chapter, *Grade Aid* features chapter summaries, learning objectives, activities and exercises, practice tests, and short answer/essay questions, to help students grasp the concepts in the text.

iSearch for Psychology contains material on conducting web searches and critically evaluating and documenting Internet sources. It also contains material specific to using the Internet in the study of psychology through Internet activities, as well as lists of URLs related to the discipline. The *iSearch* also contains an access code for entrance to ContentSelect, Pearson Education's online database of peer reviewed and discipline-specific journals. Students can conduct online research anywhere and any time they have an internet connection.

Psych Tutor, a service of Allyn & Bacon, provides free tutoring for students who purchase a new text. Qualified college psychology instructors tutor students on all material covered in the text, including art and figures. The Tutor Center provides tutoring assistance by phone, fax, e-mail, and the Internet, during Tutor Center hours. Students who bought used books can purchase the Psych Tutor for $25 at *www.aw.com/tutorcenter.*

Premium Resource CD combines a compilation of chapter-specific video clips with critical thinking questions, and links directly to the companion website. Clips include coverage of such topics as the human genome project, anorexia, alcoholism in teens, a gender study, hypnosis, lucid dreaming, phobias, and more.

Acknowledgments

We thank the following people who prepared special marketing reviews to assist us in gauging trends in the field and to provide us with their own valuable input to our draft manuscript of the eighth edition:

Lee Fernandez, Modesto Junior College
Alicia Grandey, Pennsylvania State University
Emmett Lampkin, Kirkwood Community College
Jerry Marshall, Green River Community College
Mark Mitchell, Clarion University
Merryl Patterson, Austin Community College

We also thank the following people who reviewed the seventh edition in preparation for our writing of the eighth edition:

Joseph Bilotta, Western Kentucky University
Victor Broderick, Ferris State University
Brad Caskey, University of Wisconsin–River Falls
Stephen Chew, Samford University
David Coddington, Midwestern State University
Patrick R. Conley, University of Illinois–Chicago
Randolph R. Cornelius, Vassar College
Orlando Correa, Hartford Community College
Tamara J. Ferguson, Utah State University
Scott Geller, Virginia Polytechnic Institute and State University
Judy Gentry, Columbus State Community College
Harvey Ginsburg, University of Southwest Texas State
Ronald Jacques, Brigham Young University–Idaho
James Johnson, Illinois State University–Normal
Edward Harmon Jones, University of Wisconsin–Madison
Tracy L. Kahan, Santa Clara University
Kevin Keating, Broward Community College
Melvyn B. King, SUNY–Cortland
Stephen Klein, Mississippi State University
Gary Levy, University of Wyoming
Michele Lewis, Northern Virginia Community College
Fred Medway, University of South Carolina
Jeffrey Mio, California State Polytechnic University–Pomona
Margie Nauta, Illinois State University
Shannon Rich, Texas Woman's University
Deborah Richardson, University of Georgia
Larry Rosenblum, University of California–Riverside
Alan Searleman, St. Lawrence University
Michael Selby, California Polytechnic State University
N. Clayton Silver, University of Nevada–Las Vegas
Pamela Stewart, Northern Virginia Community College–Annandale
W. Scott Terry, University of North Carolina–Charlotte
Michelle Tomarelli, Texas A&M University
German Torres, SUNY–Buffalo
Kim Ujcich, Middle Tennessee State University
Lisa Whitten, SUNY–Old Westbury
Michael Zickar, Bowling Green State University

We owe a huge debt of thanks to the people at Allyn and Bacon for their support, guidance, and assistance. Carolyn Merrill's confidence, management, support, and careful handling have been essentially important for both of us. A first-class editor and publisher, she is also a first-class person. Kelly Perkins and Anne Weaver helped us think creatively and write carefully; their insights were helpful. Allyn and Bacon's production department reinvigorated the eighth edition with the professional skills of designer/page maker Deborah Schneck and copy editor Susanna Brougham. Susan McNally facilitated the process of production at a time that we appreciated a calm, smooth, and methodical force. We also thank Joyce Nilsen and Marcie Mealia for their dedicated efforts in selling our book.

Students always deserve thanks because they teach us, and we acknowledge that situation and thank them for doing so. We thank Grant Bursek and Chris May who helped in library research. We thank several staffers, including Maxine Cogar and Pat Harrison, who helped us with logistical support. We also owe thanks to our colleagues in our psychology departments, who offered expert advice and cheerleading, each at the appropriate times. Several colleagues were especially helpful to me (LB), including Jess Feist, Diana Odom Gunn, Patrick Moreno, Cam Melville, Dena Matzenbacher, and Jan Disney.

We have friends and relatives who have supported and inspired us in various ways through the years, and their love, encouragement, and friendship mean a great deal to us. I (LL) thank Gene and Lois Green, Al and Susan Waxenberg, Stephen and Nancy Guerrera, Marcy and Jason Mallett. I also thank Frank Provenzano, Len Rosen, Ed Caress, Sandi Kirschner, and Bill Barke—each in his or her own way has helped me enormously. I thank my friend, mentor, and teacher Arnold Rubin for his enduring support; his untimely passing has left a gulf in many people's lives. And my love to my daughters, Sarah and Jesse, who inspire and bring me pride every day.

Our spouses deserve special recognition. Linda Lefton and Barry Humphus have encouraged and supported us in this daunting task, and they deserve even more than the love and thanks that we offer. They are our friends, lovers, and spouses—they are our best friends. What more can we say?

Lester A. Lefton
Linda Brannon

Two Careers in Psychology

I love teaching psychology. I hope my students here at Tulane University like the way I do it. My teaching technique and style began over three decades ago. My career in psychology began with a survey of sexual attitudes that I conducted in high school. I passed out questionnaires to the juniors and seniors, who were to respond anonymously. Then I spent days poring over, collating, and summarizing the data—which I, of course, found fascinating.

At Northeastern University in Boston, I majored in psychology and was particularly interested in clinical psychology. I took courses in traditional experimental psychology—learning, physiology, perception—but especially enjoyed abnormal psychology, child development, and personality. While in college, I worked in a treatment center for emotionally disturbed children. The work was hard, emotionally grueling, and stressful, and the pay wasn't particularly good—thus, the direct delivery of mental health services began to lose some of its appeal for me. Later, as a laboratory assistant, I collected and analyzed data for a psychologist doing research in vision. In contrast to my counseling experience, hunting for answers to scientific questions and collecting data were activities that held my interest.

My graduate studies at the University of Rochester included research in perception, and I studied visual information processing. In graduate school, my intellectual skills were sharpened and my interests were focused and refined. After earning my PhD, I became a faculty member at the University of South Carolina. My research in cognitive psychology involved studying perceptual phenomena such as eye movements. Now at Tulane University, I teach, do research, and write psychology textbooks. My goal is to share my excitement about psychology in the classroom, in my textbooks, and in professional journals.

Over time, my interests have changed, as I'm sure yours will. At first, I was interested in the delivery of mental health services to children. Later, I focused on applied research issues, such as eye movements among learning-disabled readers. But my primary focus remains in basic research issues. My evolving interests have spanned the three major areas in which psychologists work: applied research, human services, and experimental psychology—topics I present throughout the text.

I am married to a wonderful woman and have two daughters. I have applied in my family life much of what I have learned in my profession. My family hasn't been angry about it, although from time to time my "psychologizing" about issues can be annoying, I'm sure. I'm an avid bicyclist and computer hacker and occasional photographer. My life has generally revolved around my work and my family—not necessarily in that order. You'll probably gather that from many of the stories and examples I relate in this text.

I invite you to share in my excitement and my enthusiasm for psychology. Stay focused, read closely, and think critically. As you read, think about how the text relates to your own experiences—drawing personal connections to what you read will make it more meaningful. And please feel free to write me: *Lefton@tulane.edu*. Good luck!

Lester Lefton

My career in psychology began when I kept taking psychology courses as an undergraduate at the University of Texas at Austin. I was going to be a drama major, but I just couldn't stay away from the psychology courses because I was intrigued by how people understand the world in terms of language. Other areas of psychology, such as social psychology and child development, were almost equally exciting. Deciding which one to pursue was difficult, but I chose the program in human experimental psychology at the University of Texas at Austin.

During my years in graduate school, I was involved in researching language and cognitive processes. I spent many hours in the laboratory, collecting and analyzing data, and attempting to understand. The results of research studies fascinated me. I loved the data, and the printouts, and the patterns that the analyses revealed.

Toward the end of my doctoral studies, I got to teach a course in introductory psychology, and I also discovered that I loved teaching. When I finished my doctoral degree, I went to McNeese State University in Lake Charles, Louisiana. McNeese emphasizes teaching, and I taught a variety of courses, specializing in experimental psychology and biopsychology as well as continuing to teach introductory psychology.

In the early 1980s, I became interested in the developing field of health psychology. Along with Jess Feist, one of my colleagues in the department of psychology, I began to write a textbook for this new area. The result is *Health Psychology: An Introduction to Behavior and Health,* which is now in its fifth edition.

When I was a graduate student, a minority of students were women, but that situation changed, bringing changes to the entire field of psychology. It was exciting to be part of that transition and to watch women come into the discipline in large numbers. My research interest turned to gender issues, and an editor at Allyn and Bacon persuaded me that I should write a textbook on the topic. *Gender: Psychological Perspectives* is the result, and the course that I teach on the psychology of gender is one of my favorites.

I teach, do research in the area of gender, and write textbooks. In 1998, I was selected to be Distinguished Professor of the year at McNeese State University. I am married to a terrific guy, Barry Humphus, who has encouraged and helped me do things I did not think I could do, such as write three textbooks. I love movies (and movie trivia) and find wine both delicious and fascinating. I am an occasional hiker and reluctant jogger.

My students never stop teaching me, and I am grateful to them. Both Lester and I invite you to share our excitement and enthusiasm for psychology. If you want to tell me anything, contact me at *lbrannon@lightwire.net*.

Linda Brannon